UNTIL DEATH

NICOLE BLANCHARD

DEDICATION

For the bad girls who want to make the villain
*get on his knees and *beg**

CONTENTS

TRIGGER WARNINGS

Morally black hero
Morally grey heroine
Forced marriage
Forced consummation
Dub / non consent
Degradation
Humiliation
Pierced Hero
Coercion
Obsessive Behavior / Stalking
Organized Crime
Emotional / Psychological Manipulation
Graphic Sexual Content
Murder / Death
Violence / Gore
Suicide
Mental Heath Struggles
Sexual Assault

Please mind the triggers and take care of your-
selves. - Nicole

UNTIL DEATH PLAYLIST

One of the first things I do before I start writing is to create a
playlist that I listen to while I write. Scan / click the QR
code to listen along.

FOREWORD

Aiden & Catriona's story begins in their prequel, Little Death. It's not *required* to read it first, but it does add nuance to their relationship.

If haven't already and you want to dive into it first, you can find it in KindleUnlimited or in print.

Enjoy!

PROLOGUE

CATRIONA

"I s that black car following us?" I'd twist around to get a better look at the driver of the car behind me, but I don't want to be too obvious. If I could get away with evasive maneuvers, I'd try, but the last thing I need is for SENATOR GALLAGHER'S DAUGHTER ARRESTED ON TRAFFIC VIOLATIONS to scroll across tonight's breaking news. Said senator would be less than pleased.

"Stop being so paranoid, Cat. No one's following us," my younger sister, Elizabeth, says as she flips down the passenger visor to reapply nude gloss to her pouty lips. "I know it's a shock, but not everyone is obsessed with you."

I frown, certain that a car has been on our tail since we left my house, then glance in the rearview mirror. My best friend, Yasmine, meets my eyes, then rolls hers. She shrugs and glances covertly behind us, her tight black curls floating in the jets of air from the blasting heater.

"She's right. I don't think they are. They just turned at the light," Yasmine says.

"Thank you," I say, as my fingers tap out an anxious rhythm on the steering wheel. Yasmine sends me a quizzical look, probably wondering what the hell is wrong with me, but she doesn't press when I give a subtle shake of my head.

Thankfully, she's a forgiving and discreet soul who not only kept her mouth shut about my current obsession but also didn't say a word when I showed up the fateful morning after my truly idiotic plan went disturbingly awry.

And by awry, I mean I landed in the bed of a man with a dubious background, experienced the phenomenon of multiple orgasms, and left before he could wake up and realize I'd escaped. I seriously doubt any explanation I'd given would've stopped him from putting those big hands around my pretty little neck. This time, probably not in a way I'd like.

I push thoughts of Aiden O'Connor from my mind. It's over. I'm never going to see him again, and I got what I wanted. There's nothing else to think about. Absolutely nothing at all. No reason he'd want to track me down.

Punish me.

Nope.

"Hello?" Elizabeth asks in her singsong voice. She snaps her fingers for emphasis. Twisting in her seat, she flicks a look at us both. "Why did you two even make me come today if we're going to spend it driving around in circles? I'm starving, and you promised you'd take me out for lunch since I couldn't hang out with Rue and Iris."

"What?" I ask, wiping my hands on the skirt of my baby-pink long-sleeved sweater dress and blinking at the street signs even though I've lived in New Orleans my whole life. "I wanted you to come. I've barely seen you, and it's your freshman year at Tulane."

She works up a fleeting smile. I can't tell if it's genuine or if she's just trying to placate me so she can get this lunch over with. "I'm sorry, you're right. I don't mean to make you feel bad. We've both been busy."

I swallow back my automatic rebuttal and cover my guilt. I should have been home. Should have made a point to carve out time for her. I never seem to have enough time for her. Is that why she always seems resentful now?

"You realize that is the third left turn you've made, right?" Yasmine interjects before I can panic-wallow. "Who Dat is on Burgundy Street. Perhaps both of you should eat lunch before this turns into World War III. You get hangry if you skip meals. So let's focus on the road signs and use our nice words, okay?"

I swallow hard, and this time when I study the rearview mirror, I'm looking past Yasmine's concerned face to the black car I could've sworn has been tailing us since we left campus. Maybe Elizabeth is right, and I've just grown more paranoid. Hard not to after what happened the night before Halloween. And God knows Elizabeth won't want to hear anything once I mention our old house or its connection to our mother's death. She never wants to talk about her anymore.

So I swallow back all the secrets I've been keeping, triple-check that there's no black car in traffic behind me, and white-knuckle it the rest of the way to the café.

During our meal, I think I've convinced them my paranoia was nothing—until Yasmine tugs on my elbow as we're walking out of the restaurant a couple of hours later. Elizabeth weaves down the sidewalk with her phone pressed to her ear, blithely chattering to someone on the other end. She spent most of the meal swiping through her phone and glaring at everyone. The ever-present tendrils of guilt in my stomach twine even tighter. How many more secrets will there be between us?

"Seriously, I wasn't going to ask questions because you came back in one piece, but you've been off ever since, and it's been months. You don't need to tell me what happened, but I need to know that you're okay."

Yasmine has been my friend since I transferred to St. John's Prep in third grade. We both shared an obsession with 2000s Usher, abhorred seafood (which is practically illegal in Louisiana), and agreed that purple was overrated, but we could share pink as our favorite color. I've never kept a secret from her in my life—let alone one so big I want to burst.

"I'm probably just being paranoid, like she said," I reply, tugging on her arm. "It's nothing. Too much time spent watching the news."

She resists my attempt to get her to move. "You hate the news, so I know you're lying. Tell me why you've been acting like the FBI is tracking you."

"It's probably not the FBI."

Her mouth falls open. "What the hell did you get into that night, Catriona? I thought you said everything was fine." She lowers her voice. "No one saw you... did they?"

"What do you mean by no one?"

"The more you talk, the more bullshit I smell. Hurry before Elizabeth realizes we're walking at a glacial pace and harasses us some more. I swear that girl has an attitude problem no number of beignets will fix."

To be fair, Yasmine had tried to talk me out of my plan that night. But once I got the idea in my head, there was nothing she could do. Because all I care about is learning the truth about my mother's death. The police say it was an accident... but I'm not so sure. I was convinced I could find clues at our old house, where she was found.

The only problem? The Irish businessman—or at least, that's what everyone *believes* he is—who bought it.

My plan to crash the charity masquerade celebrating the opening of his hotel and casino had been dumb, not that I'd admit it to Yasmine, who would probably say I told you so. No one was more surprised than I was when I caught his attention. I nearly dropped my champagne glass when we'd locked eyes across the room. If this had been a love story and not a tragedy, it would've made great TV.

I was supposed to go to the party, sneak away when no one was watching to find my mother's phone, and be in and out of the house before anyone noticed me. What I was not supposed to do was spend the night with him.

Then, sneak out before he woke up.

"I slept with him," I say, bracing myself for Yasmine's reaction.

She laughs—and I freeze in the middle of the sidewalk, because that's not the response I'd been expecting. Recriminations, maybe. But not laughter.

"Good one, girl. Please. You would have told me before now. I asked you a thousand times if something happened, and you told me, of course not." She does a double take when she realizes I'm not next to her. There's a pause when her smile dies, and her brows draw together. "Catriona, c'mon. Tell me you didn't keep that from me. Be for real."

I can't force the lie out of my throat.

Her laughter trails off, and her brown eyes grow serious. "Catriona?" Her voice wobbles.

Guilt swirls in my stomach. I've never kept anything from her for this long. For one, I'd been terrified to say anything at first, certain that Aiden was going to track me down. And then, because I didn't know what to say. How do I explain to her the things I saw? What I did? If anyone would understand, it would be her, but I didn't even know how to explain it to myself.

"It's why I've been a little paranoid. I couldn't deal with everything that happened, and I ghosted him after."

"Ghosted him?" She turns in a tight circle, hands shoved in her curls, laughing uproariously. "And I thought sneaking into the masquerade was crazy, but I swear to God you've gone off the rails since your—" She cuts herself off before she can finish the sentence. We both freeze for a second before she continues. "I can't believe you slept with him." Another pause, and I school my face, trying to hide my fears. "Why would he be following you? Is there something else you're not telling me?"

I should tell her. The me before that night would have spilled my guts in a heartbeat. Before I'd witnessed a murder, slept with the killer, and decided I should keep my mouth shut. The person who'd entered law school intent upon sticking to her laurels feels a million miles away from the person I am now. One willing to break laws to mete out justice.

It's because I love her that I don't tell her.

Yasmine is a good person from a good family. I've spent as much time in their house as I have in my own. The Baptistes don't deserve to be tainted by this. Especially not Yasmine, who has stuck with me through everything. She has enough going on with medical school; she doesn't need to bear this burden on top of everything else.

So I swallow back the truth that wants to spill free and shake my head. "No. I never told him my name. There's no way he knows who I am. I didn't talk to anyone else. Besides, I honestly think he's forgotten about me. I'm sure it's just anxiety."

She believes that lie a lot easier.

But I still watch my rearview the entire way home to make sure.

He didn't come looking for me. It's been months. The night we spent together must already be a distant memory for him. He probably doesn't even think about me.

I couldn't have been more wrong.

CHAPTER 1

AIDEN

Eamon tosses the protesting man to the floor at my feet, then takes a step back, eyes gleeful and alight with devilish intent. Whoever it is crumples into a heap, the pungent stench of ripe sweat and what I can only describe as fear wafting up. Interesting contradiction considering his Hugo Boss suit and Gucci loafers. Someone with expensive taste and a debt to settle is my initial guess.

I lift my brow at Eamon, who is practically bouncing in his blood-splattered leather boots. I'd lecture him about getting blood on the Persian rug, but I know he wouldn't give a damn, so I've stopped trying. If parenting is anything like dealing with him, I'd make a terrible father.

"Aren't you going to open your present?" he asks as he strips out of his leather jacket and tosses it over an empty chair-back. He prowls around my office like a restless tiger.

"Is this one of those cat-and-mouse situations?" I reply.

The last thing I want is to find myself in the middle of one of Eamon's games. They never end well, and I always end up annoyed when he outwits me. I'd pay to be on the sidelines the day someone outwits him.

"Depends. Are you calling me the cat or the mouse?" he asks.

The man on the floor pushes to his hands and knees, trying to crawl away, but his ribs meet with one of Eamon's boots for his effort. Cocking my head, I study the gasping figure, trying to figure out why he thinks crawling is a good idea. Running would be even worse. Then again, he doesn't know us very well.

Yet.

"The cat," I answer and recline in my leather desk chair, flicking my attention back to Eamon, who is watching the mass on the floor with cold amusement. "You're bringing me a dead—or nearly dead—mouse because you think I'm your pet and incapable of feeding myself?"

"Does that mean I can put a collar on you and walk you around, little pet? Will you purr for me?"

The emphasis he places on little pet is not lost on me, but Eamon is best ignored when he's trying to be meddlesome. Which is most of the time.

Is it late enough to warrant joining him for a drink? A Jameson and ginger is calling my name. After six long months of business, the Emerald Isle is finally running smoothly, even if I end most nights planted face down in my bed. The exhaustion has been worth it, according to our bottom line, but will it be enough? Is it ever? No matter how much money I earn or how many bodies I bury, it seems like

I'm a hamster on a wheel, endlessly toiling, never able to reach my destination.

My bank account may be fat, but there's an ache inside of me that gnaws a lot like starvation. Depravation. And no amount of money can satiate it. Whiskey and sleep are the only ways I've found to deaden the constant, clawing sense of lacking something as vital as oxygen. The only other remedy I've found is one I'll never have again.

Rolling my bleary eyes at Eamon, I say, "Only in your fantasies, you sick fuck. Now tell me why you're bringing me strays. Didn't you know you're supposed to dispose of your toys when you break them?"

Eamon's lip curls, and he snorts. "He wishes he were mine. No, this is the mark you asked for, in the flesh. Found him in D.C. with his latest mistress. Finally got around all those bodyguards. Afraid of somethin', you piece of shite?"

I'll bet he is. Considering Cian's rapidly dwindling patience, it's better for all involved that Eamon tracked him down when he did.

The man turns up his face, and my ribs contract around my lungs as I put a name to it within one breath and the next.

Despite the fear firming his unsmiling mouth and the lines around his green eyes, he has the air of a man used to having control of a room. And the desperation of one who realizes he's lost it.

But it's the familiarities I note that leave me reeling like I'm the one who took a boot to the ribs. His blond hair is streaked with silver and closely cropped instead of so long I can wrap it around my head several times. The same under-lying facial architecture, though he has a strong jaw with a cleft chin instead of one as sharp and delicate as a fairy's, and thin lips where they should be lusciously full.

So this is Senator Rory Gallagher. A ghost of a smirk tugs at my lips, then immediately collapses into a frown as he spits blood at the rug. Doesn't he know what a bitch stains can be to get out of wool? A bead of sweat glides down his temple, and he swallows hard when I pin him with a cold, blank stare.

"Do you have what you owe Cian Lynch for your significant debts?" I ask.

Gallagher doesn't answer. Maybe he can't, the way his jaw is locked so hard as his body fairly vibrates with nerves.

Eamon shoves him with a boot between the shoulder blades, and Gallagher yelps before pushing up again. "Answer him when he speaks to you," Eamon suggests with deadly calm.

"Christ, no, okay? No, I don't have it, but—"

"Take him to the warehouse. We can deal with him later," I say, cutting off his excuses.

Gallagher opens his mouth to protest. The words commit suicide on his tongue at my expression.

Instead of doing as I instruct, Eamon ambles over to the crystal decanters lining the wall that house some of my favorite vintages. I keep meaning to hide them better because he's always finishing them off before I get a taste. The only reason I haven't is because the bastard would probably tear apart my office to find them if I did, and I can't be bothered.

"I would, lad," he says, as he takes a bottle off the shelf, studies it, and exchanges it for another, "but Rory here said he could make you a deal you couldn't refuse. I thought you might want to at least hear him out before we kill him."

"Get up," I order. Gallagher doesn't move, frozen with fear. Stretching my tense neck from side to side, I give him one more chance to comply. "Get up, Gallagher, or Eamon will help you up, and I promise that's something you don't want."

"It's something I want," Eamon says, turning from the bar with an old-fashioned in his hand, if I had to guess. I can scent the orange peel over the reek from here.

Gallagher struggles to his feet, shuffling to keep both me and Eamon in his view. Like prey cornered by two predators. I don't know if he even realizes he's doing it. He knuckles away the blood and sweat from his face and tries to muster up some of his famed self-assurance and charm.

"I only need five minutes, O'Connor," Gallagher punches out between breaths as he tries—and fails—to affect an air of confidence. Bruises bracket the lines of his nose with faint shadows. "Just five. You won't regret it, I promise." He doesn't say please, but I can hear the beseeching note in his voice, discordant and revolting.

I've learned a lot about Rory Gallagher in the months I've been hunting him like a fox after a rabbit. There's nothing he can offer I'd be interested in, nothing I'd ever allow myself to have, but despite knowing it, I find the questioning words teasing my lips, threatening to spill out between us. Thankfully, Eamon speaks before they break free of their cage.

"Begging already?" Eamon frowns behind his drink. "And I didn't even need to bring out my knives. How disappointing. Maybe I should bring him back to the warehouse and see if we can do something about his endurance. This must be how his mistress feels when he's fucking her."

"Five minutes," Gallagher repeats, holding my gaze, despite Eamon circling ever closer to him. His handsome face is white beneath the bruises at the mention of Eamon and his legendary knives.

I run a tired hand over my face and through my hair. "And why should I listen to you, Gallagher? You knew what you were doing when you refused to see me, tried to hide from me. Do you think Cian Lynch is a man who gives third chances after he's already shown more generosity than you deserve? Your time is up. Your debts are due. There are no further extensions. No interest. You pay in money, or you pay with your life. You knew the terms when you agreed to them."

Gesturing with a nod, Eamon retrieves a ledger the size of a small child. I also keep electronic records, but I like the feel of pen and paper under my hands. The physical weight of a book. Inside is a meticulous record of the reports, notes, and names of all the pertinent debts owed to Cian, the head of the Lynch Crime Family, and one of the most ruthless men in organized crime. And there is an exorbitant amount.

The only way you rise to power in this world is by being more ruthless than your opposition. And Cian is the most cunning of them all. The Emerald Isle hotel and casino I own is but one of the many businesses contributing to the wealth of our organization. But it may his as well, considering he owns me.

I place glasses on the bridge of my nose and run my finger down the rows of figures, dates, and names until I find the one I'm looking for. Whistling through my teeth, I say, "According to my records, we've been more than generous,

Rory. You've had plenty of time, practically twice as long as we normally allow to settle your debts."

Tipping my glasses down, I study his ashen face and bloodshot eyes, grateful I'm almost through with this task. The greedy ache in my gut is hungry for his death, craves it. If I can't have what I really want, then I'll settle for his blood on my hands. I've been looking forward to finishing my obligations to Cian regarding him for months. Despite how curious I am about what he wants, I almost hope it's something I can turn down so I can draw out his punishment. Which is nothing like how I usually deal with men like him. Normally, it's a bullet in the brain, job done.

"The house you provided as your down payment was only half of what you owe. So where is the rest?"

"I just need some more time, that's all. Just a little more time to get the rest of it. There are circumstances with my wife's estate he doesn't understand."

"He's already given you time and plenty of it. I'm afraid the clock—and Cian's patience—has run out." Frankly, Gallagher's lucky he's still alive. For six months he evaded Cian's reach, spending much of his time in D.C., where he knew we wouldn't dare attempt to off him.

Coward.

Gallagher rubs a hand through his hair, leaving the normally perfectly gelled strands sticking up in all directions. "I can—" His voice cuts off as Eamon prowls around the room nursing his drink.

"You can what?" I ask, wondering if he'll plead for mercy on his behalf. Maybe he'll invoke his family, not that I've ever gotten the sense he cared about them.

"I can make a deal," the sniveling man says.

Eamon snorts after we share a disbelieving look and says, "Are you seriously trying to renegotiate with Cian Lynch? Do you have a death wish? Because I can arrange that and make it much more enjoyable. For me, at least."

For the first time in our short and despised acquaintance, Rory grows a spine. Ignoring Eamon, he says, "I have something you may find useful. You said I could pay in blood."

"I doubt there's anything you have that I will find useful," I answer slowly, wondering where he's going with this. My palms grow slick, my neck hot. I fight the urge to shift in my seat. Outwardly, my mask doesn't crack.

He licks his dry lips, winking brilliant veneers that probably cost more than most four-year Ivy League degrees. "These debts. Do they specify exactly whose blood? Or would any Gallagher blood suffice?"

Eamon inhales so quickly he nearly breathes in the whiskey. "You've got to be fuckin' with me, pal. Maybe I knocked you around a bit too much. Or you've gone hard of hearing. Christ, Aiden, let me deal with this one. Save you the trouble."

I nearly sigh again. I've never minded being Cian's enforcer. But I've never enjoyed it the way Eamon does. I've never craved it. It's a duty, a job. Something to check off on a list that seems never-ending. Maybe if it gave me more satisfaction, I wouldn't chafe at the knowledge that all I'll ever be is Cian's hound.

"Spit it out, Gallagher, or I'll let Eamon introduce you to those knives he loves so much."

"What would you say if I were to offer you one of my daughters?"

What I say is nothing, and Gallagher, degenerate though

he is, doesn't miss the way my eyes narrow in interest despite myself. Can he hear the way my breath catches in my chest? He leans forward as though we're coconspirators.

"The oldest is... a challenge, but my youngest listens well enough."

My back goes ramrod straight, but he's so enthused by his own idea at this point, he doesn't notice.

"Why the hell would I want one of your daughters?" I ask.

At this, he looks more like the invulnerable man of power he pretends to be when the cameras are on him. "Because I know the thing you want the most in this world, and my daughter is the key to giving you what you want."

Eamon sneers. "And how the hell do you know somethin' like that?"

"While you've been looking for me, I've been learning all about you." He doesn't glance away from me. "About your mother. That you haven't seen her in nearly, what? Ten years, right? I bet you miss her."

I say nothing, which says everything.

The fear stitching Gallagher's muscles taut loosens at the silence. "I may not be in the family, but I've been around Cian long enough to puzzle out how it works. If you were to get married, you'd have to go back to Ireland to introduce her to all of them. It's tradition, right?"

The thought makes me sick, but my face stays perfectly blank.

"Cian would have to let you see your mother. That's why he hasn't forced the issue. Married you off to one of his lieutenant's daughters. Because he'll do anything to keep you under his thumb. His *Cú Chulainn.*"

His hound.

The name on his lips makes my stomach roll.

"You desperate piece of shite," Eamon interjects. "Tell him to fuck off."

When I don't, Eamon spins slowly in my direction.

I say nothing again.

Eamon spears a hand through his messy brown curls, but it immediately flops back in his eyes. "Jesus Christ." He wants to say more but wouldn't dare risk it in front of Gallagher. But it doesn't matter. I know all the reasons it's a terrible idea and all the reasons I may not have any choice in the matter.

"You'd really sell one of your daughters to pay your debt?" I ask, ignoring Eamon and the roll of nausea in my stomach. "I doubt Cian considers pussy enough payment for the five million you owe, Senator Gallagher. Even if it's Gallagher pussy."

I should be furious at his attempts to divert me. I should let Eamon take him to the warehouse to be dealt with, but I'm tired. Tired of fighting. Tired of wondering when the next hit will come. Tired of waiting for Cian to pull the last rug out from under me. If I have no choice, then why fight so hard to prevent the inevitable?

Eamon, who was forged alongside me in the crucible of terror that is Cian Lynch, wisely keeps his mouth shut at the blank expression on my face.

Gallagher continues, "My daughter will do what she's told. And you don't have to tell Cian everything, do you? As soon as you're married, my daughter will have access to the trust fund provided by her mother's family, the Doyles.

Then you'll have the rest of the money I owe and get the chance to see your mother."

Eamon's cackles cut the tension at Rory's words. "You really are a backstabbing bastard. You realize you're talking about selling one of your children, right? Using them—and Aiden—to pay your debt. You're pathetic."

But Gallagher won't be swayed, not even by Eamon's righteous indignation. There's a furor in his eyes, a desperation that has me examining his words with growing resignation. "Everyone gets what they want, no need to make this messy." He holds his hands up as Eamon circles him like prey. "I've spent my life arguing my way out of impossible situations, I'll admit, but you'd be a fool not to consider my offer."

That he's not wrong leaves an acrid taste in the back of my mouth. When I was a boy, all I wanted was to take my father's place at the helm of Clan O'Connor in Ireland, before it had evolved into the monstrosity it is now. I'd known from a young age that our family wasn't like others, but when he'd been at the helm of the Irish mob, it had been about honor, pride, and family. Now, the thought of going back there leaves a metallic taste in the back of my mouth.

If my mother knew I was even considering defying Cian to see her, she'd call me an eejit herself and then box my ears for the sheer stupidity.

I wouldn't give Gallagher's plan any weight if I weren't so goddamn tired. All I want is to see her one more time, to know that she's okay. To smell the familiar scent of roses clinging to her skin. To make sure she hasn't given up. To tell her I'll keep the promises I made to her. Every day I feel her slipping away. Pieces chipped away by Cian's iron fist. Soon, there won't be anything left of the mother I knew.

If Cian had considered this possibility, he never would have assigned me to deal with Gallagher. Or maybe he did, and he's testing my loyalty. Either I can take the risk, or I can face never seeing my mother again.

"Aiden—" Eamon says.

"What makes you think this is something your daughter will agree to?" Once I've decided, I don't second-guess myself. I'm almost weightless with relief. All these years I'd spent doing anything and everything Cian Lynch has ordered, and I'm willing to throw it all away at the chance to see my mother. Maybe this is what he's been waiting for all along. For me to crack. To give up. To make a mistake.

If he learns what I'm planning before the deed is done, my blood will join Gallagher's on Eamon's knives.

"My daughter will do what she's told. You understand that, don't you, Aiden?" Gallagher says when he reads the resignation in my expression.

"I'm going to enjoy carving you up when I get the chance, Gallagher," Eamon croons at the jab. "It may not be today, but I can guarantee this won't be the last time we meet. If this is a trick and you get him killed, I'll find you, wherever you try to hide, and what I'd planned for you will be child's play compared to what I'll do to you. Do you understand me?"

My mind travels back to the conversation I had with Cian the night of Emerald Isle's grand opening. I hadn't known it then, but ever since that fateful conversation, my life has been barreling toward this conclusion. Maybe even longer.

. . .

"CIAN. I wasn't aware you were coming," I say, keeping my tone neutral. Controlled. Always controlled. "Would you like a room upstairs? The executive suite should be available to you."

He turns, lifting a brow and leaving his damp tumbler on my glossy oak desktop without a coaster. My fingers twitch at my sides.

"Was I supposed to clear my schedule with you, Aiden?" Cian asks, a thin blade of a smile splitting his even thinner lips underneath his salt-and-pepper facial hair.

Of course not. My stomach knots, but I show nothing. I'd let myself believe that crossing an ocean might loosen his grip on me.

Eamon was right.

I am a fuckin' eejit.

"Never mind that," he continues with a wave through the blue mist of smoke. "I'm here because I need you to do something for the family."

I'm numb, something I never thought I'd be in Cian's malevolent presence. There's always another job. Another body to bury. Another chain lashed around my neck, dragging me down. I'm covered in so many of them that there'll be no clawing my way out. Something I have no doubt he knows as well as I do.

I'd fought it at first. But I soon learned that dealing with Cian is a lot like Newton's third law of motion: For every action, there's an equal and opposite reaction. Each attempt at freedom only ends up with people I care about hurt.

"I need you to find Gallagher."

I blink, go completely still. "Senator Rory Gallagher?"

"The one and only. The remainder of his payment is due. The house was supposed to be a down payment on the ten million he owes me. You'll find him and get the remainder. Five million and not a penny less."

"And if he doesn't?"

"Well, he has some family, doesn't he? I'm certain you can get creative."

"Of course."

Cian sucks his teeth. "He has some valuable connections here in America I don't want to waste, so the sooner the better. But I want you to make it clear to the man that I'm not to be trifled with. Either he pays in money, or we have his blood."

I nod stiffly.

"I'll take that executive suite," Cian says as he ambles to the door, leaving the sweating glass of ice on my otherwise perfect desk.

"Of course," I repeat.

"Your mother sends her best."

WHEN I FORCE myself back to the present, Eamon is glowering at Gallagher from his place by the fire, radiating murderous energy. If he were a tiger, his tail would be flicking in angry annoyance.

"It's a pleasure doing business with you, O'Connor," Gallagher says with a pleased smile.

I amble toward him and offer a hand to shake, which he readily accepts. But what he doesn't expect is the gun in my other, the barrel digging into his throat. It would be so easy to put a bullet in his brain.

I thought it would be hard the first time I ever killed a man, but it was easy. One pull of a trigger and I was safe. I could do it now and continue as I have been. Cian's debt would be satisfied, and my mother and I would be safe.

But I don't.

Because the one thing I want more than anything in the world is to see her.

And I'll use this bastard to do it, marry his daughter, defy Cian. Risk everything.

"What the—O'Connor. I thought we had a deal!" His throat bobs against the unrelenting metal. "What the fuck do you think you're doing?"

"Let me make myself exceedingly clear, you worthless piece of shite. The only reason you're still breathing and not bleeding out onto the floor is because I'm allowing it. If you fuck this up, I won't hesitate to let Eamon carry out his promise. You're only alive because of my mercy. Do you understand me?"

"Not even a bruise. You could have at least drawn some more blood." Eamon says petulantly. We ignore him.

"I said, do you understand me?"

"Yes, I understand. For God's sake, don't kill me. I understand. I understand!"

I release my grip on his hand, causing him to lose his balance and stumble backward. Wiping the sweat on my pants, I'm suddenly bone-tired and desperate for whatever remains of my bar. "You'll bring your daughter for dinner tomorrow so I can ensure she'll cooperate with your plan. If she does—"

"She will," he insists.

"—then the wedding will take place at St. Louis Cathedral at two p.m. next Saturday. My lawyers will draw up the necessary documents, and you can keep her inheritance to pay your debt. I expect your complete cooperation and silence on this matter. If you breathe a word of this to Cian before the ceremony, our deal is over. Do I make myself clear?"

Gallagher nods enthusiastically. "Absolutely. Tomorrow. I appreciate you working with me on this, O'Connor. I'll have my assistant arrange whatever you need."

I open the door to an empty hallway, more than ready to be rid of his pathetic, stinking presence. "Now leave before I change my mind."

When he's almost at the door, I call his name. "And Rory? Don't even think about coming to the Emerald to test your luck again. You won't be welcome in my establishment, and you'll be thrown out on your ass if you try. We don't accept men who don't know when they're in over their head."

Gallagher may be an idiot to get involved with a man like Cian, but he's got admirable survival instincts and a desperation to live I hadn't accounted for. Like a cockroach. I stare in the middle distance long enough that Eamon appears next to me with another old-fashioned.

"Drink up. You're going to want to blame this horrible decision on something, and it sure as hell won't be me, because I tried to warn you. I hope you'll tell that to your mother when she tries to kill me for not trying harder to stop you."

I scrub a hand down my face and accept the drink. "She'd never kill you."

"Like hell." There's a pause. "I still think this is a horrible decision," he says.

"That's because you're the king of horrible decisions, handsome. To which are we referring?" a familiar feminine voice interjects.

My gaze lifts to the end of the hall where Mara Kane stands, casually unwinding a blood-red scarf from around her neck. She ruffles her bob the color of glossy raven wings and gives us a haughty look when we don't answer her question quickly enough. We both stare at her as though we're seeing a ghost.

"Mara, love, what the hell *are* you doing here?" She allows Eamon to tug her fully inside the office as he shuts the door behind her. She tosses her Birkin onto my desk and arranges herself on one of the two chairs opposite, and Eamon plops down next to her.

"What the hell are you doing here?" I ask in a low voice. "Aren't you supposed to be in Dublin planning your wedding?"

"So many questions," she says lightly without answering. "I knew you boys missed me."

"Mara," I repeat.

"The wedding is still happening. Good God, you're as bad as my mother. You'll receive your invitations at some point. It's not like I need to plan the damn thing right away because I'm on my deathbed or something. But enough about that unpleasantness. What horrible decision have you made now?"

I can't force the words out, so Eamon does, punctuated by gross exaggeration and blatant lies, but Mara gleans the gist.

"Well?" Eamon demands, eyes on Mara as he gestures to me.

She tucks a lock of hair behind her ear, her eyes narrowing into slits. "Well, what?"

"Aren't you going to try to talk some sense into him?"

"Since when have either of you *ever* listened to reason? Especially if it came from me. I gave up trying to be your keeper years ago." She waves an elegant, manicured hand. "Besides, it's far more entertaining to witness the inevitable consequences of your own actions."

"Thanks, I think," I say. At the same time, Eamon interjects, "I listen to you!"

Mara rolls her eyes. "Name one time you've ever listened to me." She pauses as Eamon screws up his face in concentration. She gestures at him, a weary hand wave of someone exhausted from dealing with idiots. "Precisely."

Eamon sighs dramatically. "You're only saying that because you don't want to be the only one married."

I flinch inwardly. Mara's upcoming marriage to Niall Cleary, a slimy bastard who basically bought her as a teenager, is the one subject that could cause the ice princess to lose her cool. Just to be safe, I roll my chair backward to inch out of the blast radius of her infamous temper.

Thankfully, she merely crosses her legs, evidently in a benevolent state of mind, and says, "Is that jealousy I hear, Eamon? Are you upset because there isn't a person on this planet who wants to marry you?"

"I—" For once, Eamon is speechless.

"He'd have to find someone to put up with his... eccentricities first."

Mara gives an unladylike snort. "If by eccentricities you

mean his affinity for torture—and not the fun kind—then you aren't wrong."

"I'm standing right here, you fuckin' arseholes." There's a pause where his vision goes off, like he's staring at something far away. "And what kind isn't the fun kind?"

"I'm not sure there's a woman—or man, for that matter—alive who could do that," Mara says to me.

"I'll have you know if I wanted a wife, I could find one," Eamon says, and I can't imagine a woman crazy enough to consider spending the rest of her life with Eamon willingly. Then it occurs to me he could rope one in *unwillingly*, and I want to curse Mara for ever planting that seed in his mind. Maybe I'll distract him with another job. A little bloodshed will wipe the whole idea away.

"Of course you could, dear." Mara reaches over to cup his cheek consolingly and ends it with a playful smack. "Consider yourself lucky that you don't have to be shackled to a ball and chain like me and Aiden. You're free to do whatever you wish. When is the funeral? I mean, wedding?" Mara asks.

"A week." I can't tell if I'm more eager to get it over with or on edge to see the seeds of my goal for my mother's freedom finally bearing fruit.

"I'm afraid I have to agree with Eamon here. You shouldn't marry this girl for your mother," Mara says. "Believe me, she wouldn't want this for you."

"Give it a rest, you two. I know what I'm doing. Marrying the senator's daughter isn't the worst thing that could happen. Consider it a means to an end."

I can't help but feel in my gut, it will be a bloody end.

CHAPTER 2

CATRIONA

The car—a nondescript Uber I ordered for subterfuge—pulls up to the road, and I press a hand to the butterflies multiplying in my stomach. Realistically, I know there's no one following me, but it doesn't hurt to be careful. Paranoia, thy name is Catriona. My phone bleats out the sound of a call ringing and ringing, but Elizabeth doesn't pick up.

Did I really think she would?

Sighing, I end the call and wish I had the magic words to convince her to help me. But the moment I showed her my makeshift murder board, she looked at me like I'd lost it. And maybe I have.

Six months ago, when I snuck into our old house where my mother died, I found her phone and spent weeks trying to break into it. Finally, I accepted defeat and began the arduous process of interviewing private investigators to help.

Because I may be a lot of things, but I can admit when I'm in over my head.

Finding out exactly what happened that night is my number one priority, even if it costs me everything. Shoving away those worries to deal with later, I climb out of the Uber and give the driver a five-star rating before I study my destination: a small hole-in-the-wall bistro that no tourist would ever give a second glance. Which means it's perfect.

Mr. Leonardo Broussard is the name of the private detective I finally settled on, and he comes here most afternoons for a pick-me-up coffee and a treat. It's been months, and he's finally combed through most of her phone. I'm full of warring emotions. Dread for what he's found. Relief if there's news to report. Anxiety it'll be nothing, and I'll have to start all over again.

The scent of yeast and coffee greets my nose as I stride to the entrance. It may be a hole-in-the-wall, but the vibes are excellent. Inside, the bistro is little more than a walkway between the massive counter and the opposite wall. There's just enough room to squeeze in a few two-top standing tables, with more room for people at the counter. Most of the decor is sparse, but what the place lacks in design, it makes up for in quality, if the smell is anything to go by.

After a quick scan of the patrons, I realize Mr. Broussard isn't among them and let out a sigh of relief. The moments I'll have before he arrives will certainly help calm my nerves and let me go over the questions I have for him. I place an order for my favorite, a honey and lavender latte, and wait in a shadowed corner for him. The drink soothes my nerves so that when the bell rings over the door, I'm able to look up without flinching.

Mr. Broussard is an unassuming man. I recognize him at first glance because of his hair, or lack thereof. We met in person once before when I handed over the phone, and I'm struck again by the air of competence and sturdiness that surrounds him. According to his website, he's a former lawyer—is that why I feel so at home around him?—who has been a private investigator for the past ten years. He's the only one who didn't immediately brush off my concerns, so it's not like I had much choice.

I edge through the cloister of tables and patrons to his side just as he's turning away from the counter.

"Miss Catriona." He rocks back on his heels. "Have you already ordered? I can get us a table."

"I have, but thank you."

He gestures with his croissant to an empty spot. "Why don't we take a seat, and we can discuss what I've found so far?"

Sinking into a chair, I wet my tongue with a piping-hot sip from my honey and lavender latte, though I barely taste it. "Thank you again for agreeing to look into this. If it weren't for you, I was about to give up hope I'd find anything at all."

His smile is a twitch under his mustache. "Of course," he says, as he rifles through a leather messenger bag I didn't notice he was carrying. He pulls out a thick notebook. "I like to keep it old school sometimes. I have notes of my findings here with me."

"Probably safer that way, I imagine," I ramble, as my heartbeat kicks up a notch.

"I was able to unlock your mother's phone based on the

suggestions you provided and some programs a friend of mine designed. Don't ask me the details, they're not really my specialty. We recovered a log of her calls, emails, and text messages. That would be these." He passes me a folder of papers. "Going back for six months or so, to start. This is your copy."

I swallow roughly and take the proffered file. Once the knot in my throat passes with a swallow from my drink, I say, "This is incredible, more than I hoped for. Were you able to look through them and see if anything stood out to you?" Cracking open the folder, my latte forgotten next to my elbow, I pore over the lines of data.

There are numbers I recognize—mine, my father's and sister's—but there are many I don't. So many. And that doesn't include her emails or any other important information, like banking or social media. This could take a while.

I slump farther into my seat. Shit. Once, just once, I want to feel like I did when I found the phone. Like I was making some headway. But so far it's been one step forward, ten steps back.

"I know it seems like a lot," Mr. Broussard says, drawing my attention away from my pity party, "but this is a good start. I've been able to identify the easy numbers, as I'm sure you have. Yours and Mr. Gallagher's, Elizabeth Gallagher. You all called her on the day of her death."

My nose stings as I nod, remembering.

He continues, "There's another number on the day of her death that I don't have. I was wondering if you could double-check it with your contacts."

I nod. "Of course." He points at the number, and I

unlock my phone to type it into the contacts to see who comes up. My heart is in my throat, blood pounding in my ears.

But there's nothing.

"I'm sorry, I don't have it. Should I try calling it?"

"No, I wouldn't," he says after a moment's thought. "I waited to speak with you first, but my next step is to track down all the numbers and compile a list for you to go over. I also got her calendar. Will you check and see if anything stands out to you? It should be near the back of those documents."

I find the sheet and glance over it. There's not much there that I hadn't already gleaned from her social media. I practically devoured it in the weeks after her death, but unfortunately, I couldn't find anything out of the ordinary. Charities. Trips to the bank. Pilates. Drinks with her friends. Appearances with my father. Meetings with her lawyer. Nothing seemed overly suspicious.

"Nothing that stands out, no. But it doesn't make sense to me, and I don't understand why the police ruled it an accident. Despite what my father thinks. I mean, who trips and falls down the stairs?" I shake my head. My mother was a former supermodel. She could sprint a 5k in heels. Tripping down the stairs? I don't think so.

"That's alright. We're only getting started. I still have to go over all the police reports and security camera footage. Don't give up on me yet."

I manage a weak smile. "I won't. I'm grateful to you for helping me with this."

He pushes to his feet and gives me a nod, mustache

twitching. "I'll be in touch when I've gone through the rest of this. I wanted to keep you apprised of my progress so far."

I get to my feet as well, relief swamping me at the thought of finally having someone else on my side. "Thank you again for meeting with me. I appreciate it." I tuck the folder under my arm, already dying to pore through it like I would one of my textbooks.

"No, you keep it. Let me know if any of it jogs your memory. Take care of yourself, Ms. Catriona."

"You too, Mr. Broussard."

Stay positive, I tell myself as I order and wait for my Uber. The good news is we're making progress. He has accomplished more than I was able to in the past six months. There's a strange number as a lead, and he'll finally get access to the police reports and evidence. I couldn't very well ask for it without my father throwing an apoplectic fit.

The driver makes awkward small talk once I fold into his car. He tries to hint about my identity, but I deftly evade his questions. Thank you, media training. Finally, he falls silent, and I let my eyes slide closed, then immediately they snap open as the flashbacks hit, and panic surges through me. Digging my hand into my chest, I try to ease my thumping heart.

I bang my forehead on the window, trying to get ahold of myself, and then realize the time. I've missed my trusts and wills class. Because of course I did. I'd say that was an uncommon occurrence, but it's not the only time I've missed it this week. I make a mental note to email my professor as I check my location and estimate the distance to our house.

The blare of my cell phone interrupts my thoughts,

causing my heart to slam against my ribs, and I nearly jump a foot in the air.

It's Elizabeth, finally returning my dozens of calls. I answer it and press the phone to my ear, forcing my voice to remain calm so I don't draw undue attention from the driver, who's already studying me in the rearview. Maybe it's a good thing she didn't answer my attempts to reach her. Perhaps I should keep this little investigation to myself.

"Why were you blowing up my phone?" she says without so much as a hello.

"Bethie, hey," I say, thinking fast for an excuse. "How are you?"

There's a long pause. "You called to ask how I am?" Elizabeth's disbelief bleeds through the line. "And don't call me Bethie. I'm not five."

"I called because I'm heading home in time for dinner, believe it or not. I wanted to see if you'd like me to pick you up anything from Antoine's."

"You're being weird." There's a rustling of clothes and the sound of lips smacking like she's checking her lipstick. "Besides, I have dinner plans with one of Dad's friends tonight."

Red flags go up in my mind. "Which friend?" Could it be someone who knew something about our mother?

"How the hell should I know? I don't keep track," Elizabeth asks, drawing my attention back from my exhaustive mental list of suspects. Father's friends. His staff. Her known associates. Father.

"You know what? I'll be home in a few minutes. Why don't I go with you guys?"

"Is something going on with you? You're starting to freak

me out. It's a stupid family dinner with one of his old friends. It'll probably be boring. You're lucky you don't have to go."

But those old friends may have insight into my mother, and with so few clues, I can't let an opportunity to gather more information pass me by. I lament the traffic in front of me, sending my Uber driver mental signals to hurry the hell up.

"We never get to spend time together anymore," I babble with fake laughter. I'll go with you to keep you company. Don't let him leave without me. I'll be home in a few minutes."

"We're about to leave, you don't have to—"

"Two minutes. Stall for me!"

***

"That was longer than two minutes," Elizabeth says when I rush through the door. "He's about to lose his mind. You know how he despises being late. Where have you been?"

Elizabeth latches onto my arm, and I shove all thoughts of Mom and my meeting with Mr. Broussard to the back of my mind. The last thing I want is for her to ask more questions—or to have to reveal where I was and who I met. I concluded the rest of the ride over here that it's best if I keep her out of the loop regarding my investigation until I have concrete proof. I want the sister I used to have when we were kids, and springing this on her won't win me any favors.

I note her blue Alexander McQueen A-line dress with an asymmetrical hemline for the first time. In it, she looks every bit a beautiful girl of eighteen, and I stifle the knot in my throat at the wish that things could have been different. In an alternate reality, she'd be a normal girl, excited about college and the future. But with Rory Gallagher for a father, she was doomed from the start.

"I had a meeting with an advisor." That is the story I concocted when I first met Mr. Broussard. The perfect excuse to see him whenever I need to go over anything regarding the case. "I didn't know you cared so much. Aww, Bethie, I love you, too."

"I don't get what your deal is. You never come to these kinds of things. You hate anything to do with Dad's campaigns or his friends. Why do you even want to come with us anyway?"

"I'm starting to get offended that you don't want to spend time with me," I say, surprised to find the statement rings true.

She brushes off my attempt to hug her. "Don't try to get me to play interference. He's pissed. You need to change," she says with a flick of her hair. Her eyes are green like our father's, and they roll as she glances toward his study. "You should have answered his calls. We're already running late. Get dressed. Wear something nice. We needed to leave ten minutes ago."

Elizabeth studies her reflection in the mirror, brushing back stray locks of hair and fixing the line of her lip gloss, so she doesn't see me struggle to contain the rush of sadness that spears through me. When we were little, everything had been so easy. I'd loved being a big sister, watching out for her, teaching her new things and knowing absolutely everything about each other. I'd been there for every day of her life. Now, we're more like strangers than sisters, and it's as though I lost two people instead of one when our mother died.

"Do you want to help me get ready?" The words tumble

from my lips, awkward and uncertain. The last thing I want is her scrutiny before what is no doubt going to be a long, long night under our father's. But a part of me longs for the people we used to be before the world stamped them out.

She shakes her head, glossy dark blond waves floating around her shoulders. "No, but be quick, or he's going to leave without you. Whoever we're meeting must be important. He's pacing around like there's an alligator on his ass."

I give her a jerky nod, not quite meeting her gaze, and take the stairs two at a time up to my room. A glance back shows her watching my ascent with an unreadable expression, and I force my eyes forward because if I don't, I'm afraid of what she'll read on my face.

Since Mom's death, everything between us has been different. We haven't been close since we outgrew the innocence of childhood, but now there's a space the size of the Grand Canyon between us. Like we speak different languages, or are people who used to be close but haven't seen each other in a long time even though we live in the same house. She has Father to turn to because she's always been his favorite, but he's always been the hardest on me.

I race through my room, stripping off my jeans and T-shirt and dressing in a long-sleeved, figure-skimming pink midi. I pair it with some basic nude heels and a nude clutch, stuffing my phone in it as I glide back downstairs. Elizabeth waits with Father, her face carefully blank of her earlier amusement. The last thing I want to do is go to some stuffy dinner so he can schmooze, but I'll suck it up to learn more about the people he's close to, no matter the risk or how much it pisses him off.

"If you're determined to tag along, you could at least be

on time," comes my father's brusque voice. "So help me God, Catriona, if you ruin this for me, I will not be responsible for the consequences."

Sweet man, our father.

On the outside, he doesn't seem like he's rotten to the core, but I guess they never do. I can't remember a time when I wasn't afraid of him. When we were young, Mom did a good job of shielding us from his anger and violent mood swings, but there was only so much she could do.

What makes me sick to my stomach is how much the three of us look alike. Same blond hair and general face structure, though mine is a little more pointed. Elizabeth got his dimpled chin. The only thing that sets me apart from them is my hazel eyes, which I inherited from my mother. If you didn't look closely, Elizabeth and I could be twins.

As I bite back a scathing retort, he's already stalking out the door to where a sleek black G-wagon waits. I frown, realizing there's no driver as he climbs into the driver's seat. I know better than to ask, so I keep my mouth shut as I take a seat behind him. Elizabeth slides into the passenger seat. It shouldn't make me so goddamn lonely, but it does. It has always been the two of them, and now it is them... and me. It's not her fault; he's always preferred her. A fact of life that never emphasized my isolation until Mom died.

"You look perfect, as always, angel," he tells Elizabeth, as he whips us into traffic. He takes her hand and kisses her knuckles. Why does he reserve his biting words and punishments for me? God knows, I've spent years of my life trying to figure it out, but there's nothing I've ever done to deserve the treatment he directs my way.

"Thank you, Daddy," she replies with a small smile. I

turn away from them, studying the growing darkness outside my window and hoping the evening will pass quickly. "Did you let him know we're running late?" Elizabeth asks, and I wonder if she's trying to distract him from more scathing retorts.

Frequent events and socializing aren't out of the norm. We're often required to attend galas and luncheons and charity events of all kinds. But on short notice? No, something has my stomach clenching with nerves that has nothing to do with my meeting with Mr. Broussard and its harrowing aftermath.

If this were a decade ago, I would have reached for Elizabeth's hand and squeezed it three times in rapid succession. Our silent way of saying I love you. She would have turned hers over to lace our fingers together and squeezed mine three times in return. Is it possible to mourn a person when they're still alive? Ever since Mom died, it hasn't felt the same, no matter how much I try to connect with her.

Because I believe there's more to the story.

And Elizabeth believes the police and wants us to move on with our lives.

"I planned to leave earlier than expected just in case." He meets my gaze in the rearview mirror during a momentary pause in traffic. Then it flicks over to Elizabeth in warning. "Whatever happens tonight, keep your mouths shut unless you're spoken to."

It's said to me, but Elizabeth and I both respond, "Yes, Father," although she's not really paying attention. She's scrolling through her feed, the light washing over her face.

Too soon, though it's probably been a good half hour weaving through evening traffic, we pull onto Burgundy

Street and park in public parking, which Father grumbles about under his breath. He makes impatient sounds as we climb out of the car and follow his ground-eating stride down the sidewalk to a sage-green corner townhome that has me sighing in... regret? Jealousy?

It has to be a recently restored, absolutely stunning historic 1800s Gallier Creole-style building. I try not to gape at the wraparound balcony on the second floor and the private fenced-in courtyard. If I were to get my own place, it would be something like this. Right in the center of the bustling city I love so much. Smaller than the estate we used to own, but so New Orleans that it makes my heart squeeze.

Elizabeth takes several deep breaths and plasters a smile on her face as we step up to the front door. She ruffles her hair and checks her makeup in her phone camera. I should probably do the same, but I honestly don't care. All I can think about is getting home and sleeping for at least twelve hours. I do check my phone to see if there are any updates from Mr. Broussard, but there's only a Supernatural meme from Yasmine and a request to finally let her loop Reggie into my investigation. I wish I could, but I don't want to drag anyone else into my mess besides the ones I already have. At least not until we have something more concrete.

My father strides to the front door and knocks imperiously, his complexion turning increasingly gray, which makes me frown. What could he possibly have to be worried about? He steps into the light, and I swear he has bruises under his eyes.

Walking a few feet behind Elizabeth, I resolve to keep my cool. I won't let anything that happens get to me. Chances are, tonight will have nothing to do with my mother. I'll survive a boring dinner, then pore over the folder Mr. Broussard gave me to see if it contains any leads.

Soon, an older woman with soft brown hair and a round face answers the door and immediately welcomes us in. "Senator Gallagher, so glad you could make it. He is waiting for you in the dining room. If you'll follow me?"

It's a trap. My instincts scream at me to make an excuse and get the fuck away, but Elizabeth has a death grip on my arm, so all I can do is follow them. Legs leaden. Heart racing. Something inside me senses it despite there being no outward threat. I tell myself I'm being foolish, but I keep my guard up, just in case.

Whoever this guy is, he must be important. Pondering this and who the mysterious host could be, I follow Elizabeth as the older woman, who introduces herself as Frances, welcomes us into a small foyer. The walls are distressed plaster over exposed brick in an aged cream color for most of the shared left wall. Directly in front of us is a narrow set of stairs, and beyond that, another doorway and what looks like a mudroom.

Elizabeth's shoes echo on the slate flooring as we move deeper inside, passing a roomy kitchen with lots of windows, more exposed brick, and another sea of slate floors.

We march in a single file behind Frances because the tight space of the hallway doesn't offer room for much else. I, naturally, fall in line at the back. Father disappears through the open double doors to our right, behind Frances, and then Elizabeth. I hesitate in the hall, something forcing my steps to a halt, somehow knowing that if I step over the threshold, something terrible waits on the other side.

I could turn around and flee. Should give up this fruitless

search and live my life. But I stride forward, resolute, through the threshold. With a sharp eye for detail, I scan my surroundings for clues about the mysterious dinner host but find nothing. When I drag my attention back to my father for a quick assessment, I nearly curse under my breath. The tension in his shoulders could practically snap his spine. That's how on edge he is.

"Gallagher," comes a smooth, rumbling drawl to our right, toward what I assume is the kitchen entrance. He must have been in a corner not visible from the hallway. Had he watched us come in? Why hadn't he introduced himself first?

Then I recognize the voice.

One with a lilting, musical Irish accent that's been a frequent star in my dreams.

No.

"I'm so pleased you could make it."

My heart does a sickening flip in my chest and damn near breaks through my ribs. Elizabeth draws away from me as Father tugs her forward. I try to hold her hand because it's the only thing keeping me upright, but she pulls free of my grasp, and I breathe deeply so I don't pass out.

"Of course," Father answers. "I'd like to introduce you to my daughters. This is Elizabeth, my youngest." A pause, reluctance. "And her older sister, Catriona."

Turning slowly, I squeeze my eyes together and pray to a God I don't believe in that I'm wrong. That stress is telling me the voice is familiar. But it's not. It can't be. There's no way he can be here right now. I would have known. Why the fuck didn't I insist on knowing who we were going to meet tonight? Why hadn't it ever occurred to me that he and

Father could be more connected than a simple real estate transaction?

I finally muster up the balls to open my eyes.

A low buzzing fills my ears. My hands go clammy, and I brush my palms against my thighs. I'd run, but Frances is already closing the double doors to the hallway, and his tall, broad frame occupies the only other exit to the kitchen. Unless I want to smash through the doors like the Hulk, I'm trapped.

Father urges a trembling Elizabeth forward, and she bobs her head as she allows the man to take her hand and bring it to his lips.

The first thought that comes to my panicking mind falls woefully short of my horror.

Fuck.

At my whispered curse—*Did I say that out loud?*—his familiar eyes, so light blue they're almost pure silver, lift to mine as he kisses my sister's fingers. He raises a brow, the only sign at all that he recognizes me.

It's then, with equal amounts of crystal-clear clarity and sick horror, that I realize the purpose behind tonight's impromptu meeting, and why it's going to be an unmitigated disaster.

Above all, Father values connections, and he hasn't made it a secret that he views Elizabeth and me as pawns to move around at his pleasure. I wouldn't put it past him to use one of us to further his interests.

And that's something I can never allow to happen.

Because the man extending to his full height with Elizabeth's hand in his isn't a stranger at all.

In fact, he's been haunting my increasingly dark and

dangerous dreams for months—ever since I left him sleeping in the messy sheets of the bedroom where he spent an entire night punishing me for crashing his party. A punishment I'll never be able to force from my memory. Not that I've wanted to.

Clearly, expecting him to disappear from my life was a big mistake.

Huge.

CHAPTER 3

AIDEN

I still with Elizabeth's hand against my lips, already wishing I could speed up time until after the wedding. The sooner this is over with, the better. I let out a slow breath, everything inside me icing over as a sour taste fills my mouth. There is only one way tonight can end. Elizabeth doesn't notice as she chatters blithely about how nice it is to meet me. I highly doubt she'll maintain that sentiment for long.

Straightening, I release Elizabeth's hand and then... there she is. Like she never left.

Frozen in the entrance to the dining room, Catriona observes the scene, expressionless. I blink once, but it's all I need for the sight of her to sear itself into my brain. Skintight pink dress that makes her seem ages more innocent than she is. Hair in Hollywood curls flowing over her shoulders. Heels that emphasize her trim calves and shapely legs. I thought I'd imagined how good she looked. But I hadn't. Not even a bit.

Trouble. That's what she looks like. I'd known it then, and it's even more apparent now. This woman is trouble.

Ripping myself away, I shake Rory's hand and press my fingertips to her sister's lower back, guiding them to the table, place settings already out for the meal. Frances quietly sets another place for Catriona. I hadn't thought—maybe I'd hoped that she wouldn't come. It would be less of a headache if she stayed as far away as possible in the future.

"Wine?" I ask Rory. He opens his mouth and pauses like he's remembering our last conversation, and wonders if maybe I'm playing with him. I'm not, but I don't mind how it immediately sets him on edge. It'll be better for everyone involved if he stays that way. He scrutinizes the empty doorways like Eamon may be hiding in the shadows, then gives a jerky nod when he finds them empty.

Frances pours glasses of water as I move back to the kitchen for a bottle. I'd planned to abstain, to stay level-headed, but if I'm going to spend the night getting royally fucked, I prefer to do it with lubrication.

A hand on my wrist stops me inside the kitchen and pulls me back toward the hallway, where we're out of sight of the dining room. *Shite.* Not even a chance to guzzle down a bottle or two of my favorite vintages. Not a particularly promising start to the evening.

"Yes?" I ask with a lifted brow when she doesn't let go after a pointed look at where her grip holds me captive.

Her mouth parts, brows pinching together. A pulse races at the base of her throat. "What the hell are you doing here?

Is this about the house?" Her throat bobs as she swallows, and her grip tightens.

"Worried I'll tell him about us?" She releases me, and I work up a sneer. "Don't trouble yourself. Tonight has nothing to do with you."

I'd tell her to leave, but if I know her at all, that'll only ensure she keeps her sweet arse right where it is. Catriona follows closely as I cross to the kitchen shelves where I keep a couple of bottles. Choosing blindly, I turn and find her standing right behind me.

"If you're looking for a repeat, I hate to tell you, but it's not happening." The urge to call her pet is so present, I can almost taste the word on my lips, see it reflected in her conflicted hazel eyes. I wonder if she'd slap me if I did.

"Are you fucking kidding me?" She jerks her chin up. There's a beauty mark at the corner of her left eye that I hadn't noticed when she'd been wearing the mask. It twitches as her eyes thin to slits. "That's what you have to say to me right now?"

"Is there something else I should say?"

"You could tell me why you're pretending you have no idea who I am. Why you're here with my father. Because I have to tell you, what's in my head isn't painting a very nice picture of you."

"No one's pretending. I know who you are. And there's no one I can think of who'd mistake me as nice."

"And?" she demands, slapping a hand on the counter when I try to slip by her, bottles in my hands.

I level her with a look. "And it has nothing to do with anything. It was one night. And you left. We both got what we wanted. End of story. Don't make it more than it is because you will only embarrass yourself."

Trying to shift around her, she blocks my way, ignoring my scowl. "Is this some sort of power play because I left you in bed? Are your sensitive male feelings hurt because I ghosted you? Because if that's it, I have to say, that's pretty fucking pathetic. Even for a man like you."

"My sensitive male feelings are perfectly fine, thanks for asking. Now, if you don't mind, I have guests waiting." I take a step closer, invading her space. She doesn't back down. Christ. The warmth of her rage radiates off her, along with her scent. What is that? For some reason, it reminds me of mornings in the kitchen with my parents in Ireland. Floral, green, bright.

"Are you fucking with me? Is that what this is? Okay, ha ha, so funny. But this is taking it too far. My family? Really?"

I duck down, and she stiffens from head to toe. I can almost hear her heart pausing its attempt to push blood through her veins. "Such a spoiled, selfish little girl. Tonight has nothing to do with you. I don't even know why you're here. My business is with your father and your sister. But if you insist on staying, then I'd recommend not making a nuisance of yourself. We're going to be seeing a lot of each other in the future, so I suggest you get used to staying out of my way starting now, if you don't want your father knowing what you were up to."

This time, she doesn't stop me when I move around her, but the sound of her heels against the floor follows me back to the dining room.

The scent of Frances's potato leek soup is hearty and rich, but it makes my stomach twist as I take my seat at the table. I'm at the head with Elizabeth to my right. Rory takes my left, with Catriona to his other side. If it weren't my job to read people, I wouldn't notice anything amiss in her expression. I have to give her credit. Her mask is almost as good as mine.

Almost.

I don't realize Rory is already speaking until I rip my attention away from Catriona.

"Elizabeth is a freshman pursuing a degree in history from Tulane, and she can speak French, German, and Italian. She's also an accomplished violinist and quite the baker. If I say so myself," Rory boasts when I finally tune back in. No note of the panicked man from the previous meeting. No, he's the consummate politician now, all big, fake teeth and an even faker smile. I wish I could crack him open and string up his insides like Mardi Gras beads, ropes of intestines hanging from trees.

"You must be very proud," I say, waving Frances away as she tries to fill my bowl with ladles of soup. Wine will be my first, second, and third courses.

As Rory blathers on like an auctioneer at a cattle sale, I drink. Catriona glares. Elizabeth takes dainty spoonfuls of soup. Frances hovers, hands fluttering like moth wings and as graceful as a ballerina. She catches my eye from time to time, her mouth a firm line of disapproval, but she doesn't say a word. Not that she could. Rory hasn't given anyone else the chance to speak.

"Her *Gaeilge Uladh* isn't as good as it could be, unfortunately. We never had the time to go to Ireland to pick it up."

Catriona snorts. I swallow the wine souring on my tongue. My hand fists under the table as our eyes meet in a moment of unwanted intimacy that blots out the rest of the room.

"Would you like to go?" I ask Elizabeth, deliberately turning my body so she fills my vision.

"To Ireland?" Elizabeth asks after blotting her mouth.

"Yes. It's a beautiful country. I haven't been back in many years."

Elizabeth glances at her father. "Y-yes, I'd love to."

"She loves to travel, this one. All over. Must have gotten it from her mother because I prefer to keep to New Orleans when I'm not needed in DC," Rory says between deep gulps from his wineglass. He snaps his fingers as soon as Frances reenters the room and gestures for her to refill his glass before she serves the next course.

I frown at his arrogance, hiding it behind my glass.

"I was sorry to learn about her passing," I say to Elizabeth.

She drops her head to study the table with a murmured, "Thank you."

"Her mother was the most beautiful of *her* sisters, as well. Knew I had to have her as soon as I set my eyes on her. I did. It's a shame she's gone. A damn shame."

All I can spare for him is a grunt before I force myself to study Elizabeth. You'd think I could substitute her for Catriona, considering how much they look alike. But I don't feel a damn thing when I look at her other than obligation and resignation. She's too fucking young for me, but that's nothing compared to the list of my sins.

Schemes swirl in my thoughts, mixing with the lightning strike of my desire for revenge as I say to Elizabeth, "How are you liking the potato leek soup? Frances is my secret weapon in the kitchen. No one in New Orleans can compare."

Elizabeth smiles shyly. "It's wonderful, thank you. You have a lovely home. Have you been in New Orleans long? I love your accent, so I'm assuming you grew up in Ireland? Our mother was from Dublin."

"A Dub. I like the city well enough. Dublin's grand, but I like the country, myself. My family is from the western coast, County Clare."

"I've always wanted to go there. The cliffs must be gorgeous."

Catriona's loathing burns a path into the side of my skull. I hide my smile behind a deep drink of wine as Rory picks up the conversation. I wish we could have skipped this dinner altogether, but I wanted at least one meeting with the woman I'm supposed to marry before I met her at the altar. I may want to see my mother, but I draw the line at forcing this girl to go through with it. I'd rather kill Rory and get it over with.

Sensing the strange tension in the air, Elizabeth blinks rapidly and busies herself with buttering a roll and stuffing it in her mouth. She may not be ready for my life as it stands, but I could change that easily enough with enough training and positive reinforcement. The fact that I care nothing for her should be protection in and of itself.

The clink of Frances clearing the soup bowls punctuates the growing tension. Rory hasn't touched his food, but Catriona has methodically emptied hers, like a soldier preparing for battle. Her eyes keep darting between me and her sister, calculations clearly running behind that sharp glower. I recognize that look—it's the same one she wore at my estate right before she suggested we flip a coin to see if I'd let her go. She's planning something. Scheming. Does the woman ever stop her *fucking* scheming?

Curious, I luxuriate in the weight of Catriona's all-consuming hatred directed at me and say to Elizabeth, "Has Rory explained why you're here tonight, Elizabeth?"

"O'Con—" Rory starts, but I silence his outraged objection with a mild look. Christ, I'm tired of his voice. I don't think the man knows how to shut the fuck up.

"Your father owes the man I work for a great deal of money." I'm speaking to Elizabeth, but every iota of my attention is on Catriona, who stiffens at my words. If she's going to be a problem, I'd bet the Emerald she'll show her hand tonight. Once that's over with and the wedding is done, there will be nothing standing in my way of getting Cian's approval to visit my mother.

Elizabeth's face twitches as though she wants to glance at her sister, but she stops herself just in time. "Do you know what he promised me in exchange?"

Elizabeth keeps her expression blank. Impressive. "What —what did he promise you?" she asks.

"He promised me you," I answer.

The only show of emotion Elizabeth gives is her hand turning white around the stem of her water glass. "Right," she breathes, and sets the glass aside before clearing her throat and daring to glance at her father, who gives her an encouraging nod. Elizabeth squares her shoulders and opens her mouth to speak.

"Like hell," Catriona bursts out, finally unable to contain herself. She pushes away from the table, evading her father's grasp and rounding the place where I sit to stand next to her sister, her hands wrapping around the back of the chair until the wood creaks under her fingers. Her furious honeypot eyes ping back and forth between her father and me. "You can't be fucking serious. You're selling her to pay your debts? Your own daughter?"

The look she gives him would flay a lesser man, but Rory's either impervious to the disdain of others or incredibly ignorant. Maybe a little of both. I down the rest of my wine, settling into a pleasant buzz and wondering if Frances will think me insane if I ask her for a fry-up when they're gone.

"Sit down, Catriona," Rory barks, spittle flying, his sour breath a pungent cloud at my cheek. "It's done."

Catriona seems at a loss for words—a first, I have no doubt. I lean back in my seat, refreshing the wine in my glass as I settle in to watch the scene play out and hoping they'll be quick about it.

"You can't make her do this. You can't," Catriona says to her father. "She's too young. Please don't do this. You don't even know what he's capable of."

"It's done," Rory snaps again, as he cuts a hand through the air.

Elizabeth murmurs to her sister at the finality of the proclamation, and Catriona's eyes blaze. Really, her passion is an inspiration, but can't she tell it's a waste of time? Poor girl. It must be exhausting to care so deeply about everything.

"I warned you not to ruin this for me," Rory says, and I silence him with a gesture. His teeth clack together with how quickly he obeys.

Now, who's the good dog?

I lift a brow at Catriona, giving her space to speak, ready to get this over with. Her head swings toward me, leveling me with her contempt. The rest of the room drops away, throwing me back to when I'd last held her in my grasp.

"You're really going to go through with this? I don't know why I'm surprised. You're disgusting."

Her father barks, "You little bitch," before she's even finished speaking.

"Do I need to put a muzzle on you?" Rory flinches at my lethal drawl. The fact that I'm going to be related to him, even if it's only on paper, disgusts me. "Leave us."

Rory moves to drag Catriona out of the room, and I stand, causing Elizabeth to startle and leap to her feet as well. Jumpy little thing.

"No, Rory, take Elizabeth to the study for more wine and dessert. Frances will show you the way while I have a conversation with Catriona. Then we'll talk about the finer details."

The silence stretches between us like a rubber band ready to snap. I signal discreetly, with a slight nod toward the door.

Frances appears, seemingly out of nowhere, and says, "This way."

This breaks Rory out of his stupor. "What are you playing at, O'Connor? You can't renegotiate now. I swear to God, I'll—"

"Calm yourself, Gallagher. Nothing's changed—one of your daughters for your debts. Do not mistake my manners for kindness. Now do what you're told."

Hatred twists his features, but he releases his bruising grip on Catriona's arm and reluctantly herds Elizabeth out of the dining room after Frances. If it weren't my mother on the line, I'd never willingly tie myself to a man like him. In fact, if I ever get the chance, I'd love to put a bullet in his brain. I imagine it, him on his knees again, begging, the way he'd jerk from the force of impact. How he'd topple over, a pile of meat, eyes blank.

As soon as they're gone, Catriona rounds on me. "What is it?"

"What is what?"

"What do you have on him? What could he have done that was so bad that you had to take my sister? Tell me. I deserve to know."

"What happened is between your father and my boss. It's not personal, and it's out of your hands. It's best for everyone involved if you accept that now, because the people involved in this are more dangerous than you can imagine. You want to keep your sister safe? Leave it alone."

Her stony expression tells me she does not believe a word I say, not that I'm surprised. "You expect me to leave it alone when you're forcing my sister to marry you? Who are you? What are you involved in?" When I don't answer, she prods, "Does it have to do with that man I saw you kill on Halloween? Dufresne?"

I go still. Before she can continue, I say, "Stop. Just stop. The way you want to be the savior is sweet, really, but—"

"Oh, cut the patronizing bullshit, O'Connor. If you aren't going to tell me what I want to know, I'm going to find out for myself. I won't rest until I ruin you. I promise you right now, that's what will happen if you marry her."

"And you think you can stop me? You have no idea who you're dealing with."

To my surprise, she laughs. "You're such a fucking cliché. You're not the first asshole I've dealt with, and you won't be the last. But you want to know the truth about men like you? They're weak. Every. Single. One. So what'll it take to get you not to go through with this? My silence? My body? What if I were to pay my father's debt myself? How much is it?"

My throat is dry, but there's no more wine. I've drunk it all. "Neither your silence nor your body is worth anything to me, Catriona. Don't flatter yourself. And as for the debt? You couldn't afford it." She doesn't back down when I draw steadily closer. "There's nothing you can do to stop this. It's not a crusade. There won't be any justice. Don't get in my way, or I'll make you regret it."

Brave girl, with her emotion-choked eyes and knotted hands. She's trying so hard to be strong. Doesn't she know it's useless? She's going to give in. She has to see there's no way out of this. I let the relief fill me until my muscles turn liquid. I spin to the doorway before her voice stops me.

"Do you want me to beg, like I did that night? Because I'll beg if that's what you want. I'll give you anything. What you had that night and more. Everything... if you'll do this for me. Please."

The smart thing to do would be to brush her off, will the memories of her away, and leave her. I have too much going on to be distracted by her mouth and her pretty pleading. Too much at stake. Too much to lose. Entertaining her would be a mistake.

Yet.

Yet...

"What would you do for me, Catriona? Would you get

on your knees while you beg? You'd have to. To make me believe it. I remember you were so pretty that way."

She sucks in a breath, and the indecision of it wars across her face before her expression hardens. "You'd love that, wouldn't you? If-if that's what it will take for you to leave us alone, the-then I'll do whatever you want."

"Is that really something you want to say to a man like me? I realize you don't know me very well—well, most of me —but it would be in your best interest to be very careful what you're willing to do for me."

She lifts a brow, regal and perhaps so pissed off at me now that she's forgetting to be afraid.

"You're mistaken, O'Connor. It isn't what I'm willing to do for you. It's what I'm willing to do to stop you from marrying her."

"And that would be?"

Catriona takes a deep breath before tipping her face up and warming me from the inside out like the burn of a good whiskey.

"Anything. I'd do anything you want to stop this," she says. "Including getting on my knees... or marrying you instead."

CHAPTER 4

CATRIONA

The moment the words come out of my mouth, I want to suck them back in. Panic flares then rises in my esophagus like a geyser. I've always made it a point to put my goals first, much to the detriment of my sex life, so marriage has been the last thing on my radar. Being tied down to a man like my mother hasn't exactly been on my to-do list.

After tonight, O'Connor would be last on the list of candidates I'd consider chaining myself to.

But I'll do it.

Even if it's him. Despite what he's done.

Maybe even because of it. It would serve him right to be married to me, forced to face the breadth of my loathing every day for the rest of his life.

I don't examine the reasons that I can't stomach the thought of him marrying her. Would they be honorable upon inspection? Probably not.

I have no illusions about the kind of man he is, yet I still find myself incandescent with rage all over again, fists clenched and teeth grinding. I'll never admit it out loud, but fuck him for even considering this after that night. And fuck me for thinking it meant anything at all. I should know better. One thing for sure and two things for certain: I'll never let my guard down around him ever again if I can help it.

If he's determined to go through with this, then he's going to learn exactly what regret tastes like. He's going to understand his threats and intimidation won't work on me.

"Did you think about me that much?" Aiden asks, leaning close enough with his full lips parting and his voice dropping a few octaves. The mocking note grates on my nerves. My vision tunnels, and my fists clench until my nails bite half-moons into my palms. As he studies me, my skin prickles like the ghosts of those hands are trailing all over my body. Breasts, hips, thighs. All the places where my dress stretches tight over my curves.

But the man who would have touched me, found all those places and worshipped them, is gone. He's been replaced by the stranger in front of me. The one with a face so cold he could still be wearing that blank-faced mask. The fact that I fell for his act infuriates me almost as much as his words. I'll blame it on grief. We all go a little mad sometimes, right? My sins aren't as bad as murder, but fucking a psychopath and liking it feels just as unforgivable.

"You wish, O'Connor. I have better things to do with my time. The only reason I'm offering is because you're fucking with my family. Is coercion the only way you'd ever get anyone to marry you? Makes sense, based on my personal experience, but I'm willing if it means you'll leave her alone."

He pushes back, his grin turning feral. It hovers there for a moment, reminding me of the man I'd known that night—the one who had gotten so thoroughly under my defenses that I let him do unfathomable things to me. That I'd wanted him to do more.

"Your begging is cute now, but useless. What will it take for you to understand?"

Shock and fury thicken my voice and blur my vision with crimson. "You really are a fucking jerk. Why? Why does it have to be her? It doesn't have to be me, but you can have anyone you want. Anyone else. Why is it so damn important that you have to marry her, or do you simply delight in being a bastard?"

His silver eyes flick back and forth between mine, and I do my best at shuttering my thoughts and expression. I suppress the urge to look away, to give him yet another moment of vulnerability. Because I'm not lying. I would do anything to keep this marriage from happening.

Whatever is left in his face hardens, turning cold, and I fight a shiver that traces skeletal fingers down my spine.

Finally, he says, "Envious, Catriona? Afraid to be left out? That I'd choose her? Jealousy is an ugly color on you."

"Oh, fuck you, O'Connor," I say, finally unleashing a sliver of the emotions rioting inside me. Then it's overcome by fear, genuine fear, flashing through me like a lightning strike, and I know with a certainty that makes me ill he's going to stick to his word. It feels like this whole situation is a car wreck that I'm being forced to watch from the sidelines, with no way to prevent the devastation. The momentum leaves me sick to my stomach. "The fact that you think I'm jealous about this situation is a testament to how insane you are."

He crosses to me, sucking away the rest of the oxygen in the room with every step. He's close enough that I can see every shade of gray in his mercurial eyes. "If you think this is insane, imagine how much worse I can be if you push me. Hmm? But don't worry, so long as you behave, I promise I'll be good to your sister." His voice lowers. "So very, very good."

I flash a cold smile. "If you go through with this, I'm going to spend every day making your life a living hell."

For a moment, I think he'll reconsider. But the bubble of hope pops in the next instant, leaving me numb and empty.

"As if it isn't already," he says. "There's nothing you can do to change it. Now, be a good little pet like I know you can be, and accept this situation is one you can't change."

I grind my teeth together.

I resist the urge to plant my fist in his face.

Only barely.

Talking to him is getting me nowhere. I'd have more productive conversations with a rock wall.

I follow him to the study on the second floor, and it occurs to me that he could be at my family's estate. Why meet with us here and not at the fancy new house he acquired? Was the estate part of his deal with my father? How fucking connected is my father with these people? What the fuck did he do?

Aiden opens the door to find Elizabeth and Father sharing heated words on the other side. Their conversation cuts off abruptly as soon as we enter the room. Elizabeth gives me a look like she is resigned to her fate, and I redouble my vow to do whatever it takes to stop this before it's out of my hands.

There has to be something I can do or some other deal we can make to excise him from our lives. I'll never forgive my father for putting us in this position. I feel like I'm missing a big part of the picture. Something crucial. I've been so focused on tracking down leads about our mother that I've let this clusterfuck surprise me. I should have been paying closer attention.

I want to hold on to that thought as Father and Aiden begin to finalize the arrangement. I need to figure out why it unsettles me so much, but my head fills with fuzz from panic, and it's as though my whole being becomes lighter, like I could float away at the slightest breeze. My brow and palms grow slick with sweat, and the room around me, as well as its occupants, fades under a white haze.

I have enough awareness to realize it's an anxiety attack before I'm catapulted into a memory I only visit in my nightmares.

It's as though I'm in two places at once. In reality, I'm next to Father and Elizabeth, but at the same time, my thoughts are assaulted by the sound of my screams. As Aiden speaks to Elizabeth, asking her questions about her prefer- ences for the small, intimate wedding ceremony he has planned—how can it possibly be intimate if he wants it at the St. Louis Cathedral?—Father answers over Elizabeth, who merely rolls her eyes and maintains her silence. Does she even want this? Or is she going along with it so she doesn't upset him?

I sink into a chair in front of the fireplace as the memory

swells inside my thoughts, growing bigger and bigger, a wave gaining strength and speed as it hurtles toward shore. The string connecting the two moments is the overwhelming sense of powerlessness. I'd been powerless to save my mother.

And now, I feel powerless again. Powerless to stop Elizabeth from being forced to marry O'Connor. My nails dig into the leather of the chair to hold on to the present.

That night, I'd arrived home late from a long day of classes. I was supposed to be home earlier to help my mother prepare dinner for some politician or another—I can never recall who it was, though the police have already ruled them out as suspects. I'd been too late to save her. I'd found her in a discordant tangle at the foot of the stairs.

Listening as my father arranges Elizabeth's marriage to Aiden isn't exactly the same, but my nervous system doesn't understand that. All it knows is that something terrible is happening, and it feels like there's nothing I can do to stop it. Like I'm going to have to watch as everything implodes right in front of me all over again.

Why have a wedding in such a big church if there won't be many guests? Why have a service at all? It doesn't make any sense. O'Connor doesn't seem like the type, and Elizabeth is so checked out that I'm not sure she's even paying attention. Have we really changed so much in the past year that I don't know what to say to her to get her to object to this? The devastating answer is... yes.

But Aiden barters this deal with the controlling air of a king, and my father—much to my surprise—agrees with every point. They'll be married in the church, by a priest, this coming Saturday.

My heart trips over itself, my pulse pounding a staccato rhythm in my ears. I stifle a gasp as the memory repeats in my head, over and over and over. Blood-red stains my vision. They are so distracted by their negotiations that none of them seems to notice my spectacular spiral into a mini breakdown. I've grown better at hiding them, I think. So much so that I can go through it while sitting less than six feet away and not have them realize a thing.

As they wrap up their meeting, the fuzzy buzzing sound fades from my ears, and I regain my careful composure. Lock it away. Stay strong. Don't allow anyone to see you falter. This time, my mother's voice comes from another memory, a happier one. I cling to it as I carefully brush the nonexistent wrinkles from my dress, smooth my hair, and rearrange my features into placid acceptance.

Too late, I realize Elizabeth and Father are walking, heads tipped together, voices a low whisper, out of the study and to the stairs, leaving me alone with O'Connor once again. My muscles lock for a fraction of a second until I remind myself to stay loose and unaffected. He studies my face, a frown pulling at his lips. There's barely any space between us. As I rise, I move to step past him, but he grabs my elbow.

"Let go of me," I say, my voice low and dark.

Of course, he doesn't listen. Instead, his grip turns bruising, and he says, "No matter what you're thinking, I want your word you won't interfere. Your fury is admirable, but fruitless. It was one night. You really didn't think one night with you would mean I'd change my plans." At my silence, he croons, "Oh, how sweet."

It shouldn't be a betrayal, I barely know him, but after

the night we shared, I thought… Well, it doesn't matter what I thought. I was wrong. And as someone who is always right, being wrong infuriates me.

I grip his arm and shove it away, giving myself enough room to maneuver around him.

While I'd been in the midst of panic, one thing became startlingly clear. My father may be a hypocritical asshole, but he's always been right about one thing: you can't sit around waiting for opportunities to fall into your lap—you have to take them.

And that's exactly what I intend to do.

I shift to move around his imposing body, but O'Connor moves faster than I remembered he could, blocking my way. Scowling up at him, I cross my arms over my chest. The mask I wear around everyone else slips effortlessly back into place. I rarely allow myself to be vulnerable with anyone, and now that he's seen me at my most defenseless, I can't help the automatic urge to hide myself away. Let the ice princess reign.

He had a piece of me the night we spent together.

I gave him more when I begged him not to do this.

No way in hell will I ever let him have another.

He can go fuck himself.

"I'll have your word," he says, lifting a brow, his hands shoved casually in his pockets. "Cat got your tongue, pet?"

"Don't call me that," I answer, my tone calm despite the rage brewing inside me. Rage against him. Against my father. Against me. Maybe even against my mother, for whatever secrets she kept that cost her life. "After all, we're going to be brother and sister soon. What would my father think if he heard the way you talk to me?"

His jaw clenches then unclenches, and I smile. He gives me a hard look, and for a moment, I think he's going to push. Another moment, I swear he's going to take it all back, but then he steps aside so I can pass.

But I can feel him behind me, haunting me.

And I carry the weight of that awareness on my shoulders, my neck, my spine—all the way down the seemingly endless hallway, out of his house, and back into the car, where none of us says a word the entire way home.

***

I come back to myself as Father navigates the car up the driveway to our house. The impotence burning inside my stomach like acid makes me want to scream and then vomit profusely. Preferably all over O'Connor's lap. Or my father's, I'm not choosy. If he weren't such an irresponsible jerk, we wouldn't be in this situation in the first place. How the hell he got caught up with a man like Aiden O'Connor, I'll never know, but I'm not surprised.

My hands tremble with the effort to hold back my anger, and I take deep breaths to calm myself the entire way through the house. We follow him without question, knowing he'll want to debrief and denying him would only make it worse. Giving in to my emotions will help nothing. I need to figure a way out of this before everything falls apart. One positive personality trait I inherited from my father is my ability to think or charm myself out of any situation.

A clutch of nerves writhes in my stomach, agitated by the silent stillness pressing down around me. I press a hand to it, but it's useless, and the gnawing ache persists. Elizabeth prefers to handle confrontation and anxiety with glib comments and monotone whatevers. But me? I thrive on it. I use it to fuel my antagonism, which is usually to my detriment.

That's why, when Father closes his study door behind us and rounds on me, his open palm connecting with my cheek in a blinding blow that turns everything white, I'm able to swallow down my resulting cry of outrage. Hot, stinging tears fill my vision until their figures are blurs and shadows. A sharp heat spreads from the point of contact, and blood fills my mouth where my teeth have bitten into my cheek.

"I told you to keep your fucking mouth shut if you knew what was good for you. Is it really so hard, or are you just that fucking stupid?"

Elizabeth makes a sound of protest in the back of her throat, and our dad wheels around on her, a snarl on his face. Although my cheek stings with a searing pain and my vision is hazy with violence, I shove myself between them. I haven't done this in longer than I can remember, but my feet moved without thought.

I hold my shaking hands up. "You're right. I shouldn't have said anything. Trust me, O'Connor made that very clear. I'm sorry. I was worried about Elizabeth. It wasn't her fault. Please. It won't happen again."

He's breathing so hard, I'm afraid he may pop a lung. "The next time you do something I explicitly told you not to do will be the last. I don't care the lengths I'll have to go. And if I catch even a hint that you're going to sabotage this deal, I'll make your life hell. Do we understand each other?"

"Yes," I say, wincing internally at the desperation in my voice. I don't cover it up because I know he enjoys seeing us beaten down, and it'll mollify him, at least a little bit. "Yes, I understand. I won't interfere again."

Father scoffs, his bulk deflating as the weight of the night seems to press down on him. He glances at the globe near his desk, split in half to reveal a minibar inside. In less than a minute, he's gulping down a shot of whiskey straight. Then another. Elizabeth inches toward the exit. The more alcohol he gets in his system, the more vicious he'll be. She may be his favorite, but it's not always enough to protect her.

After his third, he slams the shot glass down onto his desk, wiping his glistening mouth with the back of his hand. She's almost out of the door when his head whips up, and he sees her attempted escape. I move to block his progress, but I'm still partially blind from the stinging slap to my eye and misjudge the distance, allowing him to evade me.

"Where in the hell do you think you're going?" He jerks her away from the door with a rough hand on her arm. She glares at him, eyes as sharp as knives. His eyes are too glassy to notice. I'm frozen in place, eye stinging, heart pounding. "We're not finished here."

"You're going to want to let go of my arm unless you want bruises in the wedding pictures," Elizabeth warns. They share an indecipherable look as I debate whether to interfere.

Father sneers. "Don't let your sister rub off on you. If you know what's good for you, you'll ensure your marriage to O'Connor is happy, at least until he gets his money. Am I understood?"

Elizabeth stares pointedly at where his hand is wrapped around her arm. The silence stretches until he finally releases her with a petulant scoff. "Don't worry. I won't mess this up for you. But if you touch me like that again, it'll be the last time. You understand?"

He jerks his chin at her, and we practically sprint out of his study before he does worse. We don't stop until we're on the second floor, well away from his meaty fists and biting tongue.

As soon as the door closes behind us, Elizabeth leans against the wall with a sigh, expelling all the tension from the past several hours. If I could relax, I'd do the same, but my thoughts are racing. Making plans, rejecting them. Searching for a way out of this that doesn't end up with someone getting hurt.

Before I can give her platitudes I don't mean, Elizabeth's voice breaks the silence. "There's nothing you can do. We both know he'll keep pushing until he gets what he wants." I try to soothe her, but she's so focused on getting her words out that she talks over my empty promises, pushing away from me to stalk from one end of her bedroom to the other.

"You don't have to do this," I murmur, but Elizabeth is too busy prowling to notice.

"Oh, please. We both know Father is going to get his way. The difference is I've learned to use his goals to my advantage. And you saw his place. The man must be successful. I could do worse."

That's where she's wrong.

I'm not sure there's much worse than Aiden O'Connor.

I press my fingers against my temple and join her in pacing back and forth across her room.

Elizabeth shakes her head at me. "Why do you always do this? I'm not a kid anymore, Cat. I have to figure these things out for myself at some point. Besides, if you try to interfere, Dad will lose his shit. Just drop it. It's done. We always knew he'd do something like this someday. I'll just have to make the best of it."

If we were anyone else, I'd kneel at her feet and take her hands into mine. I'd promise her I'd do whatever it took to ensure she could marry the man of her dreams. But that's not us, so I keep my mouth shut, the words trapped in my throat behind all the rest I've never told her. "If that's really what you want, then I'll respect your wishes."

If the words taste like a lie, it's because they couldn't be further from the truth.

CHAPTER 5

CATRIONA

According to my father, the inspiration behind my desire to become a lawyer has everything to do with his political career. There are countless interviews with the media where he crows about how proud he is that I want to follow in his footsteps. It never ceases to amaze me how easily his constituents eat up his every word.

Yasmine opens the door to her family's home a couple of days after the disastrous meeting between O'Connor and my father with an expression of bored amusement on her face. "Well, well, so you do remember where I live. I was beginning to wonder, since it appears your phone is broken."

I make a face. "I know, I'm sorry."

She doesn't move to let me in. Usually, I wouldn't even knock, but I knew my lack of response to her repeated texts and calls would annoy her.

Crossing her arms over her chest, she says, "So what

happened?" At my blank look, she rolls her eyes. "It's something with your father, right? You always go radio silent when he's a complete asshole."

I look away, sighing heavily, and she gasps.

Fuck. Unfortunately, the bruise from my father still shows in the afternoon sun, no matter how much makeup I cake over it. It's faded a bit, but obviously, it's still visible at the right angle.

"Reggie!" she shouts over her shoulder.

I choke on saliva. "Yas, don't."

"Reggie, get your ass out here. Bring your keys," she says, ignoring me. Her jaw works as she clenches it over and over. Maybe I shouldn't have come here after all, but I couldn't think of anywhere else to go.

Yasmine is a mix of the most important people in her life, and I love each of her facets. The stoicism that's going to make her a fantastic doctor she got from her father. Her sense of justice is a thousand percent her mother. But the calculating fury? That's pure Nana Estelle. That woman is sweet as honey with a tongue that'll sting like a bee.

Remembering this, I hold up my hands to placate her. "I'm serious. It's nothing. Let me explain."

"Does the explanation involve anything other than your father putting his hands on you?" she asks quietly. The heavy footsteps of her older brother, Reggie, sound behind her as he comes down from the second floor.

Reggie is in his thirties, and he has always treated us like his annoying little sisters. It made me feel like family, even if he spent most of the time when I was around doing his level best to ignore me or piss me off.

He is, however, now a detective with the New Orleans

Police Department. According to him, he works to put criminals behind bars, his mother tries to free them, and his sister wants to fix their injuries. I look up to him. How steady he is with Yasmine. Once upon a time, I tried, and probably failed, to imitate the same with Elizabeth.

"Yas, c'mon. Don't bring Reggie into this. He's going to make it a big thing, and there's other—"

But Reggie appears behind her, dressed in slacks and a white button-down shirt with his gun in a shoulder holster, before I convince her to keep her mouth shut.

Panic skitters up my spine in a hot rush. I really don't have time for this. Elizabeth will only be out of the house with the wedding planner for a couple of hours at most to try on dresses. Father is also out on other obligations. Neither of them has let me out of their sights this week. Probably certain I'll be up to no good... And what can I say? They'd be right.

"Ri," Reggie says with an easy smile. "Long time no see. What did I tell you, Yas? She's perfectly fine. Everything is —" Then his attention snags on my cheek, and his smile falls.

"You still think she's perfectly fine, asshole?"

"What the *fuck* is that?" he asks, already shrugging into his jacket with his keys dangling from his hand.

"Look, can we talk about this inside? I don't have a lot of time."

Yasmine pulls me inside with a huff and then grabs my chin so she can look at the bruise more closely. "I could kill him. Mom would get me off, no problem. Temporary insanity. No jury would convict me."

"Hold on there, tiger," Reggie says, resting a hand on Yasmine's arm. "Are you okay, Ri? Was this your father?" he asks, his voice laced with the hint of a Cajun accent that's always made me feel safe. It reminds me so much of his father's.

I take a moment to gather my thoughts. As much as I want to throw Father under the bus, it's not my priority. "Yes, it was, but I have worse problems."

Yasmine cocks her head to the side. "Worse problems than your father putting his hands on you?"

"Yes. Shit is seriously hitting the fan, and I need your help." To say the very least. When Yasmine doesn't interrupt or immediately call in for more reinforcements (read: her parents and Nana Estelle), I give them a quick rundown of the absurdity from the past few days. It sounds even worse when I say it out loud, but the relief of having someone else know what's going on eases the weight off my shoulders. I still don't tell them about what I saw O'Connor do the night before Halloween. They're already freaking out about my father. If I told them I was going to force a psychopath to marry me, they'd probably have me committed.

"I'm going to kill him," Yasmine says.

"Hey!" Reggie interjects.

She scoffs. "Like you don't want to."

"I'm an officer of the law, asshole. It would go against everything I believe in to kill him."

"Pussy. Are you sure you're my brother?"

"If he had a fatal accident, however, that would just be karma," Reggie muses, as he strokes his facial hair.

A warm rush of affection distracts me temporarily from the madness that has become my life. When I was younger and my house became a war zone of arguments, cold shoulders, and neglect, the Baptistes were always there to distract me with a plate of homemade food. They took me in and treated me like their own. I considered Claude and Yvonne, Yasmine and Reggie's mom and dad, my adoptive parents, and Estelle, Yvonne's mother, was like my grandmother. I spent so much time in their house during high school and undergrad that they cleaned out the guest room for me to use.

Since my mother's death, I haven't been back as much as I should, mostly because it reminds me of how much I've lost. It's a sore ache in my chest to realize just how much I've missed it. If I had more time to indulge, I'd stick around for dinner and wine on their terrace, stay up too late watching old movies with Yasmine, and crash on the too-small twin bed I've used for years.

"The most important thing right now is distracting Elizabeth. I would do it myself, but I know she'd fight me the whole way. I think she believes she's being noble by going through with everything. Or maybe she's trying to please Father. She always admired him even though he's the last person to deserve it."

During my rambling, we'd settled onto the benches in the small breakfast nook just off the kitchen. The sunny yellow walls are faded and marked from time, but the bright space does wonders for my dismal mood. Reggie poured coffee, strong and dark, and Yasmine lounged next to him in the seat across from me.

"What are you planning to do, exactly?" Yasmine asks. I open my mouth, but before I can say a word, she's already hissing in disbelief. "Do I even want to know? Is it worse than the other thing you did that I can't say in front of Reggie because he'd have to arrest you?"

"Seriously?" Reggie says with a long-suffering sigh. "How many illegal acts have you committed in the past year?"

"I plead the Fifth," Yasmine says.

"Define *illegal*," I say with a smile.

"Do you need me?" Reggie asks, all traces of humor gone. "I have a shift, but I can call in if you do. Just say the word. Nick wouldn't even give me a hard time for this." Nick is Reggie's boss, and I don't know him that well, but from our few interactions, I could say he'd definitely give him a hard time.

"Aw, Reg. So you do care."

"Brat," Reggie says affectionately as he kisses Yasmine's brow. He rounds the corner and does the same to me. "Seriously, call me if you need me. I'm only a call away, okay?"

"I will, I promise. Stay safe and thank you."

"Always," he says over his shoulder with a cocky smile.

"Are you sure you don't want me to ask him to stay?"

I sigh into my coffee. "I'd rather not drag him into this if we don't have to."

"But you're willing to drag me into it? Aw. Thanks, I guess."

"I know I was nonchalant about the whole situation after that night," I start.

"You mean the night you spent with Aiden?"

I grind my teeth. "Yes. But this isn't something I can make light of. I know you didn't want to get involved, but there's no one else I can ask. Please say you'll help me."

"Alright, lay it on me. It's not worse than crashing his masquerade, is it?" My smile grows, and Yasmine scowls. "I'm not going to like this, am I?"

"THIS IS the dumbest idea you've ever had. And that includes the time that you made me moon that car we didn't know was an unmarked cop car when we were sixteen. I almost went to jail, and I would rather do that a million times over than help you pretend to be your sister so you can marry this man. You barely even know him."

"When you say it like that, it sounds like a really dumb idea," I murmur.

"That's because it *is* a really dumb idea. I can't believe I let you talk me into this shit. We're probably going to end up getting caught and thrown in jail, and Reggie will make my life hell." Yasmine's biting retort comes from over her shoulder, where I'm quickly changing clothes. We have an hour before we're due to be at the church.

"That's why," I interject, puffing out a wheezing breath, "we have your mom."

Yasmine pulls her head in from the window where she's watching for the rental car and gives me a disbelieving look. "You think Yvonne Baptiste will go easy on you if she learns you bribed a priest? I swear to God, you are out of your fucking mind."

"It's not like I have another choice."

"This is a terrible idea, mark my words. I will not come to your funeral when he finds out what we've done," Yasmine says.

"I wouldn't blame you. After this, I'm going to owe you my firstborn child," I answer.

"Gross," she says. "I don't want children. I want vacations. Preferably to Caribbean locations with fruity drinks and men who will rub oil all over my body."

"Done," I answer. "Bahamas coming your way as soon as all this blows over. You'll have to find the men on your own. I have a feeling I'll be sick of them."

"Have I told you lately that I hate you?"

"Love you too, Yas. Now, you remember the plan?"

"You mean the one where I practically kidnap your sister so you can abscond with her jerkhole husband? How could I forget?"

"All you have to do is get her far enough away from the church so she can't come back and interrupt until it's over."

"You better hope she can't fight, because the last thing I want is a shiner to match yours."

"About an hour should do it. From what the wedding planner has explained to Father, it's going to be a quick and simple ceremony. I bribed the priest to change my name on the marriage certificate and during the vows, so unless O'Connor kills me or someone objects, that should be enough time to get it all done."

"You don't think he or your father will object?"

I'd thought long and hard about this, and I'm betting my life and my sister's happiness on O'Connor's interest and my father's obsession with optics that they'll keep their mouths shut. I'm not saying my father won't try to beat the life out of me after, but that's future Catriona's problem. My current priority is making sure Elizabeth is as far away as possible.

"I don't think either of them will want to make a scene. Or at least, that's what I'm counting on." Then I change the subject before I lose my nerve. "How does it look?"

We congregate in front of the mirror, and I turn from

side to side. I hadn't had the chance to go dress shopping, so I resorted to wearing my mother's. Thankfully, we must have been the same size when she married my father, because the fit isn't too bad. I have more boobs, and it's not quite my style, but it almost feels fitting to wear her dress today. Like she'll be with me when I attempt to pull this off. Father may notice, but if so, it'll be too late for him to interfere. Is it terrible that I'm looking forward to it?

"Like you're making the biggest mistake of your life," Yasmine deadpans.

Rolling my eyes, I turn away from the mirror and ignore the burn that rises in my throat. "Probably. Let's get this over with before I lose my nerve."

I wait in my room, staring down through a window as Yasmine strides out to pick up Elizabeth and the wedding planner. Father is already at the church keeping a close eye on things. The car door closes behind her, and soon, she's swallowed up by traffic in the distance. There's no going back. No changing our fates now that I've set these plans in motion. Elizabeth has told me time and again not to interfere, that she is fine with going through with it. No doubt when she realizes Yasmine is taking her in the wrong direction, she'll be pissed.

Am I willing to sacrifice my relationship with her at the altar of my plans? The sister I'd like to be would say no. I'd never want to see her hurt. But the person I am, the one fueled by justice and revenge, doesn't care who gets hurt. Her. Father. O'Connor. No one is safe.

Not when dread and a twisted sense of anticipation are unspooling in my stomach at the thought of what I'm planning to do next.

My phone rings as I'm pulling into the church, and, afraid it's Yasmine with an emergency, I answer it without looking at the screen. "Hello? Is everything okay?"

"Miss Catriona, it's Leo Broussard. I hope I didn't catch you at a bad time."

You could say that, I think, and almost dissolve into hysterical giggles. Moving into the church via the back door so no one can see me, I say, "No, of course not. Do you have news?"

"Yes, I was able to identify the last number from your mother's call records. The one you weren't familiar with."

I stop in a dark hallway, heart thundering, stomach protesting my light breakfast violently. "You did? Who—" My voice cuts out. I clear my throat. "Who was it?"

"A Mr. Devin Franklin. I assume you're familiar."

Devin Franklin? "My father's head of security?" I don't know who I was expecting, but that was not it. "Why would he be calling her?"

"That I can't tell you. But he did phone her several times the day of her death. According to the police report, which I'll forward as soon as I'm done, he says it was regarding security for upcoming events."

I start moving again, feeling the ticking of a clock in my veins. I only have a few minutes before I need to be in place so this all goes off without a hitch. "That's strange. But it doesn't seem out of the realm of possibility. I don't think my father ever mentioned it. Wait, wouldn't I have recognized his number? I have it saved in my phone."

"It was his personal cell phone number. I imagine you have his work contact saved."

Why would Devin Franklin be calling my mother from his personal number?

"Thank you for letting me know, Mr. Broussard. I'll see if I can talk to Devin, figure out why he was calling her, and confirm his story. I wish I had more time to go over this, but I am late for an appointment."

"Of course. I'll be in touch with further updates. In the meantime, I'll have your mother's phone returned to you. I made duplicates of her data, so I won't need to hold it."

I thank him, hang up, then stow my phone in a bag of things I packed, just in case this all goes to hell, and I need to bolt somewhere for a few days. The call from Broussard was exactly what I needed to focus.

A text from Yasmine confirms Elizabeth is safely out of the way.

Now, nothing is stopping me from putting this plan into motion.

CHAPTER 6

AIDEN

"If you had to go through with this nasty business at all, it would have made more sense to go to the courthouse. Sign a few papers." Mara reclines on a settee in the groom's suite at the St. Louis Cathedral. I'm ignoring her imperiously raised eyebrow and general air of incredulity. "The pomp and circumstance seem pointless to me."

"That's because you're a cold, hard bitch, love. Not a romantic bone in your body. Let Aiden have his moments of whimsy," Eamon yells from the adjoining bathroom, where he's spent the past fifteen minutes obsessing over his hair. I don't know why he bothers. It's looked like a messy rat's nest for the past fifteen years, and it'll continue for the next fifty. For some reason, perfectly intelligent women find the veritable mop of dark curls irresistible (Mara excluded), and I've never understood the appeal. Not when they're on the head of someone clearly psychotic. And I say that lovingly.

For the most part.

I study them with no shortness of resignation as I nibble on a pastry provided by my assistant, Finn. "Call it whatever you like, but the bigger the spectacle, the less likely Cian is to turn it into a real-life red wedding."

Eamon's snort can be heard across the world. "What a party that would make, though."

Mara quits studying her blood-red nails to shoot Eamon a look. "We have vastly different definitions about what makes a party."

Rolling my eyes, I give my black suit a critical once-over. In less than an hour, I'll know if I pulled this off. If I have, then seeing my mother for the first time in years is on my horizon. There'll be hell to pay, but it will be worth it if I can see her. It has to be. If I haven't... then death will be a welcome oblivion.

"Yes, yes, we all know what you lack in taste you make up in sheer audacity," Eamon snipes.

As they bicker, I study myself in the mirror. The lines of the suit are classic and expertly tailored. Mara tried to convince me to wear a white button-down shirt, but I opted for black on black. She rolled her eyes and muttered under her breath how I have no sense of taste or tradition, but I ignored her. The last-minute tailoring cost a small fortune, but I don't plan to be married twice, so I didn't bat an eye.

Maybe a small part of me knows Catriona will see me in this suit and feel regret that she left without saying goodbye that night. Perhaps that same part of me is also looking forward to punishing her in this way one last time.

Brushing that thought away, I run a comb through my lightly gelled hair and adjust my cuff links.

Mara shoves to her feet and prowls restlessly. "Stop preening, you little shit. You look fine."

"Maybe he's a romantic at heart, darling. Wants to do the thing properly. You're only saying that because the thought of *your* wedding is making you break out in hives." Eamon presses a red rose from an arrangement on a chest of drawers to his nose and inhales indulgently.

Mara huffs out a breath but doesn't deny it, and I hurry to interject before she takes offense and starts snarling. Mentions of her impending nuptials make her snappy. "Play nice, or I'll tie you both up so I don't have to deal with you."

"Kinky," Eamon says, moving across the room. "This calls for a celebratory shot. I'll get the whiskey. No abstaining, or I'll hold you down and pour it down your throat."

"We're in a church," Mara says dryly, patently ignoring my threats. That's what I love about her. Nothing can faze her. Not even my threats, which would cower anyone else. Maybe that's why the three of us have stuck together for so long. We're bloodthirsty, a little insane, and practically allergic to the spectrum of human emotion.

Eamon pulls a fifth of whiskey from God only knows where and retrieves three paper cups from a beverage area that has coffee and water dispensers. He fills the cups with a generous pour, then hands one to each of us before lifting his own.

"To Aiden and his blushing bride!"

Mara lifts her paper cup with a rueful smile at me, and I definitely don't turn mine away. I'm hoping the burn will wash away all thoughts of failure. I've managed not to think about it much, but I know the moment I step out into that church, I'm going to need the diversion.

I end up downing two—or was it three?—more shots at Eamon's insistence. I tried to turn the last one away, but he tackled me and did indeed pour it down my throat. After sputtering in indignation, I threw him out of the room so he could find his seat in the pews. Mara slapped me on the cheek and sauntered after him to do the same.

I take my place at the front of the church with the priest to my right. He mops sweat from his brow with a white handkerchief as he studiously avoids my attention.

Rory glowers from the first pew, shoulders up to his ears because Mara and Eamon are sitting right behind him. This entire ordeal is certainly pissing him off, and it's a sad state of affairs that his discomfort is the highlight of my wedding day.

The rest of the seats are filled with familiar faces, Rory's colleagues, his family. A fair amount of press and employees from the Emerald. I ordered as many witnesses as possible, just in case Cian did show up, to deter him from making it a spectacle. The more eyes on us, the better.

A pianist begins playing "Wedding March," and I experience a moment of hesitation when Catriona doesn't show as a bridesmaid first. A slow, cold wave of emotion crashes throughout my insides. Sweat dots my brow. I want to wipe it away, but my hands are locked at my sides. It had been easy to agree to this farce at first. Easy to tell myself it wouldn't matter who I married or who it hurt. But the thought of not seeing her one last time makes my chest tight in a way I don't want to examine too closely.

There's no going back now. I've made my choice, and I have to live with it. Once this ceremony is done, either Cian will bend to pressure or he'll retaliate. I can only hope his desire to maintain appearances will be stronger than his desire to punish my mother or me for going against him.

Elizabeth appears in the doorway. She's draped in a simple, classic white wedding dress and heavy veil, her features somewhat obscured by the material. But she looks enough like Catriona that it makes my heart catch.

I release a breath in a slow, measured exhalation, as I tell myself to get a grip. This is a means to an end. With each step she takes toward me, I lock down my emotions, carefully tucking them behind a cold, businesslike exterior.

Until I feel nothing.

Blissfully numb.

The walk up the aisle seems to take an eternity. The priest seems to think so too, because he keeps shifting from foot to foot and heaving with more sighs than seems physically possible.

My mask hardens as Elizabeth draws near. Maybe I should have taken Eamon's offer for more shots. But no amount of alcohol seems to be enough.

I take Elizabeth's hand and turn to the priest, who has gone so pale, I'm worried he may simply pass away in front of us. Father Michael sucks in a gasp before clinging to his Bible, eyes dropping to the words as he blinks rapidly through dripping sweat. I force myself to relax one muscle at a time as he begins his introductions.

Christ, I can't take in a word he's saying. Not when I'm drowning in Catriona's scent even though she's nowhere to be seen. I'm dizzy with it, tempted to search out the source no matter who's watching. I twitch violently with the effort of my restraint. The fucking woman is haunting me.

When the priest speaks, his voice trembles, echoing

throughout the chamber. "Dearly beloved, we are gathered here today in the sight of God and this company to witness the sacred union of this man and this woman in Holy Matrimony. Marriage is a solemn and holy covenant, a reflection of the love Christ has for His church. It is not to be entered into lightly, but reverently, deliberately, and with the blessing of the Lord. Today, we celebrate the joining of two souls in a bond that is meant to endure not only in times of joy but also in hardship, bound by faith, fidelity, and love."

Then the priest is motioning for me to remove Elizabeth's veil. I snap back to myself and am grateful Elizabeth is standing with haughty defiance. Gripping the fabric, I pull it over her face and behind her head, determined to finish the ceremony as quickly as possible.

And that's where my hands freeze, on either side of a face that's been a recurring star in my dreams since the moment we met.

Because the woman standing in front of me isn't Elizabeth, as promised.

The woman standing in front of me, ready for me to say vows to her, is her sister, Catriona.

She's not supposed to be here.

This wasn't in my carefully laid plans.

This is going to ruin *everything*.

Fear strikes through me, spearing into parts I thought long dead.

Catriona lifts her face to me, a devious, satisfied smile tugging at her lips.

"Hello, future husband," she says.

CHAPTER 7

CATRIONA

I glory in his expression—a sweet mixture of confusion, fury, and apprehension. I can't lie, I like it. I like it a lot. Probably way more than I should. The rush of heady control it gives me is addictive, and I *revel*.

For the first time in my life, I'm not letting anyone control my fate. I'm taking it into my own hands. The satisfaction is almost as potent as the perpetual rage that simmers just beneath my skin. Whatever the consequences, it's worth it purely for the look on his face.

I hope he feels like I yanked the rug right out from underneath him. Even better if he's panicking, stuck, thoughts racing. His eyes flick over to the congregation, but I don't check to see who he's looking at. Honestly, I don't much care. Basking in his reaction suits me just fine.

I give the priest a once-over and note the sheen of sweat on his face. Like most everyone else, the father had a price. It was merely a matter of pushing hard enough to learn what it would take to make him break. Turns out, it was a couple of thousand dollars. I didn't have it to spare, but I had my mother's diamond necklace. I hoped she wouldn't hate me too much for pawning it.

It was shockingly easy to convince him to change the paperwork and the name in the ceremony from Elizabeth Gallagher to Catriona Gallagher. Of course, this means I'm banking on Aiden and my father not causing a scene, but based on a glance at my father's pursed lips, he's not going to do a damn thing. At least, not now with all eyes on us. With the parking lot full of cameras. The pews full of witnesses.

The priest proceeds with the ceremony, and no one objects. I'm so consumed with relief that I miss most of it.

"Catriona," O'Connor says with a sharp, biting undertone. His hands grind the bones in mine against each other, and I wince, glancing around. The priest stares at me expectantly, and I furrow my brows, my thoughts a muddle of nerves and fear, but also satisfaction at O'Connor's murderous frown.

There's no way he can back down now, not unless he wants to make a fool out of himself in front of everyone. The reporters in the pews would have a field day. Maybe if we weren't in a public place, he'd find it easier to brute force his way out of this, but most of my family is here, as well as strangers who must be his associates. It's not like he can murder me in front of so many witnesses.

He should have thought about that before turning down my offer. We could have been partners instead of adversaries.

"Repeat after me," Father Michael says.

I swallow thickly and nod, but it's more like a puppet jerking on its strings. I may have maneuvered this moment, but the glare I can feel coming from where my father is sitting in the first pew is a stark reminder that he believes I'm his doll to arrange as he pleases. And all this stunt has accomplished in his eyes is to paint an even bigger target on my back. That'll be nothing compared to Elizabeth's rage.

It doesn't matter. Victory is sweet on my tongue. If they want to treat me like an enemy, then I'll be one. I don't need any of them.

Father Michael begins again, and I repeat as directed. "I, Catriona Deirdre Gallagher, take thee, Aiden Malcolm James O'Connor," I say, my voice steady despite the storm raging within me, "to be my lawfully wedded husband, to have and to hold from this day forward, for better, for worse, for richer, for poorer, in sickness and in health, until death do us part."

As I speak these words, a heaviness settles over me, the weights of my new manacles closing over my skin, pressing me into the ground. They may be of my own choosing, but they're heavy around my wrists just the same.

O'Connor produces rings, and I nearly give in to overwhelming hysterical laughter. Or the increasing urge to faint clear away. Before the compulsion can coalesce, he's handing me a man's band, identical to my own, that he helps my stiff fingers place on his in return.

I note they aren't the gleaming, brand-new silver I expect to match his eyes. They're plain gold, nicked in some places, and there's even an inscription on the inside of one band. Whose were they? Where did he get them? As soon as he finishes forcing his band on my finger, along with a solitaire engagement ring, and then his own, a sick sense of foreboding envelops me. He pulls me closer, and I have a legitimate fear that I may crumple in front of all these people, so I don't resist.

Mistake.

Because the scent of him fills my nose, leaving me sick and obsessed, exactly like I'd been the night we met. He smells like a thunderstorm about to unleash itself in the middle of a dense, verdant forest. Paired with something that makes me want to wrinkle my nose. Like the ozone after a lightning strike or smoke from a fire. I want to flay him alive for ruining the scent of petrichor, one of my favorite things.

As though he can pluck the thoughts straight from my brain, he shifts closer, filling the space between us. I don't dare pull away, despite all my instincts screaming at me, because he and I both know it would cause too much attention, and I can't afford that now.

When I come to my senses, it's to the realization that he intends to kiss me. Surely, Father Michael is going to skip the "you may now kiss your bride" business like I asked him to, but all it takes is one frantic glance at O'Connor, and Father Michael turns to me. Surely, O'Connor wouldn't dare to *actually* kiss me, but he does.

I only have a moment to squeak out a startled protest and press my hands against his chest, feeling his firm, powerful muscles bunch underneath my fingertips. Then he's so close to me I can feel his heat through the layers of his suit and my dress. I hadn't realized I was shaking, frozen with apprehension, until his warmth sinks into my skin. My breath catches, and then his hands cup the back of my skull, lifting me until our eyes meet in the moment before our lips.

My brain can't parse the conflicting responses it receives from my overwrought nervous system—the flash of white-hot panic, the memory of our last kiss. My body recognizes his, remembers how easily he mastered it. For a moment, one flash of weakness, I soften toward him, letting his looming form grow closer. There's a low rumble in his chest, and I snap to the present, cursing myself for letting my guard down, even for a second.

I try to step away, but his grip is unrelenting. My chest heaves with the effort to draw air into my lungs, but instead I'm drowning. In the scent of him, the taste. The memories. His lips brush over mine, and I sigh with relief, believing the torture to be over.

O'Connor moves back—for what, I have no idea—then his mouth returns to mine, pressing hard enough to bruise the sensitive flesh. My gasp may as well have been like spreading my legs for him because the next thing I know, his tongue invades, accepting the temporary surrender and sweeping into my mouth, his taste flooding my awareness. I try to tear away, but he doesn't give an inch.

Furious, I bite down—on a lip or his tongue, I don't know.

When I pull away, there's blood on his mouth. He lifts a hand to it, wipes the back of his forefinger over the stain, and studies it with an amused twist to his lips. My thoughts flash back to when I'd drawn blood after trying to escape him. He'd looked the same. Like a shark scenting prey in the water. Cold-blooded. Furious. But also intrigued despite himself. His tongue darts out to wash it away, and then I realize the coppery tinge on my tongue is his blood.

My face drains of color, and his smirk deepens, his eyes blazing with the promise of swift retribution.

And there's no escaping it—him.

Because I chose this.

When I shove away from him this time, he lets me, taking a step back with his hands stuffed in his pockets. Father Michael pronounces us husband and wife over the ringing in my ears.

And then it's done.

I'm married to Aiden O'Connor.

Fuck.

He jerks me down the aisle, and I hope I'm able to paste a smile on my face for the flashing cameras. When I come to my senses, most everyone has filed out of the cathedral, and I'm alone with O'Connor in the bridal suite. He's standing a few feet away now, with a cell phone pressed to his ear, murmuring at someone on the other end of the line. I press a hand to my stomach to contain the fevered mixture of relief and trepidation, then stumble to a nearby chair to catch my breath. I give myself a moment to let all the emotions wash over me before I chain them away.

Father appears in the doorway. After a speaking glare, he turns on his heel and stalks from the church. I can only hope Yasmine hasn't had much trouble with Elizabeth, that she'll stay away as long as it takes for Father's temper to cool. Soon, all that's left of the family I've always known is the echo of his boots resounding off the sanctuary's cathedral ceilings. They sound like gunshots in the cavernous building's emptiness. Final.

There's no going back now.

All too soon, O'Connor finishes his call and crosses the

room to me. Muscles tensing under his scrutiny, wary of his next move, I harden my expression because I refuse to let him have any effect on me. Despite my outward nonchalance, I still taste his blood on my tongue, the lingering scent of heavy rain and danger on my skin.

"Let's go," he says—orders. Like my father, O'Connor doesn't ask so much as dictate.

I bristle, but don't move a muscle. Too bad for him, I don't take orders. "Go where?"

His smile is as sharp as a blade. "Didn't you pay attention, *bhean chéile*? It's our wedding night. It's time to go home."

I'm not fluent in *Gaeilge Uladh*. Father had always been more concerned with his career trajectory than giving credence to our parents' Irish roots, but even I recognize the phrase. It's something my grandfather used to call my grandmother, my mother's parents, of course. My father's parents are long since dead and probably for the better, considering their progeny.

It means *my wife*.

"Call me that again, and the next time I bite you, I'll take your tongue as payment," I say, swept by waves of exhaustion and in desperate need of a shower to wash away the cold sweat and the taste of him. "And if you think I'm going to sleep with you of my own volition again, I'm not the only one who's gone insane."

Ignoring my threats like I'm a child having a tantrum, O'Connor pulls me to my feet. "You have two choices from now on: do what the fuck you're told, or I can make you. You have no idea what you've gotten yourself into. So unless you want to find yourself in worse circumstances than married to me, you'll start listening."

I jerk my hand from his grasp, ignoring the sting of his brutal grip. "Why don't you tell me what I've gotten myself into, then? Explain why my father needed to sell my sister. Is this some kind of sick game for you guys? Treating women like cattle? And disposing of people when you feel as though they've wronged you? Like that cop, Dufresne? Yeah, I still remember that night. You're disgusting."

He steps so close that the toes of his shoes disappear under the flare of my dress. I shiver at his nearness as though I can feel the coldness of his glare caressing my skin. Piercing. Dissecting. Unflinching. "Does it make it easier to hate me, darlin', if you pretend you aren't happy to be right here with my rings on your finger?"

My head pounds with a fresh headache, and I scowl up at him. The last word you could use to describe me right now is *happy*. Maybe relieved. Anxious. Annoyed, but not happy. "I didn't need to marry you to hate you, O'Connor."

"Sweet words from your lips, Catriona. Music to my ears. By all means, if you'd like to stay at the church, feel free. I'll never stop someone from repenting for their sins. But if you'd like to get out of that ridiculous dress, come with me. I have no doubt they'll be ambushing us at my house to sort out this mess." At that, he turns and strides out of the bridal suite.

Knowing I have no other options and that this whole shit show was my idea, after all, I follow. I draw in slow, deep breaths for the length of the aisle and out of the front doors to stem my rising anger. I'm assaulted once more by the crowd of socialites and reporters who press in on me, triggering a violent sense of claustrophobia that I battle into submission.

"Aiden! Aiden, over here! Tell us all the dirty details, Aiden!"

"How does it feel to be Mrs. O'Connor?"

"Aiden, let us see you with your bride."

"C'mon, this way. Give us a smile!"

I stop at the church entrance and pose for a few shots, ignoring the crush of people. I've had to fake it so many times for everyone in my life that the smile comes easily. When I'm certain they have something passable, my smile widens, and I wave before moving to the limo where O'Connor—and whatever happens next—waits for me.

I'm careful to maintain a neutral expression as I fight my way out of the crowd and to the limo. A man I don't recognize opens the door for me, and I fold myself inside.

O'Connor sits across from me like the worst kind of *un*welcome party. As I study his sprawled form, with a tumbler of whiskey in one hand and a cigarette in the other, it hits me for the first time that I did it. I stopped their wedding.

I gesture toward his glass, and he passes it over with a lifted brow. Drinking deeply, I do my best to ignore him, which I plan to do for as long as I can. Maybe if I do, this whole thing will never seem completely real. It'll stay a fever dream borne out of my darkest nightmares.

The whiskey burns my throat and settles like lead in my stomach. I pass the empty glass to him, and he refills it from a small bottle in his suit jacket, then places it back in my outstretched hand. The alcohol warms me from the inside out, and I study him.

Aiden O'Connor.

My husband.

It doesn't matter how many times I repeat it; I don't think I'll ever get used to it.

He twists to speak to the driver, and I tune it out to send a text to Yasmine, letting her know I'm okay. The limo moves, finally drawing us away from the crowd and the constant, sickening flash from cameras. O'Connor is unfazed, face blank, eyes watchful, a silver glint in the shadows.

"Well, go ahead." My voice comes out hoarse from the burn of whiskey.

"Go ahead? Go ahead with what, pet?"

I jerk my chin at him. "Don't play games with me. Your punishment, since you like them so much. For making a fool out of you and switching places with my sister. I'm sure there's something vile you have in store for me. You might as well get it over with. I may not know everything about you, but what I know is enough."

O'Connor's lips curl into a sardonic smile, the edges of which don't reach his mist-colored eyes, now fixed on mine with an intensity that sends a shiver down my spine. "Punishment, huh? Tell me, Catriona, what exactly do you think would be a fitting punishment for your transgressions? Turning your sweet arse red? Taking you until you scream?" At my flinch, his laughter punches through the small space, sounding bitter and hollow and mocking. "Is that what you think I should do?"

I swallow hard, his derisive tone slicing through the haze of alcohol-induced courage. Ignoring his last comment, I say,

"I think whatever it is, it was worth the look on your face when you got exactly what you deserved."

"So feisty. You'd think you'd be sweeter after the mess you've put us in."

"The last thing I'm going to be to you is sweet."

"You're the one who put yourself in this position. I'm not sure why you're pretending to be upset that you got what you so *clearly* wanted."

"That's right. I tried to reason with you, but you wouldn't listen. I told you if you went through with it, I'd make you regret it."

His body tenses, lithe as a tiger underneath the lines of his shirt, and he snorts a laugh. "You shouldn't have played games with the big boys. There is far more to this scenario than you could possibly imagine. If I'm able to fix this mess you've made, it'll be a fucking miracle."

Unease prickles along my spine. "If you and my father hadn't cooked up this plan in the first place, none of this would have happened."

O'Connor relaxes, and it's as though the tension immediately transfers to me. How is it he's more intimidating while lazy and loose like this than he is when he's got murder in his eyes?

Then he says, "Oh, pet, if that's what you think happened, then you have no idea what is going on here."

CHAPTER 8

CATRIONA

"Then why don't you tell me what's going on here?"

He's quiet for a long time. So long that I don't think he'll answer at first. I fill the silence with plans for every possible response. Then I imagine how the hell I'm going to get myself out of this mess. For all my plotting, it hadn't occurred to me what would happen after the wedding. All I could think about was revenge.

Am I willing to sacrifice my safety for it?

Without a doubt.

Am I prepared for the reality of those very real consequences?

Probably not.

So when O'Connor—I can't imagine ever calling him Aiden again—straightens, puts out his cigarette, and knocks back the remains of his drink, I brace myself for anything. For the worst.

His palm wraps around my jaw. His eyes are silver fire. "I'm done playing games with you. You have until we get home to convince me your bullshit is worth the trouble. Otherwise, I'll tell your father this was a mistake. I'll have the marriage annulled and marry your sister like I was supposed to do in the first fucking place."

I glare, but the part of me that knows him is melting the slightest bit. "You wouldn't dare."

"I'm so far from joking, sweetheart. You want to play games, we can play games, but I think you've forgotten that I always win."

"What do you mean, convince you?" I ask warily, my heart thudding a heavy drumbeat in my ears. "Do you want me to come up with another wager or something?"

O'Connor moves from the seat across from me to the one beside me and sprawls out, looking every inch a king. The creeping sense of foreboding washes over me, like I've been dreading and anticipating this since the moment I saw him again.

"What do you think I mean? Prove to me that all the shit I'm going through for you will be worth it. Prove to me why you're worth the trouble. Prove to me why I shouldn't undo all of your hard work as soon as we get home." When I can do nothing but gape at him, his expression melts into a smirk I want to claw off his face. "What can I say? You were right. You deserve every bit of punishment I can inflict on your tight little body for what you've done. Go ahead and fight me. We both know I'll win."

If asked, I'd say the heat flooding me is shame. A sane woman would be running in the opposite direction, but something in me unravels at the words.

"Do your worst," I say, and tip my chin up at him even though I know it's reckless and stupid. "I think we both know it'll take a lot more than threats from you to break me."

He practically purrs with savage delight. "Whatever I want, hmm? Maybe you'll be the perfect wife for me after all. I hadn't planned to use Elizabeth for anything other than a pretty prop at my side to trot out from time to time, but maybe this arrangement won't be completely worthless. After all, I already know how sweet you come for me."

Despite my whispered prayers to the contrary, my cheeks fill with color, and he chuckles.

"Yeah, I remember everything about you, pet. Why don't you show me what a good little wife you can be? We still have time before we get home." He makes a show of closing the window separating us from the driver so that we're completely alone in the dark interior.

And then I understand all too well.

Because this is the masked man from the masquerade. The one who'd conquered me in a room full of people. Who'd made me crawl for him. Made me beg. Made me want every dark, filthy thing he'd done. He sneers at me like he can read my thoughts. All hard edges. Unforgiving. Practically a stranger.

One who knows all my weaknesses.

"Come here, Catriona." His voice is dark velvet, each word dragging over me like a warning caress, settling deep in my chest, weighing me down in the seat. "Don't make me tell you twice."

My breath catches in my throat, and I instinctively inch away from him, only to have his hands enclosing my hips and pulling me back until I'm pressed against his side. The scent of his warm skin, the heat from his fingertips... It's so overwhelming that it makes my head swim with thoughts of thunderstorms and woodsmoke. I try to breathe, but I only take more of him in, clouding my thoughts with panic.

I shove hard against his chest, but he's immovable. His muscular body may as well be made of granite for all the good it does. "I agreed to marry you, not that I'd fuck you again, you bastard. Don't do this, O'Connor, or I will—" The *please* is at the tip of my tongue, but I can't force it over my lips. *I refuse.*

"You'll what? Fight me? Go ahead, I'd love to see you try." His thumb brushes over my lower lip, and his eyes are glued to his touch. Something in his stare makes my stomach twist, like it's filled with poisonous snakes. Something dark. Something possessive. "In fact, I'd almost prefer it."

A whimper claws out of my throat. "If you make me do this, I'll make you regret it."

He chuckles softly, the sound low and sinister, vibrating through the confined space like the rumble of thunder from a distant but devastating storm. "Then you'd better make it good."

"Fuck you, I—"

Before I can finish, he reaches into a pocket, and my breath catches, expecting him to pull out a weapon to threaten me, put a knife to my throat or a gun to my head. But he takes out his phone. My brows furrow as he unlocks the screen and taps until I see my father's contact card.

"You wanted this. *You* came to *me*. But if you're getting cold feet after your little master plan, we can fix this right now. I could make one call and have it all sorted in a few hours. The fact that I'm even entertaining bringing you home is a favor to you. What you should really be doing is thanking me."

The fear I've always managed to suppress with bravado coalesces into a weight on my chest. When I manage to speak, it's only to croak out, "Stop," but of course he doesn't. His thumb hovers over the call button, his eyes never leaving mine as my panicked thoughts swirl around my skull. If I thought my situation was bad before... it's nothing compared to this.

He leans closer again, his lips brushing against my ear as silence finally descends. "Would it help if I told you I've dreamed of you? How you felt around me? How greedy I am to have you again? No? That's okay. I promise I'll make it good for you."

He leans back again to study my face, and I don't know what I look like, but I imagine my expression is a combination of shock, horror, and dread. I try to control the urge to wrap my arms around myself and hope he can't see my limbs trembling.

"But first, you're going to make it good for me."

Make it good for him? Of course. It's another game to him, isn't it? I'm here for his amusement. He's got me. My future now hinges on this man. He could call my bluff in an instant, and he's right, this would all be for nothing.

Am I willing to be his little pet again to get what I want?

I close my eyes, my breath coming in sharp bursts as I try to find some semblance of control, but it slips through my grasp like water.

"Look at me," he demands, and my eyes snap open. I don't have a choice. I don't think I have since the second I saw him again.

He leans in closer, his mouth inches from mine. "You aren't going to fight me, are you? We can't have that."

"I'll do what—what you want." I lick my too dry lips and meet his mercurial gaze. "I'll do whatever you want."

Everything in me screams to resist, to claw at his eyes, to shove him out of the car, but the mess I've gotten myself into may as well be a guillotine, ready to drop the second he commands. I've traded one monster for another—and this one has me by the throat.

Even seeing the immovable will in his face, I hesitate, and he says, "You said you'd get on your knees for me. So get on your knees."

My brows pinch together until I remember. I'd told him that night of the dinner that I'd do whatever he wanted—including getting on my knees for him—if he'd marry me. I guess he's calling my bluff.

My hands are shaking as I comply, the material of my dress biting into the soft flesh, my face blooming with the red heat of shame. I could beg some more and try to find the magic words that will make him see reason. But I know there's no combination in the English language that can sway Aiden O'Connor away from something he wants, and until I have the leverage to make my escape, my only choice is to do what he wishes.

He adjusts his position in the seat, lifting his hips, spreading his legs in that arrogant, masculine way that oozes dominance. He tangles one hand in my hair, the fingers sifting through the long strands, tugging at them gently until goose bumps pepper my skin. The other is behind his head, cradling it as he watches me with hooded silver eyes. A handsome devil and I'm ready to do his bidding. The perfect little doll for him to pose and play with.

I hate him so fucking much. Almost as much as I hate that I can't walk away.

When I hesitate at the buckle of his trousers, the hand behind his head moves to guide mine over his hardness. I gulp as I feel the solid length of him, the heat searing against my palm. I'd made myself forget how big he was. Big enough that my belly tightens at the thought of having it anywhere inside me again.

"Don't make me wait," he warns idly, as his finger twists my hair in circles. I do my best to ignore the way it sends shivers down my spine. "Show me how perfect you can be for me."

Shifting away from the sensation, I move instinctively. His hand falls from my hair to lock behind his head, every inch the indolent god. I slide the strap of his belt out of the buckle, tugging until it comes loose from the prong, then separating the two until I can pull it out of his belt loops. A glance up shows him darting his tongue out to wet his lips, and I look away just as quickly. A few jerky movements later and his suit trousers are unbuttoned. The sound of the zipper sliding down the teeth seems unreasonably loud in the quiet of the back seat.

He lifts to accommodate me as I struggle to shift his pants and briefs down his hips, and then his cock bobs out, hard and long, bigger than I remembered and already weeping translucent pre-cum at the tip. It glides down his hardness, sleek in the glint of the passing lights. A hiss of pained arousal greets my ears, and I swallow back a gasp, feeling the heat of hatred burn low in my belly at the thought of him getting any enjoyment from this.

The piercing glints in the low overhead lights. An apadravya, I recall, after some late-night internet searching in the days after I left his bed. It had led me to a Wikipedia article whose pretty picture was almost as mouthwatering as O'Connor's is in real life.

Almost.

Of course, the biggest jerk I've ever met has a cock worthy of poetry.

O'Connor's knowing smirk catches my momentary hesitation.

My teeth ache to sink into his flesh. My fingers cramp as I resist the urge to tighten them until he squeals for relief. He may want to break me, but I want to *destroy* him. I hold back the impulse, but only just.

Fingers probe my lips, and I send him another startled glance. "Get them wet," he instructs in that same low, commanding voice.

Is he testing me? Seeing how far he can push me before I cower in fear? A sense of understanding crashes over me. Of course he is. He has me under his thumb. Now he's going to test my boundaries to see how much I can take. How easy I'll be to break again.

I grant his fingers entrance, and they slide over my tongue, filling my mouth with the warm surge of a taste that's solely him. They press deep, pillaging until they're nearly to my throat, and I almost choke. When I don't, his eyes twitch, and he presses farther back, triggering my gag reflex.

My body seizes as I make a retching sound, and he finally relents. He gathers the saliva in his hand and uses it to coat his cock in a measured, familiar stroke as he studies my reaction. I want to look away, but I can't, wary of what he'll do next. I'm entranced by the sight even though I don't want to be.

"So obedient," he murmurs as he thumbs the wetness coating my lips. "That's good. You're going to be my perfect little obedient wife now, aren't you? So good for me. So sweet, like I know you can be."

He moves, and I flinch, but it doesn't deter him as he delves into the neckline of my wedding dress. I can only watch, numb, as he shifts it lower so he can free my breasts from the bustier, shoving the material out of the way. His big hands cup my breasts as I quake, the rough pads of his fingers rasping over my nipples. He shifts and takes one in his mouth, his tongue flicking it into a hard point. I bite back the sound that rises in my throat. He releases me with a pop and traces the sensitive peak once more with his mouth before he pulls away. His gaze ravages what he's done like he's inspecting all his work for flaws.

Is that really what this is about? He wants to punish me even more for sneaking out that night, for forcing him to marry me, for defying him? I don't have time to think about it before he's taking the other nipple into his mouth, teeth nipping cruelly until I finally make a pained sound of protest in the back of my throat.

"You look so pretty on your knees. Just like I remember."

There's no mistaking what he's asking me to do, not with the wet sounds of his hand working his ten-inch dick and the hungry gleam in his eye. "What makes you think I won't use my teeth?" I hate myself for how my voice breaks, betraying my nerves.

His hand braces at the back of my neck in a warning. A threat. I meet his eyes and feel the thunderous surge of defiance and righteous fury flood me, washing away the woman I'd been this morning. Some of it must show because he *smiles*, and his hand on the back of my neck tightens.

"Go on, then. Make it hurt," he answers. "Is that why you won't let me back into your bed? You're punishing me, aren't you? For picking your sister? That's fine, pet. Punish me. We both know how much you're already aching for my cock."

His grip is unrelenting around the back of my neck, twisting in my hair as he pulls me inexorably forward. I shouldn't resist so I can get this over quickly, but there's an iron will inside my spine that can't give in without making him work for it—at least a little. The driver is still a few feet away, and the thought of him hearing me keeps me from screaming in protest.

"Keep your eyes up. I want to watch you as you take me."

I obey, locking my eyes with his as I part my lips and wrap them around him, going slow so I can adjust to the discomforting awareness of the piercing, heavy and cold on my tongue. He makes a sound in the back of his throat, and his hand twists even more in my hair.

"Thought I'd imagined how good you felt, but fuck if it's not better than the last time." He tugs me forward, his other hand coming to force me into a punishing rhythm as I sputter around him, trying to breathe despite my mouth being stuffed full. My hands are on his thighs for balance, and they ripple underneath me, a reminder of how dangerous and powerful he is and how completely I'm at his mercy.

As though to test me, he pushes deeper, forcing his cock down the back of my mouth, farther than I've ever taken one. I choke, unable to breathe, panic exploding in my mind. He's too big… I can't.

He keeps me there until spots dot my vision, and then, just when I think I'm going to pass out, he relents.

I pop off, my chest heaving, tears running down my face. Black, inky drops stain my dress, and I bet if I looked in a mirror, I'd see them leaving paths of despair carved in their wake. I wipe at the snot dripping from my nose, the drool trailing down my chin, the tears in thick tracks down my cheeks, and he knocks my hands away.

"Leave it. I want to see you ruined for me."

A sob barks out of my chest, but I struggle, fingers digging into his thighs until I tuck away the emotion behind a wall of impenetrable self-control.

Before he can shove his dick back into my mouth, I suck him back in and revel as his shocked inhale fills my ears. He wants me ruined? Fine. He wants me to make it worth his while? He'd better enjoy it while he can.

This time, his hands are gentle in my hair, letting me suck him at my pace, which is frantic but determined. My head bobs, and my tongue slicks up and down his length. All the while, I'm promising the first chance I get, I'm going to cut off his dick and shove it down *his* throat.

Almost like he can read my mind, his lips quirk, and he says, "Hating me only makes me like it more."

I take him deeper, wanting to get this over with so I can get the taste of him out of my mouth, and the sound of his pleasured gasps out of my memory.

He hisses, "Fuck, I knew I wasn't imagining how good you were at this. You feel so fucking good."

My traitorous body goes hot and tight at his praise. It's sick and twisted, but bolts of pleasure shoot straight between my legs. His display of dominance shuts off every neurotic thought in my brain. For the first time since the masquerade, my mind is beautifully, simply blank.

"Yeah, fuck, take me deep. Just like that."

Evidence of my submission delights him further, until he's thrusting to meet every downstroke, his fingers cupping my cheeks to smear through salt and paint me in humiliation. His eyes glaze over, and he fists his hands in my hair as he drives deeper, heedless of my struggling sounds.

The worst part isn't the violation. It's the satisfaction that burns in my chest as I watch him succumb to me. That I can find some enjoyment from this degradation is devastating to the point that when he fills my mouth with his thick, salty spend, I'm still crying. It hollows out my chest, threatens to choke me as I struggle against the quakes. It's worse than the night we spent together. So much worse, because I know the lengths he's willing to go. I know exactly how ruthless he can be now. And a twisted part of me enjoys it.

"Swallow it," he grunts after pulling out of my mouth. "All of it. Every drop. Then I want to see that pretty tongue all clean for me."

Glaring at him, I struggle to do as he tells me as I fight to breathe and stem the flow of tears. Finally, I open my mouth and stick out my tongue. His slow, sinister smile makes me want to claw it off his face.

"Good girl. Now come here."

He reaches for me before I can resist and hauls me into

his lap. My eyes bulge when I feel him still semi-hard underneath me. Then, before I have enough time to organize my thoughts or prepare a defense, he's ripped the lace thong under my dress. He pockets the tattered remnants. I hadn't realized I could feel even more vulnerable, but I do.

"If we had more time, I'd take your pretty little cunt right here, but we'll have to make this fast. Spread your legs for me."

The blush on my cheeks intensifies when he shoves my dress up my hips and finds me bare. A rumble sounds from the back of his throat. He folds himself beneath me and slides down until his torso rests on the car seat, and I'm hovering over his mouth. A bark of disbelief rips from my throat before he seals his mouth over my clit and sucks. Hard. Adrenaline lights a fiery path from the anger swirling in my chest to where the unwanted friction stokes a spark between my thighs.

"O'Connor, fuck, stop. I don't want—"

Popping off, he pins me with a look. "You'll let *me* tell you what you want."

He holds my thighs with a forceful grip, keeping me against the steady onslaught of his devious tongue as he licks me until all my objections wither and die in my throat. I try to smother him—I swear to God, I give it my all—but he doesn't make the slightest sound of protest or even attempt to get me to lift my thighs from where they bracket his head. I grip the headrests of the bench seat to hold myself upright, my fingers digging into the leather as I do everything in my power to block the sensations from converging into anything other than horror.

He may be lethal, but he's also patient and too observant

for my own good. The drive from the cathedral to our destination must be longer than I thought because even though I'm trying not to react to his relentless assault, I find my resolve weakens far sooner than I thought possible.

I close my eyes, and that seems to make it worse. I can feel every flick of his tongue as it circles the sensitized nub of my clit. He draws it into his mouth and sucks until it's throbbing and swollen with blood, tender to the slightest movement. He teases my lips and thighs with his fingers, scoring them lightly until I shake above him, muscles fighting for control over a reaction that can't be mastered. The sounds of his mouth working are obscene, filling the small space.

He plunges his tongue inside me, thick and far more dexterous than I thought possible. His nose bumps against my clit with every lick, and I swallow back the moans that threaten to spill from my throat. O'Connor is even worse than I imagined. I thought he'd use my mouth, and that would be the end. That he would revel in his display of ownership and be done with it. No, this is even worse. He is determined to make my body *enjoy* it.

The more I try not to respond, the more I find I lose control of my reactions. His hands move to cup my ass cheeks until he works my hips into a rhythm against his mouth. Everything that isn't in his control trembles in an effort to hold myself back, but I realize too late that it forces an almost echo chamber effect so that I feel every thrust or lick a thousandfold the more I try to ignore it.

He works my body into a frenzy with an unforgiving, single-minded focus that sends tendrils of fear snaking through my consciousness. By the time I realize I'm hovering on the edge, ready to throw myself off it, it's too late.

He seems to realize it before I do and wraps his arms around my hips, pulling me more fully onto his face. I try to fight him with all that I have, but it only works to rub my clit and cunt against his devastating tongue. My thighs clench around his head, and he groans as I tremble to keep my orgasm at bay.

The sound of his obvious enjoyment trips something in my brain. He eats my pussy like he's never wanted anything in this world as much as he wants to have me come all over his face. And because I don't want it just as badly, because I know it's wrong and I *hate* him for it, hearing him moan and pant for me causes me to let my guard down just enough that the waves of heat and bliss overtake me from low in my belly until they radiate upward like waves of sunlight.

His low groan of satisfaction is muffled because his tongue thrusts inside me to lap up my release, drinking it down like I'm the finest wine.

When I'm racked with aftershocks, he pulls back with a satisfied gleam in his eye, lips wet from me. He licks them clean, his eyes half-hooded, and says, "Who knew my wife could be such a good little slut?"

CHAPTER 9

AIDEN

As soon as her shaking subsides, Catriona attempts to move away, but my hand at the back of her neck is an iron shackle as I sit up and arrange her draped over my lap. When my phone bleats out an incoming call, I pull it from my coat pocket, note the name with a curse before answering, and press it to my ear as she continues her futile attempts to scrabble away from me.

"O'Connor," I answer distractedly. My dick is already rock hard again, and I'm imagining all the filthy, fucked-up ways I can have her coated in my cum. Mark her as mine. Make her pay for all the trouble she's caused. Punish her for the position she's put me in. We'll both be lucky if we aren't dead in a week.

Christ, *fuck*. I should have stayed at the church.

Fixed it all with Rory.

But the moment I'd seen it was her under the veil, fury had consumed me and rooted me to the spot.

I'd wanted to torture her like she's tortured me. Demand recompense in the form of her plaintive little cries, her tears. If only she'd done what she was told, everything would be fine.

I may have said I'd annul our marriage and take her sister instead, but I know if I say a word to Rory, it'll make Catriona vulnerable. She would have been safe if I'd married her sister. I could have made sure of it. Now her father, volatile idiot that he is, may have her square in his sights. My carefully laid plans have all gone to shit, but I've survived worse.

"Did you have something to do with this? Tell me now, or I swear you'll regret it. I should have known better than to trust you. You're lucky I haven't called Cian already to tell him what you've done."

Catriona's head snaps up at her father's shouted voice blaring from the speaker. What little color remains underneath her furious blush drains immediately.

Rory takes my silence for permission to continue his tirade. "I swear to God if you planned this, I'll do everything in my power to make you pay for making a fool out of me."

Her struggles intensify, but I keep her pinned with my hand at her throat. Loose enough that she can still rub her puffy, slick pussy against my cock. It gives me no end of delight to imagine coming all over her while talking to him. I give half a thought to turning on my phone camera so he can get a good look at all the ways I plan to defile what had once been his. To exemplify all the ways in which his words are less than useless to me in a way that I can't yet do to Cian.

"Rory, how lovely to hear from my new father-in-law. Already calling to send us your best wishes? You're so thoughtful."

I click the speaker button and place the phone on the shelf behind my head so I can still talk. Catriona's eyes flash, then narrow in warning. She glances at my phone and back to me as I cant my hips to smear my dick through her sweetness. Ah, but fuck, it isn't going to take me long to come again, and my head drops back in ecstasy as Rory's voice drones on in my ear. Even his frantic blathering isn't enough to stop the white-hot flame of heat licking over my skin.

Is this what it means to go mad? Because that's how it feels. Like the leash I've kept on my control has snapped. If I'm Cian's hound, then I've gone rabid.

My refractory period is nothing to sneer at, as Catriona well knows, but this is something else entirely. I've never been the marrying kind, but maybe knowing she's my wife is what really fucking does it for me. Who would have thought out of all my various depravities, calling her my wife would be my new favorite kink?

"I know you had something to do with this nonsense. Let's get this straightened out, O'Connor, or so help me God, not even Cian will save you from what I will do to you."

Catriona tries to move away again as I pick up a rhythm, but my newly free hand is on her hip, keeping her against me. I spare half a thought to shifting her up slightly to slide inside, but we're almost to the estate, and I want the first time I get inside her again to be in a bed with hours to devote to fucking the hate out of her. That, and I know there's a good chance if I try, she'll find a way to stab me with something.

I can't seem to stop myself. The wrath I'd felt when I

realized what she'd done has twisted into something darker. More demanding. Something so vast and consuming, I don't have the words to describe it. Catriona's glower twists with the promise of retribution and confusion, like an avenging angel. Equal parts innocence and destruction. Her hostility has me hard and leaking.

"No need to be dramatic, Rory. But your daughter is busy right now. Can I take a message?"

Busy, to say the least.

At this, Catriona's nails bite into my shoulders, and I grunt despite the layers of fabric between us. Her face is a wreck of makeup, mascara tracks from the tears still leaking from her eyes, lipstick smeared from her lips, and that's nothing on the state of her clothes. Panties missing. Dress rucked up and yanked down. The hand on her hip strays to her bare breast, cupping and lifting the weight. She's so soft. So perfect. I never imagined I'd ever get her dirty with my undeserving hands again.

"Put her on the phone now, or they won't be able to identify your body with how thoroughly I'm going to mangle it."

Catriona jerks away, nearly throwing herself back off my lap when I tweak her nipple. Tired of her struggling, I flip us both, pinning her to the leather seats with my hips as Rory drones on and on with threats. She squeezes her eyes closed, her chest heaving in an effort to control herself. But it's hopeless. I'm going to make it my life's mission that she never knows a moment's peace for what she's done.

"It's our wedding night, Rory. You'll have to call back when we aren't so...busy," I answer, and then reach up to tap the mute button as he fills the space with his expletive-ridden diatribe. "Maybe after our honeymoon in a few weeks."

"Honeymoon? What honeymoon?" Catriona gasps as I fist my cock against her, the head bumping against her clit, and even though she tries to mask it, the friction has her sweating, too. "F-father never mentioned anything about a honeymoon."

"Because he never asked. It was supposed to be a surprise for your sister. Don't worry, we'll make it work with your classes. I'll take care of everything."

"I'm not going anywhere with you."

"You no longer have a choice." I punctuate the statement by fitting my cock to the weeping entrance of her body. I slide in, just the tip, and watch as her eyes dilate. "Did you do all of this because you wanted some dick? Darlin', all you had to do was ask. You didn't have to marry me for me to fuck you again."

Her eyes flash with anger, and she whips her hand up against my cheek with a snap. The crack of her palm sounds like lightning in the back of the limo. Stinging pain erupts, and the edge of it is so sweet and her gaze so murderous that I come without warning, jerking my dick roughly and spending all over her messy, trembling thighs and ripe, rosy pussy.

The shock in her face should make me feel something like remorse, but the only emotion I register is a sick, twisted sense of satisfaction. Not what I'd had in mind, but the pain at her hands is an awful lot like pleasure. A momentary distraction. Relief.

"O'Connor! O'Connor! Answer me, you fucking bastard. You tell me where she is, or I swear to God. This wasn't what we agreed to. If I find out you're responsible for this switch-up, I'm going to make you pay for thinking you can double-cross me."

Rory blathers on some more, and I'm too distracted rubbing the cum into her skin to give a damn. I could get used to seeing her like this. Marked by me. Ruined by me.

All mine.

Unerring proof that she belongs to me. Almost as good as the sight of my mother's rings on her finger.

A glance through the window shows we're almost home, but that doesn't stop me from using the new lubrication to tease her clit with my thumb. Her face tells me she wants to kill me, but she keeps her lips zipped shut as she can't resist the resulting shiver. I reach for the phone with my other hand to unmute it.

"—need to figure this out. I have connections, so we can get this taken care of tomorrow. We'll do a ceremony at the courthouse. The press will have a field day, but you don't want—"

At her father's threats—or maybe because my thumb presses a little more insistently—she gives a full-body shudder and bites into her plump lower lip. She's going to hate me even more in the next few minutes, and I almost can't fuckin' wait. She deserves everything that's coming to her for what she's done.

"There are two things you need to remember from now on. You are a pathetic piece of shit, and she's not yours to command anymore." I give him a moment to shriek like a hyena, then continue. "And if you ever threaten my wife again, it'll be the last thing you do." I don't think she'll come again, but I enjoy how much she fights against it, especially as her eyes flash wickedly at my words. "Do you understand me, or will I need to speak with you in person?"

"You're going to regret this, O'Connor," comes his grave response.

"What I do is none of your business." Another glance shows we're nearing our destination. I heave a sigh of remorse and give her swollen, abused clit one last caress before I pull away. "We're done now, Rory. Don't threaten me again."

Catriona pushes herself into a sitting position and yanks up the top of her dress. She can't quite get it all the way up and glowers at me. The skirts flutter down around her thighs, blocking the sight of her cunt covered in the evidence of me.

I hang up on his outraged reply, then tuck myself back into my pants. Catriona won't meet my eyes, which is probably a good thing. The pleased smirk pulling at my lips would only piss her off.

"Why did you say that to him?" she asks, her voice hoarse. I try not to shudder at the evidence of my torment.

"Because the only one who gets to hurt you from here on out is me."

"Why didn't you tell him the truth? You could have explained what I did. He'd probably thank you for it. You heard him. He'd fix this all for you in a heartbeat."

Is the sullenness in her voice from what we just did or from her father? I push the thought away. "Did you think I'd let you off so easily? No, you forced yourself into this position. And I don't plan to let you out of it so effortlessly. You bought yourself a husband, and I'm going to ensure you get everything that comes along with it."

Her breath hitches, and she angles in the seat to face me, her eyes still liquid with unshed tears. "You don't scare me."

I lift a finger to trace the tracks of mascara down her cheeks, and she flinches but doesn't look away. "Tell yourself that as much as you need to, *bhean chéile*. You and I both know differently."

"I hate you," she hisses.

"Then I guess it's a good thing you've tied yourself to me for the foreseeable future. It'll give you time to get over it."

"Then you misunderstand my capacity to hold a grudge."

"And you misunderstand my capacity for patience."

She opens her mouth like she's going to argue, but then the car comes to a stop in front of my place, and it snaps closed again. Much as I enjoy arguing with her, I'd rather do it in an actual room where I can get her naked and no one can interfere for a couple of hours. Twelve would be sufficient, but twenty-four hours would be ideal.

But I have a feeling once she realizes what she's in for, she won't let me near her again for a long, long time.

Even more unfortunate, the taste of her didn't satiate the ceaseless hunger inside me. Like the night I had her, it only seems to make me want her more.

I attempt to return Catriona to rights, but she slaps my hands away. Hers may be trembling, her eyes thick with tears, but she has lost none of her bite. I'd smile if I wasn't certain she'd claw it off my face.

I take her wrists in one of my hands and grip her jaw with the other. Fire blazes in her eyes, and her ire is so intense it almost blots out the hurt. A better man would feel shame at enjoying making a woman vulnerable, but the place where my desire for her lives is the space between her anger and her ruin. Seeing her broken and vulnerable like this? I'm obsessed. Addicted.

I'd tried to save her from my attention. Wanted to protect her from everything that goes along with being mine, but she'd literally walked herself into my den of iniquity and chained herself to me.

"You'll let me fix you up, pet. I don't want you walking in there looking like this."

"Then maybe you shouldn't have practically ripped my clothes off me," she snaps. Self-possession may be a trait I pride myself on having, but I find it severely tested each time she bites back at me. Maybe this is why I found her irresistible the night she saw me at the casino, and why I haven't been able to stop thinking about her since.

That's not to say there haven't been women in my life who could hold their own. Mara would skin me alive if I were to characterize her as anything other than a staunch feminist in a man's world, but Catriona has been an intriguing combination of cold as ice and soft as silk. I can't imagine many women who'd voluntarily walk into an arrangement like the one her father had prepared for her sister. Can't imagine many who'd get on their knees for me with hatred in their eyes and leave me wanting more.

So much more.

And she thinks *I'm* the dangerous one.

"No one is keeping you here," I say, keeping my posture loose and unaffected. Lights burn bright inside on the first floor of the estate as we pull into the drive. I imagine Frances is there, preparing meals to last for the week to give us privacy. "You can leave at any time."

Catriona stills, allowing me to release my hold. When she doesn't make to leave, I pull up her dress and fix the crooked clasp that was torn when I yanked it down. A wince pulls at her lips as I straighten her bra and brush against her abused nipples. It takes pure physical restraint to keep me from taking them back into my mouth and soothing her into a more agreeable state. I wonder if I could make her come with my mouth on her nipples alone, and I have to force myself to think of the steps methodically, or we'll never get out of this fucking car.

Much as I'd enjoy showing the world how much she irrevocably belongs to me, that also means I don't want any eyes on her body but mine. The thought of anyone else seeing her like this makes me want to carve someone up, and I wouldn't particularly care who. Thankfully, we're left alone as I wet a handkerchief from my pocket with water from a bottle. Shivers wrack her body as the cold liquid comes into contact with her delicate skin. When her hands tremble again, she fists them by her side. Once I return her makeup to an acceptable state, I pass her the wet fabric and let her finish until she's satisfied.

"Did I prove it to you? Was it good enough that you won't tell your boss the truth?" she asks, her voice so raw it scratches along my spine like skeletal fingers. A sense of foreboding stills my attempt to herd her out of the limo's back seat. "I hope that was worth it, because if you ever try to do anything like that again, I'll cut off your dick and shove it down your throat."

Threats of violence sharpen her gaze, washing away any remnants of hurt she may be feeling. As I watch, she brushes the evidence of our little tryst from the wrinkles in her dress, tucks away the emotions ravaging her face, and pastes on a robotic expression. Everything inside me stills, watching her wipe away her personality like she's factory resetting a printer until all signs of the woman who makes my blood light up with sparks of life disappear.

It hollows out something inside me, scrapes me raw of every moment of triumph my little attempt at dominance conjured. The woman I thought I figured out so easily washes away those assumptions in under a minute. Frozen, I can only watch as she climbs out of the limo, her face serene and determined. The only sign that something had occurred between us at all is the bulge and weight of her panties in my pocket.

She may belong to me, in body and in name, but she'll never truly be *mine*.

CHAPTER 10

CATRIONA

Who knew my wife could be such a good little slut?

If only he *also* knew how I'm going to make him regret ever saying that to me, he would have kept his fucking mouth shut.

As we sit in a tense silence, I methodically plan all the ways I can make him miserable. Because if I think about what just happened between us... I shove the thoughts away, deep inside my mental box of shit I can't think about, and lock it down tight, along with everything else that I can't think about.

I don't have the luxury of losing it. If I'm going to make it out of this with my sanity intact, I have to focus on my end goal: survival. No matter the consequences I receive from my father, the cold shoulder from my sister, or the retaliation from O'Connor.

No matter what it costs.

Even if it costs me my sanity.

My freedom.

My sense of self.

My phone buzzes in my hand with a text from Yasmine. I fish out my phone, wincing at the missed calls from Elizabeth, and I'm instantly a thousand pounds lighter at the sight of Yasmine's name on my screen.

Yasmine
Your sister is furious. I left her at your dad's, who is also furious, FYI. If Reggie weren't with me, I'm sure he would have given me the third degree. Or worse. How did it go?

Me
As good as we can hope for. It's done. We're going back to his place.

Yasmine
You mean your old house? Really? You sure you're ready for that

Suddenly, the tight laces of the wedding dress feel a whole lot tighter around my ribs, and it's an effort to draw air into my lungs. It had never occurred to me that we'd go back to the beautiful home that had once belonged to my mother. The home where I discovered her broken body.

He wouldn't... he couldn't think I'd...

Me
I don't know

> **Yasmine**
> I'm tracking your location. Hate to break it to you, but it's your old street. Would now be a terrible time for me to say I told you so? Going to that party was a horrible idea

> **Me**
> You're telling me

A breath rattles out of my chest as we pull up to the gate of the last place I ever wanted to see again. I follow O'Connor through the garage and courtyard to the mudroom, fighting my instincts to flee the whole way. A short hallway later, we're in the kitchen. The earlier relief at Yasmine's text messages has completely evaporated. Being back in this house is like being enveloped in shadows. Thick, oily shadows that fill my throat and choke out all the oxygen. The last time I'd been here... I don't even want to think about it.

"You seem tense," O'Connor says, startling me from my thoughts. No shit. My muscles are drawn so taut, I'm afraid they could snap a bone. "As your husband, I can—"

"Absolutely *fucking* not. I'm going to stay in my—in a guest room. Don't worry," I say, before he can make an excuse to follow me, "I can find it myself."

I eye the stairs, because the only rooms down here are the entertaining spaces—living room, dining room, formal versions of both, and the kitchen. But he's blocking my path to get to the stairs. When he doesn't move, I spear him with a pointed, unamused frown.

"You'll be staying with me tonight so I can keep an eye on you." O'Connor takes my hand to lead me up to the second floor before I can offer an objection. He's moving so fast, I can only focus on not tripping on the material of my wedding dress as he drags me behind. The upside? I don't have time to linger on the spot where I'd found my mother.

It's not until we reach the top that I'm able to tear my arm away from his grip. "Stop manhandling me, O'Connor. I do know how to walk by myself. And I'm not staying anywhere with you."

He points at an open doorway—the same room that had belonged to my parents. And the one we'd shared at the masquerade. Also known as the last fucking place I'd want to be, let alone with him.

When I balk, he lifts an arm to block my escape, his eyes shifting from flat and opaque to flinty and penetrating. "After what you pulled today, you'll stay where I fucking put you, or I'll tie you to the fucking bed. The choice is absolutely not yours. I suggest you give future actions more thought than you did today."

"I don't have to explain myself to you. I tried to talk to you about it, and you left me no choice. If anything, today is *your* fault." This is the most ridiculous argument I've had with anyone, jammed in a hallway, wearing a wedding dress and caked in makeup. I enjoy dressing up in my suits and designer dresses, but I prefer that armor to this.

O'Connor starts to speak, then clamps his teeth together. He picks me up by my waist and shoves me bodily through the door, where I stumble. One of my heels breaks under the strain, and he shuts the door behind us. The lock slams home, and then he has me pinned against the wall. I forget how to breathe even though the hand he has at my throat is only a suggestion.

"Here's the deal, *bhean chéile*," he murmurs in a throaty warning, "now that you've completely fucked everything, I'm going to keep an eye on you so you can't cause further damage. You wanted a husband? You've got one. So I hope you're ready to have me at your side until we're both in the grave, because I won't be going anywhere."

"If you think you're going to control me, I hope you're ready for an *early* grave," I hiss, my throat working against his hand as trepidation rains over me. "I can easily make this hell for you, O'Connor."

"I'm starting to believe you." He releases his hold on my throat, and I'm halfway across the room before he turns. "Tomorrow, we can discuss what's going to happen going forward. For now, I trust you won't cause any more trouble if I leave you to get ready for bed?"

Before I can say anything further, he disappears into a walk-in closet and comes back a few minutes later with clothes. "These should fit. Don't worry, I've already hidden all the sharp implements, so there won't be any backstabbing tonight. Sorry to disappoint."

The siren call of a shower is too great to ignore, and I mentally table giving a damn about him being close. It's not like he hasn't already seen every part of me. I hope it kills him to know I'm in there, naked.

I snatch the clothes from his hand and stride to the bathroom. His eyes drill into my back the entire time, but I pretend he's not even there. As exhausted and emotionally drained as I am, I don't really care if he's watching. I don't care about what he means by "what's going to happen going forward." All I want is to sleep for a century, because this week feels like it's lasted that long.

Forgive me, Mom. I send up a quick prayer as I shed the now lank and wrinkled material of her wedding dress. As much as I daydreamed about getting married in this dress when I was a little girl after staring at pictures of my parents' wedding day, now all it makes me want to do is puke. I shove it into a corner, out of my sight, and a fraction of the nausea abates. I may never get rid of it, but it'll be a long time before I can look at it and picture anything positive. The thought of what we'd done in the limo makes bile rise in my throat.

I practically leap into the shower, not bothering to pull the curtains, and I let the pounding spray slough away the dregs of panic remaining in my chest. For the first time since my eyes cracked open with the dawn light spilling in my bedroom, I have a moment to breathe. Steam billows around me, clinging like film to the windows and the glass shower wall.

I clean myself all over with thick, rich soap, comforted by the lavender scent that's almost an exact match for the one I have at home, but not enough that I can stop myself from washing my body over and over again. Consciously, I know I'm as clean as I can get, but my subconscious is a stubborn bitch and thinks I'll never be rid of the stains all over me. From where he touched me. From where he thought he owned me. I don't think I can imagine anything more terrible than not having control over the only thing my father couldn't take from me—my body.

He hadn't forced me, not really. I was willing to do whatever it took to keep him from wrecking my plans.

Somehow that's worse.

While I wash myself, taking my time while O'Connor is in the other room, I make myself think of the positives. Now that I'm back in my family's home, I'll have more time to poke around—when O'Connor isn't hovering, obviously. Maybe I can get access to security footage, or maybe there are more clues in my mother's favorite places in the house. Her library, of course, the greenhouse, perhaps even this very bedroom.

I hadn't considered it when I'd come up with the insane plan to force O'Connor to marry me, but this is an opportunity I can't pass up. Mr. Broussard may have more ideas about what to do with the chance to re-examine the crime scene, even if a lot of time has passed. I make a mental note to update him during our next call so we can brainstorm.

By the time I step out of the shower, my usual alabaster skin is inked heavily in red and purple. Bruises on my throat, by my nipple, along my thighs. A red flush from the scalding water. Nails bitten to the quick from my nerves over the past week. Teeth scrubbed so hard my gums weep red rivers.

The clothes O'Connor had provided were one of his T-shirts, a white one. Thin. Almost see-through. As well as a pair of pajama pants. *Whatever*, I think with a mental shrug. It's his funeral. I'm brushing my teeth when the door opens, and O'Connor strides inside.

"What the fuck? You could knock," I sputter after rinsing my mouth.

"In my own house? In my bedroom? I don't think so." If he notices my breasts through the shirt, he doesn't comment. My sensitive nipples may as well be beacons the way they twist and jut against the fabric.

"Maybe I'll add that to whatever hostile-takeover-style negotiations you're planning," I mutter.

"If anyone is hostile in this relationship, it's you, *Mrs.*

O'Connor." He moves into the bathroom, stripping pieces of his tux along the way. I wish I could say I looked somewhere, anywhere else, but that would make me a fucking liar. "But I'll make note of your request."

"If you think I'm taking your last name, you really are insane," I say, but I don't know if he hears me over the running water. My mind is immediately filled with images of him in there. The spray buffeting his skin, splashing against the tile. How he'd looked, pleasure-ravaged and vulnerable. When he returns, he's wearing nothing but a towel wrapped loosely around his waist. Beads of water trail down his heavily tattooed body, and I freeze where I'm perched on a chair by the window, brushing my hair. My mouth goes dry. Liquid heat pools low in my belly and immediately curdles to shame. How can I even think that anything about him is attractive? My brain may be aware of how evil he is, but my body sure isn't. *The traitor.*

"Too good for my last name?" he asks, and when the towel drops, I spin, not wanting to take in the sight of him more than I absolutely have to. Not wanting to remember how much I've dreamed about him since we met.

"Please. You don't really want me to be an O'Connor. Let's be honest," I say, when I can find my voice.

His footsteps pad to the closet, followed by the sound of him pulling on clothes. I release a breath, thankful I don't have to spend the night near him while he's naked.

"You're my wife now, Catriona. Maybe you'll understand exactly what that means after our conversation tomorrow. Though from what I've learned about you so far, your levels of comprehension leave something to be desired," he says in a wry voice, and I grit my teeth so hard my jaw screams in protest.

Without answering him, I stalk to the giant bed and climb under the sheets, facing the wall. Ignoring him seems to be the best way to move forward. I try to relax despite my anger and fear, but my nervous system doesn't recognize that O'Connor's simply climbed into the bed beside me and presumably settled in for sleep. I catalog his every huff of breath or the whisper of sheets as he shifts to a more comfortable position as a potential threat. Is he moving closer? Is he planning to put his hands on me again?

As soon as the thought crystallizes, the memory of that night surges to the forefront of my mind. O'Connor commanding me to get on my knees for him. Crawl for him. Making me come in a crowded party where anyone could have watched.

But what he did to me isn't the worst part of everything that happened.

The worst is that my body remembers how good he made it feel. Craves him the way it wants all sorts of things that are bad for it, like an addiction. He's so close that I ache for him to touch me and can't stop thinking of it.

I try to think of something, *anything* else, but the first thing that comes to mind is how he treated my father—and how much I enjoyed hearing it. That must be the *definition* of daddy issues.

I don't think there's a therapist on this planet who could walk me through the seven circles of fucked up this is.

Are there medications that cure things like this? I make a mental note to look into it. I'm going to need an entire pharmacy to deal with all the trauma if I survive this marriage.

A complete chemical imbalance is the only explanation I have for hating him so much and being unable to ignore how much my body wants him. Adrenaline or mania—something. Relief. Fear. The perfect concoction of whatever the fuck forced me to find any semblance of pleasure in the worst possible moment. With the worst possible person. Is it because I'd been stripped bare, figuratively if not literally, and somewhere in the darkness of it all, there was a freedom in letting him have absolute power over me?

Does that mean I deserved it? That I'll let him do it again?

As I struggle with my thoughts, O'Connor slowly inches closer in his sleep. So close that woodsy, masculine scent surrounds me, and his electrifying warmth cocoons me. My heart beats like a drum inside my chest, and I can't seem to tell if my body is frightened... or excited.

That's what eventually has me finding enough courage to steal the blanket decorating the foot of the bed and flee to one of the walk-in closets, which I realize too late must also belong to him. As soon as I'm safely enclosed inside, I flick on the light and try to steady my breathing. Which is proven damn near impossible when I realize it's soaked in his scent, leaving me feeling more on edge than when he'd been inches away from me.

I don't sleep well after that—not that I would have, anyway. My mind races with anxious thoughts, each one more frantic than the last. Every time I doze off, I'm jerked awake by the memory of our vows. Of O'Connor kissing me. Of the night we had together. The memories echo in my mind like a haunting refrain, refusing to let me rest.

Not only is the chaos in my head relentless, but lying on

the admittedly comfortable carpet in the closet doesn't exactly scream luxury. My makeshift pillow is a pile of laundry. Each time I stir awake, I'm convinced he's about to barge into the closet and drag me out—or worse, force me to join him in bed.

That's why I'm genuinely surprised when I wake up in the middle of the night and realize I'm still alone. Curled up in a ball on the floor, I shiver underneath the blanket, my body stiff from the cramped position. The pale light of dawn seeps through the gap beneath the closet door, casting faint shadows across the floor. My chest aches with the reminder that this is my reality now—cold, uncomfortable, and endlessly uncertain.

If nothing else, at least I've lived through those things before. If I can take on my father, I can handle anyone.

A thread of violent recklessness stitches itself into my soul. At the memory of Elizabeth's biting comments and casual disinterest, my father's arrogant sense of dominion over my life and choices, and O'Connor's general malevolence, the good little girl I've tried to be all these years finally hands the reins over to the part of me who is tired. And angry. Who has been pushed so far that she can't possibly fall any further.

My last thought as I drift back to sleep, just for a little longer, is that I can't let any of them get to me. Least of all, O'Connor.

Because if I'm married to the devil, I won't win by playing by his rules.

CHAPTER 11

AIDEN

My phone vibrates on the bedside table. It's Ma. It always is first thing in the morning. Midday in Ireland is when Cian is most likely to be out of the house. Alarm shoots through me, but I don't understand why at first.

I drag the phone across the table, swipe at the screen until it connects, then press it to my ear. "Mornin', Ma," I say.

"What have you done?" she says without preamble. Usually, I love hearing her familiar, comforting voice. The sound of it brings me back to my childhood. But there's something wrong with it now. Ma hasn't been right since my father was killed and Cian kept her for himself. But there's a lucidity to her tone that's usually absent. An urgency.

"What do you mean?" I roll away from my stomach,

blinking rapidly, trying to clear my vision and adjust to the searing morning light. "What happened?"

"Cian left last night and hasn't returned home. I've been waiting all day. I've been hearing whispers. You know how the men like to talk. Worse than a gaggle of hens. They've said your name, I'm sure of it."

A shadow of unease has me sitting up, searching for Catriona's presence next to me, but she's not there. The space where her body had been when I fell asleep is barren and cold. Thoughts of how easily it'd be for someone to over-power her surge to the forefront of my brain.

"Everything's fine," I lie. "Probably nothing. You shouldn't worry."

Leaping to my feet, I reach under the bed and have my Glock 19 in my hands in seconds. Is he here? Has he found out already? Could he have gotten here without me know-ing? *Fuck.* Still clad only in my boxers, I clear the bathroom with a glance. Empty.

"I don't believe you, Aiden. Please, tell me this doesn't have anything to do with me. Tell me you haven't done anything stupid."

I unlock the door to check the hallway, pausing on the landing to listen to the first floor. But everything is silent except the sound of my heart thundering in my ears and traffic buzzing to life outside the windows. I'm itching to go downstairs to call security and check whether there's been a breach, but I also don't want to leave. I'm frozen, uncertain. What the fuck is happening to me? A dull, sick feeling takes up residence in my stomach. I hate it. I hate it more than I've ever hated anything in my life, and I have enough of the feeling to go around.

"Aiden!" Ma urges. "Tell me."

Are they safe? The words bounce around the inside of my skull. For as long as I can remember, I've only had one person to care for: my mother. Now that there's another, the balance of my life seems to have shifted dramatically.

I murmur placating words, but I don't believe them. She hasn't been safe in a long time. Helplessness has me by the throat as I search through every room, guest bedroom, bathroom, closet. I thoroughly check the study where I found her the first time, the night of the masquerade party, when she'd snuck in here and witnessed me kill that good-for-nothing cop, Dufresne. All empty. Then I remember the closets in the bedroom. She wouldn't—but she definitely would. I make my way there carefully, gun held in front of me, safety off. I'd been so distracted by the shocking turn of events the day before that I hadn't considered increasing the security here.

As I move back into the bedroom, skirting a table and the foot of the bed, I find myself forgetting to breathe. The closet door is closed. Had I closed it before going to bed? I can't fucking remember.

Gun in one hand, I open the door—and relief gusts past my lips as I find Catriona asleep on the floor there, using my clothes for a pillow with a blanket wrapped around her small body. Had she always seemed so small?

"Ma, I'll tell you everything soon, I promise. Cian isn't going to do anything to you." At least, not worse than he's already done. Not if I'm not there to witness. "Take care of yourself."

"I don't care about me, *a stór*. All I care about is that you're okay."

"I'm fine, I promise. I'll talk to you tomorrow?"

"Of course. I love you."

The words won't pass over my lips, but she doesn't mind. She knows I love her. But saying them would feel too much like saying goodbye, so I haven't in a long time.

My fingers tremble as I hang up the phone, flip the safety back on the gun, and set it on a shelf. The blanket from the foot of the bed only covers part of her body, forcing her to curl into a little ball like a child. Pink-tipped toes poking out from underneath, her knees uncovered, and her palms clasped together and pillowed under her cheek. Dark circles smear underneath her eyes, pulling my mouth into a frown. I give myself another minute to slow my breathing and get ahold of my emotions.

Then I push away from the doorframe to retrieve some clothes. Jeans. A Henley sweater I shove up my forearms. Boots. I strap on a smaller handgun to an ankle holster. Catriona may have been perfectly safe, but waking up and not knowing if Cian had been here makes my palms itchy, and I feel better with an emotional support weapon on me at all times.

By the time I'm finished dressing, Catriona begins to stir. I sit on the bed, going through my security feed as she drifts back to consciousness. From this vantage point, I can only see a sliver of her, but it settles me to keep her in my sights.

As I study the feed for the second floor and confirm that the only others coming in or out of the house have been my staff, I release the remaining tension held captive in my body. Frances answers my text a moment later, confirming she has breakfast ready for us and that she already has clothes waiting for Catriona downstairs.

Feeling much more level, I leave Catriona to her own devices for a few minutes while I double-check the third and first floors, needing to see in person that no one else is here. The rest of the house is empty. With that confirmed, I retrieve the clothes Frances fetched and bring them back to the second floor. I find Catriona waiting in the bedroom, sleep rumpled and soft. Too soft. Easily breakable.

She stands silhouetted in the closet doorway, still clad in my white T-shirt and pajama bottoms. She crosses her ankles, drawing my eyes back up to her full, flared hips, generous breasts, and finally to the scowl still sitting on her lips.

She parts them to speak, and a yawn cuts her off before she can continue. "Wha-what do you want?"

This is the morning after I hadn't been privileged enough to witness the first time we were together. Of course, I would have preferred to wake up with her naked body against mine. But there's a vulnerability to her now, before she's dressed and all done up. A side of her that most people aren't normally witness to.

"Are you hungry? I believe we skipped dinner." Her stomach growls loud enough that I hear it as clear as a bell. Her cheeks redden with embarrassment, and I say, "I guess that answers my question. I had Frances bring you some clothes. After you get dressed, we'll go down to the kitchen. We'll eat at the table there, and I'll answer three questions." I hand her the clothes without waiting for her agreement, a huff of displeasure aimed at my back.

I can practically feel her thoughts racing, wondering why I haven't berated her for choosing to sleep on the floor rather than next to me. What she doesn't realize is that I don't care where she sleeps, for now, as long as she does it where I can keep an eye on her.

Catriona takes the clothes and moves to the bathroom. She comes out wearing a light pink thigh-skimming dress made of lace flowers, her face as made up as she can get it, skin bright and clean, hair in a simple twist. Elizabeth would have been a satisfactory wife, but Catriona... It's like she was born for this. No one would doubt the man at her side. It's only too bad for her that the man is me.

I nod to the stairs, and she skirts around so she's in front of me. It soothes an ache in the pit of my stomach caused by her absence this morning to keep her in front of me. Cian has eyes everywhere, and even though I've walked through the entire house, I still feel like he's watching. Always watching. Waiting for me to let down my guard.

"Why only three questions?" she asks over her shoulder, as we move down the stairs to the kitchen.

"Because if I give you free rein, you'll turn it into a deposition, and it'll put both of us off our breakfast. Plus, I want something in return."

"Color me shocked. And what exactly do you want?"

I flick an immovable glance back at her. "To negotiate."

She follows me silently, no doubt planning and plotting in that pretty little head of hers. She simply wouldn't be her father's daughter if she wasn't, but it doesn't deter me. I've always maintained my position by being one step ahead of my opposition, and the same is true when it comes to battling *Mrs. O'Connor.*

Breakfast waits for us on the eat-in table, her favorites, of course. Frances is a known social media stalker and had no trouble perusing Catriona's profiles to find out what she likes most. The woman is a saint.

I prepare Catriona's usual lavender-honey latte—like her preferred soap, Frances had informed me—as she freezes in the kitchen doorway. Her drink of choice makes something inside me clench tighter with the realization that she shouldn't be anywhere near my life. It's too hard, too dangerous. The latte is sweet and light, two words I'd never use to describe myself. I've long suspected she harbors a soft, sensitive side hidden underneath her prickly exterior. And like me, I imagine it's hidden... way, way down deep. For her, it shows up in her preferences: pink clothes, floral scents, and ridiculous drinks.

For me... I've quickly realized that if I ever had soft spots, they were ruthlessly destroyed a long time ago.

I make a plate for her and place it at the table in front of giant bay windows that look out over the backyard. "Sit," I tell her, gesturing to the food. I'm eager to get these negotiations in place. The itch beneath my skin from this morning's wake-up call is nagging at me furiously.

She doesn't move an inch, but her eyes are glued to the plate piled high with food and her steaming latte. While she wrestles with her conscience, I make a plate for myself and take the seat opposite hers. One thing about Catriona is that she'll never turn down food. I made certain Frances stocked all her favorites, with backups of her holy grail snacks—pistachios and peanut butter with green apples.

After our night together, I'd done a little internet sleuthing myself and filed the details away like nuggets of gold I could use. For when, I wasn't quite sure, but it kept me from completely spiraling out of control. Knowing what she liked to eat. The soap she buys religiously from one small business. Her expensive-as-hell perfume. The classes she's taking (and the ones she's failing). The average number of steps she takes in a day. She was lucky I didn't hack the security cameras at her house.

She refused to tell me her name that night, but she never knew I recognized her the moment she walked in.

Finally, she takes a seat on the other side of the table, ignoring me in favor of her food. The spinach omelet, crispy turkey bacon, and fresh slices of watermelon dominate her focus. She waffles for a moment between the three and ignores all of them to inhale half of her lavender-honey latte. She moans in the back of her throat and cuts the sound off halfway through, her cheeks turning a pretty pink beneath the cream of her skin.

She contemplates me over the curve of her coffee cup. A little furrow draws between her brows, and the urge to press my lips there and soothe it away is so overpowering that I grip the chair beneath me. The words froth up against her lips, but she rolls them back as though to contain them. Silence presses down between us, but it's not an uncomfortable one, at least not for me. I finish my plate before her and make a cup of black coffee for myself.

Once her breakfast is gone and her cup drained, she pushes the dishes away and crosses her arms over her chest as she studies me. I tilt my head and stare back, inwardly amused. I've faced far more intimidating men who couldn't meet my eye, but this woman has never backed down from me, and I really shouldn't be surprised. It's why I couldn't walk away from her that night, and why I had to walk away from her when her father proposed his ridiculous scheme.

"What negotiations are you talking about?" Catriona finally demands.

"Is that one of your questions?"

She hesitates, then nods, a determined glint in her eyes.

"How about I give you this one for free? As a show of my goodwill." At that, she scoffs. "There are certain things I want going forward. I'm willing to give you some things you want in return for them." At this, she sits up a little straighter, but I stop her before she can continue. "If your questions include anything about the marriage, money, etcetera, you can save them. I won't count them against your three. Understood?"

Her mouth opens, then closes. I can't take my eyes off it. "I don't know how honest I can expect you to be, considering, but I'll bite. What, exactly, are you involved with? What sort of organization?"

Is this why she's occupied my thoughts since Halloween? Because of the intelligent gleam in her eye? The way she never ceases to surprise me? "I work for a man named Cian Lynch, head of Clan Lynch. He's the leader of the Irish mob. I take care of collecting his debts, an enforcer, if you will. He's married to my mother, Mary." The words come out tasting like chalk, so I wet my mouth with a sip of coffee so I don't choke.

"I don't know why I'm surprised. Considering what I've seen, it makes sense. Did he have anything to do with my mother's death? Did my father go to him?"

At this, she lifts her head, and I'm snared by the determination on her face. Her ferocity grips me like a magnet, hooking just behind my gut. "Your father never asked Cian anything about your mother. His only debt to us is from what he's spent at the tables. He's a shit gambler. You have my word on that."

"Will he..." I refill her latte, and she bites her tongue to keep from showing any gratitude. Brat. She pauses, blows at the beverage before taking a sip, then sets it aside before licking foam from her lips. "Will Cian retaliate for what I've done? Is he a threat to me?"

"Cian doesn't like when things act outside of his control. When that happens, he likes to throw his weight around to make sure all the players on the board know who is in charge. It remains to be seen what the consequences will be for what you've done, but they're not your burden to bear. Do you understand me?"

"Yes, but... that didn't answer my other question."

The levity disappears from my voice. "You should always consider Cian a threat, Catriona. He's not the head of the family because of his people skills." I sip the too-hot coffee to wash the bad taste from my mouth. "Last question."

Catriona nibbles on her lip, pulling it between her teeth and then releasing. "Why did you go through with it? You could have objected. Stopped the ceremony. Forced the issue, and you wouldn't be in this situation. So why did you say yes when you realized it was me?"

"Because it was too late," I say. And now she's out of questions, which is grand since I'm done sharing.

Now we negotiate.

It brings a smirk to my lips as she steels herself. Straightens her spine. Clasps her hands together. Now that she's rested, eaten, and caffeinated, her fire is back, blazing white hot all over me... and I bask in it like I've only ever lived in shadows.

She tips her head at me. "What do you want to negotiate, exactly?"

"We're married now, pet. Best we get all those pesky expectations off the table."

Catriona swallows hard, her fingers knotting together so tightly that the knuckles turn white. "I'd like this in writing."

"Of course. I'll have my lawyers draw up what we agree on, and you can look it over."

"Fine," she grinds out.

"You're welcome to consult your attorney as well."

"Obviously. What else is on your list of requirements? If you say anything related to sex, I'm going to stab you somewhere sensitive. I wouldn't sleep with you again unless I had no other choice."

"Famous last words. You can't tell me you didn't like it."

"Want to bet?" she says sweetly. Then stiffens when my smile widens.

"So vicious," I say, then force myself to get back to business. "I want to have you added to my accounts."

Snorting, she says, "Like hell. My father is clearly willing to pay fast and loose with my mother's money, but that won't be me. I'm not giving you a cent."

Her voice is stern, and I sigh, thinking maybe I should have brought in a mediator. Christ, Elizabeth would have been so much easier. "I said I want to add you to my accounts. I don't want your money, *bhean chéile*, but I find it interesting that protecting yours is your priority."

"Then what do you—"

"Keep your accounts; I don't want or need them. I won't touch what's yours." I take a languid sip of coffee, watching the confusion tighten her features. "But what's mine is yours.

I'll add you to mine as soon as possible. Spend to your heart's content."

Her eyebrows jump somewhere in the vicinity of her hairline. "But why?"

It's so cute when she's thrown off guard. I should do it more often. I like it almost as much as when she's spitting fire at me.

"I have money, though that may be hard for you to imagine. As my wife, you're entitled to it," I drawl with another smirk. She looks like she wants to slap it off my face, and my eyes drop with amusement to where her hands twitch in the folds of her dress. "For whatever you need. My mother would have my hide if I did any less, and if we're going to do this, it's expected. Your father's debts will be taken care of from your inheritance. Aside from that, you'll have a vast fortune at your fingertips."

"But—"

"As soon as it fits for our schedules, I'll take you to my man and have you added. Blow it. Leave it. Donate it, I don't give a shite. There's more than enough to fund your whims and fury. It might even humor me to see you try to spend it as fast as I can earn it."

She gathers her surprise and tucks it away. It's fascinating how she wipes her emotions and puts on a perfect mask. "I may do that. I could use a new wardrobe."

"It's yours."

"That way I can save for a future without you in it."

"Cute that you think you'll have one."

"I could really use a vacation."

"We're going to Ireland for our honeymoon soon. After that, we can go wherever you want. I have a jet."

"You have a jet," she deadpans.

"Technically, it's the organizations, but as my wife, it's at your disposal."

"I've always wanted to go to the Maldives."

"I'll pack our bags."

"You're really terrible at this negotiation thing," she muses. "So far, it sounds like I'm coming out on top of this. What's in it for you?"

"Maybe I like seeing you on top," I drawl.

Ignoring my comment, she lifts a shoulder. "I'm not going to say no to a new fortune. It's your bottom line, not mine. Don't come crying to me when I send you the bills."

"Like I said, spend as much as you like."

"What else do you want?"

"I want to know where you are at all times. I'd prefer a tracker you can wear. I don't trust you to always have your phone on you."

Catriona snorts. "Like hell *that's* going to happen."

"I guess when I said negotiations, I should have said requirements. Because this is nonnegotiable."

"You can put a leash on me over my dead body, O'Connor."

"I'm not going to compromise on your safety, *pet*. I hope you don't ever need it, but it's imperative that you're safe. My world is an ugly one, and this will bring peace of mind. Didn't we just have a conversation about how my boss is going to be pissed when he finds out about this? Do you want to end up at the bottom of Lake Pontchartrain?"

"Your peace of mind is my last priority. I don't care who you are. You're not putting a tracker on me. There has to be another way to keep me safe. I'll carry a taser. Or get a gun."

Heat surges through me at the thought. "Oh, I can teach you if you like."

"Not a chance."

I hide my smile behind another sip of coffee. "Grand. But if you aren't going to use a tracker, then you'll at least allow bodyguards. They're discreet and well-trained."

"No," she says flatly.

"I'm being quite flexible here. You're coming out on top in every way. All I'm asking is this one little thing."

"To let you stalk me."

"At least I'm informing you ahead of time," I say, lifting my hands. "But it's the tracker, the bodyguards, or I lock you in this house. You choose."

"Fine, I'll take the fucking bodyguards," she snarls. "But you'd better hope you have some bodyguards of your own, because you'll be lucky if I don't kill you myself." Before I can agree, she holds up a hand. "But I want separate bedrooms."

"No way in—"

"I'm not going to sleep with you, and I'm not going to sleep on the floor. Separate bedrooms, O'Connor, or I swear, I'll hide somewhere you can't find me."

We both know that's not possible, but all I wanted was the bodyguards, so I say, "Fine. Your own room. I'll have Frances set one up next to mine. Children—what do you say—"

"I say no way in fucking hell would I ever consider procreating with you."

"Not even—"

"There's nothing you could offer me that would make me consider it."

"Are you sure about that?"

"Are we forgetting that you almost married my *sister* yesterday? I'm pretty fucking sure."

"So you're saying you would have considered it if I'd agreed to marry you when you asked?" My voice comes out low, unintentionally, and her eyes darken.

"Don't twist my words."

I let the moment linger, then say, "Fine. I reserve the right to renegotiate this later. It makes sense for you to focus on your career first."

"We aren't renegotiating anything. I'm never going to have kids with you." A pause. "You mean you aren't going to make me stay at home and be the perfect Mafia wife?" You could cut glass with the amount of sarcasm in her voice.

"What makes you think I'd stop you from pursuing your career?"

"I don't know? My general understanding of who you are as a person?"

Ignoring her, I say, "Then again, you've been having trouble with your classes, haven't you? I'll worry about your career interfering when you're not in jeopardy of getting kicked out."

She jerks away, the china rattling on the table. "How do you know about that? What—Jesus." Placing both palms in front of her, she speaks slowly and clearly. I'm definitely not luxuriating in how good it feels to see her stunned. "You've been, what? Stalking me? Looking into my family? That stops now. You have your bodyguards, but I draw the line at you infiltrating every aspect of my life."

"That sounds like something you should have thought of before you forced me to marry you."

"If you don't stay out of my personal and professional life, O'Connor, we're going to have a problem."

"I'll do no such thing... of course, if that's something you want, I'm willing to—"

"If you say negotiate, I'll strangle you with my bare hands."

"—offer a concession."

"What do you want?" she says through gritted teeth.

"It's imperative we present a united front, especially to my boss, Cian, so that we're invited to Ireland to be presented to the other Clans in our organization. This means you'll be my wife in public, at events, and especially in front of anyone I work with. The alternative could be dangerous for us both, so it would be to your benefit to agree, but I'm nothing if not gracious and won't meddle in any of your classes."

"Why the hell would you *meddle* in the first place?"

Ignoring her, I press, "Do you agree?"

"What sort of events?" she hedges.

"Our reception on Friday. I have a few social obligations, such as a charity gala where Cian will be present, and I can introduce you. Then the dinner with the other Clans in the organization in Ireland."

She blows out a breath. "Fine."

"You won't embarrass me. You'll act like being Mrs. O'Connor is the only thing you've ever wanted, and you won't leave my side."

"I said yes. What more do you want?"

"Perfect. You're doing so well already. See how easy it is to behave?" She fairly snarls in response, but I pretend not to notice. "I'll introduce you to your bodyguards, and then the reception will be on Friday. Don't worry about attire. I have a friend who'd slit my throat if I let you wear anything she didn't choose."

"Can we be done now? I need to go home and get my—"

"Absolutely not. You won't be leaving the estate without your bodyguards."

"Fine. Then where are they?"

"They start tomorrow. Give me a list of what you need, and I'll have someone retrieve it for you."

"I can get my own stuff, O'Connor."

"If I knew you wouldn't get yourself into more trouble, maybe I'd believe you." Putting the cup into the sink, I say over my shoulder, "Get me the list this afternoon, and I'll have your things brought over. My lawyer will draw up the terms for your approval."

"You can't keep me locked in this house. I'll find a way to get out," she says to my back, and I stop, then turn and amble to the table. She straightens, wariness clouding her expression.

Leaning down, I brace one hand on the table and the other on the back of her chair. She goes so still, I'm almost positive she's stopped breathing.

"Remember what I told you before? When you thought you could play games with me? Consider that sentiment even more applicable now, Mrs. O'Connor. There's nowhere you could run where I won't find you."

CHAPTER 12

CATRIONA

"I thought you meant it when you said you loved me."

Yasmine takes an ungodly sized bite of her turkey burger, wiping a bit of green goddess dressing from her lips as she chews. She swallows, then says, "I love you very much, but have you seen my schedule? I barely have time to shower, let alone pencil in lunch. Which, thank you for treating, by the way."

We're at The Company Burger on the Thursday after the wedding, where I harassed Yasmine to join me for lunch via threats that I'd lose my mind if I didn't see her at least once before the reception. She's still in her jade scrubs, slightly faded from too many washes. Her hair is thrown up in a bun at the crown of her head with black spirals escaping to frame her face. The gray fleece jacket she wears to combat the hospital's freezing temperatures is tossed over the back of her chair.

"You can thank Mr. O'Connor because we're putting it on his tab." We haven't had the chance to "add me to his accounts" yet, but I do have a shiny black American Express card burning a hole in my wallet.

"I love your husband. He can take me out for lunch anytime." Yasmine tucks an errant curl behind her ear and sips at her Cobru shake, a cold brew milkshake we discovered freshman year. According to her, it's one of the only things keeping her upright during long days (and nights) of clinical rotations as a fourth-year medical student.

"You can have him," I say around a bite of my hot dog, piled with relish. I polish it off with a deep slug from my root beer float. "But back to the point. This is the first time I've seen you since the wedding. He could have shipped me off to a foreign country by now, and you'd never know."

"Okay, point number one, I'd never marry a billionaire. It goes against everything I believe in. Plus, my parents would kill me if I got married before they met him."

I nod because, true, her parents, while lovely and understanding people, are also devout Catholics who only want the best for their baby girl. Reggie would obviously raise objections. Not to mention her grandmother, Estelle, who we both love more than life itself.

"And point number two, see previously mentioned hectic schedule. Besides, I've been texting you every day, and let's be honest, if he were going to, he would gotten rid of you by now if he was pissed off about your interference."

"Rebuttal: You're way too cavalier about this. Maybe he won't ship me off in retaliation for forcing him to marry me. Maybe he plans to draw it out more than that. Make me go insane."

"Blame it on my lack of sleep. I don't have time to express my shock. Besides, we knew there was something wrong with him from the start. At least he doesn't have a mattress on the floor with no bed frame like the last dude I hooked up with." She dips a fry in ketchup, and her soulful brown eyes narrow. Scooting in a little closer, she lowers her voice. "Is he being absolutely diabolical? Like the movie *Gaslight*?"

Yasmine is obsessed with period noir films or psychological thrillers from the fifties and sixties, and often insists on watching them instead of newer releases.

I shrug at her because I don't possess a mental library of movies like she does.

She heaves a sigh. "It's a psychological thriller where this guy tries to convince his wife she's going crazy, but really, he's arranging it so that he can have her institutionalized and steal her dead aunt's fortune. We'll have to watch it on my next day off."

"You mean in a million years?"

"Probably. Before I'm dead, at least."

Eager to return to a sense of normalcy, I ask, "Honestly, right now I'd even take that over the way my week has been. What else would we watch if we weren't victims of the desire to obtain advanced degrees?"

Yasmine licks her lips clean of ice cream as she considers. "*Psycho* obviously feels relevant. Maybe *Strangers on a Train*, *Rebecca*. *Rear Window* would be good, too. Maybe we'll make it a whole-day affair. We could both use it. Popcorn covered in buckets of butter. Obscene amounts of candy."

"We can do facials and stuff, too. Maybe splurge for a

personal massage therapist to come by. Black Amex card, remember?"

"Yes!" she says, pointing a fry at me like a conductor. "Now you're talking. Can't have a girls' night without some spa treatments."

"You're not kidding." I sigh and practically inhale more root beer as I finally answer her initial question. "No, O'Connor's not doing anything that insane. In fact, he's being totally normal. Honestly, he works more than anything, and I barely see him."

Her long lashes flutter, and she wrinkles her slightly upturned nose. "Honey, I'm sorry to tell you, but that sounds like the opposite of diabolical."

"That's what makes it so genius," I say morosely. "He's lulling me into a false sense of security before he pounces."

"At least he's feeding you before he does it."

"His only positive character trait, that's for sure. His chef, Frances, is to die for. But enough about him." The guilt at not being entirely truthful with my best friend is eating at me. I have to change the subject before I spontaneously combust. "Tell me about how your day has been so far. I know you don't have much longer to catch up, and I'm tired of complaining about my problems."

She studies me in that way she does, where I know she understands more than I'm letting on, but I school my face until she nods. "I know, a two-hour lunch break feels like a dream, and I didn't ask the attending, Dr. Redmond, twice when he told me to get some fresh air."

"I don't know how you do these twenty-four-hour shifts. I would die."

"Sometimes it feels like I'm dead on my feet, that's for

sure." She shakes her almost empty cup. "That's why coffee is my best friend. You'll have to accept second place."

"Since coffee is also my best friend, I'm not offended. Please, tell me something that'll distract me from my life. Did you get any of those patients who have fallen on anything suspicious?" Yasmine often has the best stories. There are only so many times I can explain contract law before she has to fake her conversational orgasms with me. I don't blame her. Of the two of us, her days are admittedly a lot more interesting.

She chuckles. "No, but a kid came in with a broken crayon up his nose. He was so proud."

I'm not going to think about O'Connor's request to "negotiate" children. I won't. What in the world makes him think I'd *want* to procreate with him? Honestly. "How do these ideas even occur to them?"

I can't even imagine becoming a mother anytime in the future. Not when I'm barely even out of school and still have so many things I want to accomplish. Really. He was deluded to even bring it up.

Yasmine's laughter is throaty and a tinge tired, drawing me back from my thoughts. "I have no idea, but I'll tell you what, his mom had to bring him back two hours later because he'd done it again. This time, he had broken crayons in both nostrils."

"What an utter delight."

"That was nothing. An hour later, we had a woman who accidentally cut off part of her finger while making dinner for her in-laws."

My mouth drops open, and I'm totally enthralled. "You're kidding."

"Girl, I can't make this stuff up. But that's not even the best part."

"I'm scared to ask."

"She brought the piece she cut off in a plastic sandwich baggie. Her whole family came with her, causing a scene like you wouldn't believe. I'm half convinced she did it so she could get away from them. Redmond made me kick them out so they could wait in the lobby. For a woman covered in a ton of blood, after they left, she looked like she was on vacation."

"You sure you want to go into emergency medicine? Isn't there a tamer discipline? Like a nice, quiet family practice?"

"No way. The chaos of it makes me feel alive. Plus, you get to see such a wide range of cases in the ER. No two days are the same."

"My best friend, the badass."

"Damn right," she says, and we clink glasses. She glances at her watch and then grimaces. "Ugh, I have to go back already if I'm going to make it in time for rounds. Thanks again for this. I really needed it."

We push to our feet and make our way to the counter. "Of course, I still owe you about a thousand more meals for everything you've done for me. I know Elizabeth probably didn't make your weekend pleasant."

"To say the least, but it was mostly the silent treatment."

"Well, I appreciate it."

"You don't even have to ask. Speaking of Elizabeth, is she still giving you the cold shoulder?"

"Pretty sure I'm not her favorite person at the moment. Which has been true since Mom died, so I'm not surprised. No matter what I do, I can't seem to get through to her that this was for the best. But enough about that. Let's make plans for that movie night, okay? Maybe we can do it at my place, since I'm never allowed to go anywhere but home and school."

"With bodyguards," Yasmine says, twitching her eyebrows to my shadows, who are hovering in the corner of the restaurant.

"Don't remind me."

"One of them even looks like Kevin Costner. Think they'd let me pretend to be their Whitney Houston?"

"I think you're delirious and should go home and sleep because singing is definitely not your strong suit," I say with a laugh, as I pay and leave.

"It's not fair that Reggie got all the vocal talent, and I sound like a disgruntled cat."

"It's really a shame he doesn't sing more often. He could be on stage instead of toting around a badge."

"Like he needs his ego inflated any more than it already is." She scans her phone, then the street. "Shit, that's my ride. I'll text you tonight to make sure you're still alive. Don't believe him if he says the lights aren't flickering. Trust your truth!" she adds over her shoulder, as she hustles to a silver sedan idling by the road.

"Whatever that means!" I shout back.

"IF YOU DON'T CALL your watchdogs off, I'm going to drown them in the river," I hiss into my phone as I stride through campus after lunch. I really don't have time for this, and I have even less time now that I'm stuck taking back routes to all my classes, so I don't get caught by my friends or—God forbid—some wannabe influencer skulking around to capture my humiliation for the world to see.

O'Connor's responding chuckle is melodic in my ear, and I practically jog to keep my distance from my shadows. "You know the rules, pet. You agreed to them, remember? I have the paperwork to prove it. They're only there to keep you safe."

"They aren't keeping me safe if they keep drawing attention to me. Because if I spend one more day with them hovering over me in the library while I study, I may drown myself in the Mississippi instead. And don't call me, pet."

"And make me a widower? You wouldn't dare. I'm far too young to wear black all the time."

"You already wear black all the time," I growl.

"We can always go back to negotiations. I'm not an unreasonable person. Take the separate bedrooms clause you forced me to add off the table and think about adding children in five years instead of ten, and I'll consider only requiring one bodyguard instead of two."

"Like hell," I bark, drawing the attention of the only other person sharing the sidewalk. At the ferocity in my voice, they wisely veer off in another direction.

Bren and Tadhg keep the pace even though I'm practically running and they're in suits in the middle of the Louisiana heat. They're barely even sweating. What the hell do they feed them in Ireland? Are they part robot? Jesus.

"I said no kids, and I meant it. Not in ten years. Not never."

"Up to you, pet. Seems a minor concession to me."

"You would think that."

"You'd like sharing a bed with me. I'm an excellent snuggler."

I snort. "That, I highly doubt."

"How would you know? You've never actually slept with me."

I don't dignify that with a response. Even if he's right. "Please, Aiden. They're driving me insane. I can't concentrate with them following me around everywhere, and I'm behind enough as it is."

That's not to mention the fact that I can't continue my search for information about my mother with two of Aiden's henchmen glued to my ass. They'd report my movements back to him in a heartbeat, and I don't want to explain what I'm doing to him. Or defend what I'm doing. He'd probably tell me it's too dangerous or fruitless to continue, and I'll be damned if I have him tell me what to do about this.

This is the one thing I won't let him take from me. I wanted to do a more thorough search through the house, but the thought of them seeing me on security footage stops me. How am I supposed to meet with Mr. Broussard if they're attached to my back?

"You have my answer, Catriona. Besides, you're almost done for the day, and Mara will be waiting for you at the library to take you to try on clothes for the reception tomorrow."

I nearly groan out loud as my feet practically skid to a stop. "Mara, right," I repeat faintly. "Who exactly is Mara? Is this another assistant?"

His laughter fills my ear, and I resist a shiver. "Please call her my assistant to her face. Record it when you do. You can claim it as my birthday gift for the year."

"I'm hanging up now," I threaten, so I don't hear more of his laughter, which is unsettling. Keeping my distance is the only way I've found I can put up with him for any length of time. I stay busy with classes and studying, spending most of my time on campus or in the library, so I don't go back to his house, where space seems to be shrinking with each passing day.

I've learned far too much about him in a short span. Like that he goes for a jog in the morning while listening to golden oldies. That he calls his mother every few days. He said he had a mother, but the evidence confirming it shakes me to my core. The first time I heard him talking to her, I sped away as soon as I realized. The last thing I want to do is make him seem more human.

"Mara is one of my closest friends. She was at the wedding," he continues as if I haven't said a word.

"You have friends?" I blurt.

There's a pause. "Yes, Catriona, I have friends. Mara is obsessed with haute couture and has agreed to pick out a dress for you to wear tomorrow. Unless you've had time to pick something out yourself?" He barely waits a second before continuing. "That's what I thought. Besides, I think you two will get along."

"What makes you think that?" I grumble in response.

"She also has an unwanted fiancé she wishes she could castrate."

Well.

I don't know how to respond to that, so I say, "Do I have to? I know how to dress myself."

"Of course you do. We signed an agreement. However, if you want to renegotiate, I'm open to a discussion."

I press a hand to my head. Between catching up on all my assignments and dodging O'Connor when he's at the house, I haven't had time to think about the reception. And if he mentions negotiation or concessions again, I may resort to mariticide. "Fine. I'll let your friend play dress-up."

"*Please*, call it that when you see her. And record that, too. Better yet, record the whole thing so my other friend Eamon and I can both watch."

"Goodbye, O'Connor."

"Goodbye, *Mrs. O'Connor*."

I would chastise him for calling me that, but he's already hung up the phone. The man always has to have the last word, and it's infuriating.

By the time I'm finished with classes, I give up trying to hide and cross through campus to get to the library with my guards in tow. I've attempted to speak to them, but they mostly grunt in response or don't speak at all, so over the past week, I've learned to ignore them. I'm hoping O'Connor will eventually give up the whole concept, and I'll be free to walk around unencumbered. There has to be something other than kids—God—or sharing a bed he'd consider.

I see Mara parked outside the Howard-Tilton Library and recognize her instantly. Mostly because she's leaning against a blood-red vintage Mustang Fastback. Of course, one of O'Connor's closest friends would be drop-dead gorgeous with a smile as sharp as a knife and hair that's simply cut in a bob, but looks like it cost a thousand dollars. Maybe if I'm nice to her, she'll give me the name of her stylist. I can never seem to find one I can tolerate for more than a few sessions.

"Mara?" I ask when I get close enough. "I'm C—"

"Catriona." She holds out a perfectly manicured hand. "Of course. So nice to finally *officially* meet you. I'm Mara. I'd say lovely wedding, but I'm against the institution as a whole," she adds with a quirk of her black, slashing brows.

My cheeks go hot. "Glad you could make it?" I answer, but it ends up sounding like a question.

"Aiden tells me you need a dress for the reception party. I think I have just the thing." She rounds the front of the Mustang to the driver's side. "Well, come on, we don't have all day."

"What about my stalkers?" I say, jerking my thumb at the two men behind me. "They're supposed to follow me everywhere."

She sends them a sultry smirk. "They know where we're going, but I don't allow bloodshed in my house, so they'll have to stay outside. You understand, don't you, boys?"

Mara doesn't give them enough time to respond, slamming the door and barely waiting for me to buckle my seat belt before she cranks the car, engine rumbling, and tears out of the parking lot at a speed that makes my heart jump into my throat.

I'd wondered what a woman like her—sleek, sophisticated, and obviously successful—would be doing with O'Connor, but the way she drives the car gives me an inkling. She's controlled, but there's a spiteful aggression underneath that I recognize. I don't know her story, but I get the feeling she's not the sort of woman to be trifled with.

"So how long have you and O'Con—*Aiden* been friends?"

"He and Eamon have been attached since birth. Grew up together in County Clare. I didn't meet them until I was about, oh, thirteen, I guess. My family does business with the organization."

I can tell that's as much as she's willing to share, so I don't press for more. "Eamon?" I ask, realizing this is the perfect opportunity to learn more about my (not) husband.

Mara maneuvers confidently through the afternoon traffic, not a hair out of place or an inkling of frustration when we hit a bit of a gridlock. She's dressed in all black, skintight jeans with artful rips on the thighs, a thin, lacy black tank top and a black leather jacket that complements her skin tone, dark hair, and red lips. She almost reminds me of a fifties model, and I'm envious of how put-together she is. And it's not like I'm dressed casually. The clothes I'm wearing are designer. But after a long day of hoofing it around campus and a longer week avoiding O'Connor, I feel less than composed.

"You've probably seen him around. Curly dark hair. Always looks like he wants to stab someone?" she says with a sultry laugh. "If that doesn't strike a bell, I can always give him a ring to join us. One thing about Eamon is that he loves to cause trouble. Seeing you without Aiden hovering around would be his idea of a good time."

"Oh, yeah, now I remember." In fact, I remember him cleaning up a body after O'Connor had put a bullet in a cop's head at the masquerade. Eamon had joked about it. If O'Connor is a stone-cold killer, then Eamon is his mad-jester sidekick.

"If Aiden is Cian's right-hand man, then Eamon is Aiden's. When Aiden was assigned to come to New Orleans, Eamon followed close behind. He said it was because if he stayed in Ireland for another minute, he'd probably wind up dead."

"How long have you been engaged?"

"Seven years," she answers.

I do a double take. "Sev—" I didn't think she was old, per se, but she doesn't seem much older than my twenty-four years.

"We got engaged when I was seventeen," she answers, before I can give in to my morbid curiosity and ask.

"You were so young."

"Well, let's just say I wasn't given much of a choice," she answers easily. "In the family, you do what you're told, or you learn quickly otherwise."

"Do you at least like him?"

"My fiancé?" She laughs again, but it's a ruined, harrowing sound this time. "Not at all. There isn't a day that goes by that I don't wish I could put one of Eamon's knives in his throat."

"I guess we have that in common."

"But let's not talk about him. I'd love to know more about you." She sends me a look over her Gucci sunglasses.

"Me?" I laugh nervously. "There's not much to tell, honestly."

"I very much doubt that, darling. You got the better of Aiden O'Connor. If that's not something, I don't know what is."

"To be honest, I was mostly trying to keep him from getting to my sister. My marrying O'Connor had nothing to do with... any of that. It was reckless, really. I have a problem doing things without thinking sometimes." I don't know what it is about her that makes me admit it, only that she's as easy to talk to as Yasmine.

"Whatever the reason, consider me impressed. It's rare to find someone who will stand up to guys like Aiden or Eamon. Usually, people are too busy pissing in their pants or worshipping at their feet."

It's with those ominous words that she pulls into a parking lot at a chic apartment. Glittering buildings greet me as I leave the car with a valet and stride through the first floor. Her heels click on glossy black tile as she saunters to an elevator, which whizzes me up to a penthouse.

I've been in places like this before, and I'm no stranger to opulence, but everything from the scent lingering in the air to the furniture screams money. I thought my family was wealthy, but it seems the level of wealth I've married into may be more than I can comprehend.

Then again, my father did owe these people millions of dollars, so it shouldn't be a revelation.

Mara leads me through a white lacquered door, which turns out to be her bedroom. She points at a set of double doors that I assume lead to a bathroom. "Head in there and strip to your panties. Some of these dresses will require a strapless bra due to their cut. I'll pick out a few to get started, and then we can go from there."

It doesn't even occur to me to argue. That's how I find myself practically naked with her passing me several dresses through a cracked door. I've barely known the woman for an hour, and she's already seen more of me than my primary care physician.

We start with a classic sheath that she nixes right away. "Too plain," she dismisses. "I thought maybe it would read as elegant, but you outshine the dress, and that simply won't do. I prefer for you to complement each other. You know?"

I don't, but I change into an A-line satin accentuated with pearls next. This she also dismisses after a moment. "No way in hell. Too sweet. I want you to be sexy, sophisticated, and unattainable. This isn't only your wedding reception but it's also crucial for Aiden." She doesn't elaborate, and I'm too intimidated to ask for more information.

After several more, I wonder if we're ever going to find the right one. I almost beg her to choose any of them when she finally gasps. The top half is a corset, lifting my breasts and cinching my waist to almost nothing. It was a good call on the bra because I couldn't wear one anyway, not with the drawstring front that leaves a strip of skin bare from my naval to my cleavage. Satin material clings to my hips, bares my thigh with a daring slit, and falls to my feet.

"This is definitely it," she says. "It's the perfect amount of sexy and elegant."

I lift my brow in the reflection of the dressing room mirror. "And we want me to look sexy at my wedding reception?"

Mara's throaty chuckle fills the small space. "We want you to look like someone everyone wants, but can't have."

"If you say so," I answer. "It's a beautiful dress. Thank you for helping me. I like shopping, but I appreciate someone else's expert opinion for occasions like this."

"It wasn't without a reason. I have a favor to ask."

A ball of apprehension twists in my stomach. "A favor from me?"

"I'm worried about Aiden. I know you have no reason to trust him, but if he comes into any trouble, any at all, I want you to call me. Give me your phone, and I'll put my number in." If she'd asked, I may have said no, but I find myself passing her my phone without complaint.

Her red nails flash as she taps the screen to put in her contact. "Why are you worried about him?" I ask when she hands it back to me. I text her so she has my number, just in case.

She huffs out a laugh, and her lips twist to the side. "There's always a reason to worry about him. He's Cian's favorite," she makes quotation marks around the word, "if he could have one, you know? But he's not the sort of person you want to find yourself attached to, if you know what I'm saying."

Thinking of my father, I nod. "Aiden mentioned he may retaliate for what we've done." I press a hand to my bare throat. Isn't that something I should want? If he's taken out and I stay away from the crossfire... that'll be good for me. Right?

"A man like Cian doesn't tolerate big moves without his prior approval." She lifts a shoulder. "I could be wrong. Maybe he won't care. But a man like Cian hates being outmaneuvered. And even worse when a woman has a hand in it. I don't want to frighten you," she pauses, shrugs, "then again, fear is a good motivator. You *should* be frightened. These aren't people who fuck around."

"Aiden can take care of himself." I shiver at the memory of him killing Dufresne.

"Ah, yes, your little tryst at the masquerade," she says. Jesus, fuck. Can the woman read my mind? "Aiden may be his enforcer, but Cian is the kingpin of one of the most powerful crime families in the world. In Ireland, he may as well *be* king. There isn't a pie he doesn't dip his finger in. If you want to have a business, run drugs, guns, or hold a political office, Cian's approval is a must-have before you do."

I swallow hard, suddenly feeling like the corset I'm wearing is too tight. "And if you don't?"

"Then you're dead," she answers simply.

A chill rolls over me. "And what does O'Connor have to do with it?"

She sighs and ruffles her hair with a hand as she gathers up the discarded dresses to put them back on their hangers. "If he had the balls, he'd kill me for telling you, but because he'd never touch me, I'm going to tell you anyway. Aiden's father, John O'Connor, was the original kingpin. Cian was his best friend. When John and Cian began to disagree on how the organization should be run, Cian slit his throat."

I'm frozen to the spot as I listen, imagining Aiden as a boy. What growing up like this must have done to him. Is that why he can be so commanding? So cold and ruthless?

"Anyway, Aiden witnessed the whole thing. Cian made him and his mother watch his father bleed out. Kept them restrained so they couldn't help or get away. It basically drove his mother insane. She loved John O'Connor with every fiber of her being. If you believe in love, that is."

"Cian sounds like a monster," I say in a hoarse voice.

"He's worse," she promises.

"You think he might kill Aiden next? If that's the case, why hasn't he done it already? He's had years. Why keep him around?"

Mara huffs out a laugh and takes the dress I've been clutching from my hands. I follow her out of the bathroom as she places them back in her closet. She leads me to an elegant office and shuts the door behind us. I turn down an offered shot of vodka, I think, and after she knocks it back, she continues.

"Because he's a twisted fuck, darling. After he murdered John and let his body rot in the courtyard for nearly a week, Cian forced Aiden's mother, Mary, to marry him."

His poor mother. The little girl inside me who wants nothing more than to be held by my mom one more time can't fathom being separated from her, forced to endure her suffering for ages. Even worse, his mother watching the man she loves being murdered by his best friend and then being forced to marry his killer.

"Exactly. And it's not like Aiden could do anything about it. He was only fourteen at the time, still a kid. If he'd gone against Cian, Cian would have killed him without hesitation. I think it amused him, honestly. To watch Aiden suffer. If Cian ever got a whiff of Aiden rebelling, he'd punish his mother. Cian never had to put a hand to Aiden because he used his mother as a whipping boy."

"Why would Cian care about Aiden rebelling as a literal teenager? Why punish him if he didn't do anything?"

She stares off into the distance like she's recounting a memory. "For one, because I think he's a sick bastard who enjoys breaking someone down. Each time Aiden did something wrong, Cian got to take it out on his mother. He's the definition of a sadist, and Aiden is his favorite toy."

"And for another?" I prompt.

"Cian knew that as Aiden grew up, fueled by hatred and a thirst for revenge, he would eventually come for him—unless Cian broke him first."

"And you think Cian will see our marriage as Aiden doing something against him?"

"Honey, that's exactly what Aiden was doing. Getting married means he has to go home to Ireland to introduce his wife to the family." Mara pours another shot of vodka for herself and one for me. When I shake my head, she insists. "Trust me, you're going to need it. *Sláinte*," she says, knocking my glass with hers before we both tip them back.

The liquor trails down in a line of liquid heat through my chest and pools in my stomach. "Why does going back to Ireland have any significance?" I ask when I can breathe again.

"Because it means Aiden can see his mother," Mara says, replacing the bottle and stacking the shot glasses by a small sink.

"That's good, right?"

Mara pushes to her feet, grabbing her purse. "Aiden hasn't seen his mother in ten years. The only thing he cares about in this world is Mary O'Connor. His plan is to spring this marriage on Cian so he can see her for the first time since he was a teenager during the required introductions to the rest of the families in the organization. He'll never tell you that, but I will. If you fuck this up for him, you won't have to worry about Aiden at all—because I'll be the one to fucking kill you." She gives me one last lingering once-over as I try to discern if she's joking or not. "Now, you're going to knock 'em dead tomorrow. Aiden won't know what hit him."

I don't know whether I want to recommend my therapist to her or ask her to be my friend.

CHAPTER 13

AIDEN

"I don't have long to talk today. It's been a long week. But it's so good to hear your voice, Aiden. It always is. You have an angel's voice. Did I ever tell you?"

It's the morning of the reception. Catriona has already left for classes—I get the feeling she plans it so she's out the door before I even leave my room. A remarkable feat, considering I'm an early riser. The one time her morning classes were canceled this week, she found me in the kitchen, waiting for the coffee to brew, leaning against the counter, having a similar conversation with my mother.

"I'll keep it short, Ma. And you do, all the time," I murmur into the phone as I go through my morning routine. It's barely six, but the house is already bustling with movement. Frances, preparing the kitchen for the week, Finn working quietly at the island counter, and Eamon swimming laps in the heated pool outside, the splashes echoing through the cavernous first floor.

"Well, good. That's good. Have I told you about my blue rockets, love? They're beautiful. The deepest shade of purple I've ever seen. I can't wait to show them to you the next time you visit. That is, if you have time to visit the gardens."

My head hangs at her voice. Wistful. Dreamy. Too dreamy. Sometimes she can barely hold the thread of a conversation. There have even been moments when she forgets I'm her son and calls me John, my father's name. The only time she's fully lucid lately is when she's talking about her bleedin' flowers. I've memorized them all in my head. Oleander, daffodil, lily of the valley, mountain laurel, angel's trumpet, and so many more. I mentally add blue rockets to the list. It's my wildest dream to give her something other than the garden to look forward to.

There'd been a time when Mary Clarke O'Connor had been a vivacious woman. She'd spent most of her life in Derry with her father until he passed away, and she was sent to Dublin to live with her paternal grandparents. Her mother had died in childbirth. When she'd been married to my father, she'd dance around our house to the golden oldies, singing at the top of her lungs. Now, the only time she sings is during these phone calls.

"You haven't. Tell me everything."

Every day she still answers the phone is one where I can breathe easy. Especially since the wedding and her panicked call the morning after. It turns out Cian came home with no idea about what I've done, so I let myself breathe a little easier.

Ma goes on to describe her latest acquisition in minute detail. Sometimes she doesn't remember I'm on the other end of the phone and starts talking to herself, but I don't mind. I call as often as I can, every morning if my schedule allows, because the thought of not hearing from her sends bolts of alarm through me otherwise.

All we've had for the past ten years are these phone calls. When she gets lost in her garden, and she's grown weary of talking, she'll sing for me if I beg. The same songs she used to sing when I was a boy, like "Molly Malone" or "Danny Boy." Songs her grandparents had taught her after she moved to Dublin.

I want to tell her I'll see her soon. The words hover on my tongue, begging to spring free, but I swallow them down. We still need to get through the reception tonight, and then I'll inform Cian of what I've done. I'm banking everything on his desire to make me pay for my disobedience before he'll harm my mother. Because Cian knows if he kills her without having a leash on me, there'll be hell to pay.

"I'd better go rest now, John," she says, and I hang my head. "I'll talk to you tomorrow."

"Until then," I wheeze.

After, I brood over my coffee cup until it's no longer steaming as Eamon finishes with his laps in the pool. Turning, I drink the cool coffee and frown at the trail of water he leads in from the backyard.

"Why don't you swim at your house?" I ask.

"Did you say goodbye to Mary before I could tell her good morning?" Frances hands Eamon a towel, which he takes and sends her an exaggerated wink, which she ignores.

"That's an arsehole move. Just because she likes me better doesn't mean you should interfere in our relationship."

"The only way you'd have a relationship with my mother is in that supremely fucked-up head of yours."

Eamon ties the towel around his waist and leans against the counter. Finn, who has always been 90 percent terrified of Eamon, shies away, but tries to pretend he's not. I don't blame him. Finn is often the one who has to clean up after Eamon when he goes rogue. I imagine the poor man has seen enough to make him rightfully wary.

"You can keep telling that story if that makes you feel better. Mary loves me. Is there any of that coffee left, lad, or did you drink it all?"

Sighing, I pour him a cup. "Let me reiterate, you have your own place."

"But yours is so much more interesting. Especially since your new bride moved in. Tell me, how was the wedding night?"

I don't dignify that with an answer.

Eamon grimaces and nudges Finn's shoulder. "That bad, huh? Don't worry, I can give you some pointers if you're a bit rusty. I know it's been pretty spare since last... what, fall?"

"I'm good, thanks," I say dryly.

"Prickly," Eamon mutters to Finn, who shakes like a leaf. "That must mean she hasn't let you tickle her fancy, so to speak. Why not?"

"I need to change my security code," I mutter.

"I bet she makes you sleep on the other side of the bed." At my hardened expression, he chuckles. "If you're even in the same room... no, lad. Don't tell me she won't even sleep in the same room? That's an absolute disgrace." He pauses, considering, and I go still. A thoughtful Eamon is a dangerous one.

Before I can stop him, he's bounding up the stairs.

"May as well see what wifey is hiding while she's not home," he calls back. "I bet she has mountains of lingerie. That'll cheer you up, won't it?"

"Jesus Christ," I mutter under my breath as I follow him, taking the steps two at a time. How is the bastard so fast? "Stay out of her bedroom, you gobshite. Eamon!"

By the time I catch up, he's already in Catriona's room. His lanky form travels slowly around the perimeter at first, studying her mussed bed, clothes strewn all over the floor, and books piled on the desk crammed under a window.

"If you don't stop breaking into my house, I'm going to have you neutered."

"You'll thank me later when you're not worrying over your ma anymore."

I've kept myself so busy this week with preparations for the reception, dodging questions from Cian, and managing the Emerald, all with one sole purpose: forget the woman staying in the room next to mine. It's been hard, considering I can hear her at all hours of the day and night. From her late-night pacing as she presumably studies from her giant textbooks, to her four-thirty wake-up alarms and showers. These walls may be well constructed, but my ears seem to be specially attuned to her presence and able to catch the slightest sound.

"Does a woman really need this much pink?" Eamon asks, coming out of Catriona's closet with a froth of pink scarves around his shoulders. "She has as much of it in her closet as you do black."

But I'm too busy taking in all the sights around me to admonish him. How has she managed to make the room smell like her... feel like her in less than a week? I've been living here for damn near a year, and the entire rest of the house still seems like it belongs to someone else.

In addition to the clothes and books littering every surface—including the floor, furniture, and desks—jewelry glitters in strands and clusters on her nightstand, dresser, and even over the doorknobs. But more than anything, it's her scent. The one I've realized comes from her lavender-honey lattes and lavender bath soap. The smell that clings to her skin and haunts me.

"Fuck yeah. I found her phone," Eamon says, closing one of her desk drawers and striding to me. "Want to see what your pretty wife has been up to?"

He passes it to me, and I tap the screen to wake it, but it doesn't turn on. "This couldn't be her phone. I don't think I've ever seen her without it attached to her hand."

"Burner?"

"Why would Catriona need a burner?" I say, like it's the most absurd thing I've ever heard. "It's probably an old one. Let's get out of here. I need to go to work before the reception."

"If it's an old phone, why did she bring it here with her?"

Curiosity lingers, but I shove it away, like I have other thoughts of Catriona since she moved in. "C'mon. We have to pick up your suit from Mara unless you want to find yourself in her ropes."

Eamon replaces the phone where he found it. "Fuck that. The last time she tied me up for fun, she wouldn't let me go for two days."

"Best two days of my life," I say, and close the door to Catriona's room behind us.

We leave Finn at the Emerald after I attend to my never-ending list of responsibilities. Eamon spent most of the time terrorizing the blackjack dealers into letting him practice counting cards, and flirting with everyone from the young Black female bartender to the six-foot-six, muscular croupier. Finally, I haul him away to ensure we make it in time to dress and get to the reception.

Senator Rory Gallagher holds court in the center of the ballroom like an emperor. His exaggerated laughter can be heard around the room. Every so often, the flash of a camera punctuates his guffaws as he poses with yet another one of his admirers. Elizabeth hovers at his side, a polished fake smile affixed to her face.

Is that what it would have been like to be married to her? A life of pretension? At least with Catriona, I know the gist of what she's feeling. It's hard not to when the sheer magnitude of her hatred is present in every heated glare she directs toward me whenever we're in the same room together. But at least what she's feeling is genuine, honest. Too many people in my life like to hide behind their deference, fear, or manipulation.

"So where's your blushing bride?" Eamon murmurs, knocking my shoulder with his as he lifts a drink to his mouth. He scans the crowd, shifting and searching for something to keep his ever-capricious attention. "And when are you going to let Mara and me come over to play? You've been keeping her all to yourself."

"Never, if I can help it. You'll scare her away." A woman catches my attention, her body enveloped in white, showcasing curves I'd kill to get my hands on. Then the crowd shifts, blocking her from view. I could use the distraction of a woman. I'm overdue to lose myself in a few hours of mindless satisfaction, but none of them could ever be her, so I look away, already losing interest.

"Women love me," Eamon says with a sniff, tossing his hair as he passes me his drink, which I finish off. "It's not my fault if some of them are squeamish."

"That's right, darling," Mara says, in a swirl of black silk and a cloud of the same perfume she has me buy for her birthday every year, *Tom Ford Vanilla Sex Eau de Parfum*. "Even monsters are worthy of love and affection. Or so they tell me."

She kisses Eamon on the cheek and lifts hers for me to do the same. I almost don't see the bruises under her flawlessly applied makeup, and if I weren't so accustomed to seeing the same evidence on my mother's face, I wouldn't have glanced twice. I still, wrap a hand around her jaw, and tilt it up until the light illuminates the shadows around her eyes.

In the next moment, she shifts away, tilting her face down, her eyes hard chips of green. "Let's not ruin your night," she chides softly. "You know I can take care of myself."

Eamon has gone dangerously quiet.

"Did Niall do this?" I urge, as I scrutinize the crowd for his presence. "Where is he? I'd like to have a chat with him."

"He's not here, so you're wasting this impressive display

of machismo. Like I said, I can handle myself. And you have too many guests and too much press here tonight to make a scene. Drop it, Aiden. I mean it." She blinks. "Where's Eamon?"

Not standing next to me, like he'd been a few minutes ago. "Fuck," I bite out.

Mara puts up a hand. "You wait here. Catriona will be here soon, and you'll want to look pretty for your admirers. I'll find our demented knight in shining armor and stop him before he does something silly. Really. Like I can't take perfectly good care of myself. You're both idiots."

Then she's giving me her back and striding away. Before I can ignore her advice and follow, the woman I'd been admiring earlier appears at my side, and all I notice is the deep plunge of her dress and the way it frames her perfect breasts. But it's not until I see her face that a bolt of pure animal lust ignites and my mouth goes dry.

The woman in the white dress is Catriona.

Because of course it is. Who else would be wearing white at our reception but my wife? I guess I still haven't gotten used to the idea, though a week feels like enough time to imprint that fact on my brain with stunning clarity.

"Where are your bodyguards?" I demand, instead of telling her how incredible she looks in her dress. She does. But I doubt she'd welcome hearing it from me.

Tossing long blond curls over her bare shoulders, Catriona crosses her arms and scoffs, "You're kidding, right? They've been glued to me all week, just like you wanted. They went to get something to drink because they've been following me around campus all day. Probably walked a million steps. Is that okay with you, or are you really so heartless?" Before I can answer, she accepts a glass of champagne from a passing server and sips, waving her free hand. "Never mind, you don't even need to answer."

Bren and Tadhg finally appear, and I fillet them with a look, and they blanche. After they shuffle back to position at my wife's back, I relax, but only a little. Fucking Niall. I've already been on edge, waiting for Cian to show, knowing he's got to get word about what I've done any day now. Combined with the lack of sleep, I'm itching for a provocation to devolve into my baser instincts.

"I said to stay with her at all times."

Bren, the younger of the two, flinches. He's new, and I've had a soft spot for him since he came to the States, but he's also too quick to show his emotions. Sometimes when I look at his rounded, boyish cheeks, I wonder if I was ever that innocent. "We're sorry, sir. It won't—"

Catriona positions herself between us, and Bren's mouth closes with a snap. "Don't bully them because you're pissed at me. They haven't done anything wrong."

Bren glances at her with puppy dog eyes and looks away when he realizes I'm glaring at him. Tadhg maintains his stoic exterior. I paired him with Bren because he's been a member of the organization for as long as I can remember. Bren may be young and enthusiastic, but Tadhg is experienced and trustworthy. He'd been my father's enforcer before he was killed. Cian had no qualm about letting my most loyal friend come with me when I left Ireland.

"That would depend on your definition of wrong. They were told to never leave your side when you're in public."

"Really, of all the moronic, pedantic things to—"

"I have her now," I tell them, with one last skewering

look. "See me tomorrow morning before your shift starts so we can go over what I expect from you."

"Yes, sir," they both intone.

"Was that really necessary?" Catriona asks. I expect her to give me a verbal lashing, drawing the attention of every vulture circling us, but she keeps her voice low so only I can hear.

"The safety of my wife is always necessary."

She peers at me, focus shifting between my eyes. "I can't tell if you're full of shit or just an excellent actor."

"Can't it be both?"

Silence falls as Catriona quite literally bites her tongue to keep from snapping out a response.

Despite repeated attempts to the contrary, no force on earth can keep me from looking at her mouth. Remembering what it had been like to finally kiss her, taste her. And how much I wish I could do it again. The fact that she keeps to her room or flees before I wake up have kept me from trying again. That and the fact that I know I won't be able to catch her off guard a second time.

Flocks of partygoers stop by to wish us well, and Catriona paints a demure smile on her face. I wonder if she realizes she gets that from her father, the ability to charm an audience. I doubt she'd find the comparison a flattering one, so I say nothing.

Every now and then, I find her looking in the direction of her family, frowning. And in those moments, her face softens, vulnerable, and I imagine that's what she must have looked like as a child. Wanting to be loved. Craving the security a family should provide.

Unsettled, I scrutinize the people on the dance floor for a

distraction, and I find Eamon and Mara jerking this way and that as he interrogates her under the guise of dancing.

"Look at that. I think they're playing our song," I say stonily, as I pull her onto the dance floor.

She resists, but only slightly. "We don't have a song, you psycho. Don't grab at me."

"Well, then, this can be our song." I wrap my arms around her waist, thankful she's settled back into annoyance. That I can handle. "Smile pretty. You're supposed to be desperately in love with me."

Etta James croons "At Last" in the speakers as Catriona tilts her head up to me with a smile that doesn't reach her eyes. "Like that'll happen."

"I'm sure you've had plenty of practice faking it."

I don't realize it until we're across the room, but Catriona has let me lead the entire dance, her body pliant in my arms. One would almost say trusting. I write it off. She's probably as distracted by her father as I am trying to maneuver us closer to Eamon and Mara, who are now turning in tight circles, mouths pressed into lines. Eamon's neck is corded with tension.

"Why do you keep staring at them? Is something wrong?" Catriona pushes to her toes to see over my shoulder. Spotting them behind me, she says, "What happened? Are they arguing? *That* would make a lovely headline, don't you think? And I'll bet you were certain I'd be the one to cause a scene."

"Stop staring."

She relaxes back and twists her lips to the side as she puzzles over this new tangle. Is that what occupies her thoughts? Problems and all the ways she can fix them? Like her father? Like her sister? The last *fucking* thing I need is someone else to trip their way into my problems. Especially her.

"Did someone hit her?" she asks, keeping her voice low enough that I'm the only one who can hear it. "Are those bru—"

"Keep out of it, Catriona. You know what your job is and what it isn't. Don't think because I've been agreeable that it gives you license to nose your way into my life. Into my friends' lives."

Her mouth falls open for a pregnant pause before she snaps it closed, and her hands, which had been resting lightly on my shoulders, drop to her sides. Then she erases all emotion from her face, spins around, and strides in the other direction, moving as fast as she can to get away from me. It's only our first public outing, and she already can't stick to the contract.

I follow. Of course, I fucking do.

According to people I've worked with, when they experience adrenaline, their thoughts blur. It makes them frantic. But the opposite has always been true for me. Sure, my heart races and my muscles tense, but everything gets very, very clear. My thoughts. My perception. My next move.

Catriona's golden head bobs through the crowd. I stick close, prowling, always her predator. One who'd sink their teeth in her, if given the chance. She moves quickly, but not so fast that she'll cause any unsavory attention. She can keep her cool with anyone else. But when she's with me? It's like she can't help herself.

I seriously consider calling the entire party off. She's with a man I don't recognize. I reason with myself that it could be anyone. It's a party, for fuck's sake. It doesn't mean anything. He hands her a drink, and she smiles at him.

Smiles.

At him.

The bounds of my jealousy are apparently nonexistent because the mere sight of her with another man has me crossing the room, threading through well-wishers like a bull, and she's my red flag.

Just before I reach her, she spots me over the shoulder of her companion. Her eyes bulge, and she hisses something. The man gives her a sharp nod before leaving. I glare at his back until Catriona stalks to me, grabs me by the arm, and tugs me to an empty balcony. Classical music spills from the party, but out here, we're cocooned in secrets and shadows.

"Who was that?" I ask the moment the doors close behind us.

"None of your business," she snaps.

"You're my wife. Everything about you is my business."

"Don't be ridiculous. I'm allowed to have conversations with people who aren't you."

"Then why is it such a big deal to tell me who it was, unless you have something to hide?"

"I don't have something to hide. I just don't feel like I need to tell you every little detail of my life. Didn't you *just* say I wasn't supposed to put my nose where it doesn't belong? Maybe you should take some of your own advice."

"It's different when we're supposed to be showing the party what a perfect couple we are. I can't have you draping yourself over another man."

"I'm not doing this with you. We have to go back inside

for pictures. That would make us look like the perfect husband and wife, right?"

"We're not going anywhere until you answer my question."

"You are such an asshole."

"I'm still waiting, darlin'. I have all night."

She scoffs. "Fine. That man? His name is Devin Franklin. My dad's head of security. There. Are you happy? Can we go back inside now? You're making a big deal about nothing."

I grab her arm as she moves to go around me, and she whirls, jerking it out of my grasp. Her mask of indifference slips, just a little, but it's enough for me to note the mounting frustration.

"No, you can't go back inside. Why were you talking to him? What's the big secret?"

"Jesus, get a grip. Just because I have your ring on my finger and we've fucked doesn't mean you can boss me around."

"I'm afraid that's exactly what it means. Or do I need to remind you?" She stills, and my blood flashes hot.

"No, you've made it perfectly clear what you expect."

I herd her into the wall, one hand at her belly, the other braced beside her.

"Are you trying to make me jealous? Because those kinds of petty games won't work on me."

Catriona leans in a fraction, a shark scenting blood. "Sure seems like it's working on you. What's the matter? Daydreaming about having me begging for you again?"

My mouth goes so dry I can't respond.

"Because it'll be a cold day in hell before I ever let you near me."

"If you really want to know what hell is like, *bhean chéile*, let another man touch what's mine."

"I am not yours," she bites out, eyes glittering and hand tightening around the flute of champagne at her side.

"That's not what you said the last time my cock was inside you. Remember?"

Her breath stutters against my lips. "Hardly."

"Need a reminder? How long do you think it would take me to get you off, hmm?" I tilt my head down, skin heating as I reacquaint myself with the curves of her body. My voice lowers of its own volition. "Does it ache for me, love?"

She takes a sip from her champagne, and if I didn't know any better, I'd say she sounded indifferent to my interrogation. Men twice her size have withered at less. It shouldn't be so *fucking* hot. "Please," she says. "The only thing I feel for you is revulsion."

"Is that right?"

Her eyes bounce between mine like she can't look away. "That's right. You hate that, don't you? You hate how much you want me. That's why you can't seem to stay away from me," she taunts.

The haughty smirk falters when I don't give in to an angry tirade. "A little hypocritical, don't you think?"

"I think maybe you're having issues with your English. You don't seem to understand the definition of hypocritical."

"Yet you're the one who melts the moment I touch you. I think *you're* the one who can't stay away from me. After all, you crashed my wedding because you couldn't stand to see me marry someone else."

A furrow pinches between her brows, which smooths as quickly as it appears. "Is that what you want? For me to admit that I want you? That I care about you?" At her words, my body sways closer, an answer even though I haven't said anything. Her lips tilt up, and she lifts a hand to my cheek, slapping it lightly. "Well, you can keep hoping and waiting, O'Connor. That's never going to happen."

"That's not what it seemed like when you came all over my face. I bet you're wet for me right now, aren't you?" I grip the dress at her thigh and ruck the material up until I find skin. Her fingers claw at me, but I'm stronger. "Always such a slut for me."

Her hand is up and cracking against my cheek, this time in earnest. My head whips to the side, face already stinging. She's the personification of fury and defiance when I look back at her.

It's not until seconds later that I realize the sound of music has swelled. The doors are open.

Rory and Elizabeth spill out onto the balcony seconds later, followed by more people, cameras raised and lights flashing as they take pictures.

CHAPTER 14

CATRIONA

O'Connor's jaw *clenches, unclenches* in that way of his that I've already memorized, if I cared about memorizing anything about him. Then he's moving with a muffled curse, and I flinch, curling inward and hoping to protect my face from his retaliation. My body trembles against his until I realize he's not my father. He isn't going to fight back with his fists.

Fireworks go off—no, that's not right. There's no sound other than the music from the party. It's only the lights flashing that are temporarily blinding me. Disorientation mounts for a long minute. *Get ahold of yourself, Ri,* I hear Yasmine coaching in my head.

Not for the first time, I wish her schedule had allowed her to attend. She would have been able to tell me if I was hallucinating or not because there's no way O'Connor's arm is wrapped protectively around me. No way he has me huddled close against his body as he fights his way through a crush of spectators, ignoring my father's protests.

But that's exactly where I find myself, ears filled with O'Connor's biting warnings as we move through the hovering crowd to the ballroom. My chest is tight as my thoughts race in an attempt to figure out what his game plan is going to be. Will he move us to a room with more privacy? Will he wait for later to dispense his revenge?

I shouldn't have done that. I don't know what I was thinking. The only person I've ever hit before was him, but that was different. He'd chased me through the estate at his masquerade to stop me from leaving. The circumstances here are wildly different. *We're* different.

But now he needs me.

If he's going to get the trip to Ireland he wants, he can't hurt me.

The thought steadies me until we're safely ensconced on the other side of the room, a couple of hundred people between us and the cluster of socialites.

I go through the motions, accept another drink, and take my place at the head of the table. A plate from the buffet is placed in front of me, and I eat mechanically, suddenly ravenous and hyperaware of O'Connor sitting next to me. Mara and Eamon are on the other side of him. The trio conducts an entirely silent conversation through lifted eyebrows and smirks, in a language of their own, which ends with Eamon sniggering and Mara looking very pleased.

O'Connor stretches an arm over the back of my chair, and I stiffen. "Stop looking like I'm going to hurt you, pet, or it'll give the press more fuel, yeah?"

I eat, but I don't taste it. It goes down like lead. Like

other lawyers, I hate apologizing because it means I've done something wrong. "I shouldn't have done that. I'm—"

"If you say you're sorry, I'm going to be disappointed. O'Connors don't apologize."

It's so close to the thought I had only seconds ago that I'm speechless. Before I can untangle how to respond, we're called away for more pictures with my father.

And Elizabeth.

Which turns out to be even more awkward than my entire evening with O'Connor. Father and Elizabeth get through the whole ordeal without saying a word to either of us, but still paint beatific smiles on their faces for the cameras. They don't say a word about the scene they witnessed, but I do catch Elizabeth sending vicious glares my way.

Remembering my promise to O'Connor, I position myself at his side, wrapping one arm around his waist and placing my hand on his chest to display the rock of an engagement ring and matching band on my finger. He stuffs his free hand in his pocket, tilts his chin up imperiously, and winds his other arm around my waist. This is the only time Father and Elizabeth break character. It doesn't make my smile deepen, just a little. It doesn't make me shift closer, just a little. And I don't feel vindicated.

Not at all.

What the fuck is he doing to me?

LATER, after we say our goodbyes.

After Eamon and Mara eye us with discerning gazes.

After O'Connor speaks with the man I've learned is his

assistant, Finn, to hopefully stop the release of those pictures to the masses.

After I flee upstairs to my room and lock myself in the bathroom.

I finally let myself think of O'Connor's face after I slapped him. How good it had felt. How he'd looked.

Instinct had told me he was pissed. That there's no way he'd let me get away with it. That he'd retaliate.

But as I sink deeper into the bubbles and scalding water, I don't think the look on his face was fury at all.

It was hunger.

The memory of it has my hands slipping over my body, caressing my breasts, teasing my pebbling nipples, and biting my lip to contain the twist of pleasure. His voice fills my ears over the music blasting from my earbuds. *"Does it ache for me, love?"*

Here, safely behind a lock, I admit to myself that it does. It does ache for him. I ache for him. And even though it makes me hate myself, I slide my other hand between my thighs, breath rushing out of my lungs as shocks shoot up from the contact.

My fingertips swirl over my clit as I center my thoughts on the memory of him pressing me against the wall, his mouth grazing my ear. His sexy, throaty, threatening voice. This is so wrong. I hate him, but I can't seem to make myself stop. Two fingers plunge inside, the heel of my hand exerting delicious pressure against my clit, but it's not enough.

Growling, I release the plug and let enough of the water drain out so the tub won't overflow. I pop out a bud, ears straining for some hint of where O'Connor is, but I can't hear anything over the flow of water, and, if I'm being honest with myself, a part of me wants him to hear.

To wonder.

To want.

Whoever designed this room must have been a woman because the faucet has a detachable head. I adjust the settings until the spray is firm but not too stimulating, then angle the shower head just where I need it. Hooking my heels over the sides of the tub, I pull my body into position, letting the jet of water give me the perfect pressure and freeing up my hands to cup my breasts and tease my nipples.

In this secluded place, where I'm alone and safe to fantasize without judgment, all I need is the memory of O'Connor to get me close.

He's not here, so I don't stop myself when I finally come, and the name I whisper is, "Aiden."

It's Thursday, what feels like a century later, when my phone pings with a text from Broussard asking me to meet. I'm just replying my affirmative when it rings in my hand. All I want is to go home, soak in my giant bathtub—without thinking of O'Connor this time—and turn my brain off for a while. The other girls in my class keep stealing glances at me, as the sound of the incoming call reverberates off the walls.

Despite O'Connor's best efforts, it hadn't taken long for word of my scene at the reception to spread locally, as everyone in attendance began sharing online. Especially when Father's opponents caught wind of the news and used it to attack the core of his "family man" focused narrative.

The gossip and attention, which had ebbed in the months since my mother's death, reignited with each salacious clip.

A glance at my phone screen shows it's from Judge Landry's office, and my stomach sinks. While the story isn't the most flattering, I was hoping it wouldn't be serious enough for the judge's office to get wind of it. My clerkship with her after graduation is absolutely vital to my ten-year plan.

"Hello?" I answer breathlessly, as I start shoving my belongings into my bag.

"Hello, this is Patricia Sterling from Judge Landry's chambers. I'm calling for Ms. Gal—forgive me. I mean, Mrs. O'Connor. Catriona O'Connor."

I'll never get used to hearing that name. "This is she."

She makes a humming noise. "Yes. Do you have a moment to speak with her regarding a matter that's come to our attention?"

My stomach sinks. "Of course. When?"

"Please hold, and I'll transfer you."

Throat dry, I mumble my agreement and sink into a chair. She doesn't want to make an appointment. She wants to speak now. Not a good sign. My fan club is still here, waiting. Watching. I smooth the emotion from my face. No matter what happens, I won't give anyone more to run their mouths about. The moment I'd walked into class Monday morning, it had been to complete silence with all eyes on me.

Yasmine finally badgered me into looking at the videos two days ago, and I wish I hadn't. Short clips of it are everywhere. Aiden towering over me, eyes glittering and unhinged. One arm blocking my way. The other at my hip.

Next clip, my hand whipping up. My face pinched with

fury. The sound of the slap echoing over the balcony. The way O'Connor presses closer for a moment before the phones start flooding the space with lights.

But it's the last clip that gets me. The one where my face goes white with panic, when I flinch. At the time, it had been out of fear, with the memory of Father hitting me at the forefront of my thoughts.

The phone clicks, and Judge Landry's businesslike voice fills the line. "Mrs. O'Connor. Lovely to speak to you again."

"Same to you, Judge Landry. I hope you're well."

I've always admired Judge Landry. Born and bred in Louisiana, she also graduated from Tulane Law and began her career at the Louisiana Division of Administrative Law, where she's been a judge for twelve years. Prior to becoming a judge, she was an assistant attorney general. She's no-nonsense and highly respected for her unwavering professionalism—a characteristic I would have said applied to myself prior to my mother's death.

"I've been better," she says briskly, and I begin to sweat, despite the chill swirling through the lecture hall. While she was present during my interviews, this is our first real conversation about something other than my future employment prospects. "I'm sure you're aware as to why I'm calling. Your father has brought some things to my attention."

"My father?" I sound like I've swallowed rocks. "Judge Landry, before you say anything, I'd like to state I take complete responsibility for my regrettable actions, and I'm happy to make a statement to that effect. Whatever my father has said, I urge you to—"

"While I appreciate the sentiment, unfortunately, our role requires the utmost professionalism from its employees to maintain an impeccable reputation with the public. As such, I've decided it will be best for now to go our separate ways. Your father is a man I highly respect. You'd do well to consult him on this matter."

"Right," I whisper. The irony isn't lost on me.

"Human resources will be in touch with the requisite paperwork." There's a pause, and she sighs. "It's a pity. I thought you were going to be a fantastic asset."

She hangs up before I can respond.

"Did you really slap Aiden O'Connor at your wedding reception?" one of my classmates demands a few minutes after I hang up from my call with Judge Landry. "That's him, right? Lucky. I gotta tell you, smacking him around would have been the last thing on my mind if he were my husband."

"I'm sorry, what?" I say, as I glance up to one of the girls who'd been smirking and giggling throughout the lecture, to find her pointing at the door—where O'Connor waits with a shoulder against the doorframe.

Seeing him again has my cheeks flaming. Because of what I'd done... and my call with Judge Landry. If I'd been thinking clearly and not on edge from my short, unproductive conversation with Devin, I wouldn't have let my guard down in the first place.

Since the reception, I haven't seen O'Connor for more than a few minutes in passing, by design. I couldn't imagine looking at him, knowing the things he'd said to me had a thread of truth.

"Well?" Vanessa pushes. She's not the first to stop me this week, wondering what happened to cause the pictures that had been splashed everywhere. "I've been dying to ask you about the videos."

Ignoring her, I push my way past and resign myself to interacting with him. It should surprise me to find him here, but I'm not. He's been trying to get me alone since the reception.

He looks out of place among the leggings and oversized T-shirts, and business-casual attire in his crisp suit. It should be against the law for a man to look this good.

The rest of the class filters by him, and he turns sideways to squeeze his way inside, his eyes on me the entire time. If he notices my classmates giving him curious glances, he doesn't pay them any mind. Vanessa tries to catch his eye, but finally gives up when she realizes he won't look away from me. By the time I get to him, the girls who'd been gawking at me all week long are blessedly gone.

"What are you doing here?" I ask, glancing around him to confirm the hallway beyond is empty.

O'Connor rocks back on his heels. "What? I can't want to see my wife?"

"Yeah, right." I shift from foot to foot as I hold my bag in front of me like a shield. "Is something wrong?"

"Nothing's wrong. I've been trying to speak with you all week, but you've been hiding since the reception, so you left me no choice but to corner you here. I don't mind, though. You know I like the chase."

I run a hand through my hair. "Is there something wrong with you? If you need someone to annoy you, I have two I can recommend. They love nothing more than to follow people around."

"But the only one I want to annoy me is you. Besides, we have unfinished business."

"What unfinished business?" Naturally, my thoughts

flash back to the night of the reception. The tension that had flared to life between us. That's not what he's talking about... right?

"I'd love to know where your thoughts went just now. The way you're staring at me is interesting. But we don't have time. If we don't leave now, we're going to be late."

Without giving me an answer, he guides me out of the classroom with a proprietary hand on my lower back and keeps it there as we navigate through campus. My mouth opens and closes, unsure whether I want to see him follow through or lodge a more vehement protest. The indecision lasts me most of the walk to his car and the drive across town.

On the sidewalk, he lifts an arm to guide me to a brick building with ivy growing up one side and a fancy sign trimmed in gold that reads Global Wealth Management in a discreet, understated way that I know, from experience, means expensive. Why would he bring me here after what happened at the reception? Any other man would be serving me with divorce papers, not giving me access to his fortune.

O'Connor leads me inside, and the beautiful assistant at the entrance offers a cheerful grin when she sees him. "Mr. O'Connor. Right on time. I'm Anne, and I'll show you where you're going. Mr. Bennett is waiting for you in the conference room. I'll take you right back."

"Now? You want to do this now?" I hiss at his back.

"No time like the present."

"What kind of game are you playing? Have you seen what they're saying about us? Why would you still want to—"

He looks over his shoulder with a killer smile. "Anne, if you'll give us a minute, please."

The assistant brushes her hand over hair the color of aged copper and glances curiously from O'Connor to me and back again. My brows furrow, and I do the same, to find O'Connor smiling at me like he has a secret. A thrill of anticipation rolls through me like I've touched a live wire.

"Of course, Mr. O'Connor. Mr. Bennett is waiting for you here when you're ready."

"I'm leaving." Letting him bring me here was a mistake. If I hadn't been so distracted by the call from Judge Landry, I never would have let him. Stupid, stupid, stupid.

"Didn't I tell you the first time we met, I'd never hurt you?"

I freeze.

"Didn't I?" He moves closer, his warmth searing a path throughout my system. "You flinched. Thought I was going to hurt you. I may be a lot of things, Catriona, but I would never raise a hand to you." A huffed breath ruffles my hair. "At least not in ways you wouldn't like."

"It pains me to say this, I hope you know that. But I shouldn't have hit you. It was—"

"If I wanted your apologies, I'd ask for them. But if you really need my forgiveness, then go to this meeting with me, sign all the papers, and don't put up a fuss. Otherwise..."

"Otherwise, what?"

"Otherwise, you'll have to come up with another way to make it up to me."

Fat chance that's going to happen. I study his face, trying to read him, but his expression is carefully neutral. At my silence, O'Connor takes my hand, and we move down a brightly lit hallway to a conference room in the middle of the floor surrounded by glass. It reminds me of a giant fishbowl.

A man with carefully cropped white hair and a groomed beard gets to his feet as Anne leads us into the room. He's rotund, with glasses and rosy-pink cheeks.

"Mr. Bennett, Mr. and Mrs. O'Connor are here."

"O'Connor," Mr. Bennett says in a booming voice. "Lovely to see you. Pleasure to make your acquaintance, Mrs. O'Connor. I'm sorry it's taken so long. We normally don't like to delay this business so long, but our schedules finally synced up."

"No problem, David. You have everything we talked about?" O'Connor pulls out a chair for me, and I sit, my eyebrows still raised in astonishment. He takes the seat next to me, across from Mr. Bennett, and places a proprietary hand on my thigh underneath the table. I try to discreetly shrug away from his touch, but he resists, clamping down on the muscle as he focuses on whatever paperwork Mr. Bennett slides in front of him.

"Standard contracts we've discussed. Life insurance. Wills. Living will. Investment and brokerage accounts. Trusts, etcetera."

"Excellent."

"Your lawyer has already gone over everything and sent his approval, Mrs. O'Connor. If it all looks agreeable to you, we'll just need your signatures on the lines we've flagged."

"Right," I whisper.

Mr. Bennett clears his throat. "We'll just need your signature next to Mr. O'Connor's, please. It's marked with the tabs." He pushes a sheaf of papers across the glossy surface of the table to me.

"O-of course," I stammer. "Shouldn't we discuss this some more? It seems—" My gaze flicks around the room, but Anne has made a quiet retreat, and Mr. Bennett is arranging the paperwork for me to sign. No one is listening to me.

I put pen to paper.

O'Connor's hand tightens. Slips higher. I try to push it off, to no avail.

As I go through the paperwork, Mr. Bennett places account summaries and investment plans in front of me, as well as others I don't fully comprehend. But the number of zeros on the statement lines makes things pretty fucking transparent. I nearly swallow my tongue. Aiden's hand tightens again. I sign my name. This process repeats several times until we get through the impressive stack.

In the end, I've been added as a beneficiary to his retirement and investment accounts, and I've been made a secondary account holder on all his (and there are many) banking accounts. Even if we get divorced, I'll be a rich woman. Vastly, vastly rich. Even without my mother's inheritance.

"That'll be it then," Mr. Bennett says when all is done. My hands are numb, and there's a ringing in my ears that won't quite go away. This... this entangles us in a way more permanent than marriage. Money is sticky. Messy. It can ruin you. I could take everything from him, yet he's... giving it to me. It doesn't make sense.

As I'm puzzling through it, O'Connor finally lets go of my thigh to push to his feet and clasp Mr. Bennett's hand in a firm handshake. They exchange slaps on the back and small talk while I have a mini panic attack about what I've just done.

"Of course, take all the time you need," Mr. Bennett is

saying when I tune back in. He nods at me with a congenial smile before pushing away from the table and leaving.

I flick my gaze around the fishbowl conference room, but no one seems to pay any attention to us even though there are open office doors and cubicles less than ten feet away. My heart beats a frantic rhythm in my throat, chest, and ears.

"I shouldn't let you do this," I say on a shuddering breath.

"Let me?" he scoffs. "Are you going to stop me?"

"Yes. This is insane. You're insane. We've only been married for a few days."

"Almost two weeks."

I roll my eyes, ignoring the way my cheeks heat. Has he been counting? "Fine, two weeks, but that doesn't help your case. You don't know me well enough to trust me with this. I can't in good conscience agree to taking half of your money. O'Connor, you're a billionaire. That's a *lot* of fucking money."

"I can make more, pet. Besides, I like the thought of you wearing things I've bought for you. Of you flaunting my money in your father's face. If it helps, you can think of it that way."

My breath catches in my throat. "I don't—"

"You don't have to worry about it. I know what I'm doing."

"You can have me added to your accounts all you want, but it doesn't mean anything," I reason.

"Of course not. But you're welcome to use it. Go on a shopping spree. Donate it to your favorite charities. Renovate the estate or buy another one. Blow it at the tables."

"Maybe I'll donate it all." I try to sound confident, but I'm certain he can hear the way my voice quavers.

"Do it," he insists. "Which charity? Should I have Mara show you to her favorite designers? I'm sure she'd love to indulge you."

"I'm a little afraid of Mara, if we're being honest. When she helped with my dress for the reception, she told me she'd kill me if I fucked things up for you."

A smile tugs at O'Connor's lips. "Trust me, that's practically her saying she loves you."

"Your friends are strange."

"So we'll start with charities. We're organizing a charity gala. Why don't you give a generous donation in our name?"

"A gala?"

He nods, relaxing into a wide-limbed sprawl. "Plated, black-tie, you know."

"All too well."

"It would be a great opportunity to clear up our image after the reception."

Wincing, I say, "Right. Of course."

"I'm going to have to spoil you like this more often. It's worth giving away my fortune to see you this speechless."

I narrow my eyes to slits. "Don't get used to it. Anyone would be shocked by being offered that amount of money. But I get to keep my mom's inheritance, not that it would mean anything to you. And everything I make on my own." It makes me feel greedy, but while he may be eager to give away everything he owns, I feel like I need to hold on to it with everything I have.

"Whatever's yours remains yours. I would never take it from you." He leans close and palms my hair, his hand coming to rest on my shoulder. "So you're just going to have to deal with receiving for now."

"What about what my father owes Cian?"

A sad smile. "I told you I've taken care of it."

"I should slap you more often. You aren't planning to do anything dangerous, are you? Out of the norm, I mean? This isn't a dying-wish situation, is it?" The thought grabs me by the throat. Has Cian said something? Done something? It hasn't occurred to me until this moment that there may be men out there who want to do to O'Connor what he does to others. Christ, what have I gotten myself into?

"No, Catriona," he says, the words colored by a smile, which he presses into my hair. It shocks me so much that I don't react, and then it's over before I can. "Nothing out of the usual, anyway."

"Screw law school, I should have just become a findomme."

He tilts his head. "A what?"

"A findomme. Financial dominatrix. A woman who dominates men for money."

Shoving to his feet, he *clenches, unclenches* his jaw again. "Let's get out of here."

CHAPTER 15

AIDEN

The silence on Catriona's side of the car during the ride home grates. What I'd give to know what she's thinking. This week has been a bitch. The waiting. For the news of the reception to break. But even more, for Catriona to come to me.

Five days and she hadn't.

So I'd finally given in and gone to her.

Both because I needed to ensure her safety if something were to happen to me, and because I wanted to see her face. Gauge her reaction. The concession in our constant battle was worth it.

Frances greets us, and dinner is served—steaks, asparagus, and sweet potato, but I barely taste any of it. The little liar is hiding something, and getting her to let down her guard the slightest bit had been the first step. I don't want to push her, but I know there's something about her interaction with Devin Franklin that doesn't sit right with me. Something she's not telling me.

She may have only wanted me as her husband for her sister's sake, but now that she's got me, I want everything from her.

Especially her secrets.

My plans are thwarted as soon as both of our plates are clean. Frances appears in the doorway with a grinning Eamon at her side.

"Well, isn't this nice?" he says, giving a jaunty little dip at the knees. "Dinner with the missus. I hope I'm not intruding."

"Yes."

"No," Catriona says at the same time.

I flick her a dispassionate look, and her lips press together. To Eamon, I say, "You're always intruding. Now, what do you want so you can go?"

Eamon rests against the doorjamb, crossing his ankles. "I'm stealing you for the night."

"No."

I see Catriona sip on wine out of the corner of my eye, a cautiously amused smile semi-hidden behind her glass at the byplay.

"You haven't even heard what it's for."

"I don't need to hear. Besides, we're occupied." I gesture to the plates.

"You're done. Surely, you can survive being away from her for a day."

"We—"

"Of course you can have him for the night, Eamon. I have readings to do. And a new clerkship to find. So I'll be busy for the evening." Pushing to her feet, she nods at me before rushing out of the room.

"Now look what you've done," I say flatly.

"You're the definition of a happy groom," he says, twitching his eyebrows at me. I try to escape to my study without him, but he doesn't get a clue and follows. "I always thought marriage would suit you," Eamon adds at my back.

"I can't wait for the day when something like this happens to you," I answer through gritted teeth, as I pour myself a glass of gin. I knock it back, appreciating the floral notes and, with pride, noting that the brand is from Ireland: Dingle Gin. No wonder it's excellent.

It's almost like she knew what I was trying to do, I muse to myself, as I sip more. *Did she sense I was trying to get her alone? Needle information from her? Clever little wife.* Of course she did. My brilliant, ruthless Catriona. If any other woman has offered me half as much amusement, I can't pull them to mind. Ever since she stole her way into my life, every other woman has been lackluster in comparison.

Eamon chuckles, throwing himself into a chair with that infuriating grin of his. "There isn't a woman alive who could knock me off my feet."

Ignoring his sarcasm, I take the chair opposite him. Maybe if I get him drunk enough, he'll pass out, and I can interrupt Catriona's studying. "Why aren't you on a job? What do you want?"

Slumping dramatically with one hand on his chest, Eamon says, "You think I'd let you get married without doing something special to celebrate? You wound me."

I glare at him over my drink. "I'm *going* to wound you, you gobshite."

He gestures, and I sigh before handing him my glass for him to drink. Will I ever get to finish a drink in my own house?

"You seem like you could use a bit of distraction." He gestures with the now-empty crystal tumbler. "And I'm your favorite distraction."

"What you are is a giant pain in the arse."

He shakes the glass for a refill, and I retrieve the bottle and another cup. "Not telling me anything I haven't heard before. Besides, you love me. Want to know what I have planned for you?"

"If it's not a bullet to my brain, I'm not interested."

"You always know just what to say."

I think of Catriona upstairs and rub a hand over my face. "Fuck it. Tell me your plans."

"Really? I thought it would have taken more convincing. Mrs. O'Connor must really have you in knots."

I make a rolling motion with my free hand. "Do you ever stop running your mouth?"

Tsking, he says, "But I have so many interesting things to say."

"Start with what the hell you're doing here," I suggest.

He shifts the bag at his side that I didn't realize he'd brought with him. "We're going to start with this."

"You think now is the right time?" I question drolly.

Eamon smirks. "Why? Are you planning to consummate tonight? I didn't think Catriona was interested, based on the videos I've seen this week."

"It'll be in your best interest to refrain from commenting about me fucking my wife." I throw back the rest of my gin. "I'm not going to be able to talk you out of this, am I?"

His expression turns rueful. "'Fraid not."

"Do I get a choice in what or where it is?" He gives me a look that says how can you be so stupid. "Fine. Get it set up. I'll pour more drinks."

"I'm surprised your pretty bride isn't wondering what we're up to."

I scoff, trying not to imagine what she's doing right now or if she's wearing any of those negligees I'd seen in her room. How tonight *could* have gone if we were any other people in the world. "I'm sure she's pleased you're keeping me busy."

While he sets up his supplies, I retrieve a bottle of Teeling vintage reserve single malt whiskey from behind my desk. Despite the fact that I haven't been to Ireland since long before the Emerald Isle opened, I still prefer Irish whiskey. By the time it's poured, Eamon is ready. Gesturing to him, he grins wide, and I pour us two generous measures.

"*Sláinte!*" Eamon toasts after knocking his glass to mine. "I take it by the look on your face, marriage isn't the happily ever after you always dreamed?" Eamon snickers, bringing me back to the present as he arranges his supplies on a sterilized tray: tattoo gun, needles, ink, petroleum jelly, and a bunch of other shit I don't know the name for. I find myself looking forward to this. Maybe Eamon, the bastard, isn't such a gobshite after all.

"Shut the fuck up unless it's to tell me what you're planning on putting on me."

At this, his grin spreads wider, and he pulls out the stencil from his bag.

I lift a brow at him as I study it.

"You can't be serious."

"As a heart attack, *mo chara*."

I think about Catriona and how she'll react when she sees. She'll be pissed, no doubt in my mind. Probably call me crazy. Honestly, I think it may be worth it.

When my lips pull into a smirk, Eamon says, "I knew you'd love it. It won't take long, and then we can drink the rest of this whiskey."

"Like hell. It's for special occasions."

"Lad, you married Rory Gallagher's daughter. It's either a special occasion or we're toasting to your impending funeral."

He isn't wrong. "Alright, fuck, I'll drink, but you're going to finish the bottle on your own."

"I thought you'd never ask."

BY THE FOLLOWING MORNING, I'm cursing Eamon's name for convincing me to finish half the bottle with him—sneaky bastard. When I'm done, I study the tattoos and imagine Catriona's reaction—ire, disgust, and confusion, probably. But what I'm really hoping for is outrage. She'll do all sorts of interesting things if she's pissed off with me. Hit me. Yell at me.

Tell me all the things she's been keeping from me.

Let me pin her down and fuck her into submission.

Maybe all of the above.

I listen for any sign she's awake, but the room next to mine is still and quiet, and there's no indication she is when I peek out into the hall. A shower is the first order of business, to wash away the reek and peel off the bits of film covering my fingers. Eamon has done most of my tattoos. Some of them were at my request, but most were because I liked the pain and he needed the distraction. Over the years, I've accumulated so many that I'm running out of room as his canvas. One of these days, he'll have to find a new one.

The Saniderm comes off relatively easily, though it always feels like I'm peeling off a layer of flesh, no matter how much I soak the surrounding area. I wash the sensitive skin with antibacterial soap, then dry the new tattoos with a clean towel and apply a light film of Aquaphor. They're small, but they're on my hands, so they'll require a little more attention than tattoos in a less exposed part of my body.

Or maybe I want to baby them because of what they are.

A bottle of water clears away some of the muddiness from my thoughts, and aspirin does the rest.

When I glance up, I see Catriona in the fogged-over mirror, standing at the doorway to the bathroom, wearing a pink camisole and jeans. Her shoulders are bare, framed by delicate straps of lace on her upper arms. Her golden-blond hair tumbles from a clip at the back of her head.

Having just spent the past half hour thinking of her, seeing her appear out of nowhere does something primal to me.

"Do you have a second?" Her voice is still husky with sleep, but her eyes are clear. Based on the way she doesn't look away from my face, I can tell the sight of my half-naked body is distracting her. "Or I can come back. I didn't want to wake you, but I heard the shower, so I tried to call for you." She swallows hard. "The, um, door was unlocked."

My chest warms under her attention. And she hasn't

even seen the tattoos yet. "Good morning to you, too, Mrs. O'Connor," I say, just to see her eyes flash with indignation.

Catriona sucks in a breath, and my eyes drop to her mouth, where she's biting her lower lip. "Right. Yes. Um, good morning." It doesn't escape my notice that she doesn't correct her name. Pleasure rolls through me, but I don't let it show on my face. "Well, I don't want to keep you. I just wanted to give you a heads-up that I have a meeting with my, um, advisor this afternoon. So I'm going to be a little late. I didn't want Bren or Tadhg to freak you out, so will you give them a heads-up?"

"Of course," I say, and use another towel to blot the water streaming from my hair.

She blinks. "I'm sorry, are you still drunk right now? Because if I'm not mistaken, you just agreed with me. Are you sure you're feeling okay?"

Giving her a sly smile, I move to leave the bathroom, and she holds her position until I'm within inches of pressing against her from knees to chest, then she backs away to let me out. Her footsteps are close behind as I move to the bedroom, the one I'm supposed to be sharing with my wife, but that is noticeably lacking any of her things. When had I gone from wanting her as far away from me as possible to imagining her here every morning when I wake up?

Maybe it's her name inked into my skin, my ring on her finger, and that she carries my last name that's causing me to lose sight of all my previous objections to having her as my wife.

I study the bed and give half a thought to persuading her to lie on her back instead of letting her go to school. She'd fight at first, but if I got my mouth on her cunt, I bet I have a fifty-fifty chance I could convince her. Maybe seventy-thirty. She seemed to like the things I could do with my tongue.

She makes a sound of discontent in the back of her throat, and my attention returns to her face, then trails down her body. "Stop looking at me like that."

"Like what?"

Before she can answer, she zeros in on the thin, glossy patches of skin on my knuckles as I turn on the overhead light in the closet. Whatever she's going to add dies in her throat as I shift to pull clothes from drawers. Humor tempers any lingering hesitation, and recklessness has me undoing the towel, twisting more than necessary as I pull socks, briefs, and whatever the hell else from the drawers.

Enjoying her attention, her indignation, I retrieve a shirt and slacks from the closet. The room is dark and quiet, still as midnight, so I can hear her harsh breathing... and I can hear when she stops as she finally puts the pieces together.

"What the hell is that?" she demands, taking my hands in hers. She's so shocked, she doesn't even comment on my nakedness. Should I be offended?

Eamon would die to be here to see her reaction to his handiwork. "They're tattoos."

She turns a lovely shade of red. "I know what they are. Why do you have my name tattooed on your hands? Is this some sick joke, O'Connor?"

I glance down at where she's cradling my hands in hers, her pretty lips pulled into a frown as she tries to find the words to express her frustration. Surrounded by irritated red skin are the dark, black-inked gothic letters, one on each knuckle.

C – A – T – R on my right, and I – O – N – A on my

left. When she arranges my hands next to each other, it spells out her name, inked on my skin forever. The thought sends a delicious thrill skating over my nerve endings.

"It's Eamon's idea of a wedding present," I say in a low, gravelly voice. Her hands are on me. Who knew all I had to do to get them there was shock her a little? "I'm sure if you asked, he'd be willing to give you one, too. What do you think? Want my name on you?" At her silence, I muse, "Probably not on your hands, though. Somewhere you can hide under all your pretty pink suits."

She's frozen in place as I shift toward her, unmoving as I lift a tattooed hand to those red-tinged cheeks. Her eyes draw up my body, studying the ink on my chest, skating over my lips, until she meets my eyes. Now she notices I'm not wearing anything. The clothes I'd gathered are in a pile on the floor by my feet, forgotten. Her breath hitches as I inch closer, and I take in her lavender and honey scent, letting it fill my nose.

"What about here?" I whisper, thumbing her wrist where she could hide a tattoo with long sleeves.

"Have you lost your mind? Why would you get my name tattooed on you? Is this another one of your stupid family traditions?"

I could lie, but I don't. "This? No. This was all Eamon. He does most of my tattoos."

"And, what, you couldn't tell him no?"

"Maybe I thought it was a good idea. More convincing."

"So this is just another twisted way to make your stepfather believe this is real?" She searches my face for answers. "Well, I have to give it to you, you're dedicated."

"Maybe here would be better," I say, instead of giving

her any answers. My hand glides up her arm, over her shoulder, grazes her breast, and rests just underneath on her ribs, so I can feel when her breath catches. "Yeah, I like the thought of it here."

"I don't think so," she says. Her hands are on my shoulders, clutching or preparing to push me away, I'm not sure. A heartbeat passes, and she doesn't do more than grip me tighter. "Ribs would hurt like a bitch."

A smile teases at my lips, and my hand moves to her lower back.

"A tramp stamp?" she snorts. "Over my dead body. Before you suggest it, there's no man on Earth I'd be willing to tattoo on my ass."

We're so close our lips are almost touching. "Then where?"

"This is insane. I'm going to be late."

"So tell me, and I'll let you go. Where would you get it?" I should drop it. I should let her go and banish the thought from my mind. But I pull her closer with my hand on her back.

She chews her bottom lip before she reaches across to guide my wrist around, so my hand is flat against her belly. Our gazes catch, hold. She urges my hand down, across her button, down her zipper. Fuck, I don't think I'm breathing. But she skims over the front of her until my hand is gripping the curve of her hip, nearly the top of her thigh. My thumb presses intimately close to the heat of her. My dick is hard and leaking. I'd give anything for her to touch me.

"If I were to get a tattoo of a man's name—"

"My name," I interrupt.

"—this is where it would be."

Is it just me, or are we somehow even closer? Did she move, or did I? My typically organized mind feels like it's in the center of a tornado.

I imagine it there, branding her. Another way to show the world—and her—that she's mine. Something inevitable holds me in its grasp.

She doesn't back away when I shift my free hand to thread through her hair, but her eyes are flashing in warning. Her hands shove at my shoulders, but I'm immovable. I pivot until she's against the wall, no way to escape, at my mercy. She strains against me, then realizes how much I'm enjoying it, and she freezes.

"Don't you fucking da—"

I capture the words with my mouth, swallowing her protests.

Her hands fly to my biceps, and she tries to push me away, but I pull her closer to me with a bruising grip on her hips. When she gasps, I deepen the kiss, feeding her my tongue, letting her nip at my lips until she softens. It's only for a moment. Just one where she kisses me back. But it's enough to have her tearing herself away.

She shoves me and brings a hand to her tender mouth. "What the hell are you doing?" she whispers.

"Kissing my wife."

"*Don't* kiss me again," she says, ignoring my comment. "I swear to God, I'll break something valuable the next time you try."

I brush the hair that's fallen into her face. She flinches away as I lift my hands, and at that, I let her go. "Whatever you say, Mrs. O'Connor."

"I'm going to go. Remember, I have that meeting this

afternoon. It may take a while, so have Bren and Tadhg wait in the car. I don't want them embarrassing me in front of my advisor," she demands, chest heaving. "But if you ever touch me again, I'm going to make you regret it." As she talks, I get dressed, ignoring my protesting dick. "I hope you're prepared to laser those off as soon as possible."

I don't dignify the laser removal comment with a response. If anything, her reaction to them has ensured they're never coming off. "I'll let them know. Is there anything else you want?"

Her jaw clenches, and she crosses her arms over her chest. "I mean it, O'Connor. Laser them off, or I'll figure out a way to tattoo over them myself."

"If that's what pleases you."

"I doubt you care about what pleases me," she mutters behind my back, still following me as I move to the bathroom to brush my teeth.

I meet her eyes in the mirror. "I care very much about what pleases you."

She scoffs. "Don't be ridiculous. Just keep your hands to yourself, O'Connor, and I'll do the same. There's no reason we can't be civil."

"You? Civil."

"What's that supposed to mean?"

"What if I don't want you to keep your hands to yourself? What if I don't want to be civil?"

She makes a disbelieving sound in the back of her throat. "You're only saying that to fuck with my head. I don't even know why I'm having this conversation with you. Tell Bren and Tadhg what I said. And for God's sake, don't do anything else like this while I'm gone today."

I watch her all the way out of my room, then I call Bren and Tadhg to give them the day off.

My wife is up to something.

Because she wouldn't have let me kiss her otherwise.

She wanted me to. Let me touch her. Get close to her. And she never would have done that unless there was something she wanted. Or wanted me to ignore.

And I'm going to find out exactly what it is and why.

CHAPTER 16

CATRIONA

Me
Emergency meeting. Please tell me you're not at the hospital.

Yasmine
I'm always at the hospital. You'll end up burying me here. Why? Do you need a doctor? Call 911, you idiot.

Me
Can't you stop saving lives for once? I don't need a doctor. This is what I'm dealing with.

picture of my name on O'Connor's knuckles

Yasmine
He didn't. Are you shitting me? Why is this so hot? It shouldn't be, right?

Me
He did. I'm going insane. I need to talk to you about this. Girls' night? SOON. And it's not hot. It's demented.

Yasmine
Color me intrigued. Tomorrow? Movie night at your house 😊

Me
You're on.

Yasmine
The people of New Orleans are lucky I'm such a consummate professional. Otherwise, I'd leave them to their various traumas to dive into the drama. I'll be there after my shift at 4.

Me
I'll try not to make any terrible decisions until then.

Yasmine
What terrible decisions.

I swear to God, if you don't answer me, I'm going to kill you myself.

What terrible decisions?!?!?!?!

Just for this disrespect, I fully support your husband getting your name tattooed on his hands.

Count your hours, Catriona Deirdre O'Connor (that's right, full government name)

My phone buzzes in my pocket with texts from a thoroughly annoyed Yasmine, and I try to pull it out to text her back so she doesn't worry, but I'm interrupted by a brusque masculine voice.

"Catriona."

I whirl around, heart hammering, and find Mr. Broussard leaning out of the window of a nondescript beige sedan. The locks click, spurring me into action, and I skirt around the car before folding into the passenger seat.

"Thank you for picking me up, Mr. Broussard. I realize this is highly irregular."

"No need to thank me, this is nowhere near the most bizarre thing I've done this week, let alone in my career. Where to? The same place?"

I shift uncomfortably. It may be irrational, but I've become even more paranoid about someone spotting me out in public while I'm chasing down information about my mother. It had been bad after her death when my father was so concerned about our public image, but with how entangled O'Connor is with my father's gambling debts, I highly doubt he'll want me doing the same thing, and I can't risk it.

"Is there somewhere more private we can go?"

Broussard shifts the car into gear, strokes his mustache, then says, "Sure, I know a place."

He fills the silence with small talk about my classes and

interesting tidbits about cases he's worked on. I wonder idly as he navigates the streets to a neighborhood on the outskirts of the city if he has a family. Or does he keep a job with varied hours to fill the time because he doesn't have a regular one? When I was younger, I used to wish I had a father with Mr. Broussard's disposition. Someone steady, dependable, and trustworthy. Though I would have settled for a kind man.

He pulls the car into the driveway of one of several identical cottages. They're spaced far enough apart that I'm not worried about privacy. And I'm kind of curious what the inside of his house looks like. It's almost like getting a peek at the inner workings of his brain.

"Is this where you live?" I ask.

"Yes. I hope that's alright."

"Of course. I'm sorry for intruding."

"Not at all. This will make it easier to demonstrate what I've found so far. I keep all of my equipment in my office."

Broussard leads me into his home, shrugging out of his patched suit jacket and hanging it on a honey-colored pine hall tree. Photos fill the space, though they're covered in a light layer of dust. The room is well-loved but neglected. I know then, without asking, that he must have lost his wife at some point. There's a woman's touch to the decor, the attention to pictures, especially, that screams he was married and that he loved her desperately, if the adoration in his eyes in each image is any indication.

He gestures to a hallway lined with more family photos. "My office is the first door on the right. I'll get us some sweet tea, or I have water or soda if you prefer."

Touched by this insight into his life, I smile warmly. "Sweet tea would be perfect."

The pictures in the hall don't show any children, so it's just Mr. Broussard. His wife was a slight woman with a floof of white hair and a luminous smile. They seemed so happy. My heart squeezes in my chest at the thought of him being alone. At how different his marriage must have been compared to my parents'.

I huff a laugh. Or even mine.

"Here we are, Catriona." He hands me a glass of sweet tea with a wedge of lemon on the rim and a glass straw.

"Thank you so much."

Gesturing, he says, "Please, take a seat. I'll pull up what I've found since our last conversation. I'm afraid it isn't good news."

Steeling myself with a deep pull from the straw, I sit on a fluffy chair next to his substantial oak desk that has enough gouges and scars in its surface for me to conclude he must have had it for a long time. "At this point, all I want is to know the truth, no matter how bad it is. I thought Devin would have more information, but our conversation was interrupted. Not that it matters. He said his car had a loose battery connection. Had it towed and everything."

"Hmm. Just like the police report." Broussard rubs his mustache with a thumb and forefinger, and, despite the topic of our conversation, I have to hide a smile. Dammit, I don't have the emotional bandwidth to care about anyone else, but I've grown a soft spot for this man.

Forcing myself to focus, I consider his words. "I don't know anything about cars. Is that a plausible explanation?"

He makes a so-so gesture with his hand, tipping it from

side to side. "Ehh, most people familiar with cars would see it right away. But if he's more focused on his job or has never been around cars, I assume it's a plausible explanation."

"Well, I guess that's what we call a dead-end."

"Maybe. We'll put a pin in the car for now. I did have luck accessing your mother's banking information with the information I found on your mother's phone."

I perk up. "Really? I'm assuming, based on your call, you found something." A sick, greasy feeling twists my insides into knots. All I want are answers, but at the same time, I'm terrified of what I'm going to find. The sweet tea helps, but only a little.

"Most of the transactions were innocuous. Insurance payments for bloodwork, charities, the medspa, lawyers, clothes, dinners, etcetera. But several transactions occurred after her death. Transfers from your mother's accounts to your father's."

"How is that possible?"

"Because they were her personal accounts, he couldn't touch them until the court appointed him executor. He had to take the death certificate and the letters testamentary to the bank before they'd move a dollar." He pauses, throat working as he drinks from his glass. "Not altogether suspicious, but there was one transaction on her account right after he got access as executor that drew my attention, so I thought I'd mention it. It's labeled as an estate account, but a little more digging shows that's not the case."

"So where is the money now?"

"That I do not know, unless we got an accounting of your father's." He studies me over the desk. "I have people who can do this, but I wasn't sure if that was a step you wanted to take. It's not strictly legal."

I imagine the circus that would be. If I didn't have a gut feeling my father was involved in her death, I'd drop it and wouldn't consider doing something illegal. The man clearly has no affection for me, but accusing him of murdering my mother without concrete proof would do more harm than good.

"I took the liberty to do some more digging." My gaze shoots to his as he continues. "Around the same time, Devin Franklin started spending more. A lot more. A new house. Brand-new car. Expensive watches and dinners at exclusive restaurants." He worries his mustache some more. "It may be a coincidence. He could have come into wealth on his own, but the timing itself is suspicious, so I thought it worth mentioning."

"That would explain why he was so cagey when I tried to corner him at the reception. If he helped my father cover up the details behind my mother's death in exchange for cash, then it would explain his lifestyle changes."

Could he have been the one who killed my mother? If his supposed car trouble turns out to be a hoax, then he would have been at the house at the same time she was.

"There has to be some way to place him there at the time of her death. Maybe the money was payment for... for killing her." I can barely force the last sentence through my tight throat.

"It's an option, but I can't say anything for certain without more information."

"Of course. No, you're right. But it's not a good look."

"It does seem damning at first blush," Broussard admits,

palming his head. "I'm going to search the area for additional footage. Maybe the police missed some home security systems from nearby properties that would have something useful. Especially if they weren't looking for anything because they thought it was an accident."

"They were pretty damn convinced from the beginning. Even my friend at the department, Reggie Baptiste, thought it was strange how quickly they leaned into the accidental death determination."

"Happens more than you would think. The simplest answer is usually correct, but it's also the fastest way to close a case, and sometimes things aren't always as they seem."

Touched all over again by his willingness to simply believe me, a rush of affection has me beaming at him. "Thank you. Sincerely. You can't know how much it means to me to have someone actually listen to me and take my concerns seriously."

"Six years ago, my wife was coming home from her shift as an ICU nurse at Louisiana General." I nod as it's the same hospital where Yasmine does most of her rounds. "She was hit by a man who'd fallen asleep at the wheel. She died instantly, but he made it out with only a few scratches. I knew he'd been drinking, but he was a prominent local businessman, and somehow his breathalyzer results mysteriously disappeared. Nothing I did brought her any closure. So I understand all too well the need for justice."

"What was her name?" I ask, remembering her cheerful smile from the pictures. His unwavering devotion.

"Sylvia. Her name was Sylvia." He looks down, emotions warring over his face before he gulps the rest of his sweet tea. I look away, giving him privacy. After a moment, he clears his throat. "Right. Well, like I said, I'm going to focus on footage from nearby cameras, and hopefully, something will turn up. I'll also see if I can rely on my sources to get some clarity on your father's financial dealings. If he's in debt for gambling, like you say, then I'd bet my hat there's something in his finances that will shed more light on what happened."

"Is there anything I can do to help?" Not that he would ever give me access to his bank statements. I'm pretty sure if I showed up to his house, he or Elizabeth would slam the door in my face... or worse.

"I'm afraid not. But if you can talk to Devin again, I think he'll be the one to crack first out of everyone. He was nervous, you said?" At my nod, he continues, "Then I would keep up the pressure. It would be worth it to have another conversation with him."

"I'm not sure when I'll get the chance..." My voice trails off as I remember O'Connor's insistence that I attend the charity gala with him. "Actually, there's an event in a month or so that I could invite my father to that he may not be able to refuse, and if he attends, then Devin will absolutely be with him. It might be the perfect opportunity to confront him again."

"Perfect. When is the—"

The doorbell interrupts, and Broussard checks his feed on his phone and sighs. "Excuse me. My neighbor has more packages delivered than she knows what to do with. They're always leaving them here instead."

"Sure thing," I say, with a *don't worry about it* gesture.

As he heads to the front door, my thoughts are already shifting to how I'm going to convince O'Connor to invite my father. He was receptive to my half-assed seduction this morning to distract him from what I was really doing this afternoon. Maybe it could work again?

The doorbell goes off again.

Kissing him hadn't meant anything. The only thing I'd felt had been disgust.

The lie sits in my thoughts for a second, just long enough for me to feel how disingenuous it seems—before I hear the gunshots.

I'm on my feet and running toward the sound before I think twice. Over the sound of my flats slapping against the floor, there's the glaring lack of any other noises—no screams, no moans, nothing. *Please be okay. Please be okay. Please be okay.* I can't do this again.

The front door is open, and Mr. Broussard's body is sprawled half in, half out of the threshold. A pool of blood spreads underneath him. Before I fall to my knees beside him, I fist a doily from one of the side tables and press it into the blood seeping from his shoulder.

Retrieving my phone with my free hand, I somehow manage to call for an ambulance, whispering reassurances to Mr. Broussard.

My brain goes fuzzy and white for a minute, or maybe longer than a minute. Nearby, an older couple spills out of an identical cottage. Someone is screaming, shouting, but all I can take in is the blood. Instead of Mr. Broussard's body, I see my mother's. Instead of the sidewalk, I see the grand staircase of our former home, where I found her the night she died.

By the time the nightmare releases me from its grip, bystanders hover, phones pressed to their ears or cameras poised to photograph the morbid tableau. I stare numbly at nothing for so long that an ambulance and several police cars materialize seemingly out of nowhere, right in front of me.

The paramedics take Mr. Broussard, and I push to my feet, still clutching the bloody doily, as I experience everything through a layer of cotton. It's not until someone shakes me, hard, that I focus on the person in front of me.

My brows furrow when I recognize Reggie, Yasmine's brother. Dressed in jeans and a button-down shirt, he has his badge and gun strapped to his waist.

Nick Donovan, captain of the New Orleans Police Department Homicide Unit, strides toward us. *What is he doing here?* I think dully. Did Reggie hear my name and call in the cavalry? That's absolutely something he would do. They shuffle me to a sedan with darkened windows, and Reggie shoves me inside before climbing in after me.

"Catriona!" Reggie says, one hand cupping my cheek. "Are you hurt? What happened? C'mon, sweetheart, you've got to talk to me. Donovan," he shouts through a crack in the window. "Get a medic here for her. I think she's in shock. Can you hear me, Ri? C'mon, girl, say something."

Time telescopes around me. I'm here, and I'm not here. Someone is begging to go to the hospital. To follow the ambulance and Mr. Broussard, and once Nick and Reggie finally agree, I realize that the person begging was me.

"What were you doing here, Ri?" Reggie demands, his deep baritone comforting in its familiarity. "Can you tell me anything about what was going on? Give me a clue here. Did you see anything that happened? When I heard your name at the station, you nearly gave me a heart attack."

Crossing my arms over my chest, I try to remember the cover story I'd come up with at the first meeting with Mr.

Broussard, but the truth spills out instead. "He's a private investigator. He's been helping me look into my mother's death. We were having some tea when the doorbell rang. He thought it was from"—I swallow hard, then push the panic from my mind—"a deliv-delivery. The next thing I heard was the gunshots. I found him in the doorway. I don't know anything else, I swear."

He curses fiercely. "Jesus Christ. You got so fucking lucky. They could have hurt you, too." There's a pause before he continues, "I can't believe you didn't come to me. I would have helped you. Does Yas know about this?"

I shake my head. "Not everything. But she knows I'm looking into it. I couldn't drag you into it, too. It was a long shot, anyway. I guess it's a good thing I didn't, in retrospect. I mean, look what happened to Mr. Broussard?" My voice cracks by the end. "I couldn't live with myself if something happened to you or Yasmine."

"Goddammit, Ri. I care about you. I don't give a fuck about the department—sorry, Cap—"

Nick waves him away.

"I would have helped you. Yasmine mentioned you were torn up over your mom, but she never said you thought someone killed her. Christ, Catriona." He scrubs a hand over his close-cropped hair. "You're practically walking into bullets for fuck's sake. Yasmine is going to kill me, bring me back to life, and then kill me again when she finds out what happened."

"It's okay, Reg. I'm fine. I promise. I'm just worried about Mr. Broussard. This is all my fault. Are we close to the hospital?"

"We're almost there," Nick says with a no-nonsense

voice. "Did you get a look at the person who rang the doorbell?"

I catch Nick's gaze in the rearview mirror and try to school my expression despite the panic. As a former behavioral analyst with the FBI, he's the kind of man who I swear can sometimes read what you're thinking just by looking at your face, as evidenced by his direct, penetrating stare. They used to call him the human lie detector because until the year he left the FBI, he was never wrong.

And the one time he was, it resulted in his leaving the FBI altogether.

"I was in his office. I didn't see anything."

I let out a breath when we pull into the hospital parking lot, and he has to look away. Reggie bustles me up to the floor where they brought Mr. Broussard, and I let him tuck me into a waiting room while they attempt surgery to repair the damage. Because I'm not family, I'm not privy to any more information than that. Reggie tries to get me to leave, but I won't budge, and he won't tell me anything more than they're still processing the scene.

"I knew something was going on when you wouldn't answer my text messages."

I glance up at the familiar voice, and my face crumples at the sight of Yasmine standing in the doorway of the waiting room, her familiarity a balm. She drops to her knees in front of me when I dissolve into tears for the first time in... I can't remember how long.

"Shh," she says, and I suck in a desperate breath, breathing in her familiar scent of vanilla from her favorite perfume laced with traces of antiseptic and mint.

"When Reggie called me, I knew it was you. I nearly had

a heart attack. You're not ever allowed to do that to me again," she says into my hair.

"He's a little tattletale. Always has been."

"I'll make sure to tell him you said so."

When I finally suck back the tears, I give a watery laugh. "I'm sorry. I know you're probably busy."

Yasmine takes the empty seat next to me, and I don't resist when she arranges me until my head rests in her lap. "Shut up."

I do, letting myself relax completely as she runs her hands through my hair. Time passes, I'm not sure how much, and I drift in and out of reality, reliving the moment I heard the gunshot over and over and over again, like I do when I'm caught in memories of my mother. God, I hope he's okay. I don't know if I can handle losing someone else.

"I know you've been keeping things from me," she says after a while and cuts me off before I can object. "Don't try to deny it. You're a shit liar. I've known you were up to something since you came back the night after the Halloween party, looking like you'd been through the wringer. You're going to tell me what's going on, and it better be the truth."

"What would you say if I told you O'Connor isn't just a billionaire businessman?" I swallow hard. "What if I told you he's something much worse?"

"I'd ask if you need me to help you disappear. I'm sure we can hustle you up a fake ID or something. I've seen enough movies to figure it out."

My responding chuckle is watery. "He'd find me."

"Seriously," she says, tugging at my arm until I roll over to face her. "Do I need to worry about him? You can tell me."

I press a hand to my tired eyes. "No, I can handle him.

But I didn't want to involve you any more than I already had. His life is dangerous. Really dangerous. And you're the most important person in the world to me. It wouldn't have been fair of me to drag you into it."

"You're going to need to explain to me what you mean by really dangerous," she says gravely.

"Not here, but maybe when you come over for that girls' night? We can do it at your place if you'd be more comfortable there."

"No, I'd rather go to yours. I don't want my parents or Reggie eavesdropping."

"I—" Then I hear the raised voices in the hallway, and I sit up, trying to discern what they're saying.

One of the voices I'd recognize anywhere.

"Where. The. Fuck. Is. My. Wife."

O'Connor is here.

CHAPTER 17

AIDEN

As soon as I know she's unharmed, I'm going to strangle her.

Advisor, my ass.

The little manipulative liar. If I weren't so worried I'll find her in one of these hospital beds, I'd be tempted to bend her over my knee again.

"Where. The. Fuck. Is. My. Wife."

The nurse in front of me goes bone white, and I inhale deeply through my nose so I don't cause an even bigger scene in the middle of the hospital.

"Please," I add through gritted teeth, for good measure.

"Like I said before, Mr. O'Connor. Your wife isn't a patient here, so I can't help you."

I strive for patience, which is usually a quality I possess in multitudes, but seems to have evaporated from my arsenal completely. "She was brought in with a shooting victim. Where is the waiting room? I'll look for her myself."

"You can stop causing a scene. I'm right here."

The sound of her voice is enough to transform my ire to relief. Turning, I find her standing in a doorway several meters away, next to a tall Black woman in scrubs, who is studying me with shrewd brown eyes behind gold-framed glasses. She looks familiar, but I'm so focused on Catriona, I can't place her.

Before I can say anything, Catriona continues, "What are you doing here? How did you find me?"

I certainly can't tell her the truth—that I'd followed her from school and watched outside the cottage. That I'd waited, debated with myself for precious moments about giving up my cover to break into the house and demand the truth. But if I'd gone to her, she would have been even more defensive than she is now. I'd known she was stubborn, but living with her these past few weeks has shown me she has an iron core that bends for no one. Especially not me.

"I got ahold of him," Detective Baptiste says from behind me.

"Reggie?" the doctor by Catriona says, giving me the impression they're familiar. Now that I see him next to her, they favor each other. Cousins? Siblings? "Why would you do that?"

"How would you even know him?" Catriona says at the same time.

Baptiste and I share a glance. I clear my throat to answer. "He was involved in the investigation of the disappearance of a police officer last year." I meet Catriona's accusatory gaze. "Officer Dupont."

"Dufresne," Baptiste corrects, flicking an unimpressed glance my way. He'd put up an admirable fight trying to fit the pieces of that particular puzzle together, but I wouldn't be where I am if I were stupid enough to get caught.

"Care to tell me what's going on, pet?"

The doctor wrinkles her nose and scoffs, "Pet? Is he for real?"

My focus is only on my wife despite the two looking on with twin expressions of interest. She's not hurt, but she's covered in blood. Hands and face are clean, but it's soaked into her jeans and her pretty pink top. I can't help but think it's a physical manifestation of being married to me. This is what life will be like for her when she's linked to me, always.

The woman turns until she's standing between us and puts her hands on Catriona's shoulders. "Are you sure you're okay? Redmond would understand if I needed some time."

But Catriona is already shaking her head. "I'm fine. Not a scratch. Besides, you don't want to get behind."

She pulls Catriona into a bone-crushing hug. "Don't ever scare me like that again."

"No promises."

"Don't think this means you're going to get out of movie night tomorrow."

"I wouldn't dream of it."

Detective Baptiste's gaze drills into my back as I collect Catriona under an arm and guide her to the elevator. The moment the doors close behind us, she shoves me away.

"You can quit the concerned act now. No one's watching." Her words are sharp, but she can't meet my eye.

"You've been keeping something from me. Was that your friend? The one you text that night."

"Yasmine, yes." She huffs out a laugh and crosses her arms over her chest. All I can see is the blood speckling her chest, her throat. The places where she'd missed cleaning, probably during a hasty trip to a bathroom with bad lighting. "Don't act like you don't keep things from me. Please. This isn't a real relationship, unless you've forgotten. I'm not obligated to tell you everything about my life."

"You are if it puts your life in danger. You're forgetting I need you." Her eyes fly to mine. "That's right. Did you need me to admit it to believe me? If you get yourself killed, my whole plan falls apart. So unfortunately, we're stuck with each other. I hope you can remember that next time you try to lie to me."

Her smile is cold. "I didn't get myself killed. I'm fine. And what I'm doing isn't any of your business."

"The man you were with, your *advisor*," I sneer the last word. "I bet he knows what you're keeping from me. Maybe I'll come back and ask him. If he survives his surgery. Two bullet wounds to the chest are going to mean a bitch of a recovery."

The elevator opens with a cheerful *ding*, and several people wait for us to disembark. Witnesses promptly put an end to our conversation. We're lucky there aren't more photo-happy journalists, but considering how fast the media jumped on the last story about us, I don't think it'll be long before this one makes its rounds.

I guide her with a claiming hand on her lower back through the labyrinthine hallways from the lobby to the emergency room parking lot, where I parked my SUV to sweat bullets and wait for someone to call me. I'd hoped it would have been her, but of course it wasn't.

"I can't believe you know Reggie," she finally says, breaking the silence as I pull out of the hospital and into traffic.

"Yasmine's brother?" I guess out loud.

"Yes, so if you ever do something to him—"

"Settle, *bhean chéile*, I'm not going to do anything to him."

She pushes both hands through her hair. "Forgive me if I take that with a grain of salt, coming from you."

Silence fills the car, and I let her stew in anticipation of what I'm going to say. Maybe it'll be half as stressful as it had been to hear those gunshots and—for a split second—think they had been meant for her. I'd been out of my car and halfway down the street before I realized I couldn't say a damn thing without giving myself away.

I'd caught sight of the shooter slipping into a nondescript black SUV. As much as I wanted to stay with Catriona, make certain she was okay, my priority was finding the fucker who put her in danger, and having his head for decoration. They managed to lose me in traffic, and I was contemplating calling in every marker owed to me to track them down when Baptiste called to inform me that Catriona was at the hospital. When I heard hospital, my heart stopped. For a moment, I thought she'd been hurt. And then I realized he was saying she was fine and he'd taken her to see the victim.

The oppressive silence follows us from the car to the estate. Every sound seems amplified in comparison: the slam of the car doors, her shoes against the marble floors, my heartbeat in my ears.

Time slows and speeds up simultaneously as every worst-case scenario plays on repeat in my head. The choices

I'm about to make... they could have far-reaching conse-quences. But I can't seem to make myself stop. While I trail her, the blood all over her sears itself into my brain. Needing her, wanting her, seems as inevitable as my next breath.

It had only taken nearly losing her for me to admit it to myself.

Catriona stops in the kitchen with the island between us like a shield. "I'm not telling you anything." Her voice is reso-lute and stern. I wonder if she knows how beautiful she looks right now. Fierce. Determined. With fire warming her eyes and blood painting her skin. Hundreds of years ago, she would have been considered a queen.

I school my face. "If you're going to keep secrets, then I want some concessions in our contract." Electricity tingles under my skin as though lightning is about to strike. My body tenses, sensing danger.

She scoffs. "You're renegotiating on me? Why does that not surprise me?" Her nails click on the granite countertops. *Click, click, click.*

"Considering new evidence that's come to light, I think I have new bargaining power."

"What evidence?" She crosses her arms over her chest when she notices me watching her nervous tic.

"You're hiding something from me. I want to know what it is." A bead of sweat rolls down my back, but I keep myself loose and indifferent. I hold up a hand when she starts to object. "Consider how far I'll go to find out your secrets. These concessions could be nothing in comparison."

"To *you*," she mutters under her breath before straight-ening her spine. Fuck, but that shouldn't do anything for me. Her stubbornness. Her courage in the face of a man like me.

"Fine. What do you want? Bear in mind that if you think fucking is on the table, I'll walk out of here."

A taunting smile twists my lips to the side. "Is that where your mind goes, pet? Good to know. However, the only thing I want is for you to move into our room."

"Move," her voice starts at a higher pitch, before she catches herself. "Move into your room?"

"Ours."

She barks out a laugh. "You know I'm hiding something from you, but you're willing to let it go if I move into your room?"

"Our room."

"And if I don't?"

"Then I'll use every weapon in my considerable arsenal to torture the information out of you."

She shuffles back a step. "T-torture it out of me? You're insane."

"I've been tested. I'm legally mentally competent."

"Right."

"If I remember correctly," I say, voice lowering several octaves. "You liked my particular brand of torture. But I have some new tricks that might interest you."

Lips parted, she struggles for words before her tongue darts out to moisten the pink flesh. "You're a sadistic bastard."

"I never claimed otherwise. But if I'm a sadistic bastard, then you're a filthy little liar."

"That's the definition of a power couple," she taunts.

Silence falls again as we standoff over the kitchen island. Her glaring, me patient and watchful. Because I never play a hand when I can't anticipate the outcome.

Huffing out a breath, she says, "Fine. I'll stay in your room."

"And move all your things in there."

"Yes," is bitten out between her teeth. "But I'm going to keep my room in case you piss me off, which I expect will be often. And because I need a place to study without you hovering over me."

"I don't hover."

"You're always hovering."

"You're not here enough to draw conclusions like that."

She leans on her elbows, fluttering her eyelashes. "Aww, that sounds like you're missing me, husband."

For the first time since she moved in, I let my gaze rake over her body. From her pouty lips to her wicked curves. Propped up on the counter as she is, she's practically on display for me. Realizing it a little too late, she straightens with a scowl.

"Don't take this as an invitation," she snaps.

"I wouldn't dare. But why don't you go upstairs and... clean up. You've still got blood on you."

She looks down at the stained shirt and crimson specks all over her arms and chest like she's seeing them for the first time. Her body goes unnaturally rigid, triggering every instinct inside me. I start toward her, then stop, unsure.

"Catriona?"

No answer. Her shoulders jerk with ragged inhales.

"Catriona?" I round the island, but she doesn't seem to realize I'm there. It reminds me of the night we had dinner with her father and sister to organize the wedding. When we'd gone to the study after and she'd turned white in her seat—seemingly for no reason—and it was like she was somewhere else in her mind.

Carefully, I turn her to face me, but even though she's looking at me, I don't think she sees me at all. "C'mon, *bhean chéile*. Come back to me."

Nothing.

I bite out rapid curses under my breath as I scoop her up into my arms and take the stairs two at a time. Bursting into our room, I cross blindly to the bathroom, where the shower takes too fucking long to heat. When it's warm enough, I step us both under the spray. She clings to me—and that's how I know something is terribly wrong. She'd never let me hold her like this if she were in her right mind.

Her body quakes, and she's curled into a ball against my chest. I sit heavily on the bench inside the shower, holding her as close as possible. The water helps, I think, but what do I fucking know? I'm used to breaking bodies, not healing them.

The sight of the blood was what seemed to put her in this state, so I grit my teeth and maneuver her shirt up and off her shoulders. She'd probably skewer me if I tried to take off her bra, so I don't. It's not stained anyway. Then I pump a few squirts of soap into my hands and lather it over her skin.

By the time I have all the evidence of this afternoon erased from her, she's breathing a little more easily. My hand keeps going back to her throat to feel the throb of life beneath her skin for reassurance. Her heart beats steadily under my palm. We're both soaked through, but I barely notice. Seeing her react this way is like a knife between the ribs, snaking past the defense of bone to land a direct hit to my soft organs.

She gives a full-body shudder, and then she blinks rapidly, before tilting her head back. Her cheeks flood with color, and I let out a breath. Thank fuck, she's coming back to me.

"There you are," I murmur, resisting the urge to run my hands over her body to make sure she doesn't have any injuries they missed.

"You really will do anything to get me out of my clothes," she says in a voice so low, I can barely hear it over the shower spray.

"One thing about me is, I'll always be an opportunist. Do you think you can stand?"

In answer, she pushes herself to her feet and only sways a little. "I can take it from here. Let me go."

"Don't—" I clear my throat when the word comes out ragged. "You can barely stand."

That mask she wears when she feels vulnerable locks down her emotions. "I can take care of myself. Thanks, but no thanks."

I leave her standing in the shower in her bra and jeans, my slacks and button-up dripping onto the tile, as I move to the attached walk-in closet to strip, dry off, and change into briefs. Leaving my wet clothes on a hook in the bathroom, I keep my eyes averted, no matter how much I want to see what's behind the foggy glass.

Panic attacks.

She has panic attacks.

Brought on by her mother? Violence? Blood? All of the above?

I don't want to know. I shouldn't care. Usually, there's a line I can draw between most other people and me. One that protects them and me from the consequences of my life. But that line? It's getting harder and harder to see when it comes to her.

The water cuts off, and I tense, eyes snapping to the bathroom doorway. From the space underneath, I watch the shadows of her movements and smile wryly to myself. This is what I've been reduced to. Watching my wife underneath the bathroom doors.

A moment later, she appears wrapped in a towel before beating a quick retreat to her walk-in closet. Thankfully, I kept some things there for her in case the time came when she agreed to stay with me. I wince, thinking of the selection of revealing negligees stocked in there. A nicer man would have offered something more comfortable.

Unfortunately for her, I've never claimed to be a nice man.

"What about this movie night tomorrow?" I ask from the bed, where I'm reclining with my hands behind my back. I know if I try to bring up what just happened, she'll deflect and reinforce all those walls that keep her nice and safe.

"What about it?" comes her cautious response. She makes a sound of derision, and I can't help but smile. She must be surveying the offerings in disgust. At least she's not white with shock.

"Your friend Yasmine mentioned movie night tomorrow when we were at the hospital. Did she mean here?"

There's a long silence from the closet. Amusement curls my lips at the thought of her needing privacy after the things I've done to her body. But I'm not going to argue what makes her feel comfortable. She's here, and for now that's enough.

"Do you really care?" comes her voice.

"I wouldn't ask if I didn't."

"It's nothing special. We don't get a lot of time to spend together, so she's going to come over for drinks and whatever to catch up. Maybe take a swim in the pool. I told her about you. Who you are. She basically knew already."

She finally emerges from the closet, and my heart trips over itself. The pink negligee she's wearing consists of barely enough material to be called pajamas. Straps so thin that all it would take is one yank to have them come undone. A slit up the thigh of a short, silky skirt. And *Jaysus* I'll be damned if she's wearing anything underneath.

A masochist is what I am.

Catriona frowns at the bed, then heaves a sigh before lifting the covers to slide in. I try not to stare at where the negligee rides up her thighs. Try not to obsess on how close she is to me, how she smells like honey and lavender all over again.

"I'm not going to do anything to her for knowing. I'll even invite Eamon and Mara over after I take care of a few things. We'll make it a proper party. Frances can make dinner and some appetizers. What's your favorite?"

She's studying me warily, but doesn't say no. "She doesn't have to do that. I was just going to keep it small and probably get takeout or something."

"This is your best friend. I insist."

There's a stiff silence before she says, "Don't pretend you care."

I turn on my side as she clicks off her lamp. The light from mine is the only illumination left in the room. She's on her back, the golden silk of her hair draped over her pillow, arms crossed protectively over her chest. Always so defensive. Ready to attack.

"Eamon will feel left out, and you don't want to get on his bad side."

"Whatever you say. I'm not going to argue against food from Frances. She's the best part about being married to you."

Chuckling, I turn off the lights so she can rest. There are bruises underneath her eyes, and I know that panic attack must have sucked the rest of her energy.

"Good night," I say to the darkness.

"Good night," she says when she thinks I've fallen asleep.

I WAKE BEFORE SHE DOES. I know because she would have leaped off the bed if she woke up to find me plastered to her back, legs tangled, and my hand low on her belly. My cock strains against her ass, hips moving against her as I shake the last remnants of sleep from my brain. When I realize what I'm doing, I still, but it costs me.

All I can think about is the security footage I'd watched the night of our reception. When she'd gone to the bathroom and touched herself. How she'd whispered my name. I know she wants me. I could make her tell me, show me. But it'll be so much sweeter when she comes crawling to me.

Lying there is torture, but the twisted parts of my soul urge me to wait, to see what she'll do when she wakes up and realizes where she is and who's behind her. It doesn't take long. She's an early riser, and the moment the sun is up, so is she.

Her slow, deep breathing cuts off with a gasp, and her body stiffens against mine. I only manage to swallow back a groan as her hips jerk in surprise. This is the best kind of fucking torture.

This is how I wanted to wake up after the night we spent together. With her all sleepy-soft and dazed. If I'd had the time and the luxury, I would have pressed her forward into the mattress on her belly. Pressed kisses into her skin from her neck down between her legs. Made her come with my mouth first and then taken her slowly from behind, fists in the length of her hair.

The soft groan pulls me from my filthy fantasies, and I realize her hips are pressing back against me. My fist tightens against her stomach before I remember myself and relax in increments. Her breath comes faster, her hand coming to clasp over mine. For a second, I think she's going to arch back into me and make herself come from this alone.

But a second later and with a soft curse under her breath, she carefully extracts herself from my grasp and leaves me in the bed.

Alone.

CHAPTER 18

CATRIONA

"I'm not gonna lie, I'd marry a mafia boss, too, in order to have access to this pool again. I've missed it."

A laugh bubbles out before I can stop it. "Yasmine!"

She doesn't even lift her head from the float. "I said what I said. It's a heated pool. After days on my feet, this is my definition of heaven. I don't even care if my hair gets wet, and I have to spend forever on it afterward. This is worth it."

"I still have all your products with me. You can use our shower after if you want."

Yasmine perks up. "Really? Your parents', right? They had a double shower-head. I didn't understand what a slut I was for good plumbing until now. Living with my family is great, but sharing one shower between three generations is getting old."

"What's mine is yours," I say, and let my eyes slip closed again. This is the first time in what feels like a century I've relaxed. As long as I don't think about waking up next to O'Connor, I keep a tenuous hold on this rare sense of peace.

Needless to say, Yasmine had guessed the broad strokes of what O'Connor is involved in. According to her, *"I've read enough smut to know the basics. Mob right?"*

"So how does this work? Being a mafia wife. Is it all blood and drama? If something wild is going to happen, I don't have rounds, and I can crash here." When I pause, she cracks an eye open. "If yesterday was anything like what goes on, then you may need a doctor around."

"Fuck. Don't call me that. But yeah, basically it's been all drama so far." I hesitate, then say, "But are you really sure you're comfortable being here? I'd really understand if you weren't."

"After the things I've seen in the ER, it'll take a lot more than him to shock me. As long as I'm not roped into any illicit activities, I'm fine with it. Nothing, not even the mob, can keep me away from you."

Chuckling, I close my eyes and relax into the bone-melting warmth of the pool. "Your parents don't know anything about this, do they?"

Yasmine snorts. "Of course not. They'd flip. Could you imagine? Reggie is already laying eggs about it. You're lucky he didn't decide to tag along with me. It makes sense now why he was keeping tabs on you after the wedding."

"He was? No, scratch that. Of course he was. You two love being in the center of trouble. I swear, there was a time when my life wasn't so exciting."

"When was that again?"

I splash water at her, and she shrieks and kicks her feet until she's out of my attack radius. "Truce, truce."

Part of me feels guilty about taking a moment to enjoy this. There are so many things I should be doing: finding another clerkship, figuring out who shot Mr. Broussard, smoothing over the media for Dad's campaigns, and studying. But I can't seem to force myself to do any of them. I'm tired of being a crusader—of fighting for the truth when no one else does, of facilitating familial relationships when all I get from them is pain or no reciprocal effort.

Unbidden, the memory of O'Connor showing up at the hospital floats to the forefront of my thoughts. I squash it down and blame the momentary lapse on too many margaritas. The margaritas, of course, were requested by Yasmine to fulfill my lifelong debt from the night of the masquerade. It seems the repercussions from that monumental mistake will follow me forever.

Finally, I'm able to lure Yasmine out of the pool with promises of watching whichever movies she wants. I used O'Connor's bank account to pay for the snacks and went a little overboard: popcorn with every possible topping, little boxes of candy like we're at the movies, and a variety of sodas and mixers. If I'm feeling any guilt, it's hidden behind the satisfaction of bending a small part of O'Connor to my will.

Yasmine makes us more drinks, and then we settle on the sofa. I pass her a giant bowl of popcorn topped with a ton of butter and give her a box of Raisinets. She flips through the TV and picks a movie—one that I haven't seen before. As it starts to play, I sip at my margarita and open a package of peanut M&Ms. A strange feeling radiates through my chest, and it takes far too long for me to realize that it's happiness. God, I didn't know how much I needed this—a minute to breathe, to relax with my best friend, and do something that doesn't require 1,000% of my focus.

"We should do this more often," Yasmine says around a mouthful of popcorn.

"I was just thinking the same thing."

"Twins!" She lifts her drink for me to cheers. God, I love her so much.

This continues through several movies and many more drinks. Scents waft out of the kitchen, where Frances is making dinner. I tried to tell O'Connor it wasn't necessary and that he didn't need to invite his friends, but naturally, he didn't listen to a word I said.

I snort out a laugh at the thought, because even though this marriage is fake, that particular trait fits every definition of a husband I've ever seen. It's not really a problem. Frances's food is the best I've ever had.

We are knee-deep in our second movie when the front door finally opens, and a godawful cacophony fills the air. Yasmine and I both jerk from our lazy positions on the couch to sitting upright.

O'Connor stumbles into our view, carrying a blood-soaked Eamon.

Beside me, Yasmine chokes on popcorn, coughing to clear her lungs and slapping at her chest. "Jesus Christ," she wheezes. "I was joking when I said your life was all blood and drama."

I leap to my feet, and the bowl of popcorn I'd been holding tumbles to the floor, kernels exploding everywhere, but my eyes aren't on the mess. They're on O'Connor. "What the hell?"

"That's what I said," Mara says, coming up behind them.

Yasmine sets her popcorn aside instead of throwing it everywhere and pushes to her feet. She's already pulling up her sleeves and putting on a pair of gold-rimmed glasses as she strides across the room to the two men. "What happened? Knife wound? Gunshot?" She gestures imperiously to O'Connor to put Eamon on the empty dining room table. He complies, trying to hide a smile as I gather pillows from the floor.

"Why do you say that like it's something nefarious?" Eamon grunts. "Maybe it was a cooking mishap."

"You? Cook?" Mara says, lips twisted with disdain.

"If I weren't bleedin' like a stuck pig, I'd be offended," Eamon says.

Yasmine gives them a cool look. "Do you want me to take a look at that, or would you rather snipe some more?"

"Don't worry, love, it's just a bit of craic."

I put the pillows behind him to prop him up as Yasmine goes into doctor mode.

"Crack?"

"Banter," Mara clarifies. Then spotting the makings for margaritas, she makes herself at home mixing a drink. "You want another?" she asks me.

I already have enough tequila swirling around my system; more would be a decidedly terrible decision considering the circumstances. "What happened?"

O'Connor situates himself behind me, and I pretend not to notice. "Nothing you need to worry yourself about, darlin'."

Mara hands him his drink and says, "I wish you both would stop dragging me into these situations."

"What situations?" I ask. My eyes are glued to Yasmine.

She carefully unbuttons Eamon's white shirt. He's reclining against the pillows, lightly assaulting her with a grin, and I realize I don't think I would ever want him to look at me like that. A shiver racks my body.

"What's your name?" he asks her.

"Dr. Baptiste," she answers coolly before leaving for the kitchen, followed by the sound of splashing water.

Oh no. Maybe bringing her here was a mistake. I should've tried harder to keep these two parts of my life separate. The last thing I want to do is pull her any further into the madness. It's exactly why I haven't looped Reggie into my investigations. Yasmine will have to keep secrets from him, and I know if he ever found out the truth about Dufresne, he'd never look at either of us the same again.

I open my mouth to object, but she returns, drying her hands and saying to Eamon, "If you keep looking at me like that, I am going to make this so much worse."

Unfortunately for her, that was the absolute wrong tack to take with him. He opens his mouth to comment, but O'Connor silences him with a look, and Eamon frowns like a kid who just got told he couldn't have another piece of birthday cake.

"It is a gunshot, through and through, to his shoulder. Should just need disinfecting and stitching, but we can handle this." O'Connor's gaze shifts to me, and I cross my arms over my chest even though I'm wearing a light cardigan to ward off the chill, because a shiver goes through me at his attention. "We were closer to here than anywhere else, and I wanted to get this treated with discretion—but we'll leave if that'll make you feel more comfortable."

At this, Eamon protests, but it could've been because

Yasmine stripped more of his shirt, and he's playing for false modesty.

A dull feeling squeezes my chest. "What were you doing that caused you to get shot at?"

The words are out of my mouth before I think about them, drawing O'Connor's gaze down to my lips.

"Does it matter?"

I can feel the three other people in the room watching us, riveted. I should be self-conscious, but all I can focus on is the dread knotting up inside my intestines. "Of course it matters. Weren't you just pitching a fit because someone was shooting at me?"

"Pitching a fit?" Eamon cackles until it's cut off with a groan as Yasmine inspects the wound. She hasn't even touched him yet, and he's being a giant baby. I'm starting to think the psychotic man I thought him to be is only one side of him, and I don't know if that's reassuring or terrifying. "Were you pitching a fit?"

Out of the corner of my eye, I can see Yasmine taking supplies from Mara, who had disappeared into the house. Where she got them from, I don't know—must've been O'Connor's office. I should be the one doing that, helping Yasmine, but I can't seem to make myself move from where my feet are planted. Is this what my future is going to be like? Patching up wounded men in the dining room after God only knows what.

O'Connor ignores him; he hasn't been able to tear his eyes away from me, like he can read the thoughts flitting through my brain. I tighten my arms more securely around my chest and return his stare. He may unnerve me, but there's no way in hell I'm backing down.

"Why should I tell you what I've been up to? Are you going to be a proper wife to me now? Keep all my secrets. You can't have it both ways. Either you're in or you're out. What's it gonna be?"

"Weren't you just railing at me yesterday because I did something without your say-so? Maybe I just want equality?" My breaths are coming in little pants like I've been running a marathon.

We're in our own little bubble, staring each other down, unable to look away. Outside of the bubble, Mara teases Eamon as he fakes pain under Yasmine's care. Their voices are filtered through cotton, and they may as well be miles away.

"You want something. I'm willing to give you whatever you want, but it'll cost you," he says.

"I said no such thing." Haven't I already given him enough?

"I'll make you a deal. I'll tell you where I am and what I'm doing."

"I should have asked for a tracker on you when you insisted I have bodyguards." The words fall out of my thoughts and my mouth before I can stop them. Fuck, I shouldn't have let Yasmine talk me into so many margaritas. I lost track of time and thought I'd be able to sober up before he got home.

His intensity amplifies. Somehow, he's inched closer to me, herded me into a corner of the dining room, blocking Yasmine and the others from my sight, and I let him, body soft as melted wax, pliant for him. *Goddamn margaritas.*

"Let me get this straight. You want all my secrets, but won't tell me yours. Is that what you consider equality?"

"I'm in your bed every night, what more could you possibly want from me?" I ask.

"I want you to wear the rings I gave you."

My eyes drop to my bare hand. I tried to wear the rings in the beginning but stopped out of spite. It seemed like a little thing at the time. A rebellion no one but me would notice. Apparently, I'd been wrong about that. He'd noticed. The sensitive skin at the back of my neck prickles in warning.

"You want me to wear my rings?"

"That's right."

"And you'll tell me what happened?"

He nods and inches closer until our fronts brush. A flash of heat has sweat beading on my hairline, behind my knees. My pussy contracts, and I swallow a gasp. He's too close. It's too soon after this morning. The memory of his hard cock pressed against the crease of my ass is too fresh.

"Go get it, and I'll tell you everything."

Yasmine and Mara are still contending with Eamon—who's putting up a fuss and enjoying all the attention—so I duck under O'Connor's arm and practically fly up the stairs, heart in my throat and pounding in my ears the whole way. This could be the answer to learning more about his boss and what ties they may have to my family. Or information I can use to my advantage in the future. It's too good an opportunity to pass up.

Downstairs, the rings clasped in my sweaty palm, I find Yasmine finishing up the bandage on Eamon's wound. Mara has a near empty margarita in her hand as she sways to music from the movie's end credits, lost in her own world. Eamon is trying everything to ruffle Yasmine's feathers, but he's not making much headway. Nothing can derail Yasmine, not even the full force of his twisted charm.

O'Connor is exactly where I left him, except now his blood-smattered—*don't look at them*—sleeves are rolled up, exposing his tattoos. He's taken off his tie and unbuttoned the top few buttons of his shirt. The death moth at his throat ensnares me. I want to put my mouth on it. Bite the skin. Suck until the whole thing is purple.

My breath catches in my throat, and I fumble with the rings. Before I can shove them on my ring finger, O'Connor slips them from my nerveless grip.

"Let me," he says, his voice a rumble in his chest.

"I—"

But whatever protest I'm going to make dies on my tongue as he slides the gold band and diamond solitaire over my knuckle. They're slightly too big, so it shifts as he brings it up to admire.

"Good night," he calls over his shoulder without looking.

I double blink, then search the vicinity for Yasmine and find her grabbing her stuff. She makes the *call me* gesture, and I nod, unable to form words.

"Good night, lovebirds," Mara calls.

Eamon exaggerates a limp even though his legs are in perfect working order and grumbles behind them. He keeps flicking glances at Yasmine as they all walk out.

"Where were you?" I ask. Emotion swirls in my chest, and I'm not self-aware enough to identify it. Disdain? Dread? Fear? It causes the margaritas, popcorn, and candy to slosh uncomfortably. "What happened?"

"You look like you need a whiskey," is all he says before taking my hand. "C'mere."

He leads me to what used to be my father's study. Not much has changed except there's a distinct curl of smoke in the air. Cigars, maybe? I try not to think about what tying himself to me could mean. Wearing his rings. Sleeping in his bed. God only knows what he'll ask from me next.

Am I willing to risk it all just to know what he's been up to?

I take the glass of whiskey he offers and sip, wincing through the burn.

Yes. Yes, I am.

He sits behind the desk with his own glass, the only light a small lamp on a side table. It glints off his hair as he drinks, watching me.

"Well?" I prompt.

O'Connor seems to have come to a decision. "If you want to know what I've been up to, I've had Eamon tracking down the person who shot your *advisor*. Broussard?"

I nearly choke on my whiskey. He stares over his, the corners of his eyes crinkled with amusement, until I can speak again. "You're what? How—why... *what?*"

"You didn't really think I was going to let you run off without someone watching over you? You should know better by now."

"You followed me?" I rasp, wishing there was something other than whiskey to soothe the burn in my throat. "Who was—"

"One question at a time." A sip of whiskey. "Of course I followed you. You seem to think your little pink suits are made of Kevlar, but they're not. I do what I have to in order to make sure you're safe. And I don't know who he is. At least not yet."

I ignore his comment about keeping me safe. "But you must have some idea. That's who shot Eamon?" The thought makes me drink the rest of my whiskey in one gulp. It burns going down my throat. Probably not a good idea to mix with margaritas, but I can't be sober for this.

I should call Reggie, tell him O'Connor has a lead, but my lips stay glued shut as O'Connor gestures to a chair across from him. "Sit."

I plop down before I can think twice, my limbs heavy and warm. "What are you going to do when you catch him?"

His lip quirks. "I'm going to ask him a few questions."

"Oh, really?" I say sarcastically. Then I pause. Do I really want to know the dirty details? I think of Mr. Broussard in a hospital bed, seeming so frail, hooked up to monitors and wrapped in white sheets. He'd done nothing to deserve this. Whoever had targeted him—us—deserved whatever they had coming to them. Yes, I decide. I do want to know. "You'll tell me what happens. Who it is. Won't you? We did make a deal."

He nods. "Eamon got too close, and this guy's trigger-happy. Running scared. But don't worry, Eamon will find him. Probably by tomorrow."

"Should he be doing that in his condition?"

O'Connor waves this away. "He's been through much worse."

I don't know what to say about that, so I shake my head. "I don't understand. Why would you do this?"

"You're my wife."

"So you're going to hunt this man down and interrogate him?"

"I'll do what I have to do."

"I didn't ask you to do that."

"You didn't have to."

"I didn't want you to interfere."

"You're my wife. Your safety is important to me. So if anyone threatens it, I'll take care of them."

"Are you going to make a habit of fixing my problems like this?"

He tilts his head, his smile sharp as the edge of a knife. "Probably."

CHAPTER 19

AIDEN

The man on the floor in front of me howls in pain, but I let the knife in his ribs dig in a little deeper, savoring the way his body tightens. He doesn't dare jerk away for fear it will cause the knife to sink into his flesh even more. I don't usually resort to blades, but for this, I'm willing to make an exception.

"I promise, I don't know who hired me. He just said to shoot the old man and follow the girl, I swear."

I tap his cheek with my palm, but he barely seems to notice. It doesn't surprise me. After hours of this, he must be growing weak and ignorant of most of the pain he's in. "You know, I'm not sure I believe you. And what am I to tell Mrs. O'Connor about this? How is she supposed to feel safe at home when you nearly killed her, and you're walking around scot-free?"

At this, he devolves into pitiful pleas, fat tears rolling down his grimy face. I sneer at him as I let him go, gravity sinking his body to the floor of the warehouse, and he crumples into a pile of bones at my feet. I'd kick him for good measure, but I don't want to get more blood on my shoes. Messy is more Eamon's forte. The more blood, the better. My methods are more... clinical.

Cian may call me his hound, but I prefer a clean kill. A bullet to the brain. Enjoying it makes me feel too much like Cian, who prefers to draw it out. There's nothing he loves better than watching the life slowly drain out of his victims' eyes. As evidenced by the many, many years he's enjoyed torturing me for the fun of it.

My phone rings. I flick a glance at Eamon, who covers the weeping man's mouth with two hands. Eamon whispers something that makes him go white, but at seeing the name on the screen, I'm already turning away from the gruesome tableau.

"Catriona," I answer, stepping farther away so she can't overhear the man's muffled whimpers. "To what do I owe the pleasure?"

"Where are you? We're supposed to leave for the charity gala in an hour."

"I'm finishing up, and I'll pick you up in twenty minutes. Did you see what I left for you on our bed?"

"I did," she says dryly. "I hope you're ready to go to bat for me against Mara. She was offended when I told her I wasn't wearing what she picked out."

"You let me handle her. I'll see you soon."

"If you aren't here in twenty minutes, I'm leaving without you," she says, then hangs up the phone.

"You're so whipped it makes me sick," Eamon says

without rancor, as he ambles around me with a blade in his hand. He's cleaning it meticulously with a cloth.

"I'll make it even worse if we aren't cleaned up and ready to leave in ten." I shoot off a text to a cleanup crew who will get rid of the body.

Eamon chugs a bottle of water, then wipes his mouth. "I really thought he'd have more information. It was a bitch to track the bastard down. He was damn near to Florida by the time King and I caught up with him. Spent most of his money on a fancy rental car."

King is an American tracker and former hitman I lean on from time to time to chase down leads. His knowledge of the American criminal enterprise is extensive, but he doesn't come cheap. After Catriona came so close to death when Broussard was shot, I hired him to help me find the person who did it. I didn't buy the coincidence. In my life, there are no coincidences.

And it turned out I was right. Someone had hired him to follow Catriona.

Someone else is very interested in whatever secrets she's keeping.

The man Eamon and I have been working over for the past forty-eight hours is a professional. Someone *really* wanted Broussard taken out. The transaction took place online, anonymously, with payments made in untraceable crypto. He never even knew the name of the person who hired him. And after the torture we put him through, anyone would have caved. Hell, if I were at the receiving end of Eamon's knife, I would have caved. But all this sorry sack could say was he was hired to take out the old man and shut the stupid bitch up. Naturally, he had to die for calling her a bitch.

"Nothing we can do about it now. You stay here and meet the cleaners to take care of this, then I'll see you at the gala."

He waves a disgruntled hand, and I leave, my thoughts turning from the dead man and dead-end to tonight. All these weeks of planning and tonight will finally be the culmination of the biggest gamble of my life. Cian will be obliged to grant me a seat at the table, and I have to be prepared for the revenge he metes out for forcing his hand.

When I get to the estate, Catriona is nowhere to be seen. I check my watch and see we have plenty of time to get to the gala before we're considered late. The tux I'm wearing is waiting on a hanger by the front door—*thank you, Mara*— and I change in my study. I have time enough for a drink to settle my nerves, so I pour some whiskey and sip while I wait at the bottom of the stairs, one shoulder to the wall.

Heels click on marble. My head lifts, glass to my lips, whiskey sliding down my throat. Heat warms my chest as my gaze glides up the column of gold satin, the fabric sparkling under the light from the chandelier. Nude heels peek from the hem. The material glides around her legs, so thin I can see every part of her as though she were naked. It could be modest if it weren't for that and the plunging neckline, which makes it very apparent she's not wearing a bra. Whatever magic she's used keeps her covered, but hints that if she shifted just right, I could see every inch of her tits.

Fuck, I'd give no small amount of money to see them. Taste them. It's been so long, I don't even remember what they looked like. The times I'd been with her hadn't been enough to drink my fill.

Throat dry, I drain the rest of my drink and set the glass on a nearby table and move to the bottom step. Her hair is up in a twist off the back of her neck. I want to put my mouth there and kiss her until she squirms. Thin straps that I could rend in a second are all that's keeping her dress from slipping off.

"You look incredible, darlin'," I say, and take her hand to kiss the back.

"What's gotten into you?"

"Can't a man tell his wife she looks good enough to eat?"

"I'd give you indigestion," she says.

"It'd be worth it."

She flicks a look over her shoulder as we move to the front door. I manage to tear myself away from imagining taking a bite out of her ass. "Shouldn't you be focused on tonight?"

"I have a great attention span."

"Well, direct it toward what you need from me, please. I don't want another mess like the reception."

"Whatever you say. The foundation I run puts on galas like this and the masquerade"—at this, she has the grace to blush—"a couple of times a year for a variety of charities and causes. This one is important because Cian will be attending. He likes to come stateside every few months to check on his investments. I'll explain to him what's happened, and he'll be obligated to invite us back to meet the others in the organization."

"How does that all work? Why is it important?"

By now, we're in the back of a limo, rolling through the

streets of New Orleans. It would be so easy to divert to the airport. Take her away somewhere hot and tropical, where she could spend most of the day naked. I wouldn't have to share her with anyone.

"Traditionally, when a member of the organization with no other family marries, it spins off their own clan. So for me, that would be Clan O'Connor."

"What about your... um, father? Didn't he—I mean, wasn't—"

"Yes, we used to have Clan O'Connor before his death. Several families currently make up our organization: the Lynches, Carrolls, Moores, Kellys, Burnses, Clearys, Murphys, and O'Briens. There used to be more—many more —including the O'Connors. But after Cian took power, he was ruthless about cutting out those he thought weren't loyal, starting with my father."

She sucks in a breath. "So you marrying means you're breaking from his Clan and starting your own?"

"To put it simply. When Cian killed my father, anyone who was of Clan O'Connor was absorbed into Clan Lynch. Eamon is a Murphy, and he has a younger brother with a family, so they maintain his Clan, though it's mostly for looks at this point. Eamon refuses to take his place and draw Cian's attention."

"Great, so we're walking into the lion's den. I hope you have a plan."

"To a very dangerous lion. I need you to stick close to me tonight. Don't go wandering off." Before she can object, I raise a hand. "You can galavant all you want on any other night, but not tonight. I need to focus, and I won't be able to do that if—if I'm chasing you down."

"I'll stay in your sight at all times. I promise. Thank you for, um, inviting my family at my request. I'm hoping we'll be able to mend fences." She's looking out of the window at the lights speeding by.

"Anything you need, I'll give it to you."

She directs an amused smile my way. "I highly doubt that."

All too soon, the limo pulls up to the Emerald Isle, where a red carpet leads to the central entrance. A small contingent of photographers lines either side, lights flashing. "Last chance to turn back."

"I thought O'Connors didn't walk away from a challenge?" she teases, then opens the door, extends a shapely leg and folds herself out of the limo before I can help her. I'm too stunned by her including herself as an O'Connor to do more than gape like a fish.

We manage the gauntlet, posing for pictures, and Catriona plays her part to perfection. She curls against me with a hand on my chest and the other around my waist. If I didn't know any better, I'd say she was born for this.

The Emerald Isle is part luxury resort, part riverboat casino. The casino itself is in a 30,000-square-foot steamboat on the pier behind the resort. It's not like me to want to impress people. I normally rely on intimidation to do my introductions, but I find myself studying Catriona's face for her reaction.

I'm not disappointed. She observes her surroundings, her mouth falling open on a gasp. Pleased, I guide her through the main floor, evading several patrons along the way, to bring her to the elaborate ballroom in the hotel where the event is taking place. It's already packed with people, who all turn in a wave the moment we walk into the room.

Catriona presses closer to my side; the only betrayal of her emotions is the way her grip tightens on my arm. I loop an arm around her wrist and guide her through the crowd to our table. Mara and Eamon are already seated. I lock eyes with Eamon, and he gives a nod, confirming the body has been taken care of.

"I tried to tell him to put you in pink, like we agreed, but he wouldn't hear a word about it," Mara says, gesturing with her glass toward Catriona.

"He doesn't listen very well," Catriona says, nodding at the server for a glass of wine.

"It reminded me of your dress from the masquerade."

If I weren't paying such close attention, I would have missed the way her breath catches at my admission.

"Are you going to tell me what you were up to before you got home?" Catriona angles to me and lowers her voice.

"If that's what you want."

Her gaze sharpens. "Yes, it's what I want."

"Eamon tracked down the man who shot your adviser, Broussard."

"Wily bastard," Eamon interjects with a scowl. "Complete pain in my arse."

Catriona jerks. "What? You did? Who was it?"

"You sure you want to get involved with these two, sweetheart? Once you do, it's a slippery slope. Soon you'll be the one with blood on your hands." Mara must have been at the bar for a while now. Her eyes are bright, and her cheeks are stained red. We ignore her.

"A gun for hire. Not connected that my contacts can tell. Someone hired him to take out Broussard and follow you."

"Did he say who it was?" Catriona asks.

She's leaning so close to me, I can see down the top of her dress practically to her naval. My cock thickens, both at the sight and her nearness. Sleeping next to her has been a lesson in torture the likes of which leaves me aching and desperate every morning.

"The transaction was online, anonymous."

"So a dead-end?" she huffs and slumps back into her seat.

I already miss the sight of her sweet tits. Lamenting, I gesture to a server for a beer, needing something to wet my dry throat.

"Potentially. An associate of ours will dig deeper. He's got a fair hand at computers. If anyone can find a connection, it would be him. Speaking of Broussard, how is he?"

"Glad to be out of the hospital, finally. I'm going to go see him tomorrow, actually. Check on how he's doing. And yes, before you ask, Ren and Stimpy can follow me."

I assume that means Bren and Tadhg, and I'm pleased she's not going to fight me on them. Fuck knows I feel better knowing where she is. If something were to happen and she were to be taken—

"He's here," Eamon interrupts.

"Stick close to Bren and Tadhg until I'm done speaking with him." I press closer under the guise of pressing a kiss to her temple. "If I find you have to sneak off again, at least take them with you, yeah?"

But my teasing doesn't wash away the tension in her eyes, and I feel her watching me as I leave her. There's nothing I can do about it. Cian pauses at the entrance to the ballroom on the highest step, where he can lord over everyone below him. Even though most people here in the States have no idea who he is, they still part to give him a wide berth. Can they sense the insidious darkness inside him?

You wouldn't know it from the outside, like most monsters, because Cian is a good-looking man in his sixties with a trim beard and all his hair. He takes care of his body and dresses in expensive suits. You'd never guess he could kill a dozen men with his bare hands without losing his appetite for dinner.

He rocks back on his heels when he sees me coming toward him. Two men flank him in matching dark tuxedos, the bulge of weapons protruding from their sides.

"Aiden, there you are. It's been too long."

"Cian."

"Let's go to your office, shall we." It wasn't a question.

I seek out Eamon from across the room, and he gives me a nod. But it does nothing to assuage the dread writhing in my stomach.

Cian, the two men, and I ride the elevator to the top of the casino, where my office has a fishbowl view of the whole building thanks to the walls of windows and its central location. Has it really only been six months since he was here, demanding I reap a pound of flesh from Senator Gallagher? It feels like a century.

The two men take up perches on either side of the door as I lead Cian inside and make him a drink to keep my hands busy.

"I've heard you have some news for me," he says, as he accepts the drink.

"I do." Does he already know? Sweat pops out on my neck.

He gestures for me to go on.

"Senator Gallagher was able to come up with the money."

"Really? And how did he manage to do that?" Cian drawls.

"He used his daughter's inheritance."

"Of course he did," he says with a snort.

"There's more."

"Well, spit it out."

"It was with the requirement that I marry his daughter first."

The door to my office opens, startling me from my carefully planned explanation. Four familiar men stride inside, and that's how I know my carefully laid plans have gone to shit.

CATRIONA

"Shouldn't you go with him?" I spin to Mara and Eamon and send them an accusatory glance.

"He doesn't need a babysitter," Eamon says, as though this is the most ridiculous thing he's ever heard.

"We'd only make it worse." Mara's pinching brows and her inability to look away from the doorway where O'Connor disappeared belie her words.

"You're making *me* feel worse," I grumble into my glass, frowning when I find it empty.

"Aiden knows how to handle Cian Lynch. You're better off keeping away until it all settles down." Eamon scoots over to Aiden's vacated seat and wraps an arm around my shoulders. The caramel and coffee scent that seems to follow him everywhere envelops me. "Don't worry, love. We'll keep you company."

"Fantastic," I murmur, scanning the faces around me for my family—and Devin Franklin.

Father could never turn down a good opportunity to schmooze and the crème de la crème of society is out en force. But it's always possible his disdain for me will outweigh his desire to network. Maybe I put too much faith in his insatiable greed.

"Looking for someone?" Mara asks with an all-too-knowing smirk.

"My father. You haven't seen him around, have you?" I figure it wouldn't hurt to have more than one person looking out for him. Wherever he is, Devin is sure to be.

"Ugh, pass. I'm going to go find a drink." In a swirl of perfume, Mara gives us her back and strides away.

"Charming woman," Eamon says fondly at her retreating figure. Then he turns to me. "Tell me about that best friend of yours. Is she coming tonight?"

I slide him a glance, distracted from my frenetic searching. "Nooo," I say, drawing out the word, then lowering my voice. "Why do you want to know? Is your wound still hurting you?"

"Is she always so prickly?" he asks, avoiding my question. He tosses his hair back, but there's no denying the way he focuses on me, waiting for my response.

He's not... interested in her. Is he? My eyes bulge. "Yasmine? She's not prickly. She's very direct, especially when she's working. Don't get any kind of ideas. She'd chew you up and spit you out."

He rubs a thumb over his lips, and I can't tell if that horrifies or entices him. "Pity she's not here. Playing with her would keep me out of trouble."

"What sort of trouble?" But he's already pushing to his feet and striding away. I blow out a breath. O'Connor's friends are the worst.

I don't want to sit at the table all by myself so I lurch to my feet, the hulking bodies of Bren and Tadhg following at a respectable distance. I barely even notice them anymore. Oh no, I'm starting to get used to having them as my shadows. The weight of the ring on my finger hardly even bothers me now. I sleep like a goddamn baby in his bed.

This wasn't how it was supposed to go, but I can't think about that right now. I have to keep focused. I have a mission tonight, and it's not to worry about O'Connor or his psycho friends.

"You certainly look the part," says a voice that has me stopping in my tracks. My shadows do the same a few feet away.

Elizabeth rounds a column with a glass in her hand. I almost laugh at myself that my first thought is that she's too young to drink. Father has given her a glass of wine with dinner for the past decade. The older sister impulses are getting old. She's never cared for my consideration, so why is the urge always there, just underneath the surface?

"Bethie." I haven't called her that since we were kids. We're in the center of the room. The last thing I want to do after the mess of our last public outing is make a scene, and she seems primed to throw down. "I'm glad you're here. Can we talk?"

"Why would I want to talk to you? You humiliated me in front of everyone."

"That wasn't my intention."

But she doesn't seem to hear me. "Do you even care? Did

you ask me about what I wanted or let me know about your plans?" I open my mouth, but she keeps going. "No, of course not. You never do. You always assume you know best. That you can do no wrong. I bet you've barely thought of me since you married him, have you?"

"That's not fair," I say in a low voice, hoping the music and conversation is enough to drown her out. "I wanted to call, but I knew you were upset with me. I was giving you time to cool down."

Still, it's like what I'm saying doesn't register to her because she's talking over me. "It's always what you want. You never stop to think or ask me how I feel. It's like you still think I'm six years old and in need of protecting. God, do you know how selfish that is? I'm an adult, I make my own decisions. Decisions that have nothing to do with you."

Each word is like a lash and I take them, fists knotted at my side, feet glued to the floor. I deserve this for going behind her back. Marrying O'Connor and for being there the night Mom died. I let her spew her venom and don't say a word.

"A'right, that's enough," Tadhg says, and grips me by the arm. "Mrs. O'Connor is needed elsewhere."

Elizabeth's protests follow, but I barely hear them. Tadhg pulls me from the crowd and deposits me near the bar. "Thanks," I say, tilting my head up to his face. He's the older of the two, with a bushy dark red beard and close-shaved head. "Maybe you guys aren't so bad to have around."

Tadhg grunts. Which I suppose in bodyguard-speak is his way of showing gratitude.

"I have three sisters myself. That could have been way worse." Bren is younger, and of all the men I've met from

O'Connor's organization, he's been my favorite so far. Doesn't seem as hardened or dangerous as the rest. If I weren't so pissed off about being followed all the time, I might consider him like a younger brother.

Blowing out a breath, I claw my emotions back into place. I don't have the time or the luxury to indulge in a world-class breakdown right now. I can do that after I find and interrogate Devin. After I know O'Connor is safe. After I learn the truth about my mother.

"Thanks for having my back, guys."

Bren smiles, and Tadhg crosses his arms, which I take to mean he's my eternal servant. Most of the guests, here for whatever charity The O'Connor Foundation supports, have finished their sit-down meal and are now mingling and dancing in the center of the room. If Elizabeth is here, that means Father can't be far behind, and wherever he goes, Devin goes. This may be my only chance to interrogate him again.

As though in answer to my prayers, a swarm of people surges to the front doors, and there they are. Senator Gallagher and his entourage. Devin Franklin takes up the rear. I study them from across the distance, wondering if they really have the capacity to murder someone in cold blood. Devin has been with my father for as long as I can remember. Former Secret Service, he was hired the moment my father took office to make Senator Gallagher feel safe, when in reality, I think he wanted to feel important. Or maybe there were legitimate threats to his life I never consid-ered. After all, I had no idea he had a gambling problem or that he was mixed up with organized crime.

"Alright, gentlemen," I say, turning to my ever-present

shadows. "There's something I need to do, and you can either come with me, or I'll do it without your help. Which will it be?"

Tadhg jerks his chin. "Franklin already knows you're here. If you want, I'll follow him and keep him company so you can have your conversation."

"I—" That wasn't what I was expecting. "I—yes, that would be great. Thank you."

Bren squeezes my shoulder. "We're a lot more helpful when you're not trying to run away."

Mirth bubbles up. "Right."

"I'll stay with her. Shoot me a message when you've got him," Bren says to Tadhg.

Between one heartbeat and the next, Tadhg disappears into the crowd. Bren holds out an arm to escort me around the room as we wait.

"I didn't expect that you'd help me," I admit.

"It's easier to keep watch of you this way. Otherwise, you could get yourself into real trouble, and then O'Connor would really have our hides." It doesn't take long for Bren's watch to ping with a notification. "By the elevator. Tadhg will follow him up, and then we can follow."

At his words, I cast an eye around to find Devin. There— right by the elevators with Tadhg at his back, just like he said. Devin glances around, hands in his pockets. The elevators glide open and he steps inside.

I must start moving toward him, because Bren lays a hand on my shoulder. "Wait. He's not going anywhere. We don't want to draw too much attention. Tadhg will keep him for us."

Impatience sizzles beneath my skin. I'm so close. All I

need is for Devin to break his composure. Just once. For him to give me something I can use to nail him to the wall.

After an eternity passes where I don't look away from the elevator or breathe, Bren shoots me a wide-mouthed grin. "Let's go."

Oxygen surges back into my lungs as he tugs me across the room. Luckily, no one stops us along the way. I force myself to calm, to slow my heart rate. This may be my last chance to get Devin alone. I can't waste it.

A bell dings with each floor. First. Second. And then it stops at the third. The doors glide open, and there's Tadhg with Devin in a headlock. My nerves disappear, and I hide a smile. A good lawyer, someone who respects the law, should hate the use of violence against another person. But as a woman who has spent so many years under the thumb of men, it's satisfying to have one at my mercy instead.

I shoot a glance around me, but the hallway is empty. We could find a room, but I don't want to linger, and I'm too eager to get answers to wait.

Devin tries to laugh, but it comes out more like he's choking against Tadhg's muscular bicep. "Mrs. O'Connor." He struggles, and Tadhg tightens his arm around Devin's throat until I gesture for him to stop. The rush of power is so heady, I shake my head to hear his next words. "I should have known you'd stoop to sending your stooges after me. Is O'Connor rubbing off on you already?"

I lift my chin. "You've been lying to me about what happened the night my mother died. You sabotaged your car for an alibi. I want to know why."

"As I told you—and the police when they interviewed me—I have nothing to hide and I had nothing to do with your mother's death." He struggles against Tadhg's hold, but Tadhg doesn't let him move an inch. "Do I need to have your father speak to you about this? I'm sure he'd be interested in knowing you think I was involved. He did say you were struggling. It's understandable after what you've been through. Especially considering the circumstances surrounding your mother's death. I know these things are hell on your mental health."

A wave of black hatred roils inside me. Even though Tadhg and Bren are a threatening presence, Devin isn't swayed. Why did I think he'd crack so easily? Wishful thinking? He's hiding something. I knew it. "What are you covering up? All I want is the truth."

"You're wasting your time with me, you stupid bitch. You'd better run along to school and keep your nose out of places where it doesn't belong."

"Enough," the normally cheerful Bren snarls. He shoves me behind him and I stumble until I'm leaning against the wall next to the elevators. "You have a chance to tell her what she wants to know. You'll have one more because we're feeling benevolent. Tell her, or we'll make you tell her."

"You'll regret it if you do," Devin says, his face hardening. It sticks in my brain for reasons I don't quite understand, not with adrenaline crashing through my system. He locks eyes with me. "You think you're so smart, but you've got all this completely wrong. Your father was right. You're nothing but a pathetic little slu—"

Before he can finish the word, Bren's fist is driving into Devin's face with a sickening crunch. I jolt against the wall at the violence, but a part of me, as sick and twisted as the man I'm married to, delights in it. So I don't ask Bren to stop.

When Devin's face is bloody and mangled, Tadhg nods to Bren, who finally halts.

"Tell her what she wants to know," Tadhg orders calmly.

Devin must realize Bren isn't going to stop, whereas there are lines I can't—or won't—cross. He looks at me like I'm going to save him, but I tilt my head as I wait for his answer. I may be unwilling to kill to get what I want, but I care more about justice for my mother than I do about whatever morals remain when I take murder off the table.

Maybe he's right.

Maybe O'Connor is rubbing off on me.

I sigh when Devin clamps his mouth shut. Bren looks at me, one eyebrow quirked, and I shrug. He lays into Devin again, erasing whatever protests he must have had. It should make me sick. The most violence I've witnessed has been at the hands of my father. But as I watch Bren drive his fist into Devin's face over and over again, all I feel is gratification. I know he had something to do with her death. If he won't give me answers, then I'll take whatever I can get. Even if it's this.

Finally, Devin makes a sound of surrender, and Bren backs off, his chest heaving from the exertion. Pulling a handkerchief from his pocket, he begins to lazily wipe the blood away from his knuckles. Devin is a mess. Blood streaks most of his face, his lips look like ground meat, and he probably has a broken nose, loose teeth, or worse. I can't find it in me to feel sorry. Has this ruthless person always been inside it, and did my mother's death and O'Connor's influence bring it out?

"Tell me what I want to know, Devin. This is your last chance."

Blood bubbles from his mouth as he speaks. "You don't understand. He'll kill me if I say a word."

My thoughts scramble, and my knees go so weak that I have to hold the wall to stay upright. "Who will kill you? Who are you afraid of? My father? Did he have something to do with my mother's death?"

His lips press together to form the words, and my head goes so light I legitimately worry I may pass out. "Y—"

But he's interrupted at the worst possible time by the elevator opening.

Frantic, I gesture to Tadhg to deal with Devin as Bren and I whirl around to see who is inside. Grunts and shuffling sounds are at my back as O'Connor appears. As though he can sense me, he lifts his head, and our eyes lock.

Fuck.

He hesitates and then seems to resign himself to a course of crossing the short distance to me. Bren tenses at my side, but O'Connor only has eyes for me. "You can help Tadhg with whatever mess she's dragged you into. I have her now."

"Yes, sir," Bren says before sending me a glance full of concern.

"I—"

"Cian's ready to meet you," is all he has to say to get me to shut up.

"Now?" I choke out.

Instead of answering, he tugs me into the elevator. The short ride is quiet and tense. He takes my hand in his when we reach the first floor, and then it's a quick walk to the attached casino and another short elevator ride up to what must be his office.

I thought I was prepared for this.

But as I follow O'Connor's tense frame, the pit in the bottom of my stomach tells me nothing could have prepared me for this.

"What does he want?" I'd tell myself it's not a whimper, but I'd be lying. The monster I've built up in my head from everything I've learned about the man is larger than life. Thoughts of Devin and my mother are drowned out by sheer terror.

I want to cower behind O'Connor, but I force myself to straighten, throwing my shoulders back. My survival hinges on backing O'Connor's play 100 percent, and a lifetime spent as Rory Gallagher's perfect daughter may finally be useful.

"Nothing good, I can promise you that." We pause at a door. He lifts a hand like he's going to cup my cheek, then it drops to his side. "Whatever happens, follow my lead. But keep your mouth shut."

CHAPTER 21

AIDEN

Cian waits in my office, but he's not alone. Four familiar faces now surround his spot behind my desk. He pauses in lifting a tall glass of water to his lips, drinks, then wipes his mouth and places the glass down. "There he is. And this must be the lucky lady. Come closer so I can get a good look at the woman who finally got Aiden to settle down. You must be quite the catch."

Catriona is moving to the desk before I can prompt her, and despite the tension simmering in my body, I find myself reluctantly impressed. I can tell by the rigidity of her spine that she's not oblivious to the danger we're in, but that fucking self-control she projects is in full force. She takes a seat in the space across from Cian, and I follow like I'm magnetized to her movements. The thought of her near him sets my teeth on edge, so I don't sit.

She doesn't say a word, and he makes a scoffing sound at

the back of his throat. With a careless wave of his fingertips, Niall Cleary breaks from the line of men at Cian's back and comes to a stop by Cian's elbow, where he hands Cian a phone.

"Yes, I can see why Aiden's been making a fool of himself." He doesn't wait for me to respond. Instead, he tosses the phone on the counter between us. On it is the video from the reception. Catriona slaps me over and over again. "Niall brought this to my attention a few days ago. Not the sort of image we like to project, is it, Aiden? In fact, I'm wondering what the point is of attaching ourselves to Senator Gallagher at all if this is the sort of press that results from it."

My stomach burns as I move closer to Catriona's chair and brace my hands on the back. "I've handled it."

Cian gives me a wry smile. "I have no doubt that you'll try, but I know a thing or two about dealing with a willful wife. They require a strong hand. In fact, everything I've learned about your Catriona reminds me so much of your mother. Same fighting spirit. I understand the appeal. However, I'm afraid our organization can't support this marriage if your wife doesn't understand what it means to be a part of this family."

I say nothing, knowing he's already decided what he wants. In front of me, Catriona jolts, but wisely doesn't say whatever scathing retort she's conjured. Cian doesn't give a fuck about what my wife does. It's a thin justification, and we both know it. He wants to take advantage of whatever excuse he can to back me into a corner. Niall, who has always been jealous of the fact that Cian consistently chooses to place his focus on me, never backs down from an opportunity to knock me down. The cruel line of his mouth hardens even more as he unabashedly drinks in Catriona's figure.

No matter how many times I've offered to get rid of him and save Mara the trouble, she's brushed me off. I regret listening to her now more than ever.

Catriona must feel him ogling her, but she doesn't move an inch. She's as cold as ice. Cian must notice her unnatural calm. If it rattles him, he keeps it from showing on his face. If nothing else, her lack of response sharpens his attention.

Cian softens his threats with a smile that doesn't quite reach his eyes. "Normally, we'd arrange for a potential wife to travel to Ireland to meet with the family, obtain the approval from the Clans. Celebrate." His gaze drills into mine. "But since you've decided to do things out of order, without our approval, you've left me no choice but to come to you."

"Congratulations, by the way," Niall says with a sneer. "We hate that we missed the party. When Cian told me, I couldn't say no to his invitation to tell you in person."

Unease twines my guts into knots. I'd hoped I'd be the one to tell Cian the news. Catch him off guard. But someone had beaten me to it. I study the other men in the room, realizing I've been so focused on Cian, I haven't paid any attention to the other three newcomers. Aside from Niall, the three others are older, harder. But they're also heads of the top Clans in the organization.

Everything inside me turns cold.

Cian contemplates Catriona mildly before studying me. "Your wife is too strong-willed. Defiant. Though you knew that when she forced you to marry her. She needs to be broken. To understand who she belongs to. You'll show me she knows her place tonight, or there's no way she'll be accepted. I could say no outright. Make you deal with this situation you've created. But I'm willing to give you a chance for you both to show me where your loyalties lie."

"And how do you propose we do that? Follow you back to Ireland early for a vote?"

Niall snorts. "You wish it could be that simple, don't you?"

"Quiet," Cian barks. It's subtle, but Catriona flinches. My hands twitch where they grip the chair. The three other representatives are guys who clawed their way to the top after I was essentially exiled, so I'm less familiar with them than I am with Niall, and that doesn't make me feel any better.

"This is exactly why marriages are carefully orchestrated. Why I've never chosen a wife for you. It requires a delicate hand. Careful thought. One disrespectful spouse can upset the balance."

I bite my tongue until I taste blood to keep from telling him to get to the fucking point.

"You'll show me she knows her place tonight, or I will intervene. Traditionally, this would entail two of the highest-ranking family members watching the consummation on the wedding night. Back then, it was about lineage and virginity. Neither of which is my concern. What is my concern is your Gallagher bitch knows she wears a Lynch collar."

"You want to watch me fuck my wife?"

Cian's smile is as sharp as the crack of a whip. I swear I can feel its lashes as though they're striking my skin. "I consider that a bonus. What I want is her obedience."

When I speak, my voice is low, controlled. But the anger rising inside me is anything but. "That's not going to *fucking* happen."

Cian doesn't seem surprised, only disappointed. "I had a feeling you'd say that." He gestures to Niall, who pushes a box across the desk. Something simple you'd wrap a gift in. Like jewelry. Apprehension twists inside my chest, slithery and cold. "Open it," he orders Catriona. "I think you'll find its contents motivation enough. Tonight, Aiden. Or you'll live with the consequences. This isn't negotiable, *son*."

I stare at the box for a full five minutes before Catriona reaches for it.

I jerk it from her grasp, knowing somehow, I want to protect her from whatever's inside. The bloody contents tumble from inside it, thud onto the desk, and roll to a stop between us. There's a heartbeat of silence before I snatch it up and shove it back inside, closing the lid so I don't have to see it again.

My eyes lift to Cian's. "I'll leave you to... discuss. You have ten minutes. Then I want your answer."

After they leave, I begin pacing.

Catriona tries to follow, but I can't look at her, let alone ask her to do something like this. I may be a monster, but she's where I draw the line.

"Are you really going to make me fucking chase you down after that?" she storms after me, huffing as she stalks me around the office.

"Please, Catriona. Give me a second." There's something inside my skin trying to get out. I want to run. I want to confront Cian and slit his fucking throat. Bathe in his blood. Make him choke on his own fucking dick.

But I can't.

I can't.

I can't.

I can't.

My mother. Everything I do affects her.

And everything I *don't* do.

Christ. Now the same consequences apply to Catriona.

I can't *fucking* win, no matter what I do.

"Tell me what the fuck that was, O'Connor? You better start explaining right fucking now." The words come at me like knives I can't dodge. I'd leave if I could. Find some bodies to rip into. But I can't leave her here. Not when I know Cian's right outside. Not when he's got me by the throat and the balls. I feel caged, trapped. Like the walls are going to close in around me.

I turn and walk away. She grabs my hand and jerks me to a stop at the top of the stairs. "Stop walking away from me. Tell me what's going on. Who does that...belong to?"

"You already know who it belongs to."

"Then why won't you look at me."

"I said to drop it. This isn't your business." I shake off her hold and jerk away, shoving myself in the direction of the exit. A mistake, considering this is the last fucking place I want to be.

"I'm your wife," she says, stalking after me. "I'm making it my business. And you're supposed to tell me, anyway. So explain."

"Just drop it. I'll have Bren and Tadhg come up to keep an eye on you while I take care of this. I'll meet you at home later." When I try to move around her, she uses her weight and the momentum to shove me against a wall.

I scowl down at her, fisting my hands at my side. "You done?"

"Not until you tell me."

The box I'm holding in my chest can't weigh more than a few ounces, but it feels like it contains an anvil. I shove it at her, then push away, unable to watch. Afraid that if I do, it'll make me sick. She makes a surprised sound in the back of her throat, followed by cardboard rasping against itself as she pulls it open.

Her gasp feels like a shard of glass is sawing through my chest, leaving it raw and gaping. If it had been anyone else, if I'd married her sister like I'd planned, I don't think it would have hit me as hard as it does. I would have been able to keep the way this makes me feel under lock and key like I've done for most of my life.

But because it's Catriona, fierce, strong, sweet Catriona, I feel it a thousand times worse. She cracks me open with just one look. Confusion. Empathy. Outrage.

"Tell me." She pauses to clear her throat when her voice cuts out mid-word. "Tell me the truth."

I breathe in through my nose and out through my mouth, muscles tense from waiting to hear her scream. It'd be easy to lie to her. To tell her it's someone who doesn't matter to me, but I can't force the words out of my mouth. Not when I want her to see me as something other than the monster I've become.

"It's my mother's." I whisper the words so low, I'm certain she can't hear them until she gasps and crosses the room to me in a few quick strides.

She cups my jaw in her hand and lifts it until my gaze meets hers. "What the fuck?" she whispers. "Is she...?"

My eyes drop back down to the bloodstained box she drops to the table. At the sight of the severed ring finger, still bearing a wedding band and a five-carat diamond ring. She'd never been able to take it off after my father died, no matter how much Cian punished her. He'd never force her to do it, because that would ruin the point. Cian's always been more interested in slowly breaking his targets than dominating them. It's why he hasn't given up on me, even after all these years. His success, if it were to ever happen, would be all the sweeter because in his eyes, he would have earned it.

But every time he does something like this, I wonder if he's getting just that much closer.

"You heard him. If we don't consummate this marriage with his men as witnesses, he'll kill her."

I expect her to shout in outrage. To scream at me. To flee as fast as she can in the opposite direction. Knowing it as sure as I do my name, I brace myself for her shouted recriminations.

"Does he want us to do it here or somewhere else?"

My head snaps up. "What?"

"Here?" she repeats slowly, but not unkindly. "Or somewhere else."

Brows pinching together, I clear my throat. "H-here, probably. Now."

"Fine," she says, and I jerk back like I just received a blow.

"Fine?"

"That," she says, pointing at the box on the table, "is a warning, right?"

"Yes," I punch out.

She draws in a long breath. "Then fine. I'll do it."

CATRIONA

Cian's lackeys guide us to a room he had fitted with cameras linked to screens in the office. I'm surviving on nothing but fear and adrenaline. I feel numb, disconnected from my body. They shove us inside, then lock the door. Releasing a breath, I'm grateful they aren't in the room with us.

"You want to watch, fine," Aiden had said once he told them of my decision. "But the only way I can make this happen is if you watch over the cameras. Is that acceptable to you?"

Niall—no wonder Mara hates him—started to object, but Cian cut him off.

"I wouldn't be able to perform in front of an audience like this either. We can watch from the security feed in your office. But Aiden, don't try anything stupid. You'll show me you can both behave, or I'll make you pay. Starting with her. Do you understand?"

He'd agreed.

Of course he had.

I'd told him to.

But that doesn't mean I'm not shaking like I'm in the middle of an off-the-charts earthquake.

"You'll do it?" he repeats incredulously, once we're alone. "Are you fucking insane?"

"Don't ask questions, or I'll change my mind. Now get undressed. They're already watching." His phone buzzes, but he puts it on the side table, ignoring it. Something inescapable pulses in my chest and electrifies my blood.

"I don't want them to see—"

"We don't have a choice," I say in a low voice. I can't see the cameras, but I know they're there. My skin prickles with the awareness that we're being watched. I want to press a hand to my roiling stomach, but I don't want to show them an ounce of fear.

"W-what should I—" I'm shaking with nerves despite the fact that this isn't our first time together. That night with him seems so far away now. Like a fever dream. Is he really going to go through with this? Does it even matter to him? He's kept bodyguards on me, given me money, but none of that means he gives a damn about me aside from protecting his investment. There was that moment in the shower when he'd held me, but does he only do those things out of obligation? For his commitment to his mother? Would he have forced me to do this if I hadn't offered?

I have to push away all thoughts, or I won't be able to go through with this. I'm probably stupid for even considering it. But I can't walk away, knowing his mother would be punished. Neither can he. But it's there, linking us as surely as the rings on our fingers.

Without a word, Aiden undoes the cuff links at his wrists, pocketing them as soon as they're unclasped. His silver eyes, devoid of emotion, snare mine as he tugs the tail of his black shirt from his waistband, and there's something vulnerable about seeing a man like this with wrinkles in his shirt—a crack in his well-manicured facade. I wish I wasn't sharing him like this. I don't want anyone else to see him half-dressed and mussed, but I don't have a choice, so I focus on undressing as well.

All too soon, the zipper on my dress is undone. Before I can doubt myself, I draw it away, stepping out of the cloud of fabric, trying not to think of the hidden cameras and the disgusting man observing them. Looking at the dress as it falls to the floor now, I try to scrub them from my thoughts.

By the time my attention returns to Aiden, he's divested himself of his Armani button-down shirt and is working on removing his pants. The sound of his buckle clinking echoes in my ears, and I feel the tips of them ignite with the flame of embarrassment. All I can do is keep going, stepping out of my shoes. Finally, I'm left in nothing but lace and my wedding rings.

I nearly gasp when I glance up again and find Aiden nearly naked in front of me, a pair of tight black briefs the only remaining clothes on his body. If my ears were burning red, now they're scalding, despite my rational side screaming for me to close my eyes.

I wish it weren't like this. I wish we were anywhere else.

You'd think I wouldn't be affected by how absolutely

devastating his body is since we've been sharing the same bed, but no. As much as I've been trying to delude myself, he is nothing if not a work of art.

My brain can't decide which part of his body it wants to focus on. It computes only in flashes of understanding. The delicate, intricate black tattoo art decorating his body from his ankles to his collarbones, with only his nipples, hands, and face unmarked. The winking piercings from his nipples. But the more time I get to spend with him, the more I've begun to understand the real story—one written on his skin by the man who forced us into this situation.

Underneath the swirls of black ink are the thin, raised lines of scars decorating rippling muscle. There are so many, I can't tell if it's from one injury or from thousands. I hadn't been with him long enough the night we spent together to see them. Across his sculpted pectorals. Along his corded forearms and bulging biceps. All down his carved eight-pack and Adonis belt.

My hands are still in the process of wrapping around my body as I practically gape at him, then I stuff them under my armpits so I don't reach out to touch them. Question him about them.

I will fuck this man, give him my body, let the others watch, but I won't let them see him vulnerable.

When it becomes apparent he's going to wait for my direction, despite Cian's interest in seeing me cowed, I whisper under my breath, "I don't—" in a hitching voice, and I point to the bed.

Without hesitation, Aiden turns to the bed and yanks back the stark white duvet and sheets. He gestures for me to climb on, and I slide under the sheets, unable to look away from him now. The only way I'll ever be able to get through this, knowing anyone is watching, is to focus entirely on him. Pretend that we're the only two people in the world. Imagine that I never left him in the first place. That the subsequent events never happened.

Aiden may despise me for tricking him, may tease me and torture me as retribution, but if there's one thing I know for certain, it's that he wants me. He has since the moment we met. He wants me so much that he nearly married my sister to prove exactly how much the thought of me being around petrifies him.

I'm completely at his mercy once again. To use. To overpower. To hurt, if he wanted. He could do anything to me, and I'd be completely powerless against him. It should be terrifying. I should be mindless with panic.

Aiden's climbing on the bed, giving me a front-row view of the rippling muscles along his expansive chest and abdomen. Despite everything that's going on, my breath hitches. My blood heats. He flicks the covers over our bodies, and a knot of tension inside me releases. It covers most of the important things, which doesn't help much, but what the cameras can see of me is blocked by Aiden's body.

He hovers over me, kneeling between my slightly parted legs. I've never felt more vulnerable in my life. Not even when he had a gun pressed to my head or when he had me on my knees in the limo. This feels like giving him a part of myself I've been holding in reserve.

"Ease up for me, love," he says, his voice whisper-soft as he slides his hands up my thighs to grip my panties.

I nod while biting my lip and trying to control my emotions, my ears damn near burning with the force of my embarrassment. I'm grateful I styled my long, wavy hair down because it covers the blush that spreads from there to my neck and the top of my chest as he peels the material over my hips and down my thighs.

For a moment, his attention catches on the shadowy place between my thighs, and a shudder escapes his lips. Heat that has nothing to do with embarrassment glides over my sensitized skin in a rush.

The tingling in my fingers disappears completely, and I fight a whole-body shiver at the way he seems wholly consumed by the mere sight of me. I try not to watch and fail miserably as he shifts to shove his briefs down his legs and kicks them somewhere over the side. His cock bobs free, already hard. There's enough light from the lamps on the bedside tables for me to see every delicious inch of him. The intimate flesh is flushed a beautiful pink, slightly darker at the head, which is already weeping with beads of translucent pre-cum.

I swallow hard as he palms his erection and squeezes the base. Fear and desire collide in a cataclysmic chain reaction. One ratcheting the other up in a vicious cycle primed by a history of this man and the way he's always mastered my body. I still don't know if this is an act for him dictated by Cian's ruthless demands, but the wetness gathering in my core doesn't seem to care. Even so, I find myself glancing around, searching for light reflecting off the hidden surface of a lens.

A hand wraps around my jaw. "You keep your eyes on me, you understand?" He punctuates the statement with a hard, thought-melting kiss. I can't look away from him as his tongue dominates mine. When he pulls away, I'm already breathless. "Tell me you understand me, pet."

Despite telling myself not to show those bastards my nerves, I jump at his command and nod vigorously. I do as he says and don't look away from his hard, stormy eyes while he reaches under me to undo the clasp of my bra. My nipples pinch the moment they're bared to his heated gaze.

Before I can protest—not that I can—he's hinging at the waist to grip my arms and drag my body closer to his. It forces my thighs to part for him, making room for his powerful body between them. My anxiety disappears somewhere in the journey, forgotten. My gasp fills the too-quiet bedroom, but it's not so loud I don't hear Aiden's huff of breath as my legs go around his hips. His cock thrusts between us, hard and impossible to ignore, and goddammit, I ache for him. I have been for weeks. Maybe months. Maybe even since the moment I snuck away from his bed.

For reasons I don't care to comprehend, Aiden licks his thumb and applies gentle, but inescapable pressure to my clit and strokes it to life despite all my unvoiced objections. The last thing I want is to enjoy any part of being forced to fuck this man, but that's exactly what I do. I try to look away, think of anything else, but his frustratingly beautiful body is the only thing that fills my vision. His scent, masculine and clean, envelops me in that same strange intimacy until all I can focus on is how his skin is distractingly warm and smooth against mine even though his expression is cold.

When I can't look away any longer, our gazes connect like they are magnets. I don't want to crave the licks of fire that spark to life low in my belly. I don't want its embers to travel along my nerve endings, showing me every place where we touch until my body revels in the brush of my thighs against his waist, the heat of his cock branding my skin, his thumb working me into an effortless frenzy.

It occurs to me that I may come from this, and the idea terrifies me, so I force myself to breathe with intention. I won't give them the satisfaction, even if it denies me some slice of pleasure. My fingers dig into my thighs as I force myself not to move into his touch, but it's too fucking good to ignore.

My eyes pop open when his fingers move from my clit to the entrance of my body, and he dips two fingers in to test my wetness. I bite back a groan at the sensation of his thick, wicked fingers stretching me. I haven't been with anyone since... him, and this is a terrible moment to be reminded of how big he is and how much work it is to take him.

My cheeks blaze red, and there's no way he doesn't see, but he doesn't taunt me. In fact, his light eyes darken somehow as he meets mine. His teeth bite down on his lower lip as his hand moves between my legs, thrusting in and out until he's certain I'm wet enough that it won't hurt.

Then his hands retreat, and he fists them in the sheets beside my waist.

"If I were a good man, I'd tell you to leave this room and run the fuck away from me," he says through gritted teeth. It's low enough that whoever is watching won't be able to hear. "No decent person would put you through something like this. But you've known since the moment you met me that I'm not a decent person. I thought maybe I could keep you from the horrors of my life, protect you. The darkness in me was always going to stain you in some way. It should make me feel guilty." His silver eyes flash in the half light, and a tenor of foreboding clamors inside me. "But I can't deny the thought of claiming you in front of everyone has its appeal."

"Aiden," I protest, twisting underneath him. Wanting him to give me space so I can think straight. Wanting him to drive into me. Wanting to push him onto his back so I can sink down on him and show the bastards watching who really owns this man.

My hands go to his chest, and I try not to think about the way his muscles ripple underneath my palms, or the cold metal of his piercings as they rasp against my skin.

"That's right, love. Focus on me. Only me. I've got you." He shifts to hitch my thighs up, spreading me obscenely so he can wedge himself closer. I can feel my pussy contracting around nothing, responding to the stimulation of his words. "Fuck, you're so perfect for me. Look at you. Always so greedy for me."

One hand grips my waist until it's definitely going to leave a bruise, but I don't care. The other is guiding the fat head of his cock to where I'm slippery and desperate for him. I wrap a hand around his shoulder, needing something to hold as he shoves himself inside the slightest bit.

He makes a sound of anguish in the back of his throat, and then his mouth is on mine. Demanding, conquering. I submit, feeding him desperate whimpers that I try but fail to smother.

His hand retracts as I take him completely, wincing a little. He's girthy to the point I have trouble working him inside. It takes several thrusts before I can, swirling my hips to achieve it comfortably. His hands fly to my hips, and I focus on him, only to realize he's arching his neck in restraint, his throat appealingly bared to me. I have to resist the urge to bite him there, the ferocity of my desire taking me by surprise.

I shouldn't want this. Shouldn't like how it feels, but especially not like this. Not after the limo, not after my sister. Not after the way he's used me and, even more regrettably, made me like it. Made me crave it. Made it to where every time I caught sight of my name tattooed on his fingers, I imagined them wrapped around my throat in a fucked-up necklace.

I both hate and covet him. This twisted game we are playing makes me sick, but it's because I know if I give in and let him win, I'll lose a part of myself that keeps me safe. And nothing about Aiden O'Connor is safe. Nothing about Aiden says he isn't anything but a snake, biding his time, waiting for the moment to strike.

Even though I know this, even though I have all the rationalities spinning through my thoughts, his dick stretches me to the point of discomfort, making my skin burn white hot and clouding away those rational thoughts. My hips wiggle from side to side as I search for a comfortable fit. The piercing rubs inside me, stroking all sorts of new places to life with weighted fire.

Through the haze of my thoughts, his hissed exhalation reaches my ears, but I can't parse out what it could mean.

Lightning moves along my skin, arcing out of where we're connected and fizzing through my blood. For the first time since that night, I feel the same attraction to him I did when I'd tumbled into his bed against my better judgment. I'm so wet, his dick is soaked.

My eyes fly open, which is a mistake of epic proportions

because they clash with his again, and I feel the connection like I'm drowning in the quicksilver depths. His pupils are blown wide, eating at the silver, and the tattoos on his throat aren't enough to cover the ruddy flush spreading up his skin. I'm doing this to him.

"Are you gonna come for me, *bhean chéile?*"

His words barely penetrate as a haze descends on me. I shift my hips, angling until I can maneuver without pain, and then I find a rhythm that has both of our faces contorting out of our careful masks of indifference. It shouldn't feel good, but his cock is so fucking perfect it's almost impossible not to work myself against him, chasing the pleasure.

I would have thought he'd press me down into the bed, pound into me with abandon until he got what he wanted, and then it would be over. Some sick part of me wishes that's what he'd done. It would have been easier to take, in a twisted way, than this. Than for him to allow me to dictate the pace, getting me ready and forcing me to be present in the moment. Fucking him this way means I can study his every reaction. Somehow, he's both given me power and taken it away in one act of submission.

That's the only explanation for why I find my hips rolling in a fluid motion against him, working my clit against his pelvic bone until my breath comes out in harsh pants. If he's going to make me enjoy this, then he's going to do the same.

The moment the thought occurs to me, I search out the signs of everything he likes, determined to ruin him and make him feel just as vulnerable as I am. Make him feel what I feel. Distract him from this nightmare.

"I will if you make me," I pant in a low voice.

His Adam's apple bobs, and his gaze narrows at the challenge in my tone. His fists bite into my hips before he can stop them, and it doesn't escape my notice that he has to force himself to gently release his fingers one by one. I grind against him, taking him so deep it's almost painful, and his muscles twitch between my thighs.

"I don't have to make you, do I?" he taunts. "You're already almost there. My fucked-up little wife. Are you going to get off on this? Letting me take you. Knowing they're watching and they can't have you."

Coasting on his dark, twisted words, I draw his head down until his mouth caresses my nipples. "Get them wet," I say, and his face goes slack. At first, I think it's with fury or shock, but then he wraps his lips around one tightened peak, and I realize it's with pleasure.

Fuck. *Fuck.* I throw my head back as he traces my nipple, then sucks it deep and nibbles. Bolts of heat shoot straight between my legs, and my thoughts go hazy. My need for vengeance and my body's desire for him are a twisted knot that grows more tangled with every thrust and lick.

I force myself to focus on where he moves to my other breast, lifting it to his mouth. He doesn't stop until they're both glistening and as hard as knots. I cup his jaw with both hands, urging him to thrust into me with slow, grinding movements.

"So obedient," I murmur in a low voice so that the cameras won't pick it up, as his silver eyes gleam down at me, hazy and starstruck. "You're doing so good for me. My good husband doing what he's told. Just like I knew he would."

Triumph flares inside me, sick and warped, when he moans and drops to his elbows until we're pressed together from hip to chest. I'm not fucking sorry to say I am ruthless, hunting his pleasure until he's as taut as a rope above me.

I'm so enraptured by his trembling hands, the carved lines of his contracting pectoral muscles, and the grimace of pleasure and pain sculpting his face that my orgasm takes me by complete surprise. Stopping it is beyond my ability.

He comes with a deep groan I feel throughout my entire body, and it's the power that washes over me, the sheer control of this man who has mine clenching around him, sucking his thick cock deep inside me, and milking every last drop of his release until he collapses into a limp mess on the bed.

I go to move, and he rasps out, "Wait, don't," and stills my retreat. Aftershocks have my pussy clenching down on his hardness still inside me, and it's an effort to keep from how good it feels from showing on my face.

CHAPTER 23

CATRIONA

Aiden's weight pressing me into the mattress should make me struggle for freedom, but it anchors me to the moment when my head is as light as a balloon, threatening to drift right off my shoulders. He reaches the bedside table, his fingers moving as quick as lightning on the screen of his phone. Not even a minute later, he puts it back on the table, and his hands land on either side of my shoulders, his wide frame blotting out the rest of the world. Somehow, my palms find their way to his chest, and all I can do is touch him. Give in to the impulse because I don't know if I'll get another chance. The smart thing to do would be to get away from him as quickly as possible.

But I can't.

Not after seeing the raw panic on his face at the realization that his mother had been harmed.

Dammit.

Anything else I could have guarded myself against.

But not that.

He's studying me, shifting to balance on one palm as the fingertips of the other drift over my skin, memorizing. The heaven of his touch on me lulls me into a false sense of security, if only for a moment. I take in his attention greedily, sucking it down like its marrow.

When I speak, it's with a rasp. "We should probably, um —" Caught at a loss for words, my comment trails off. I don't know what the fuck we should be doing. An angel and a devil are on my shoulder arguing. I should push him away. I should pull him closer. I fought him for so long because I knew the moment I let him touch me, have me, I'd be lost again. Isn't that why I ran from his bed? Why I refused to give him my name?

He lists to the side, taking me with him, and I end up half draped over his body. God, it would be easier if he didn't smell so good, like sex and man and damp forest. I shake with the amount of restraint it takes to keep from smelling him all over.

One of his wide palms is low on my back. The other reaches across to nab under my knee and pull me more fully against him. We stay that way for a few long minutes, not talking. But I swear it feels like we understand each other more now without words than we ever have before.

Finally, he breaks the silence. "They're not watching now. He wants us to meet them back in the office in a half hour."

"Ho-how do you know they're not watching?"

"He got what he wanted," he says simply. "C'mon. Let me get you cleaned up."

What feels like a moment later, we're naked in the shower. Aiden lathers his hands with soap from a dispenser and drags them over my sensitive skin. It's...comforting. Not a word I ever thought I'd use to describe him. He'd done this before, after Mr. Broussard was shot. He's not...caring for me. Is he?

Yasmine is the only other person in my life who I'd go to for any kind of comfort. And even then, I try to keep it to a minimum. She has her own stresses with medical school, and I would never want to take advantage of her. Even Mom hadn't done this sort of thing for me. At least not since I was very young. His blatant concern over the past few hours makes me tender with fragility. Like I'm made of glass and covered in spiderwebs of cracks. One rough touch and he could shatter me.

Water spills over my hair, washing away the sweat coating my skin and the evidence of him between my thighs. Fuck, we forgot to wear a condom. How could I have been so fucking stupid? I have an IUD, but we've never had that conversation. I never thought it would be a necessity. Sleeping with him again had never made it to my to-do list.

So much for those plans.

All it took was the look in his eyes, the resignation pulling his face taut, for me to realize he was willing to lose his mother to keep from having me exposed. There's more to it than that, I'm sure. There are mafia politics at play here that I don't fully understand, but it's how I feel. Despite the threat to the most important person in his life, he wasn't going to make me do it.

Why would he do that? It doesn't make sense to me. I want to ask him, but I can't seem to make myself move from underneath the spray. I'm frozen in place, weighed down by all the questions and fears battling inside me for dominance.

I keep my eyes squeezed shut, unable to chance looking at him. Afraid the loose emotions tonight will give him too much that I want to keep close to the vest. These past few weeks here have been easy. Maybe too easy. It took practically no effort at all for me to lull myself into a false sense of security.

Needless to say, any sense of security in this situation is completely shattered now. I'd known Cian was a formidable enemy, but I hadn't realized how formidable. He has Aiden by the throat, using his mother as leverage. Anything Aiden does that Cian doesn't like, and his mother will be the one to pay the price. Tears sting my sinuses, and I breathe in the hot, humid air to keep them at bay.

This has been his life since he was a teenager? I can hardly fathom it, and mine hasn't exactly been a picnic. It was easier to push what Mara had said to the back of my mind. I had to in order to keep Aiden at a distance. To keep my hatred for him flaming hot. The thought of what Cian could have done to him throughout the years, of what Aiden would have been like if Cian hadn't killed his father, has me turning until the spray hits my back. I find Aiden standing across from me, blond hair dark and sleek and slicked back from his face. The inky swirls of his tattoos contrast against the white shower tile, making them stand out in stark relief against his tanned skin. He holds his hands loose at his sides now, his expression unreadable.

"What happens now?"

"Now, we do as he asks. Then I'll take you home. Next week, we go to Ireland."

"What about your mother?"

"What about her?"

"Is she...do we know if she'll be okay?"

He tugs me to him, and I let him arrange me against his chest as he blocks the spray. "Like I said, he won't hurt her anymore unless I'm there to watch." I don't know how I can tell, but I can hear in his voice that he doesn't fully believe what he's saying. But he says it anyway because otherwise, wouldn't the thought of being unable to protect her drive him a little insane?

I'm the first to move when all he does is hold me. After I wrap up in a towel, I realize he hasn't moved, so I turn off the water and pass him a towel. It finally spurs him into movement, and we both dress quickly after that. Me, with trepidation because now the dress that had reminded me so much of that night is thoroughly tainted. All I want to do is burn it and then sleep for a century.

When he's back in his suit, I nod, then head for the door.

His voice stops me. "I won't let him do this to you again." I look over my shoulder, my thoughts half on what's waiting for us. The indecision and confusion must be apparent because he continues. "I won't."

"There are some things even you can't control," I say.

He reaches for me, hands bracketing my jaw, lifting it. He stamps a brutal, punishing kiss on my tender lips. "Don't tell me you're afraid now, *bhean chéile*. You were doing so well."

"Don't be a jerk."

"He'll try to get a rise out of you. Don't let him. It'll only make it worse. Stay by me. I'll take care of you." He starts for the door, but I stop him.

"I can handle him. I just don't want him to hurt you."

"Worried about me?" he says it like it's the furthest thing from reality. But the truth of it cuts me to the core.

I don't know why I'm trying to console him, but as I stare at the man standing across from me, I realize I have two choices. I can keep fighting this marriage—fighting him—with everything I've got. I can keep focusing on school and tracking down Mom's leads. I can ignore him at home when we cross paths.

My second choice is that I can stop fighting *myself*. I've wanted Aiden since the moment I met him. No matter what's happened since then. No matter what he's done, I can't seem to stop wanting him. I'm tired of fighting this battle on all fronts by myself. The thought of having someone like Aiden in my corner...it feels a lot like hope that I won't have to be alone.

Something I've desperately been missing since my mother died.

Someone to have my back.

Tonight felt like the first time we were united against our opposition, and as fucked up as it was, it felt good. Knowing I could do something so important for him. Knowing how much he'd sacrifice for me.

Making my choice, I take a step toward him, and his gaze grows more intense with each step I take. "Yes, Aiden." I rest my hands on his chest as I tilt my head up to look at him. His eyes are practically mercury as he realizes I'm not calling him by his last name for the first time in a long time. "I don't want him to hurt you."

"There is nothing to worry about. If something happens to me, you're taken care of. You know that."

I step closer, our sensitized bodies brushing together. "This has nothing to do with your fucking money, and you know it."

He moves so fast, I barely finish my sentence before I'm pressed against the wall, hands fisting my arms against the glass, back and ass pressed against the freezing surface. "Tell me exactly what you mean, pet. I don't want to misconstrue our conversation."

I hiss at the intensity of his stare, resulting in a wash of gooseflesh dimpling me from head to toe. "I'm saying if you get yourself killed, I'm going to raise you from the dead and kill you myself." I swallow hard, hoping I'm not making a colossal mistake.

He kisses me softly, languidly. Like we didn't just go through hell. Like we aren't two fucked-up, horrible people willing to go to devious ends to protect the people we love. When he pulls away, his hands are buried in my hair, and we're pressed together from chest to thigh.

"Do you trust me?" he asks, and I nearly choke.

"I don't know if I'd go that far."

"I'm going to need you to try, just a little."

"You're scaring me."

"I know, but you're doing so well. Be brave for me a little longer. Okay?"

"Okay."

"Let's go," he says, just as softly as his kiss.

CHAPTER 24

AIDEN

I'm as cold as ice when I walk back into my office. Niall and the others frown at my entrance, but Cian is carefully unreadable. He's wary. Waiting. Certain I'm going to do something that will justify him killing me. He wants it so badly that he's willing to do anything. At the same time, he enjoys the hell out of watching me squirm.

He probably didn't even care to watch. Just knowing he had me under his thumb was likely enough for him. The others, though? They're pissed I blocked most of the view. But there was no way in hell I was letting them see my wife any more than they needed to.

Before, I would have killed them. Done something to get myself beaten to earn my way back into Cian's good graces. But all I want now is to get Catriona out of their sights. Get her home, away from their grasp.

"Now, was that so hard?" Cian asks when we've settled

in front of him. I keep to my feet, unable to sit due to the energy coursing through me. Catriona takes a seat at the desk, managing to master her expression into something like cool indifference.

"I do like a bitch who knows her place," Cian drawls once we settle. "I have to admit, I didn't think she had it in her."

"She had something in her, alright," one of the men mutters.

"That's enough," Cian barks, and Catriona barely withholds her reaction. "Aiden here has done what he was told. Besides, we have business to attend to. Tell me, how is my investment faring?"

"As it turns out, very well. You were right about an American expansion. We're celebrating a record-breaking first year. I knew you'd be pleased."

Catriona tugs at my arm, and her body vibrates with unease in front of me, but I smooth a hand over her shoulder, and she settles. It makes everything inside me go still, but I force myself to focus on Cian's response. He chuckles, sharing amused glances with the four others who eye Catriona hungrily.

"Good, that's good to hear. And what about this charity?" He says the word like he's talking about the plague. "How much of my money did you decide to donate? I suppose it makes sense to cultivate a good image for the Americans."

Niall scoffs, his gaze roving over Catriona like he has X-ray vision. "Pointless. I don't know why you let him get away with this shite. He shouldn't be doing a damn thing without your say-so."

Cian makes a silencing gesture. "Let him speak. He more than earned it tonight." His lips twist as he turns to Catriona for a long moment.

"A million," I say.

There's a long silence.

The three other men laugh, like it's a joke.

The smile falling from Cian's face tells me he knows it isn't.

Catriona presses closer to me, but I don't look away from the men in front of me as I continue. "You were right to send me here. There are boundless opportunities and many, many powerful families with deep pockets and a demonstrable lack of self-control. Consider Senator Gallagher, for example." Beside me, Catriona jerks like she's going to pull away. I still her with a gesture. "Tonight's fundraiser was in honor of Deirdre Gallagher. All the funds raised were to fund scholarships in her name for women at local colleges. How could I resist donating some of our profits to a charity so dear to my wife's heart? Of course, it not only means lots of press for the Emerald but also for my wife and me. Her mother. Americans do love their charities."

Cian's face could be carved from granite with how hard and cold it is by the time I stop speaking. I can feel Catriona looking at me, but I keep my focus on the men in front of me.

The moment stretches until Cian smiles. "Yes, they do. And aren't I so lucky to have such a good dog to take care of these things for me? I knew it would only take a little discipline to get you back in line. Now that this business is taken care of, we can arrange your visit back to Ireland."

Niall turns red but doesn't object. "We've called in the families for next week," he confirms.

"Meeting you is all Mary's been talking about for weeks." Cian directs this to Catriona, who, impossibly, stiffens even further from his attention.

"I'm looking forward to meeting her," she manages.

Cian pushes to his feet and gestures for the other men to precede him out of the room. Niall does so, but not without throwing angry looks back at us before he finally disappears through the door. Crossing the room, Cian stops beside us to study Catriona's face. He lifts a hand to tuck her hair behind her ear.

"Welcome to the family, Catriona. Or at least, you have my vote. There are still several others you'll have to convince." He leans closer, like he's telling her a secret. "Don't worry, though, sweetheart. From what I saw on camera, you'll fit right in."

He signals to Niall. "Let's go downstairs to see the spoils of our investment."

I give Cian a curt nod, lock eyes with Niall, then don't breathe until the door closes behind them.

When I turn, Catriona is already pushing to her feet. "We should go too. The party is probably already winding down. You should be seen." She's got her public face on. The one she uses to paint over any emotion. But this time, I see the strain behind the facade.

I have to get her out of here. I don't want her close to Cian for a moment longer than she has to be. "You're right. Let's go say our goodbyes."

We find Eamon watching over Mara as she locks eyes with Niall. "I'm going to check with Niall about the meeting logistics. Eamon, you'll wait with her?" He nods, and I tear myself away from her.

"One of these days, you're going to give in to me," Niall is saying when I get close.

"One of these days, you'll do me a favor and drop dead," Mara responds.

Niall catches my eye over Mara's shoulder. "If it isn't the disgraced prince. Ready for another show?"

"Ready to stop begging for Cian's scraps?" I retort.

Niall's eyes widen, then narrow. "You're pretty ballsy for a man who says how high whenever Cian says jump."

"Cut the shite, Niall. I've come to talk. Do you have a minute?"

He studies the room, notes Cian chatting with a visibly pale Senator Gallagher, then returns his attention to me. "Let's talk."

Mara clutches my arm. "Aiden—"

"We'll only be a minute."

"Aiden, don't—" But I'm already walking away with Niall nipping at my heels.

CATRIONA'S HEAD lolls on my shoulder. I wrap my arms more securely around her. I can't seem to make myself let go of her. This is exactly what I'd been worried about when I saw her again. Exactly why I knew she was going to be trouble.

I carry her inside, climbing the stairs one weary foot at a time. What a long fucking night. We've got a long week coming up, but the end is in sight. We have to hold on until then. I peel her out of her clothes, noting all the raw places on her skin. If I wasn't bone tired, I'd pepper them with kisses. But all I have the energy for is to drag off my clothes and climb into bed next to her.

I didn't think I'd be able to sleep, but my eyes slip closed within minutes.

THE WEEK FOLLOWING the meeting with Cian feels endless. Preparations. Worrying. But each morning, I wake up next to Catriona, and each night, she's pressed against me in bed. I haven't allowed myself to do more than that despite how much my body screams for me to take advantage of every second we have left.

It's Sunday, and we're in the bedroom, and I'm watching Catriona fuss over what to pack before we leave for Ireland tomorrow.

"You don't think this is too much? I feel like I over-packed. I probably won't even need half of this. It's been so long since I've traveled. I'm overthinking—"

"I know why, little wife. I can read you like a book. Why don't you model everything you're bringing? I'll tell you what you should keep and what you don't need. Even the lingerie... Especially the lingerie."

She pulls off the blood-red dress she was trying on and switches to another as I drink in every second when I should be packing my own bags. Everything hinges on it going according to plan. I don't have time to be ogling her. Fuck it. If I'm going to die, my last meal would take place between her thighs.

She pauses, distracted. "Are you sure you—"

"Yes."

Catriona stops mid-selection, still clad only in a black

lingerie set. I wish I could tear it off with my teeth. "You don't even know what I was going to ask."

"Because the answer is yes."

"To whatever I ask?" she questions with a sultry smile. If she moves just right, I can see her pussy lips through her panties. I'm salivating over her and wondering if she'll be mad if I make us late for dinner with the Baptistes. "I don't believe you."

"That's right. Do you want me to prove it?"

Her eyes flash with challenge at the words that have become a kind of game between us. "Then I want you to find another clerkship for me, better than the one with Judge Landry."

"Done."

"I want to burn Cian's place down to the ground after we're finished."

Fuck. She's so fucking beautiful. Have I ever told her? I wonder what I'd have to do for her to let me fuck her again. This time without witnesses. Are apologies enough? Words never seem to hold weight to me. They're easily disguised. Is it enough to give her everything that belongs to me? It doesn't feel like it. And after what Cian's done... what he could still do, nothing will ever be enough.

"Consider it ashes, love," I croak.

At this, she pauses, considering, and my skin tingles in anticipation. "Are you trying to butter me up so I'll fuck you again?"

Heat floods my veins. "Maybe. Is it working?" My grin turns wicked as a flush spreads up her chest.

"I don't know. I don't think you've earned it yet. Maybe you should get on your knees and beg for me." She says it with faux innocence, but there's a spark of defiance in her twinkling eyes. She's teasing. Doesn't believe I'll do it. When I don't speak, she huffs a laugh and returns her attention to the closet—dismissing me.

I forget the shirt I'm buttoning up as I consider her words. It gapes open, buttons forgotten as I move to where she's musing at her closet, now bursting with the purchases she's been sneaking in since I gave her my AmEx card.

Catriona gasps when she twists to look at me and finds me right behind her. "That what you want, pet?" She shivers as I draw her back against my front. "You want your husband on his knees for you?"

She shoves me away with her shoulder, and I fist my hands at my side, so I don't grab her in my eagerness. "That's right."

"Come here."

She considers me for a long moment, then says, "No. But if you don't threaten, intimidate, or murder anyone while we're at dinner with the Baptistes tonight, then you can have your chance afterward. If you do it well enough, maybe I'll let you fuck me again. Considering we may not make it through this week."

Don't think about that.

I nip at her mouth until her hands climb up to twine around my neck. "I'll behave."

She shivers, and I don't insult anyone that night.

Out loud.

AFTER DINNER, where I charmed the Baptistes—even Reggie, who was begrudgingly tolerant—I do my checks on the security team and make sure the coffee machine is prepped for Catriona's lavender and honey latte in the morning, then go in search of her.

I find Catriona naked in our bathroom, leaning against the counter with an imperious eyebrow raised in my direction. As though I should have already been kneeling between her legs, and I'm disappointing her.

When I drop to my knees, she straightens, startled. I've never given her a reason to believe I'd be the sort of man who could beg. It never did a damn thing for me the few times I'd tried other than to make me look weak.

But she's right.

Next week hinges on every detail falling into place perfectly. One wrong move and the results could be catastrophic. And I'm not willing to go to my grave with her not understanding the lengths I'd be willing to go for her.

Maybe it's selfish.

Okay, considering my entire personality, it's absolutely selfish.

"You look pretty like that," she says, breaking me from my thoughts as she crosses the room to stand in front of me, looking like a goddess come to life. "But I'm not hearing a lot of begging."

"I—" My throat clamps around the words. They're too important. Too big. And I've never been the kind of man good with them.

My hesitation amuses her. "Huh. Need a little direction? That's okay. Maybe I'm learning I like telling you what to do." She threads her fingers through my hair lazily. "Why don't you start by kissing my feet?"

I hold her eyes until the discomfort at the angle is too much, then I drop them. Starting at her thighs, I scatter kisses over her skin, working my way down until I reach her delicate ankles. The only thing I can hear is the sound of her erratic breathing and my heart beating in my ears. And Cian's voice, threatening everything I've cared about.

Folding down, I press my lips to her feet, feeling the strain in my back and my knees protesting the hard floors. But there isn't anywhere I'd rather be.

"You're surprisingly good at that," she observes from above me.

I grunt in acknowledgment because I'm too busy kissing the tips of her perfect pink toes, then up the other foot.

"Up," she directs, and reaches down to tug at my shirt. I do, hiding a wince as my kneecaps grind into the floor. Her hand cups my jaw. I'm level with her lower belly. I can smell her arousal and want nothing more than to press my face into the cleft between her thighs, but I keep my head tilted back. "So obedient."

I arch a brow. "Is that what you want?"

Her smile is slow, wicked. "You know what I want."

Wrapping my arms around her thighs, I say, "No."

Lips parted, she huffs, "What?"

"You heard me. There are no words I could say that you'd ever believe. No begging that could ever satisfy. But what I can do is worship at your altar. I can show you I repent every day for what I've done. That I won't let anything ever happen to you again. No matter what."

She contemplates me, a goddess observing her unworthy

peasant. For a moment, I think she'll tell me to go to hell, but then she tilts her head and says, "Good enough for now."

But I know it's not. Nothing will ever be.

Minutes later, she's facing away from me in the shower, one foot propped on the stone seat, her hands on the wall so she can push back for every thrust. She's mindless. Needy. My palms are filled with the generous weight of her breasts as I pinch her nipples between my fingers. Her moans echo off the tile, and it's not until she flutters around me that I realize she's got me inside her bare. Again.

"Condom," I pant and pull out. "Fuck, let me—"

She reaches a hand around and grabs me by the dick. Before I can choke out a protest, she fits me back inside her and takes me so deep I forget how to speak. "You don't need one. I have an IUD. I was tested before you, and I'm good. And you know I know you are, too. You left the test results on my pillow a week after the wedding, where I'd find them."

I forget how to breathe. At my silence, she says, "So all I had to do to get you to shut up is fuck you bare? I would have done it a long time ago if I'd known."

Fisting my hand in her blond locks, I yank her head back until her breath rasps from the effort. "You want me to make a mess of you like the little slut you are? Is that it? Want me to fill you up until I'm dripping out of you?"

"Make a mess out of me," she gasps out. "Please come inside me. Please. I want it. Make me forget."

There's a desperation in her voice. One that's not only from her desire to come. One that was present in her tentative smile all night. One that knows we're walking into danger soon and may not make it out.

Unable to do this without looking in her face, I pull out,

fit my arms under her thighs and gently slam her against the shower wall. When I slip back inside her, we both moan, and her nails bite into my shoulders as she tries to scrabble away from the intensity, but there's nowhere for her to go.

"Trying to run away so soon? After making me beg for you, little wife?" I wrap my hands around her throat, a parenthesis of suggestion, and force her to look at me. Always look at me. It's the only way I truly know she's thinking about me. I don't ever want her to look away. "You won't ever get away. I made you mine the day we said 'I do' and that's not something that's ever going to change."

Maybe I need to remind myself as much as I need to remind her after what happened. Perhaps we both need this more than I thought.

She constricts around me, her body seizing as she starts the climb toward orgasm. "Wait, Aiden, it's too much. I don't think I can take—"

"I'll tell you what you can take." I huff out a gasping laugh, feeling myself losing hold on the leash of my control. "Poor little baby girl, trying so hard for me. Taking me so deep in her perfect pussy. My dirty little slut."

She tries to turn her face away again, her cries a dead giveaway that she's overwhelmed, but I lock a hand around her jaw, keeping her in place. I use my other hand to lightly slap her cheek, three times in rapid succession, ripping a startled gasp from her abused throat. "You're so close, aren't you? Going to come all over my cock. That's right. Oh, don't be so shy now. You're gonna be so pretty when you do." Her cries fill my ears, and she thrashes against me, but I keep her pinned. "Gonna fill this pussy up, but first I want you to give it to me. Give it to me, Catriona, or I'll make you. Fucking come on this dick, baby, so I can fill you up."

She arches beneath my grasp, and her pussy clamps down on my cock, drawing my orgasm from me and ripping a growl from my chest. "There you go, baby. Fuck yes." I keep fucking her in long, deep strokes as I come. Imagining the thought of her growing full with our baby as I do.

"You're mine," I say, hand on her throat. "You're mine, and I'm not ever going to let you go."

It's a promise. To her. To me.

A panicked feeling has me gripping her tighter. Her blush is a violent red streak on the highest crests of her cheeks. I should stop and check to see if she's too sore, but I can't. My gaze drops to where I'm drilling into her, cock still half hard. I'm covered in our cum, and it drives me a little mad. I slap at the shower controls until the water shuts off and drop to my knees. Catriona makes a sound of surprise, and then it turns into a moan as I seal my mouth over her dripping cunt.

"Aiden, oh my God. Please. I can't come again."

I nip at her inner thigh, the scent of us filling my nose. "One more for me, *bhean chéile*, I need you to come on my face."

"I can't do it," she whimpers.

"You can. Or I can make you," I answer as I lick the taste of us from her pussy. "Doesn't matter to me."

CHAPTER 25

CATRIONA

"The flight will be about ten hours or so," Aiden says as we board the luxury jet the next week, his voice dripping with that infuriating self-possession. "You can sleep most of it, if you want."

I glance at him over my shoulder, my nerves simmering just beneath the surface. Under any other circumstances, I would be ecstatic to visit Ireland, but in the aftermath of all that's happened, it's the last place I want to be. I close my eyes as we settle into our seats and go over the steps again.

We'll fly into Dublin. Drive across to Doolin where Aiden has a house. Then the day after, we'll go to Cian's monstrosity of a former castle turned hotel, turned fortress, where we'll meet Mary. And the rest of the heads of each Clan. I don't know which part I'm most nervous about.

Remembering to respond, I say, "Sure, thanks."

It helps that Aiden is distracting. So thoroughly distracting. I don't know what we're doing together, but it's enough to quiet my brain. Somehow, I keep coming up with the moment I had him on his knees. The ravaged beauty on his face as pleasure ripped through him. It should make me sick, but all I feel is powerful. I'd done that.

There's a sickness beneath my skin demanding I do it again. And again.

"What rules will you have for me now? No leaving the confines of whatever hellscape is my prison? No sightseeing? No leaving the bodyguards behind? Hell, you may as well slap me in handcuffs and gag me." Bren and Tadhg lumber onto the aircraft after us. It helps to resort to our earlier back-and-forth ways. That, I understand. That, I can control.

"That can be arranged. If you weren't determined to escape them every chance you get, maybe I'd give you more freedom. But I promise you, the last thing you want to do is run into a rival Clan unprotected."

"I promise I'll be a good little girl and stay near the house. If I leave, I'll take Ren and Stimpy with me."

He lifts a hand and ghosts it over my cheek. My body goes as tight as a bow string. A smile teases his lips. "This will all be over soon. I promise." His brows lower, and the laughter leaves his face. "If all goes well, you won't have anything to worry about for a long time."

My conversation with Mara tugs at my memory, and despite the rational voice in my head screaming it's a bad idea, I say, "Tell me about your mother."

I don't expect him to answer, but he says, "Why don't I tell you what she was like when she met my father first?" At my nod, he continues, passing the time as they ready the jet. "She went to school for history. Loved nothing more than a stack of books and a cup of tea. Met my father at a library, but she didn't learn until later that he was only there because he followed her in."

"*That* sounds familiar," I snark.

"He kept showing up until she agreed to a date. She was a soft, kind soul. Loves roses and has the greenest thumb you've ever seen. My dad was crazy in love with her."

"Must have been nice."

"It's why Cian killed him, you see. He'd been in love with her, too."

The words come from nowhere as the jet lifts off. I don't know if it's the sudden motion or the frankness with which he speaks that takes my breath away.

"I found out much later that he'd been planning it since before I was ever born. Maybe from the moment my parents met, and she chose my father over Cian. He didn't care about her roses or her books. He cared about collecting her. Having her because she belonged to my father." He looks off in the middle distance and huffs a breath. "And he's spent most of my life lording her over me because I'm my father's son."

I'm afraid to speak, but I don't want him to stop. It's like I'm getting access to forbidden knowledge. Precious. Terrifying. "Why—"

"Because he harbored a lifetime of resentment toward me for all the things my father had, and he didn't."

"We have to do something to save her."

"That's not for you to worry about," Aiden says, as though it's that simple. He gestures to the flight attendant, his tone shifting to one of polite authority and clearly trying to change the subject. "My wife gets motion sickness on flights. Could you bring us a glass of ginger ale with ice and two meclizine, please?"

"Right away, Mr. Aiden," the flight attendant replies.

I stare at him, gobsmacked and off-kilter. Momentarily distracted from our conversation. "How do you know I get motion sickness when I fly?"

He gives me an unimpressed glance. "You're my wife," he answers, as though it's that simple.

I'm about to demand a more detailed explanation when the flight attendant returns with the drink and medication. Aiden passes them to me without another word, as if it's the most natural thing in the world for him to be attending to my needs.

"Thank you so much. If you don't mind, we'd like privacy until it's time for dinner," he says smoothly.

"Of course." She reaches into the storage panel above our seats. "Here are your blankets and pillows. Let me know if you need anything else. I'll close the window panels and privacy screen."

"Thank you," Aiden says, his attention already back on me.

I stare at the glass in one hand and the medication in the palm of my other. I don't want to feel like we have anything in common, but we do. I'm willing to risk anything to find out what happened to my mother. And he's willing to kill to free his.

"Take the medicine, Catriona," he urges. "I promise it's safe, and you'll enjoy the trip more if you aren't nauseated."

I shake my head, but for once, I do as I'm told and swallow the pills with a sip of ginger ale.

My hands clutch the armrests as the plane climbs, and I

don't even realize Aiden's arm is beneath mine until we're well into the sky. Even then, he turns it underneath mine and holds my hand until the medicine takes me off to a fitful sleep.

What's even more shocking is... I let him.

THE RIDE FROM THE SMALL, private airport an hour outside of Dublin takes a few hours, during which I fall in and out of sleep. Aiden grows more and more tense the closer we get to our destination, and I spend it staring out the window as the countryside blurs around me, wishing my mother were alive to go on this trip with me. She and my father had met in Ireland. He'd been visiting family in Dublin—his parents were first-generation American immigrants—and she'd been learning the ropes of her father's shipping corporation. Supposedly, it had been love at first sight. Within six months, they were married, expecting me, and living in New Orleans.

She'd never returned to work or got to go back to Dublin like she'd wanted even though she used to tell me those were some of the happiest moments of her life. I can almost feel the ghost of her next to me as the green hills dotted with sheep race by. My chest aches with longing, but I force myself to suppress the emotions building and steady my breathing.

Aiden knocks on my window. Giving myself a little shake, I realize the car has stopped. He's standing outside my door, surrounded by vast fields of tall grass. Beyond him are pastures full of fat, lazy cows, and even farther, the fields give way to nothing but deep blue water as far as I can see. Despite myself, my heart catches in my throat. I've seen many beautiful things in my life, but nothing has compared to this.

Aiden opens the door for me, but I ignore him to take a step closer to the cliffs, the water. I barely notice the sprawling stone structure to our left. My feet carry me a few steps toward the path that leads to the cliffs when he takes my arm.

I jerk in his grasp and whirl. "Can't we—"

His silver eyes dance with amusement, as though he enjoys riling me up, but he releases my arm. "Settle, darlin'. There'll be time to see the cliffs, but first, you need to eat. They've left us dinner inside the house." He jerks his chin at the cottage settled among the fields of grass. "Bren and Tadhg are in the guest cottage down the way so they can keep an eye on the road."

"Who left us dinner?" I ask, ignoring the rumbling in my stomach.

"The couple who I've employed as caretakers for the house. It's been a long time since I've been home, and I'm afraid they've gone overboard as a result. Humor me about this, and I'll take you on a tour after you've eaten. They're good people."

As he speaks, I see a curtain flutter in a window, and my stomach growls again. He's not wrong about eating. I'm starving, having slept most of the flight.

"Food sounds wonderful," I answer.

Aiden nods to the driver, who moves to the trunk to unload our luggage. He takes my hand again and leads me to the red front door. When I pull away, he looks at me but doesn't comment.

The house isn't much to speak of from the outside, but the breathtaking landscape overshadows it. The red door is the only punch of color against acres of gray stone and fields of tall sage-green grass. With Aiden's hand now pressed against my back (I swear now that he's started, he can't seem to stop touching me), I step through and find a small vestibule with several pairs of black rain boots lined near a closet door like little soldiers. Next to them is a small table, where he tosses his wallet and keys before he moves to the left through a doorway.

I follow, taking in my quaint surroundings, feeling a little off balance and out of place.

This home is nothing like I would have imagined him to possess. It's homey, quaint. Comfortable. I associate him with the elegance and opulence of his life in New Orleans. With gambling, guns, and blood. Machinations and manipulation.

My head reels as we enter the main rooms, skirting around a cozy staircase that leads to the second floor. Had his parents stayed here? Grandparents? What would his life have looked like if he hadn't been born into the Irish mob?

A sweet older couple greets us, giving him a warm hug and kiss on the cheek. I barely hear their words but offer a nice smile to them as they walk him through the house, presumably updating him on the amenities. I'm too busy feeling jet-lagged and off-kilter to be more welcoming than a cursory hello.

I study the space and try to reconcile it with the man I

thought I've always known. Had he ever been allowed to spend his days here?

A giant wall of stone divides the main living space, the living room on the far side and the dining room and kitchen nearest the front door. A double-sided fireplace is in the center, filling the room with a crackling warmth. All around are large floor-to-ceiling windows with views over the pastures that have incredible vistas of the cliffs.

My heart lifts at the sight. Traveling had never been very far up on my father's list of priorities. It was too dangerous. Too inconvenient. Didn't work with school or his campaign schedule. Then I had college and law school. There had never been time for anything I wanted when his needs were so big they blotted out everything else.

Maybe I can slip away while Aiden is doing... whatever it is he has to do. I can go to town and play tourist. Pretend I'm here with my mother and visit the cliffs. My heart aches for her so badly that I can feel it deep in my bones.

"Catriona." Aiden's voice breaks me from the melancholy.

I turn to find him with his hands shoved inside his pockets, standing next to the dining room table. "Yes?"

"Dinner's ready. Guinness stew. Sit and I'll bring you a bowl."

"I can make it myself."

He gives me an unimpressed look. "Do you always have to fight me? Sit down so I can feed you before you collapse."

Now that I'm paying attention, the rich, savory scent of stew fills my nose and washes away any of my complaints. So I do as he says, but only because my stomach twists uncomfortably and I'm practically drooling.

He sets a large bowl, crusty bread, and a bottle of apple cider down on the table in front of me. I tuck in without a word, nearly moaning at how good it tastes. Because I'm not seated at a table with my father or his guests, I don't bother with being ladylike. I finish the meal in under ten minutes.

When I look up, he hasn't touched his food, and he's pressed back in his seat, watching.

Always watching.

"What?" I ask, on edge, angry with myself for forgetting he was here, even for a second.

He clears his throat, unable to meet my gaze for once. "I'm going to touch base with Cian tomorrow. He'll want us over for dinner soon. So you have plenty of time to rest and settle in before then. I don't know when I'll be back, but the caretakers' number is on the fridge, and Bren and Tadhg will be close by if you need them."

"Of course. I'll be fine."

The corner of his mouth lifts and crosses to me to press a sad smile into the top of my hair, which I try to ignore. "Try not to give them the slip. Don't leave the property without them, do you understand?" I'm glad I'm looking in the opposite direction so I can roll my eyes without him seeing.

"Of course. Trust me, I've learned my lesson."

"I shouldn't be long."

"Just don't come back with more tattoos of my name all over you. Or maybe you want to do my portrait this time, really drive it home how obsessed you are with me."

CHAPTER 26

AIDEN

> **Me**
> I want an update every half hour. How is she?

> **Bren**
> Same

I pocket my phone reluctantly the following morning, with all my instincts screaming at me to turn around and go back to the cottage immediately. But she's safe there. Cian has never learned of the property and wouldn't dare kill us before he had a chance to do it publicly, now that we're in arm's reach. He enjoys the spectacle too much.

And I'll deal with him.

Soon.

But first, there are a few final details to put my safeguards in place.

Pointing my rental car in the direction of town, I drive aimlessly, pausing every now and again to glance in my rearview mirror. The car that had followed us from the airport is still a few lengths back. Fuckin' amateurs.

I know it's not Cian, but it could be any number of Clans loyal to him. The Carrolls and Moores come to mind. They've all been placed in positions of favor since Cian came to power. Or it could be one of the others trying to make a power play to gain more esteem. Because that's what happens when you build a house of cards on blood. Everyone is willing to kill to get to the top.

I'm willing to kill, but I couldn't give a fuck about becoming a leader. Power corrupts absolutely, and I'm corrupt enough without that mantle.

I lead my pursuer on a winding, leisurely route through Doolin, before finally pulling to a stop at a local pub. One that wasn't here the last time I visited over a decade ago. Despite that, when I walk inside, it still feels like home. Worn, durable red oak bar top. Gleaming brass rails. The scent of hops, sweat, and wood polish.

I glance around for the person I'm waiting to meet, but it takes him a while to arrive. I make myself at home while I wait. Studying the faces around me to see if one of them is the tail who'd been following us. No one I recognize.

All too soon, the door jangles a greeting, and I glance in the mirror, dread pooling in my stomach as a familiar face takes a seat next to me.

"O'Connor," Niall Cleary says. "I almost didn't think you'd have the balls to show."

"You seem awfully concerned about the state of my balls."

"He could kill us for this, you know. Don't fuck with me."

"I wouldn't dare."

"Of course you wouldn't. The only reason I agreed to this is because you have something I want. Do you have it?"

I swallow hard. Wishing I could do anything else. "I spoke with Mara. She's agreed to marry you like you wanted. Provided that you do what you said you would."

"Oh, I will. I'm not a pussy like you. I know how to go after what I want."

I ignore him. "And the rest of the Clans? Do you have any willing to work with us?"

"Murphy agreed, of course. He's terrified of his brother. Burns and Kelly as well. They're tired of being so afraid."

The clock ticks on the wall behind the bar, but he doesn't continue. "That's it?"

He levels me with a glare. "You're lucky you have that many. You better be worth your word, O'Connor, or I'll make you regret it." Niall downs the rest of his drink. "That is, if we make it out of this alive. You tell Mara I'll be in touch so we can finally set a date for the fucking wedding."

God help him, she may kill him before he gets her down the aisle. But that's a problem for another day. I stay long after Niall leaves, hoping I'm doing the right thing. Trading Mom and Catriona's safety for Mara's freedom makes me feel about an inch tall. But when I brought it up to her the Tuesday following my meeting with Cian, she agreed. "It was going to happen sooner or later," she'd said. But that doesn't make me feel any better about any of it.

It doesn't take long for the tail that had been following us from the airport to make himself known once Niall leaves.

He appears next to me, his face grave and determined. I recognize him immediately. This is the man Catriona was with on the night of the reception, and the one she'd gone to see when she gave the guards the slip. He's tall, almost gangly, with unremarkable features and short brown hair. I dismiss my jealousy almost immediately. She wouldn't want him. He's far too soft. She'd break him the moment she sank her claws in.

There aren't many other people on a Wednesday morning, but he takes a seat next to me, eyes on me instead of the beer and liquor behind the bar.

"Why are you following us?" I ask, sipping at my gin for a taste of home. "Or do you have a death wish in general?"

"I'm Senator Gallagher's personal security. He's asked me to reach out to you regarding Miss Gallagher."

"I think you mean Mrs. O'Connor, and I know who you are. Devin Franklin, right?"

A slimy smile. "Of course. A scotch on the rocks," he tells the waiting bartender.

"You've come a long way to order a drink. Don't they have scotch in the States?" I ask mildly.

"Your wife is asking questions, and I'm sure you'll understand that the senator would prefer she stop. She's stirring up trouble."

"She does tend to do that," I say into my drink.

"Then you understand our predicament."

"I understand that I gave Senator Gallagher a warning. I told him if he ever threatened my wife again, he'd regret it."

He sighs, like this is one big waste of time for him. "Don't make us get nasty, O'Connor. We can make this a nightmare for you, too. For her. If you don't want to play ball, you can kiss her graduation goodbye. Her future in law? It'll be DOA, you understand. Dead on arrival. Your casino? Maybe your business permits get canceled. Your liquor license. The building gets condemned. There are a million ways we could make this go bad."

"Nasty, you say?" I finish my gin and throw some notes on the counter. "Sounds like a threat."

"It's not a threat. It's a promise."

"And if I said I wanted to make a deal?"

Franklin leans back and finishes his drink. "I'd say you were a smart man."

"Let's take this out back then, so we have some privacy," I suggest, and like a fucking eejit, he agrees.

"I knew you were a reasonable man," he says to my back, as I lead him through the pub, down a darkened hall to the back alley. If he knew any better, he'd realize I didn't consider him a threat by giving him my back. "Catriona, that girl has always been trouble. Sticking her nose where it doesn't belong. I'm sure she means well, but honestly, she's a stubborn little bitch. But I suppose you know that already, what with being married to her and all."

"Oh, I know."

The alley is clear except for a drunk who toddles off with one sharp look from me. Then we're alone. The shadows from the nearby buildings are thick, allowing me to conceal the gun I pull from my waistband.

"I told Mr. Gallagher you would. You seem like a reasonable man. He didn't think you would agree, but I insisted."

"Of course." I peer around us for cameras, but none cover the alley that I can see. Perfect. "About that deal."

"Yes. The senator is willing to put in a good word for you with—"

Unfortunately, I don't get to figure out the ways in which Rory Gallagher is willing to sell out his daughter, because the moment Devin Franklin turns around, I have my Glock pointed between his eyes.

"You know, I never thought I was much like the man who raised me. I prefer to think I got most of my personality traits from the man who made me, but I guess now, I know for certain there's some truth to the nurture aspect of that whole debate."

"You're going to regret this."

"Oh, I don't think I will. Because you see, Franklin, I told Rory if he ever threatened my wife again, I'd have a problem, and he didn't listen. Now—let's not embarrass ourselves with tears, Franklin. You need to take this like a man." I pause. "Where was I? Right. Now, the man who gave me life, he would have made some overtures. Gave you some hints. Knocked you around. Took a few fingers." At this, Franklin whimpers. Pussy. "But the man who raised me, well, he was from a different school of thought. He didn't believe in overtures."

"Look, you need to understand, your wife is—"

"What my wife does or doesn't do is not your concern."

"I'm telling you now, man to man, she's going to get herself hurt."

"Well, then it's a good thing she has me, isn't it?" I flip the safety and cock the gun. "I want to know everything he's said to you, and what she's told you."

"N-nothing, I promise. She was just busting my balls about her mom, man."

I consider this as I back him against the wall. "What about her mom?" I ask carefully.

"Shit, I don't know." He runs a hand through his thinning hair. "She keeps cornering me, asking questions about the night her mother died. I didn't have anything to do with her death, I swear."

The barrel of the gun slides through the gloss of sweat coating his head. "Are you sure about that?"

"Y-yes, man. Please. Let me go. I won't say anything."

"You know, I was there the night the man who raised me killed my father. Sounds like something you'd see on TV. But you want to know what I remember the most about that night?"

"Fuck, fuck, yeah, whatever you want."

"I remember how my father was on his knees. It had been raining, and he was freezing. My mother was next to me, watching. And all my father could do was say please, please. Please don't do this. Please don't make them watch. Please."

"You don't have to do it, man. I'll leave her alone."

"I learned that night I'm more monster than man. That I'd have to grow up to be more like the man who raised me if I wanted any hope of killing him. Payin' him back for what he did to my family."

Devin Franklin moans. Perhaps he realizes there are some fates you can't escape. Something I had to come to terms with myself.

"Tell me, did you have something to do with the person who took shots at her and the old man, Broussard?"

"I don't know anything about that. Fuck. Please."

If he were going to admit it, it'd be now. With my gun

carving a dent into his forehead and my hand fisted in his suit jacket. If he's lying, he's doing a damn convincing job of it. And I know what it's like to look a liar in the face.

I lower my gun and take a few steps back. Then I pause, aim it at his head, and say, "That's too bad. You would have been more useful if you had more information."

Then several things happen all at once: there are footsteps behind me. Shite! I give a half-turn automatically to look in the direction of the sound. My finger pulls the trigger, and the bullet misses Franklin by a hair. He screams and ducks, nearly falling to his ass among the garbage.

Turning, I scan the space to my right for the source of the sound, but find nothing. I do the same on my left and see a figure moving toward me. What little light there is in the alley glints off the silver of a knife arcing toward me. I manage to turn on instinct, and the hot fire slashes through my shoulder.

A grunt punches out of me at the searing pain, but experience tells me it's not a mortal wound. The attack unbalances me enough that I crash into the brick wall of the building, and my head glances off, sending sparks through my vision. My knees buckle as darkness encroaches.

Devin hisses at them to leave before I get up. And then the darkness, my old friend, swallows me whole.

"Hey! You. Get out of here before I call the garda." There's the rustle of footsteps. "I mean it! I don't want any trouble."

I jerk to my feet at the first sound of the voice. My head and shoulder scream in protest, but whatever happened, I don't want to be here if the proprietor follows through on their threats. Stumbling, I find the end of an alleyway, wincing as the sun stabs into my brain.

By the grace of God, I find my rental and climb in. By the time I settle behind the wheel, the memory of what happened comes back to me in a sickening roil.

Devin Franklin.

The knife.

Fuck, no wonder my arm aches like a bitch.

I peel out of my jacket, grimacing as it screams in protest. The slash is only a couple of inches. I got fucking lucky. Then I find my phone and check messages.

9:33 a.m. Bren
Same

10:02 a.m. Bren
Same

10:36 a.m. Bren
Same

11:01 a.m. Tadhg
Same

11:39 a.m. Tadhg
She's leaving the property to shop in town.
We're following close behind.

3:11 p.m. Tadhg
She's heading back to the cottage

A quick check of my watch shows it's 5:38 p.m. Mouth tasting like the inside of a gin bottle, I drive back to the cottage, stopping first to check on Bren and Tadhg and clean up. Bren, who took an emergency medicine course, stitches up the wound on my shoulder.

The call from Cian, summoning us to family dinner at eight-thirty, comes as we're finishing up.

I leave them with instructions to contact Eamon and find out all they can about Devin Franklin and his known associates, and to make sure he's already left Ireland. Because if he hasn't, when I find him, there's a bullet with his name on it.

CHAPTER 27

CATRIONA

I glance up from the chess table where I've been staring for the past quarter hour, going slightly insane. The game I've been half-ass playing with myself hasn't been able to catch my attention.

It's been hours since I've seen or heard from Aiden. I'm not worried. I shouldn't give a damn what he does with his time. He certainly doesn't need to check in with me even though he said he would. The only reason I keep looking out of the front window is because I'm waiting on my jailers to pull out behind me so I can kill time in town.

When my phone rings next to me, I nearly jump out of my seat. "Aiden?" I croak without looking at the screen.

"No, Catriona, this is Broussard. Leonardo Broussard."

I nearly choke. "Mr. Broussard. I didn't expect to hear from you. Sorry about that. How are you? Still recovering okay?"

After the shooting, I went back to the hospital several times to check in with him. He spent most of his recovery resting, as he should, and no amount of my apologies or impassioned arguments would deter him from the case. If anything, it only seemed to serve as further motivation.

"Yes, I am. Practically as good as new, thank you for asking. I was wondering if you'd have time to meet today. I'm afraid the news I have is rather urgent."

"Today? No, I'm so sorry. I'm in Ireland on… business. Would it be possible to discuss over the phone?" There's a long pause, where I wonder if we've been disconnected. "Mr. Broussard?"

"It's not ideal, but I've come across something interesting in your mother's records I thought may be relevant."

I wipe my sweaty palms on my jeans. "Then I'd rather know sooner than later. What did you find?"

"Do you recall when we went over your mother's calendar and finances that she'd been to see a lawyer?"

"Vaguely, yes. What would that have to do with her death? It wasn't a routine meeting? She dealt with lawyers all the time."

"No, I'm afraid. When I looked deeper into her emails, I found reference to a change in her will. Did she ever mention it?"

"Really?" My mind comes up blank. "No, she never said anything to me. Why would she do that?"

"I wish I knew. I'm going to reach out to the law office, but I wanted your approval first."

"Of course. Whatever you have to do."

Afterward, I don't remember if I asked Broussard any

clarifying questions. Which means I certainly don't remember the answers.

The words echo in my head as Bren knocks on the door, with Tadhg in the car waiting out front. I load up with them, make conversation, but it's as though someone else is in control of my brain, my body. It takes what feels like an eternity to drive from the cottage on the cliffs to the center of town. Bren and Tadhg speak, but I barely hear any of it. My mind keeps replaying the conversation with Broussard.

Changed her will.

Changed her will.

Changed her will.

As I wander the picturesque streets with quaint little shops made of what looks like white plaster and stonework, my fretting over Aiden's whereabouts rematerializes. Where the fuck is he? He wasn't supposed to take this long. If he's so goddamn worried about my safety, why isn't he here to make sure I'm actually fucking safe?

If this were really our honeymoon, he should be here, patiently letting me look through each cute little shop and urging me to buy whatever my heart desires.

It's then that I give in to the little devil on my shoulder. The one that tells me to send Aiden a giant fuck you for believing he's allowed to order me around.

So while I'm browsing around the shops, I buy whatever my heart desires and pay extra to have them drop it off at the cottage. With the sheer number of purchases, it would be impossible to fit it all in our tiny little rental car. It's an odd request that garners a few befuddled looks, but if there's one thing my father's taught me, it's that money talks. I doubt my little shopping spree will put a dent in the black card Aiden gave me, but I do my level best. Maybe if he bothered to show up, he'd be able to stop me.

Really, it's his fault I end up with stacks and stacks of books, one-of-a-kind jewelry, an entire wardrobe to fill the empty walk-in closet at his place, and wine bottles by the dozen. I treat myself to a lengthy, indulgent lunch at The Ivy Cottage in their lovely outdoor seating area, followed by a few gin and tonics at Gus O'Connor's Pub (no relation, thank God).

I haven't been keeping track, but I wouldn't be surprised if I'd managed a quarter of a million dollars. A small fortune was spent on handmade merino and cashmere alone. I couldn't resist when I learned the nearby Aran Islands are famous for their sweaters. It's not only because they're expensive. Maybe I love a good knit.

By the time we drive back to the cottage, I'm pleasantly worn out and slightly buzzed from the glass of champagne the lovely barkeep provided in addition to the gin and tonics, when he learned I was on my so-called honeymoon. I've all but stewed myself into the perfect rage for a major confrontation with Aiden, but the driveway is empty of his rental car, and the lights inside the cottage are still all off.

He's not back yet. It's nearly evening. How long could a conversation with Cian take? If that's what he's even doing. How am I supposed to know for sure?

I'm not disappointed.

Or, if I am, it's only because I was looking forward to showing him exactly how much I don't care that he's not there.

After telling my bodyguards I'll be at the cliffs—and no, they don't need to follow me—I change into the rain boots and stomp my way through the muddy fields again toward the cliffs. I have half a mind to stay out here and lose myself in their wild expanse.

What if I never went back? What if I gave up the impossible task I've set myself and disappeared instead? It's so open here, I feel almost anonymous. With the endless sea of grass and blanket of fluffy white clouds, I could be someone else other than Rory Gallagher's daughter or Aiden O'Connor's wife.

It's almost dusk, but I plant myself on the edge of the cliffs and stare out into the water. I try to clear my mind of all worries, but it's impossible when they're so loud they drown out the sound of wind, waves, and birdsong. If I keep going down this path, there will be no stopping me. Like an avalanche, I'll destroy everything in my way.

I don't know how long I sit out there, lost in the mire of my thoughts. Long enough that the chill seeps through one of my new sweaters and light jacket and for the sun to slip down until the horizon almost swallows it up. When the light around me changes from gold to lavender, I know I should head back in. I'm already pushing my luck as it is. It's a miracle O'Connor hasn't come back already.

I push my fingers into my eyes, hoping it'll give me some clarity, but all I see are the impressions of starbursts over my vision.

Vertigo assaults me when I try to stand. Flailing for balance, I remember how close I'm sitting to the edge of the cliffs and how insane it is that there's no safety fence to block idiots like me from falling to their deaths. I fall on my ass, screwing my eyes shut again and knotting my fingers in the grass as though it'll keep me safe, nails driving into the loamy soil.

When my vision clears, I find Aiden staring down at me, one hand on my jaw, the other on the ground beside me.

"What are you doin' out here, love?" he asks, face flushed with exertion. "How long have you been out here?"

I tell myself it's fear that makes the bottom drop out of my stomach at the sight of him, incandescent with rage. I tell myself it's apprehension that has my breath stuttering in my chest and my hands trembling where they go up to grip his wrist.

There are a lot of things I tell myself, and maybe if I repeat them enough, I'll start believing they're the truth.

"What does it matter to you? Anything could have happened to me today and you wouldn't have even known." If I were a smart girl, I'd learn to shut my mouth.

His eyes grow wide, and I almost smile in his face. "What does it matter to me? What does it—" He breaks off and studies me with liquid eyes. It's then that I notice the wound on his head, hastily put together with Band-Aids.

My heart is in my throat. "What happened?"

"It's a long story. I'm fine. Let's go back to the house."

"Did Cian do that?" He doesn't answer. "I thought we were past secrets, *O'Connor*. Or are you just completely full of shit?"

He studies my face for a long, long moment, as though he's trying to decipher my thoughts written into my expression, like they're in an unfamiliar language. "It took longer than I thought. But that's not what you're mad about, is it?"

I look away. I don't know what I'm doing. Running around. Blowing money when so much is at stake. Wanting his attention? *Worried* about him? Trying to piss him off so he'll come back to me? No man has ever driven me this crazy. I swear, I was normal before he came into my life.

"Forget about it," I mutter, face burning now. I want to shove to my feet, but he's too close. It had been easier to have him on his knees. To humiliate him. It covered up how much I wanted him. Gave me a way to force him to give me what I needed without admitting anything. Is that how he felt the night we met? Is that why he did what he did in the limo? It was easier to keep me at arm's length to take what he wanted?

As though he can fucking read my thoughts again, he crouches in front of me. "Is that what you want from me, wife? You need me to show you what happens to bad girls who don't do what they're told?"

I don't answer him. I couldn't even if I could get the words to form on my tongue. My eyes feel as wide as saucers as he shoves me back into the grass. If I were in my right mind, I'd push him away and tell him where he can shove his filthy mouth, but when he tugs off my boots, unbuttons and unzips my jeans, the only thing on my mind is a gentle buzzing that blots out absolutely everything else.

He's here. He's okay. He's here.

His hand is scalding against my chilled skin as it slides into my panties. He reclines next to me, blocking out the path in case anyone were to wander out here, but due to the time of day, it seems unlikely. It doesn't matter. All I want is for him to keep filling my thoughts with nothingness.

Just for a little while.

It's the lightest touch of his middle finger against my clit, barely even a whisper of sensation, but it rockets through me like dynamite. I suck in a breath, the sound swallowed by the low roar of the wind, and my whole body tightens, muscles clenching in sweet anticipation.

A low chuckle rumbles close to my ear.

"Is that how it is? You've been waiting all day for me to come back? And I thought I was a glutton for *your* attention. Were you missing me while I was gone? Daydreaming schemes to piss me off enough that I'd come find you? I don't know how I feel about that, darlin'. I'm supposed to be the one fighting for you to pay me any mind. Is there a reason you want my hands on you now?"

I lift my hips, unable to tell him to stop talking and start making me come.

"That's okay. You don't have to answer. I'm going to enjoy the fuck out of this."

In my head, I scream at him to move, to apply pressure or drive his thick, long fingers inside me, but he keeps his touch teasing, rubbing my clit with practiced ease as though it's not growing increasingly dark by the second. The breeze teases the skin exposed by my hastily pushed-up shirt. It makes me hyperaware of the fact that we're in the middle of a popular tourist destination. It's remote, but not so much that people never wander along this path. My heart pounds with the possibility of being caught.

I sob for breath even though he's barely touching me at all. The relief of my brain shutting off makes even those slightest sensations a thousand times more powerful. Maybe it's because I know the kind of person he is that makes it so easy to demand these depraved things from him. Perhaps it's because I have no illusions about what he's capable of.

Aiden is a monster, a cold-blooded killer.

But he's never hidden that from me, not even the night we met.

His mouth descends on my throat, his teeth nibbling at my jaw, then teasing my ear. When his breath brushes against me, I shiver violently, causing his fingers to slip down. Without conscious thought, I lift my hips to catch them and the slightest tip slips in. That one small contact has my breath hitching.

"Naughty wife. Trying to take what I haven't given you yet. Is that why you haven't asked me? Because then you'd have to admit you can want someone like me? Because you'd have to admit a small part of you cares for me?"

His finger thrusts in the slightest bit, just enough to whet my appetite, to drive all rational thought from my mind. *Yes.* He's emptying me out and filling me at the same time, and despite knowing how wrong it is, I've never wanted anything more in my fucking life.

"That's okay. I know you want it. Want me to punish you for craving something so wrong?" I sob, and he takes it for the admission of guilt it is. "That's what I thought."

His thick, rough finger fills me, and the ache is so delicious it takes me a beat to realize it's not just one, or two, but three. The stretch soothes something inside me, breaks something inside me so completely that my brain turns off.

Because that's my terrible, horrible truth.

Despite what he's capable of, despite what he made me do, I want him to erase my thoughts. Want the punishment of his hands, his mouth, his cock. His absolution and damnation all in one destructive collision.

When my cries grow so loud that I worry we may attract every tourist in the vicinity, Aiden seems to read my mind.

He flips me over, yanks down my jeans and underwear, and plants his hand in the grass in front of my face, his body hot and hard over me. "Bite down if you can't help the screams, Catriona."

Had I been screaming? Unable to muster up the perception needed to find out for certain, I do as I'm told and bite down. The hot, salty taste of him fills my mouth. I have one moment to suck in a bracing inhalation before his fingers are back, driving inside me with an abandon that cares nothing for if it hurts. Because it does, but so deliciously that it draws tears from my eyes to streak down my cheeks. The constant threat of being caught, even if his body hides most of what's exposed, sends my arousal rocketing to new heights.

He twists his hand, fingers knocking against something vital and white-hot. I forget to breathe, and it doesn't escape his notice. "That it, huh? Are you going to come for me? Soak my hand? Leave me smelling like you for hours until I'm forced to wash it off? Come for me, and I'll fuck you right here, where anyone could see."

That's it. His words are the spark, and I'm the kindling. I tip my hips for him, arching my back, ready to accept the bone-melting pleasure.

In my desperation, I reach back for his shoulder, and he cries out, but it's not a sound of pleasure.

"Aiden?" I ask, twisting to see his face. He pulls his fingers out and sits back on his haunches. A small, dark stain appears on his shoulder. I know I was clawing at him, but it wasn't enough to draw blood. The desire that had been building in my stomach cools. "What's wrong? What happened?"

His pupils are blown wide, mouth hard with desire and

flinty with stubbornness. He puts his fingers to his mouth and licks them clean at a leisurely pace that causes my stomach to twist with confusion and apprehension. Despite how erotic the sight is, the mood is ruined.

"The cottage," he says, as I pull up my soaked underwear and my grass-stained jeans. "Not here."

The ruined orgasm still flutters through my muscles, pulses sweetly through my veins, and I'm hyperaware of how wet I am as we move silently back to the path that leads to the house.

He stops at the gate to open the padlock that will allow us into the small cattle field where cows graze lazily on tall, sweet grass. He takes my hand and pulls me through the gate. I can't stop looking at it wrapped around mine as he practically drags me from the cliffs back to the cottage.

My name, permanently marked onto his skin. My ring on his finger. I shouldn't like anything about it, but it makes something inside me twist with pleasure. It feels a lot like claiming someone. Having power over them. And for someone who has had very little power, it's an addictive thought.

Dangerous.

CHAPTER 28

AIDEN

A million shopping bags are scattered in the living area, ones that I must have missed when I got back to the cottage and realized Catriona wasn't there. I hadn't been thinking straight when I burst inside and found it empty. I'd been stupid to leave her, even with Bren and Tadhg watching, but the meeting with Niall couldn't be postponed. I should have brought backup with me. I'm getting arrogant and sloppy. And I can't afford to be. The thought of leaving her alone haunts me worse than Cian's specter ever has.

"Hope you don't mind," she says when she notices where I focus my attention. "I took myself on a little shopping trip today. You'll be pleased to know how much your money has gone to support the local community."

If Cian weren't waiting on us, I'd give her plenty of suggestions, all right.

Tugging her forward by her wrist, I move to the

bedroom, where a dress I picked out for her waits with all the appropriate accessories. "You should get changed. Dinner is tonight. I thought we'd have more time, but apparently, he can't wait."

Catriona plants her feet, stopping in the doorway to the bedroom. "Aren't you going to tell me what happened? Is that his handiwork? Why were you late?"

I could lie and come up with something plausible. But... she's been calling me Aiden. I can't remember the last time she called me by my first name. Is that all it takes for me to be on my knees for her?

"Aiden," she barks.

And I know my answer.

She brushes by me and notes the clothes with a raised eyebrow. I move to give her privacy, but she's already peeling off her sweater, kicking off her boots, and pushing down her jeans. She unclasps her bra and her tits bounce free, tipped with berry-pink nipples already twisted into points.

The sight of her practically naked withers my demands, and I sink to the bed. My throat goes dry. The thoughts of making her come again come roaring back from where I'd buried them way, way down. Along with it comes all the emotions I didn't want to feel. The fear of finding the cottage empty. The stomach-dropping realization that I couldn't just push the threat of losing her to the side. That it would matter to me if she wasn't here. How disappointed I am in myself for letting her matter, even the slightest bit. When I'd found her on the cliffs, I nearly wilted with relief.

"Your man, Devin? Devin Franklin?"

She scoffs, standing only in her light blue panties that complemented her blue sweater. There's a wet spot that outlines every delicious curve of her lips. It takes every ounce of my self-control to keep from pushing her to the bed so I can feast.

"He's not my man," she's saying, but I'm still talking.

"He followed us here."

"He... what?" The last is said with a growl.

"I noticed the tail when we left the airport. Thought it was a coincidence until it stuck close until we reached the cottage. I left this morning to see if they'd stayed overnight and if they'd follow me out. They did." I keep going, mostly because she's so shocked she's standing there, tits out, and I get to look my fill. It makes admitting my mistakes a little easier. "He walked right up to me at a pub in town. Admitted your father told him to come, to stop you from asking about your mother." I manage to tear my gaze from her body. "Want to tell me what that's about?"

"Why should I?" she challenges, lifting her chin. Defiant. Fuck. I've never seen anyone so strong and sexy. This woman hasn't given me an inch since the day I met her. She's fought for everything she's wanted, no matter the cost. Is it any surprise I'm obsessed with her?

But I know if I force her, if I move too fast, she'll balk, like a colt. She's brave and determined, but she's also guarded. And so fucking stubborn. I want her to come to me more than I want to break her again.

"Because he didn't come alone, someone was with him."

She studies the dress and the lingerie laid out on the bed. Mara chose them for me, knowing what would be required, and sent it along before we'd flown out. She'd also helped me pack a bag for the short overnight stay. The dress is another in white, this one simple silk with thin shoulder straps. The lingerie is nude and designed to be practically invisible underneath.

I'm already seething at the thought of Cian's eyes roving over her, drinking in her bare skin. It will be a monumental test of my self-control to make it until morning without putting a knife in his gut or a bullet in his brain. Over the years, I've fantasized a thousand different ways for him to die and, despite my extensive education in murder, I've never settled on a favorite.

Her feet pad lightly against the wood floors as she crosses the room until she's standing in front of me. Her nipples are nearly eye level. The mattress strains under my grip.

"What happened next? How did he hurt you?" Against my command, my body sways toward her like I'm a plant and she's the sun. I nuzzle between her breasts, hands going to her hips to tug her against me. The scent of her arousal teases my nose.

"I'll tell you if you tell me why you keep asking him about your mother." I give in, kissing the soft, creamy skin and feel her breath catch under my lips. "What is it you think you're going to find?"

She tries to hedge, moving away from me, but I catch her by the hips so she can't move an inch. Her glare doesn't deter me, and I hold her there until she bites her lip and shifts from foot to foot. Either she can start to trust me—even if I don't deserve it—or we can keep this dance of blades until one of us falters.

I have time, either way.

My fingers tighten on her skin, and I force myself to gentle. I won't push her in this. No, I want her to come to me. To give this piece to me.

"I've been looking—" She pauses, gulps, then takes a deep breath. "I've been looking into my mother's death. I know it wasn't an accident."

That's my girl. "And you think Devin had something to do with it?"

Her lips twist. "Broussard, he's not my adviser."

"He's not," I say with deadly calm.

"He's a private investigator."

"A private investigator."

"Are you just going to repeat everything I say?" She tries to put her hands on her hips and realizes I'm still holding her, then crosses her arms over her tits. I frown at their loss. "We have reason to believe Devin was present the night she died and lied about it, among other things."

"I knew I was right when I put a tracker in your ring. Devin probably followed you straight to him the day he was shot."

"You put a tracker in my ring?" she shrieks. "When?"

"You're damn fucking right, I did. The day after they put him into the hospital. And apparently for good reason. Running off, putting yourself into trouble. It's a full-time job just keeping you alive."

"There are so many things wrong with what you just said, I don't know where to start."

Before she can work herself into a lather, I distract her with, "What would his motive be?"

She sends me a scathing look when she's unable to jerk free of my grasp. If she's not careful, she's going to wind up with bruises peppering her thighs.

It sidetracks me for a moment of blazing-hot need. Catriona has a body that's stolen so many hours of sleep, I'd wondered if I could die from it. Unique in every aspect, her curves, freckles, dimples, and skin are so soft, all I could think about is seeing it blushing red and bruised from my punishing hands.

Because oh, how I wanted to see her painted in my marks. Mottled with my whorls and loops. Necklaces and bracelets gifted on her skin, semi-permanent, tender and aching. A reminder for the next time she tries to sneak away from me like she did that night.

"I don't *know*, that's what I've been trying to figure out with Broussard," she says, when I'm able to focus on her. "I found my mother's phone at the estate during Halloween and—"

"You sneaky little witch. *That's* why you were there that night? I could have killed you when I found you."

"I didn't have another choice. There were no other leads. The police were stonewalling me. My father wouldn't hear anything I had to say, and Elizabeth pretends it never happened. What else did you expect me to do?"

"Stop risking your life, for one."

She waves this away. "I knew it was the last place her phone could be, and I was right. I found it. Broussard has been helping me go through it to find leads."

"I'm sure." I'm not jealous of an ancient old man. I'm not.

Catriona levels a look at me, and I don't know if she realizes it, but she's shifted closer. Her nipples are close enough that I could wrap my lips around one. "Now tell me what happened. Did he go home?"

No man could withstand these circumstances. With a hand on her spine, I pull her forward, take one nipple between my teeth, groaning as fire shoots through me. I lave her nipple with gentle flicks, teasing with my teeth, until she knots her fingers in my hair and exerts inexorable pressure until I release her so I don't cause her harm.

She tilts my head back. "Don't distract me, Aiden O'Connor. Be a good husband and tell me what happened."

Fuck. She ruins me.

I crack a smile. "Husband. I like it when you call me that." Her fingers twist, and I wince. "Fuck, fine, woman. I had him out back with a gun to his head when someone came out of nowhere with the knife. I got knocked into the wall and passed out. They were gone by the time I woke up."

The fingers in my hair go slack. "They could have killed you. You were passed out with no one there to protect you, and they could have fucking killed you. You go on and on about me having bodyguards and threatening to put a tracker on me, yet you walk around with all these people after you."

I wince. "It turned out alright."

Her fingers slide to my shoulders as her expression turns pensive, and I give a half-hearted thought to taking her in my mouth again, but brush it away with no small amount of regret.

"So he's working with someone. And Dad is trying to cover up what happened. Whatever it is."

"When we get back to New Orleans, we'll figure it out. But for tonight, I need my wife by my side. You understand? There are some things I haven't told you about how this goes."

"I'm sure," she says. She takes a step back, and her panties drop to the floor, leaving her beautiful body completely bare to me. I study the shadowed heaven between her legs, and she's fucking dripping.

"You're a cruel, cruel woman," I say, unable to look away.

"I take it I don't have time to clean up?" she asks, and I can hear the smile in her voice.

All I can do is shake my head. The cave dweller part of my brain is delighted at the thought of her walking around still wet from wanting me.

We spend the ride to Cian's place in silence, our earlier ardor cooled by the growing threats looming ahead of us. The muscles along my back and neck twitch with repressed energy mingling with excitement. As much as I'm dreading being back here with Cian and having Catriona so close to him, I get to see my mother again. Introduce her to my wife. It almost doesn't feel real.

As though I called her with my thoughts, the front door to Cian's home opens to reveal her standing in the doorway. I freeze as emotion assails me, my lungs seizing, my muscles tightening.

"Ma," I say, my voice a ragged, boyish croak.

She's the same as I remember, yet altogether not. Or maybe it's because I've grown that she seems so small and vulnerable. Even more than I remember when I'd been forced to leave her. Her light brown hair is still the same, just long enough to brush her shoulders and frame an elfin face. Blue eyes a couple of shades darker than mine. A wide smile that flickers before wobbling with happy tears. If I also notice the lines carved into her skin, the missing ring finger she tries to hide, and the way she's thin, too thin, I conceal them so I can have this moment. Just one, where I get to feel relief.

I draw her against my body and wrap my arms around

her for a protracted moment. It's been so long. So long that there was a point when I began to accept I may never see her again. It feels like this is the first time since I lost her when oxygen finally reaches my brain.

"Aiden," she says, breathing heavily into my shirt. "My boy, I've missed you very much. I'm so glad to see you."

She squeezes me tight, and I breathe in the floral scent of her so deeply, I want to draw it into my marrow. Her hands tug at my clothes trying to pull me closer.

"It's good to see you, too. I thought I wouldn't see you until dinner."

I hold her until she starts laughing and pulls away. "I've missed you, too, my boy. There was no way I was going to wait to see you again. God, you look just like your father. So handsome." She squeezes me with bird-like hands. Dainty and easily broken. She presses her mouth against my cheek. "Please. Don't worry anymore. Everything is going to be okay." And then she turns to Catriona, and I wonder if I misunderstood her. "And you. I've been waiting to meet you." She releases my hands and steps around me to give Catriona the same treatment. "Aiden's told me so much about you."

Is it me, or is she not able to look at me?

Catriona stills, her eyes going wide and flying to mine as Ma wraps her in a hug I know must be boa-constrictor tight. She's stiff for a long moment, and I see the second she gives in, relaxes, and hugs Ma back. It's almost like she's forgotten the feeling, and I realize maybe she has. Her mother died nearly a year ago.

I turn away from them and study my surroundings blindly so I don't let myself think about it for too long. The last thing I need to be tonight is distracted. And thinking about Catriona lost and alone after the death of her mother hits a little bit too close to home.

"I'm Catriona. It's lovely to meet you, Mary. Aiden has missed you so much." Her voice ends on a choked sound.

"Catriona," Ma says warmly, and I can't remember the last time I've heard her so... happy. The light, carefree tone in her voice is happiness. Has it really been so long that I'd forgotten what it sounded like? The thought guts me so completely I go still as a standing stone. "Please, come with me. We have a bit of time before we'll have to be at dinner. I would love to show you my gardens, if you'd like."

"I'd love that," and Catriona sounds so sincere, even I believe her.

Ten minutes later, I have my hands in my pockets as I trail behind the two of them. Ma has both of her arms clutched around Catriona, but my wife doesn't seem to mind. Their heads are bent close together as Catriona replays our wedding ceremony for her benefit. It's then that it occurs to me she didn't get to see it. She'll never attend my wedding. Just another thing Cian has stolen from us.

I look away, jaw flexing, as I study the perfectly pruned flowers to get myself back under control. Only, the sight of them doesn't give me the respite I'd hoped for. It only reminds me of the gilded cage she's endured in my absence.

With effort, I'm able to rejoin them in the rows and rows of my mother's most prized possessions: her flowers. It eases something in me to see them together. For my mother to have a moment of respite from Cian's dominion.

"I couldn't resist the opportunity to meet the woman

who bested my son. I don't know whether to tell you congratulations or offer my condolences."

She'd be well within her rights to disparage me to hell and back for what I've done since we said our vows. I wouldn't blame her. Being near my mother strips me of all my defenses in a way that nothing else can. I'm a sitting duck for her here, easy pickings.

But instead of listing all of my many faults, Catriona smiles kindly. "You have a lovely garden here, Mrs. Lynch. And you should be proud. Aiden is remarkable. The charity work he does, how fast his business has grown. I wish you could have made it to the wedding. I would love to show you around if you ever make it to New Orleans."

Mom's smile crinkles her eyes, and at that moment, I know I'd give Catriona whatever she asked. I'd turn her father's house into ruins. I'd bare my throat for her. Because she didn't have to be nice to my mother. She didn't have to give her the impression our union was anything other than fifty ways of fucked until now.

She's given me the one thing I haven't had since I was a boy—a moment of peace where my mother is concerned. When we leave here, and my mother is once again alone with the evil that is Cian Lynch, at least it will console her knowing I have a good woman at my side. Ma won't have to go to bed worrying about me being on my own to deal with Cian forever, which is more than I can say for her.

It disarms me in a way no other person has ever been able to. Wrecks me completely.

No one in this world has ever had the ability to cut me off at the knees like this.

Except for maybe Cian.

And isn't it a terrifying thought that my little wife has as much power over me as the man who's had me by the balls for most of my life?

Their conversation continues as they stroll through the garden as Ma shows Catriona her favorite varieties: snow drops, daffodils, primrose, bluebells, buttercups, and a half-dozen others in addition to what seems like every variety of rose under the sun. I trail behind, letting the sight of them together center me.

"These are lovely," Catriona says, stopping to sniff a fat yellow rose with her eyes closed. "I can't believe you tend to them yourself. I'm afraid I have a black thumb. I get so excited that I buy everything in the store and six weeks later, it's like a massacre."

My ma laughs. She fucking *laughs*.

"Why don't I give you some tips? As in real estate, it's all about location..."

They talk for what feels like hours. Catriona keeps looking back at me, checking my expression, for what I'm not sure, but I give her a nod to let her continue. Ma and I could never talk like this; we've never been this comfortable outside the hugs we share when we see each other again. The man I've become is always at the forefront of her mind, and the atrocities she's had to endure for me or because of me are at the forefront of mine.

So I don't dare interrupt them. Instead, I drink in my ma's expressions and stow them away to remember later. Catriona doesn't bring up the truth about our wedding, though Ma must have some idea. She talks about school and how much she's been struggling since her mother died. They share another long hug, because Ma's always been the empathetic sort, unable to stand by when someone else is suffering.

By the time night has truly fallen and the gardens are lit only by moonlight, my chest aches something fuckin' awful. Not only because I don't know if I'll ever experience this again, but because the sound of footsteps reaches my ear.

Cian's here.

CHAPTER 29

CATRIONA

"I see you started the family reunion without us, sweetheart."

Everything inside me screams to get Mary and Aiden out of here—shield them, hide them, kill the man stepping onto the gravel path in front of us—but one glance at Cian's eyes locks my knees into place. He's got two armed men at his side because of course he does. Aiden may be ruthless and a trained killer, but going against three armed men? I wouldn't want him to risk it.

"Cian," Mary says, her eyes growing duller with each passing second. She pulls her arm out of mine. Her calm seems unnatural. How can she face him without cowering in his presence? Especially after all this time as the recipient of his brutality?

Cian's mouth curves, but on him it's not a smile. It contains no warmth. No emotion. Just the threat of teeth.

As though by wordless instruction, Mary leaves us to go to Cian's side. Her movements are careful—is she hurt?—and her breathing is even more measured. She tilts her cheek to him, her lips pressed into a line, and he presses a perfunctory kiss to her brow.

But his gaze never strays from me.

Aiden shifts closer, instinctively sliding an arm around my waist. It's a claiming I'm not certain is altogether wise, but Cian only grunts, the cold blue chips of his eyes raking over us. They glimmer with anticipation.

"Well," he says, his voice smooth as oil. "Let's not keep everyone waiting."

He spins, taking Mary along with him, and it takes everything in me to keep from ripping her from his grasp. She seems so fragile compared to his formidable presence. Like he could swallow her up. Or maybe that he already has.

My temples throb, and the only thing keeping me upright is the grip Aiden has around my waist. A sense of foreboding turns my muscles to jelly. We shouldn't have come here. We should have figured something else out. They're going to kill us. I know with an innate sense of certainty. Cian wanted Aiden humiliated and broken. Ready to walk into his death on a false mission to save his mother.

I forget how to breathe.

How are we going to get out of this?

We never should have gotten on the plane.

I try to think of a play, something to get the three of us out of here alive, but I come up with nothing. Aiden's hand tightens around me, and it grounds me, but only a little. Nothing is going to save us from bullets if they decide to put a few in our brains.

Finally, we end up at a pair of double doors after a long march through labyrinthine hallways. Cian pushes them open to a dining room that feels more like a tribunal than anything else. The table stretches the length of the room and is filled with harsh, cruel faces. The heads of each Clan and their bodyguards? I don't know. I try to remember the names of each of them, but draw a blank. Then I recognize the ones who'd been in the room. Who'd watched us. Fear crests through me. There are so many of them.

We're never going to get out of here.

Their eyes snap up to us as we enter. My lungs constrict even further, and my head spins. "Breathe," Aiden says in my ear. Or maybe I'm imagining it. More armed men file in to block the exits with guns at their ribs.

Cian gestures to the table to a seat at his right. Mary takes her place at his left. With a steady hand, Aiden leads me to a chair. I fall into it, grateful to be off my nerveless legs. I try to catch Mary's eye, but she won't look up from her ruined hands. The sweet, happy woman I'd met seems to have disappeared. More than anything, it makes me want to cry.

She deserves so much more than this.

Everyone sits but Cian, who strolls behind the chairs of everyone in attendance, calling out names I don't remember. I stay unnaturally still as he circles, my senses tracking him like a prey animal scenting a predator. Aiden's hand finds my thigh. The grounding touch provides a little comfort.

Cian stops behind me. "Life is full of surprises, isn't it? And no one knows that more than Aiden."

Muffled chuckles ripple around us, but not everyone laughs. Some men shift, their expressions tightening as they remember their own families, wives, children. It's easy to forget that evil is at your door when it's terrorizing someone else a continent away or a woman hidden behind closed doors.

"Speaking of, Mary, why don't you pour us some wine so Aiden can see how well trained you've become. Almost as good of a dog as your son." There's a general shifting of the men at the table. A few laugh, but many less than before.

My muscles are solid stone as I imagine all the ways I'd kill this monster if I could.

Mary doesn't seem to acknowledge Cian's instructions at all. I wouldn't even think she heard him because her face doesn't lose its serene mask. Instead, she crosses to a sideboard where there are bottles of wine and glasses. She busies herself with her task, and I quickly peer up at Aiden to gauge his reaction.

Cian is doing the same as if anticipating Aiden to blow a fuse. He doesn't. Cian falters for a moment. Then Mary returns with two glasses of wine. She hands one to Aiden and takes one for herself. Servants provide the rest, who shift uncomfortably.

"We're gathered here to celebrate the marriage of Catriona Gallagher and Aiden O'Connor. With our blessing, they will join our organization, and their union will bless us for many years to come. If you'll join me in a toast to the happy couple?"

Reluctantly, we raise our glasses. I hold mine to my lips, but I don't drink. Aiden lifts his for a second before placing it back down. Some drink a sip, some more than one. Mary downs hers faster than anyone else at the table, and Cian isn't far behind.

I glance at Aiden, who is watching his mother with a frown carved into his face.

"To the Clans!" Cian jeers, distracting me, and they chant it back to him.

"And now, for the evening's entertainment," he says, rounding the table to where Mary is clutching her wineglass like a lifeline. She stares into its emptiness like she's going to divine her future. Cian's hands settle on her shoulders, but she doesn't move. She doesn't seem to even realize he's behind her. My blood is ice in my veins. Aiden is stone beside me.

"We have a special guest joining us tonight."

My teeth grind together. The man sure has a penchant for theatrics, but I really wish he'd get on with it.

The room is silent now. A captive audience.

It's so quiet I can hear heels clicking against the floor on the other side of the door.

It opens.

Devin walks in, and behind him...

Elizabeth?

I jerk hard enough to rattle the silverware on the table. My body tenses so hard, I'm afraid I'll snap in half. "Bethie? What—what are you doing here?" I double blink, certain fear has me hallucinating, but no matter how much I try, the vision of them doesn't go away.

"Come in, come in. Why don't you have a seat?" Cian pulls out a couple of chairs next to Mary.

"What's going on?" I look from Elizabeth to Devin as my brows draw together. "What are you doing here?"

"Like I said," Cian interjects. "You got started on the family reunion before all of the family was here."

"W-what?"

"Please. Quit the innocent act, Catriona. I'm so sick of it." Elizabeth leans forward on the table. "You know, I used to be jealous of you. How close you and Mom were, how she would exclude me. I bet you didn't even notice."

"What? No, Mom loved you. Elizabeth, you've got it all wrong."

"No, *you've* got it all wrong. Mom never loved me."

"Stop, of course she—"

Elizabeth smacks a fist on the table. "Don't treat me like a child. You're so fucking clueless, Catriona. I thought for sure you would have figured it out by now."

"Figured out what by now?"

"That Dad wasn't the one who killed Mom, despite what you've been trying to prove for months."

I suck in a breath. My eyes flit around the room like I can find someone to help, but with Cian prowling the perimeter, delighted by the display, no one else dares to move. Aiden is blank and unmoving at my side. "H-how did you know that?"

"Because you aren't as smart as you think you are. Otherwise, you would have put it together that I was there that night."

"No, you weren't. Devin's vehicle was the only one there."

Elizabeth rolls her eyes. "Didn't your husband piece it together? Devin was my alibi. I rode with him to the house. We've been in a relationship for months. He disabled it so it would look like he was stranded while I hid until it was safe."

I'm shaking my head. There's no way. She couldn't. She wouldn't.

Elizabeth continues, blotches of color high on her cheeks. "Poor little Catriona. Mom's little princess." She spits out the word like it's poison. "She loved you best, she always did. And do you want to know why?"

I lean forward. "No, she loved you. She did."

"She asked for a divorce after you were born. Did you know? Said she couldn't put up with Dad anymore. Claimed Dad raped her. That she could barely look at me as a result. That's why she was always distant from me. She doted on you but treated me like I was a monster."

"No, she—no, I can't—"

"She told me she couldn't stomach living a lie anymore. That night, she caught me in bed with Devin. I tried to explain that we were in a relationship, but she kept screaming that it wasn't right. That she knew I was like our father. Always lying and keeping secrets. That she knew I was rotten from the start."

I press a hand to my mouth to cover a retching sound.

Elizabeth's face is alight with glee. "That's when she told me she'd changed her will. That neither Father nor I would ever see a penny from her. After all the years Father invested in their relationship, she was just going to write us off like that."

"Please—" Catriona says. "Don't—"

"So I pushed her," Elizabeth says.

I've never been a violent woman.

Angry, sometimes.

Prone to impulsive decisions? You bet.

Too stubborn, clearly.

But I've never felt the urge to inflict injury on another person.

Until now.

"You... you what?" I whisper.

At this, Cian, who'd been circling us like a shark, stands behind me and puts his hands on my chair. "Devin, here, contacted me, smart man. Told me he worked for Gallagher and could give me a fortune and a US Senator all in one go, as long as I could clean up the mess his woman made. Gallagher has always had a bit of a heavy hand at the gambling tables, but his wife's murder would put him in a position he couldn't refuse."

Aiden is rigid next to me. Face carefully blank. Hands resting on his thighs. Fuck, how does he sit there without reacting when it feels like my entire world is falling apart?

When had Elizabeth learned this? How had I been so blind to her? Was this what caused us to grow apart? Fresh horror rolls over me. She'd been the result of rape, and Mom lived with this secret for decades? Elizabeth was right. How could I have been so clueless?

"And now you want me to drop my investigation into her death."

"And sign over everything she left you," Cian says, inclining his head. "Your sister will get a split, of course. I'm not an unreasonable man."

I rock back against my seat, remembering my earlier conversation with Broussard. Mom had made an appointment with her lawyer. To write Elizabeth out of the will? Then Elizabeth found out, and that was the straw that broke her. She used Devin's connection—and Father's?—to Cian to arrange for the cover-up. Did Aiden know about this? Did he have a hand in it?

"Don't," Aiden says beside me as he pushes to his feet.

Cian nods to one man—one of the Burns family, maybe? I don't fucking know—who takes Aiden by the arms, and slams him back down in his seat, pinning him there. Aiden doesn't even put up a fight. I want to scream at him, beg, but I know that's what Cian wants, so I swallow all of it back and don't resist as someone slams me back into my seat.

"I don't think he'll be going anywhere, Nolan. Just keep a close eye on him, yeah?" Cian says as he leans back against the chair.

"I'll do whatever you want. Just don't hurt him."

I take a mental note of the man holding Aiden: a blunt nose, close-shaved bright blond hair, watery blue eyes, and a short but stocky build. He shoves Aiden's shoulder as though enjoying seeing someone who normally intimidates him being brought low. Why isn't Aiden fighting back? He's more than strong enough to take one man. Aiden's fierce gaze is locked on Cian, promising death. But will he be too late?

Cian barks out orders that I can barely hear over the ringing in my ears. I marshal my panicked thoughts into order. As much as I want to dig his eyeballs out with a spork, I need to focus. Play his game. I've done it enough times with my father. I can do it for Cian, too. Men like him just want to feel in control. I can do that.

"See, Aiden?" Cian is taunting. "If only you were as well-behaved as your wife. Your sister may say you're not smart, but it seems to me that you know when to listen. Maybe you need another demonstration of what I do to people who defy me."

Cian moves—too fast. One moment, he's standing with a hand on Mary's shoulder, and the next, his hand blurs, and when I blink, she jerks in her seat. A sharp, gurgling noise fills the air. A knife, her own goddamn steak knife, is buried in her throat.

I leap to my feet, but there's nothing I can do. I'm powerless. The man behind me slams me back down.

Blood pours from the wound in her neck, bright red and cruel. Her cry of pain had been a silent one, and the grimace of it still lances across her face. Before anyone can do anything, Cian rips the knife away, and blood flows faster now, staining her pretty dress, pooling on the plate in front of her where her finger still rests.

But what's even more horrifying is the acceptance in her face as she stares into Aiden's. Their eyes hold for a long, long moment before she blinks, and then she's gone. Her life winking out like she's fallen asleep. Slowly, her body slumps forward until, finally, she's still.

It feels like it's taken an eternity, but the whole ordeal couldn't have lasted more than a couple of minutes.

A sharp cry comes from my throat, my hands covering my mouth. I can't move. I'm frozen, like this is a night terror I can't wake up from.

Cian wipes the knife on a cloth napkin and sighs. "I hate that she outlived her usefulness, but clearly, she no longer played her part when it came to keeping you in line. I have to admit I'm going to miss her." He straightens, leaving the knife on the table.

Don't look, don't fuckin' look.

Aiden struggles, momentarily throwing off the man who restrains him.

"Want me to put a bullet in his brain? Get it all done and over with for good?" the man asks, once he has Aiden restrained again.

No one's eating anymore. Terror tends to do that to people. Whoever was serving the courses has also made themselves scarce, so no dessert will be forthcoming as a distraction.

"What do you think, sweetheart?" Cian says, his wine-sour breath wafting over my cheek as he presses his mouth to my ear. "Would you like me to get rid of him for you so we can have some time alone?"

This seems to snap Aiden out of whatever trance he was in. "Let her go."

"Ah, he speaks. I was afraid I'd gone and broken you for good, boy. I don't think I will. She sits pretty for me, doesn't she?"

Aiden jerks forward, and the man slams him back against the seat hard enough to make him grunt. "Let her go. This is about me. Let her go, and I'll give you whatever you want."

"You'll give me what I want, no matter what. Won't you?" Cian rests a hand on my thigh. From Aiden's vantage point, he's close enough to see exactly what's happening, and I stiffen, causing Cian to huff out another sour-smelling laugh.

Behind me, Cian's quaking, his skin hot against where we touch, and his hand trembles as he palms one breast, squeezing too tight before he lets go with a hiss, pressing the hand to his head as though he's in pain.

Does it make me a terrible person to hope all the wine is giving him the worst headache of his life? He hadn't eaten much at dinner. No doubt he was planning how best to make Aiden suffer, so the alcohol is probably going straight to his head.

I adjust myself on his lap to better gauge how drunk he is, hoping he's a lightweight.

"Boss, you okay?" Nolan asks when he sees the twisted grimace on Cian's face.

"M'grand." Cian grabs a blood-splattered linen napkin from the table and dabs at the profuse amount of sweat pouring from his face. His complexion underneath has gone pale. "Just hot in here from all the excitement." He punctuates the statement by dropping the sopping-wet napkin and pawing at my chest again.

At this, the table explodes. Someone leaps from the table, his face a familiar one in the sea of strangers, but I can't place him immediately. Cian's arm tightens around me as he pushes us to standing. The knife is back in his shaking hand, where he fists it dangerously close to my exposed throat.

Niall. It's Niall. Mara's fiancé. The one who'd been there watching the cameras. Except he's tossing a knife in Aiden's direction. In a flash, Aiden has slashed the bellies of the men restraining him. He leaps up, blood-splattered and chest heaving. But no one moves to confront him. The men nearest who aren't twitching on the floor back away, chairs squealing against the floor.

"Is that really—really what you want to do, John?" Cian taunts. "I have your pretty wife by the throat. Don't push me."

"Boss?" one of the men asks, Aiden forgotten. "What'd you call him?"

Cian squeezes me tighter. "What the fuck are you talking about?"

"You called him John," another says. "This is Aiden, his son."

My eyes clash with Aiden's for the first time since Cian pulled me into his lap. I don't know how this is going to end, but I don't want my last potential memory to be of Cian's hands on me.

But his expression is so soft at first, I think maybe I'm imagining it. He's never looked at me this way before and it's disarming. I forget what's going on for the briefest moment.

"Shut the fuck up, Michael. Don't be an idiot. I killed John a long time ago, just like I'm going to do with his son once I've had *his* wife, too."

"Let her go, and I'll let you live," Aiden says without breaking eye contact with me. I want to tell him he doesn't have to say that, but the edge of the blade presses more insistently against my throat. So close, I can't even swallow for fear of it slicing through the delicate skin.

"The only reason you're still alive is because I allow it." Cian goes to shout again, his body tensing with the effort, but then his hand spasms and the knife slices into my throat before it falls to the floor. I cry out in pain, but he quickly wraps his arms around me in a viselike grip. "Ah-ah, you're not going anywhere."

"Cian, you have less than a minute to come to your fuckin' senses before I rip out your heart with my bare hands for touching *my wife*."

Niall pushes his way through the masses, passing another gun to Aiden. He has several others at his back, guns raised. Between one blink and the next, there's a line of weapons on one side of the table and one on the other. Elizabeth and Devin cower at the far end, faces white. The bodies of the two who Aiden has already stabbed are quivering puddles at his feet. A trail of blood from a small cut on

Aiden's eyebrow streaks down his nose and coats his lips. He either doesn't notice or doesn't bother wiping it away.

Spearing a glance toward the rest of the table, Aiden says, "Either you come for me now like men, or I'll pick you off after. It's your choice."

No one moves.

"Go to hell." Cian is pouring sweat behind me, and his whole body quakes. As Aiden steps closer, he sways and stumbles.

"Doesn't look like it'll be too hard, old man. Losing your touch?" Aiden jeers. "Maybe all those sins are finally catching up with you. Seems like you aren't doing so hot. Afraid?"

"Of you?" He huffs a dry laugh but doesn't sound as confident, now that Aiden is prowling closer, unrestrained.

Aiden's eyes catch mine and then drop to his hands, which motion for me to get down. Instinct has me complying immediately, and I drop my body weight, catching Cian off guard. I fall on my ass and immediately scrabble away as Cian jerks in surprise, the movement sending him off balance and crashing into his chair until he's slumped over the arm.

A line appears between Aiden's brows as he takes in Cian's sweating, unsteady form. Cian clutches at his chest, his breath coming out in unsteady pants.

After a moment of study, Aiden barks out a laugh. "No," he says and twines his fist in Cian's shirt. "You don't get to go out like this after what you've done. You will suffer. Do you understand me?"

"What's happenin' to him?" one of them asks.

"Christ. Look at his face. Is he havin' a fuckin' heart attack?"

"I would, too, if I threatened O'Connor's wife. Easier way to go out," says a voice I don't recognize.

Cian claws at Aiden's hand in his shirt, gasping for air. "I can't breathe."

"Good, but I think we can do better than that."

Aiden pulls a shaking Cian to his feet using only his handhold in the collar of his shirt, then shoves him back down over the table. Dishes rattle, and wineglasses spill over, staining the white tablecloth a deep crimson. Those still sitting shove to their feet and back away from the table. Aiden takes the knife Cian had used on his mother, the one he'd pressed to my throat.

Niall shouts, "Don't you fucking dare," at a man raising a gun to Aiden.

Cian's eyes are rolling in the back of his head. With fear? Pain? He tries to focus on Aiden, but it's clear he's having trouble. Aiden slaps his cheeks until Cian's eyes swing to finally meet his face.

"You're going to watch, just like you've made me watch." Aiden straightens and gestures to a slack-jawed pair next to him. "You two, why don't you hold him down for me?"

They twitch until Aiden glares at them. Spurred by what they read in his gaze, one takes Cian's right arm, the other his left, and they pin them to the table over the remnants of dinner. Cian is so out of it, I don't know if he notices. Grunts of pain punch out of his mouth in staccato bursts, and his legs jerk fruitlessly against Aiden, who hovers above him with malicious glee.

"Leave, Catriona," Aiden says, his voice deceptively void of emotion. "I don't want you to see this."

I'm shaking my head, but he can't see me. When I speak, my voice comes out like I've walked days through a desert. "I'm not going anywhere."

I don't know if he can hear me because Aiden leans down and says to Cian, "I told you one day you'd regret honing me into a killer."

Then Aiden plunges the knife into Cian's chest, causing a visible recoil throughout the rapt audience. I have to clutch the chair beside me to keep my knees from buckling like wet paper. The scent of blood fills the air, droplets of it flying to land on every surface. The only sound is Cian's choked gurgle, followed by the squelch of the knife hacking through muscle, then the dull thud of it hitting bone.

I don't know how long it continues. Long enough that I can feel myself growing woozy from having to lock my knees to keep upright, but I don't dare move.

At the crack of Aiden breaking open Cian's rib cage, I give a full-body jerk, and the room goes white for a second before it comes back into focus.

When the sparks clear from my vision, I find Aiden standing in front of what used to be Cian's body, his heart clutched in his hands.

"Cian. You have less than a minute to come to your fuckin' senses before I rip out your heart with my bare hands for touching my wife."

Based on the faces of his audience, they hadn't believed he meant it.

He holds on to the heart for a long moment, and the silence is so all-encompassing, aside from the steady *drip,*

drip of blood falling from the table to the floor, that my ears ring. Aiden lets the organ fall from his fingers to plop onto the table. It rolls for a second, making an obnoxious wet sound, until it comes to a stop next to a saltshaker.

Chaos reigns around me. Men go for guns. A cacophony of gunfire erupts, buffeting my ears, but I can barely hear it over the screaming of my rage. Elizabeth and Devin are the first to leap to their feet and try to make it for the door. I jerk in their direction, crawling between bodies, unwilling to let them leave before I exact retribution. For more than a year, I've been desperate for answers, and the last person I thought would be involved is the one who took my mother away from me.

When they reach the door, Devin turns and sees me only a few feet behind. He lifts a gun from his side and aims.

But he jerks before he can squeeze the trigger, a hole appearing in the center of his forehead.

I twist around and find Aiden lowering his gun to pistol-whip another attacker. "*Go,*" he mouths. I know he's trying to tell me to escape while it's safe, but I can't let Elizabeth get away. She has to pay for what she's done. Mom deserves to finally know justice.

"Elizabeth! Get the fuck back here, you backstabbing bitch!"

Of course she doesn't turn around, but it feels good to shout at her. I back away as she pulls out a gun and fires off bullets in my direction. Why hadn't I thought to go for a gun? She's going to kill me before I can catch up to her.

I trip over a body at the door of the dining room, falling to land on it and recoiling. Then I spot a gun in its hand and rip it free. Checking the safety, I make sure it's flicked off, and then I peer through the doorway. A bullet drives into the doorframe beside me.

Ducking, I whip the gun around and fire off a shot in the dark. "You're not going to get out of here. There's no place to run. I'm going to find you, and they won't be able to identify you when I'm done. Show your face, and I'll show you mercy."

I'm in the hallway now, but it's dark. The lights are on, but the walls are a dark green with dark wood. She could be anywhere. There's a sound, and I fire off another blind shot. I try to control myself, but fear and adrenaline are coursing through me.

"Fine! I'm coming out!" she shouts.

Whirling, I find her coming around a corner. Fast. Too fast. Her hands are raised, a gun in one of them. I lower mine, I don't know, out of instinct? Hesitation to harm my sister. But her face twists with fury, and her arms drop. My shot catches her in the chest before she can squeeze off a round.

I don't know how long I stand there, looking at her unnaturally still body, when Aiden finds me.

Rushing to me, he barely notices her at the foot of the stairs. "I thought I told you to get out of here."

"I couldn't help it," I whimper. "She wouldn't stop."

A pained sound rips from his chest, and he yanks me to him. My arms go around his waist, despite the carnage covering him from chin to thigh. I shake against him until his hands coast over me, soothing me from the height of panic.

"I'm so fucking sorry, love. Let me look at you. Did she hurt you? Are you okay?"

I claw back the tears, but it's a losing battle. "I'm fine. Are you okay? What the hell was that?"

The tension dissolves from his body, and he tightens his hold around me. "I'm alive." The words sound as though they're being scraped from his throat with a rusty spoon. "But I need to get you out of here. Most of them are dead or gone, but I don't want to stick around. I want to torch this place, and you can't be in here when I do. Niall is handling everyone else."

"Why? What's happened?"

"No time. I'll explain later. Meet me out front. I have to get—" He bites off, looks away. "I'll meet you there. Go. Now."

I do as he says, rushing through the house like there's a monster on my heels. I don't know how I manage to find the exit, but I do. As soon as I burst outside, I breathe in the fresh air like I haven't had oxygen in a week. After several long minutes, I sniff, realizing the scent of smoke is teasing my nose.

Oh God.

Then Aiden comes out, his mother's body over his shoulder. My hand flies up to press against my mouth. His face is a mask of determination. When he reaches me, he carefully lays her body in the bed of a truck. "One more," he says. "Stay here."

Soon, he's back, this time with Elizabeth's body. My throat closes.

LATER, after Bren and Tadhg have taken over managing the aftermath. After "cleaners" have come to deal with preparing

Mary and Elizabeth for burial. After we're finally alone in the cottage by the cliffs, Aiden pulls me to him.

"I thought I was going to lose you."

"You didn't. You didn't lose me. We're going to get through this. I'm still here."

He pulls back enough to meet my eyes, his bloody hands coming up to palm my cheeks as he studies me for a long time. "I'll send you back on the first flight. We can have the marriage annulled. I'm sure there's someone I can bribe to fix this for you."

My heart crashes violently against my ribs. "Wh-what?"

He rests his forehead against mine. "I tried to save you from this, Catriona. That's why I didn't want to marry you the first time you offered in Elizabeth's place. This is who I am, this life I live... I don't want you to be a part of it. I didn't want it to touch you this way. When he had his hands on you, I thought that was it. That he'd torture me with you like he had my mother, and it broke me. I can't do this to you anymore. I'll give you a divorce."

I swallow around the knot in my throat. "You want a divorce?"

Aiden makes a choked noise. "No, I don't want one. Christ, I can't look at you when you're all covered in blood to have this conversation. It's making me want to kill someone."

He moves, but I remain with my feet planted on the stone beneath me.

"What's wrong?" he says as he turns. "Catriona?"

"I'm not going."

"What?"

"I said I'm not going. You can't make me. I'm your fucking wife, and I plan to keep it that way, Aiden."

CHAPTER 30

AIDEN

I hold a bloody hand to Catriona's pale cheek, tracking each emotion as it flashes over her face: terror, relief, horror, dread. "You're in shock. You don't know what you're saying. Christ, after what I've just put you through, it's no wonder. Let's get you cleaned up. You'll feel better after we can wash all this off you."

Fuck me, she's covered in his blood. Handprints on her cheeks. Flecks of crimson in her blond curls. Her white dress is already drying stiff with the stuff. I want to burn it. Want to scrub her myself until she's washed clean of this.

Of me.

It had been selfish of me to bring her here, knowing what atrocities may lie in wait for her. It was selfish to want to see my mother again, if only for a few minutes.

Cursing myself, I drag her along after me until I find an empty room. I nearly stumble at the realization of what I've done. That I'll never see Ma again—had it only been a couple of hours ago?—but right myself and lock the door behind us. I'd been smart enough to keep a weapon in our things and, after the carnage I wrought tonight, I don't anticipate anyone trying their luck so soon.

I killed Cian. Soon there would be families to deal with, and the deal I made with Niall already weighs heavily on my shoulders, but I can't think about that now. Not when Catriona is shivering in my arms and covered in Cian's blood.

I tug her through the room and to the shower, depositing her next to it as I turn the faucet on to as hot as I can stand. "Do you want me to help you?" I ask, nodding to her clothes.

She glances down and goes stock-still, as though she just now realizes the mess I've made of her.

Cursing underneath my breath, I close the distance between us and say, "It's all right. I'm going to help. We're going to get you clean. Can I?"

At her silent nod, I kneel, starting with the buckles on her shoes. She lifts one foot for easy access and puts a hand on my shoulder. A sound of relief escapes her throat as I massage the feeling back into her toes. When she's steady, I reach up and pull down her panties before tossing them aside. Getting to my feet, I turn her away from me to draw down the zipper of her dress, skim the straps off her shoulders, and let it fall to her feet, leaving her only in a bra, which I make quick work of.

She turns back in my arms to face me and says, "Your turn."

Before I can put meaning to the words, she drops to her knees and pulls my feet out of bloodied socks and shoes.

Disarmed, I can only watch as she stands to help me out of my shirt, then unbuttons and unzips my slacks, skimming them down.

Together, we step under the spray. Bloodstained water swirls down the drain, and she closes her eyes, tipping her head back into the deluge. I take a cake of soap and lather my hands, then use them to glide over the worst spots, careful to clean the cut on her neck and not to get any in her eyes. She keeps her face tilted up and her eyes shut as I wash her. Somehow, she must understand my primal need to care for her, inspect her to make certain she's okay.

When there is no more blood staining her skin, I let her do the same to me, letting go of her for as long as it takes for her little hands to scrub me clean.

"You could have stopped him. Why didn't you save her? You've been planning this takeover for how long? Months? Years. We could have done something. I couldn't save my mom, but we could have saved her." Her words come soft at first, falling from her downturned lips, then gain steam, ending on a demanding note as she scowls up at me.

I thread my hands through her hair on either side of her skull. "No, we couldn't." The words are scraped from the raw wound somewhere in my chest. If tears fall, they're washed away by the spray. "She didn't want to be saved. I tried to help her for a long time. I-I was too late."

"How can you say that? It's never too late to try to save someone you love."

Pulling her close is the only thing that keeps me from falling apart. "I agree... but she didn't. I didn't want to see it. Haven't wanted to for years. But she's been trying to tell me for years that she was ready to go."

"What do you mean?"

I press kisses into her hair like it will do something for the pain. But it carves a place in my soul I know won't ever heal. It will only get easier to endure. "Her flowers? The ones she showed you. They're all poisonous. I didn't understand for a long time why she grew them. Then it hit me like a freight train. She was planning to use them." I swallow hard when my voice gutters out. "She'd waited until she was certain I wouldn't be alone before she did."

Catriona's head presses into my chest. "No, why would she—"

"Yes. She suffered it all. Years of his rape. His torture. Of being without my dad. Of being alone here. Worrying about me. She lost herself because she knew if I didn't have her, I'd be lost too. She dealt with so much because of me." The words make the ache inside me throb viciously because I know they're true. We've both fought so hard. It kills me to think she'd clung to a life that had abused her only for my sake. Could I have saved her the torment if I'd let her go?

"Oh, Aiden, I'm so sorry."

"Even if we had been able to do something, she gave up a long time ago. There was no saving her now." I say the words like they're for Catriona's sake, but I know they're really for me. Not that they help the guilt rising in my throat.

"Why not?"

"She called me a few weeks ago, listing another plant she was cultivating. Blue rockets she called them. Cian never cared to learn her flowers. She was less than nothing to him. If he had, maybe he would have realized. She'd given me a vial in the gardens. It was empty. She whispered in my ear that she'd already taken it, so I didn't have a choice."

"She…"

"Blue rockets, also known as wolf's bane or monkshood, can kill you in less than two hours. She was already dead when we got here." When I can bear to look at her, fat tears stream down Catriona's face. "She laced his wine with the same poison to help us."

"She poisoned him?"

"If she had this all along, she could have killed him years ago," I say bitterly, ashamed of myself for even voicing the words.

"With you gone? Someone could have retaliated. Killed you." I don't know how it happens, but now she's comforting me. "Plus, she probably wanted to see you one last time so she could say goodbye. You can't blame yourself."

"You have to go," I tell her, needing to change the subject. My voice is so low I'm not sure if she can hear me over the pounding of the water. "It's not safe for you to stay with me. I can come and find you when things are settled."

"You can try to make me, but I'll just come back," she answers just as softly. "I'm guessing you made a deal with Niall."

"You're too smart for your own good. Yes, I've been building allies for years. He finally gave me an opening after… after the charity event. He's not much better than Cian, and Mara is… she's collateral. But we'll fix it. I'll fix it." I crush her body against me, enjoying the life-affirming sensation of her skin against mine. "I wish you weren't so fuckin' stubborn. What if something like this happens to you again? Like my ma. Do you have any idea what people like him could do to you simply because you mean something to me?"

"I know exactly what they could do to me, and I'm still saying I don't want a divorce. Are you going to tell me you know what's best for me? Because I'll tell you right now, that's a great way to piss off a woman when you're naked and vulnerable. You fought to have me for too long. I'm not going to let you get rid of me so easily."

"So fuckin' stubborn," I repeat into her wet hair, but there's a lightness in my chest that suffocates all of my carefully prepared objections.

I want her more than I've ever wanted anyone. The thought of losing her to Cian the way I had my mother? It knocked me sideways as much as watching Ma die. The feeling took me by surprise so thoroughly that I'll never forgive myself for that moment's hesitation that led to his demented hands roaming all over her. The image is seared into my brain. Every time I close my eyes, I'll see her panicked expression.

"You've known I get what I want for a while now, so you can't pretend ignorance. Remember our wedding? I won't leave you alone to face this, Aiden."

"I could make you leave if I wanted. Tie you up and throw your arse on the plane."

"Do that and see what I do to you," she practically growls.

"You have to know that the next several months—hell, it could be years—are going to be complete madness. There won't be a day when you aren't in danger because you're my wife. They were afraid today, but not all of them will be happy with how things have turned out. Cian gave a lot of them leeway to do whatever the fuck they wanted. That's not how I want to do things."

"After this, I know what I'm getting myself into. They can't scare me away."

I sigh brokenly into her skin. "What do I have to do to get you to realize this isn't a good idea? You're already testing the limits of my better nature."

"There's nothing you can do. I've already made up my mind. Maybe if I hadn't met your mother, I'd feel differently, but I did. I saw what she meant to you. Look at me, Aiden."

I listen. God, there's nothing I wouldn't do for her.

She cups my cheek. "You meant something to me that night, too. It's why I left before you could get my name. It scared me."

Groaning, I pull her closer, wrapping my arms around her until she probably has trouble breathing. "You shouldn't have told me that, *bhean chéile*."

"Why not?"

"Because after tonight, I'm not ever going to want to let you go."

She lifts onto her toes and presses her lips to my throat. "So don't."

Later, when we aren't in the belly of the beast, I'll mourn losing my mother. I'll give her the grief she deserves, but now, I can't afford to be overwhelmed by those thoughts and memories. Catriona pressed against me is a welcome diversion, and my blood screams with leftover adrenaline. She arches against me as my hands turn more insistent. She presses her breasts into my chest and nips at my throat.

"I should have told you a thousand times before, but you're perfect."

"You did tell me before, remember? Called me your perfect little wife."

I chuckle, surprised, as the sound rumbles out of my chest. "Still mad at me about that?"

"Don't worry, I have plans to pay you back."

"I'm looking forward to it."

I capture her mouth, using the sweet taste of her to wash away everything else. She moans into it, lifting her hands to thread through my hair. The movement causes her nipples to rasp against my chest, and her breath hitches.

Tearing my mouth away, I say, "We don't have to do this now. It's been a bitch of a day, and I have things to see to before we can get some sleep."

She nods, reluctantly hiding a yawn, and allows me to help her from the shower. I wrap her in a towel like she's something precious, and she dresses in a matching pajama set I recognize from one shop in town. It should piss me off all over again, remembering how she put herself in danger to get my attention, but all I feel is grateful that she's still alive.

"What things do you need to take care of now? Isn't everyone gone?" she asks, when I've redressed in a clean pair of pants and a long-sleeved Henley shirt. I keep my 9mm close by just in case. I'll have no qualms about killing the next bastard who threatens me.

"I need to make some calls before the news spreads too far. We can talk about it all in the morning. You need to sleep."

"I'm not sure I'll be able to by myself. I'd like to wait for you to get back."

Now that the blood is cleared away, I can see the dark shadows of stress underneath her eyes. The fact that she's still holding it together is fucking remarkable. "Okay, I won't be long. Lock the door behind me. I'll be back in less than fifteen minutes, I promise."

I wait outside the door until I hear the lock click and then go in search of Bren and Tadhg to make certain they'll keep watch throughout the night.

When I come back, she's almost asleep. I climb into bed and tuck her close.

"You don't have to leave again, do you?" she says into my shirt.

I should fight more. Convince her to leave. But instead, the words that come out of my traitorous lips are, "No, I don't."

"Then stay with me," she says, tugging me into her arms.

CHAPTER 31

CATRIONA - 4 WEEKS LATER

"You're not going to tell me where we're going?" Aiden asks, frowning and tugging at the silk tie wrapped around his eyes.

"You do this to me all the time, Aiden, so don't pretend to be upset."

Yasmine makes a gagging sound in the back of her throat. "Please, I really don't want to know what kinky shit you two get up to. Catriona, I swear to God, I will leave you both on the side of the road. Putting up with your friends for dinner every Sunday is bad enough."

I gasp, cheeks burning, and shoot her a glare from the driver's seat. "Jesus, that's not what I meant. I just mean he—"

She holds up a hand. "Nope, no. I'm only here because I want to see him—"

"Don't ruin it!" I shriek.

"There go my eardrums," Aiden says drolly.

"You're fine," I say and pat his shoulder. "Now be a good husband and don't peek."

"I'm the best husband. Anyone else would have bailed twenty minutes ago. One of you has been shrieking since we got into the car."

"We have not," we protest at the same time.

"My point exactly."

"We're here!" I singsong, trying to cover my nerves. He's either going to love this or hate it. He'd never tell me to my face because he doesn't like disappointing me, but I'd know.

I pull the tie away from Aiden's eyes. He looks at me first, gaze flitting over me to check to see if I'm okay, then he peers at our surroundings through the windows. "We're at City Park? That's the big surprise? Darlin', I would have come here with you any time. You didn't have to kidnap me."

"Nooo, we're going somewhere *in* City Park," I announce, barely able to contain the mixture of nerves and excitement. Aiden seems dubious, but as always, he's willing to follow me wherever I want to go. "And I didn't kidnap you."

Yasmine climbs out of the car. Her expression is guarded, but I know she's just as excited as I am. Between moments at the hospital, she's been here right alongside me. I tried to tell her not to waste her precious free moments, but when she learned what happened to us in Ireland, she threatened to move in with us to keep an eye on me. This little project has soothed both of our nerves.

"You can't kidnap someone who's willing," Yasmine mutters as she tosses her hair and winds a scarf around her neck.

I narrow my eyes at both of them as I scramble out of the car and tug at the neck of my peach turtleneck. "You two are both going to be demoted. Aiden, smile and get out of the car. I promise you're going to love it."

Aiden's smile is more confused than anything, but I'm practically bouncing for joy. It's been an exhausting, grueling week at my internship. Aiden hadn't been lying when he said he could get me another—better—opportunity. Not that I asked how he accomplished it. The woman I'd been before him and my mother, one who fought tooth and nail for everything, would have turned it down when he offered it to me because I didn't "earn it." But a clerkship at the US Court of International Trade is an opportunity I couldn't pass up.

I'm sure the fact that the connections I'll make there will be lucrative to Aiden's interests had nothing to do with his recommendation at all, I think wryly as we move through the pathways. Aiden is no longer tied to the Irish arm of the former Lynch Crime Family, but that may not always be the case. There may be a time when he chooses to go back, wrest back control from Niall, and when he does, I'll do anything it takes to be there to support him. Part of me still doesn't quite believe he's given it up to stay here, to be with me.

The moment we got back from Ireland, this idea has been percolating in my brain. I didn't waste any time reaching out to my mother's various acquaintances in the charity circuit to find the right contacts. It didn't take much convincing—or money, really—to be granted a space in the park for my purposes. Besides, Aiden is always telling me that his money is my money, and I knew this was something he'd want. After everything he's done for me, I wanted to do something in return.

"Are you going to tell me what the surprise is now?" Aiden asks.

"It's just up here, I think. Yes, here it is." I find the placard and hold my hands together at my chest. My stomach is jumping like I've had several shots of espresso. I barely blink as I wait for him to read the plaque and put two and two together.

The patient, indulgent look on his face persists for a few minutes as he looks around, not really getting it. Studying the plaque, he mouths the words at the same time. Then his eyes bounce around the plants around him, seeing their little identification cards. The ones I remembered from his mother's garden that I could cultivate here.

He spins to me, brushing a hand over his forehead. "What did..." He swallows hard. "Did you do this?"

"You haven't really had time to mourn her, and you don't have a place to visit her here. I know we had the funeral, and she has a gravestone in Ireland, but I thought it might help if you had something here to remember her by that you can visit. Mourn. I know it's hard for you, not being in Ireland as much as possible. We'll go as soon as you want. Whenever you want. But your memories with her are there, and I just thought—"

He crosses the space between us in two long-legged strides. His hands thread through my hair, and he crushes his lips to mine in a deep, emotional kiss that has tears burning at the back of my eyes.

"You did this for her? These roses—they're the same as the ones from her garden?"

I'm nodding, clearing my throat. "Yes, or as close as I could get. Not all of them, of course. And I spent quite a bit of your money to get everything perfect. The New Orleans Botanical Society has never been so thrilled."

"I can't believe you did this," he says, his voice hoarse. Then he's turning again, shoving his hands in his pockets, his shoulders lifting at the effort to breathe deeply enough to calm his emotions. He keeps his back to me as he walks through the aisles, stopping to read each little metal sign with the flower's name and a brief description. They're all roses. None of the poisonous plants she'd used to end her life. Only the ones that had brought her such joy when she'd described them.

Under each, it says, *Donated by the family of Mary O'Connor.*

Each time he reads her name, he jolts a little.

I glance behind me to Yasmine, who is trying, and failing, to hide a smile. She came to the garden with me and bullied me as I agonized over the right varieties and despaired over the growing costs. She takes my hand now as we watch Aiden touch almost every flower he passes, and I think maybe she finally gets what I've seen in him since the beginning.

"Do you promise you like it?" I ask after we drop Yasmine back at the Baptistes' house. He's said he does every time I ask, but I like hearing it. "If you don't, I can have it renamed. I donated a lot to the botanical society, so they won't care what we call it."

As he drives down St. Charles Avenue under the canopy of massive oaks, he takes my hand where it's knotted by my thigh and brings it to his lips. "No matter how many times you ask, the answer is still going to be the same. I love it. Thank you for giving it to me."

"The gardens?"

He pauses at a stop sign and catches my eye. "Peace."

I'm grateful for the honk behind us because it tears his attention away, and I can breathe again. Somehow, he still has that heart-stopping effect when he focuses all that considerable scrutiny on me.

"Where are we going?" I ask as historical homes crawl by outside the window. I've always loved this street. The history. The ties to the city. Mom and I would plant ourselves here for the parades. Ride the streetcar for fun before Father became too notorious to be out in public. Since we got back from Ireland, I forced Aiden to take a tour of my favorite places, regardless of the attention. Restaurants. Tourist hot spots. Tarot readings in Jackson Square. Walking tours through the cemeteries. "Did you want to ride the streetcar again?" I tease.

Aiden doesn't answer. Instead, we pull to a stop and park on the side of the street. "Maybe another time. C'mon."

I glance around. All I see are houses and the lacy overhang of trees. Sidewalks of people strolling by. "Come on? What are we doing here?"

But instead of answering, he's already striding up the sidewalk to a house with a green construction barrier surrounding it. I jog to keep up with his ground-eating pace. When I reach him, he's punching a number into a lock on the fence. My mind is on the internship and keeps fluttering back to Aiden's face when he realized what the garden meant as I read a sign next to the gate. *This property, Allain-Cavaille House, has been listed on the National Register of*

Historic Places by the United States Department of the Interior. Maybe it has something to do with one of his investments? I've given up trying to keep track of his various business ventures and charities. His poor assistant, Finn, must be run ragged by the vastness of his empire.

The gate swings open with a squeal of protesting hinges. Aiden strolls through, then stops when he realizes I haven't followed. "You comin'?" he asks over his shoulder.

I creep closer, glancing around and expecting a security guard to come running at us. "Should we be here? I don't know how much more Reggie can put up with, you know. Breaking and entering will be another notch against us at this point."

His mouth curls up on one side. "We can't break into a place we own." With that, he continues up the half-circle drive and through the double front doors.

"Own?" I mouth at his back, then scramble up the steps and follow him through. "What do you mean *own?*" But the demand trails off as I take in the interior.

Glossy acres of wide-planked heart of pine floors. A twinkling chandelier. Massive staircase with intricate millwork on the rails. It's stunning. And empty. Most of the spaces I can see are finished, but there are also areas still clearly under construction. Blank. Full of possibilities.

"The owner owes the casino quite a fair amount. I offered to clear his debts in exchange for the property. It's unfinished, as you can see. The exterior is about 60 percent completed. The interior is less. But it's got potential, I think."

"I'm pretty sure that arrangement wouldn't hold water in court," I say with amusement. But I'm too awed to give him too much of a hard time. "Aiden, it's beautiful. But you do realize we already have a house. Several, if you include your townhouse."

He comes to stand behind me and presses a hand to my belly to pull me against him. His mouth flirts with my ear, voice low. "I know you don't like the estate, baby. It reminds you too much of your mother, and not in a good way anymore. I wanted to give you a new start." I open my mouth to object, but he interrupts me before I can say a word. "Don't say anything yet. Let me give you a tour first before you make any decisions. Please?"

I shiver at his touch. We've been so busy since we got back from Ireland that there hasn't been much time for intimacy beyond sharing the same bed. First, there was his mother and my sister. It had been a nightmare. Understandably, the mood hadn't been right. Then he had many, many long nights of calls to Niall, which left him moody and exhausted. Mara tried to explain to him that she was a big girl who could take care of herself, but Aiden still hated putting her in the crosshairs.

Not to mention my father, who was still missing in action. The police are convinced he's been kidnapped or something equally dramatic, but the truth is, when he heard Cian was dead and Aiden was gunning for him for colluding with Elizabeth to have me killed, he ran scared. Aiden's guy, someone he refers to as King, is supposedly tracking him down. But I'm determined to look to the future. Cockroaches like my father will always scurry away. It's only a matter of time before they get squashed beneath someone's boot.

A breath escapes me. "If you insist."

He tugs me through, but instead of narrating his thoughts, he lets me study the space without comment, and

I'm grateful. I wouldn't have been able to force responses from my dry throat. The entryway is grand, at least ten feet wide with soaring ceilings. The staircase is immediately to the right, next to a space that could be for a table or extra seating. To the left is what I think should be a formal living space with a fireplace and lots of windows. It feeds through a small walkway—a half bath to the left, a closet to the right with doors that go through to the main entry—with a formal dining room on the other side.

The dining area is unfinished, with no walls and construction materials covertly tucked out of the way. Ceiling stripped, innards exposed. But there's a massive bay window on the far side and another fireplace. Looks like it's original to the house.

Aiden shadows me like a ghost as I move across the main hall. To my left is a back door. On the other side of the hall is another open space. This is where he finally breaks his silence. "This would be a family room, breakfast area, maybe. And then the kitchen to the right." I can see it. It makes my throat close around my response, so I only nod. "Want to keep going?" he asks.

At my nod, we go back to the staircase and climb up to the second floor, arriving at a landing with a hallway and several open doorways to more unfinished rooms and another flight of stairs leading to a third floor. Christ, how big is this place? Aiden tugs me to the left and through a door.

"This would be the primary suite," he says. There's an eager note to his voice now. Hopeful. The walls are bare to the studs again, but double doors lead to a wraparound balcony. Polished floors. A side room meant for the bed with arching windows. A giant bathroom with a massive walk-in closet.

"And if we go this way by the stairs, there's the laundry room. And three more bedrooms for guests or...or whatever..." Two of the bedrooms share a jack-and-jill bath. The third has its own, and all have generous walk-in closets. Off the bedroom with its own bath is access to a rooftop garden, or it would be if it weren't empty.

"So much space," I say loftily and see him sweat.

I hide my smile as we climb the stairs to the third floor. It opens to another landing. A bonus room sits to the right. Aiden's anxious now, tugging me through a door to the left and then I realize why he's so excited.

One side of the wide-open space is missing a wall, also bare to the studs like so much of the living spaces, but the rest is covered with original paneling, rich and warm wood decorated with a vast expanse of empty, original bookshelves. Up a half-step at the far end is a space for an office with more shelving and wide windows. Off the office is a nook inside what I can only describe as a turret. The walls in the nook are mostly windows with a view of the city outside. I can already see it filled with old rugs and comfy seating. The perfect reading nook. My breath catches.

Through the windows in the nook space, I glance down and see a pool, also in need of work, but filled with bright blue water. A little oasis in the lush backyard. More towering oaks line the property boundary.

When I turn, finished exploring, I find Aiden in the office space, hands shoved into his pockets.

Waiting.

CHAPTER 32

CATRIONA

"Are you going to tell me what you think or will you keep me in suspense?" he asks, his posture deceptively casual. If I didn't know him better, I'd think he didn't care about my answer. "If you don't like it, we can find somewhere else. There are other—"

"I love it," I say as I cross the creaking floor to his side, careful not to trip on the half-completed step up to the office. "It's perfect. But you didn't have to do this. I would have gotten over my issues with the house. It already doesn't bother me as much."

I'm not trying to bullshit him. Each day since we've been back from Ireland has been a little easier now that I know the truth about what happened to my mother. Now that I have justice for her. Of course, considering the circumstances, it wasn't like I could go to the police. That would have put Aiden in an uncomfortable position. I suppose what I really needed more than justice was the truth. Now that I have it, it feels like the puzzle inside of my chest has been solved. There isn't an aching emptiness where the pieces should be, waiting to be filled.

Aiden pulls me to him when I get within reaching distance. His expression is solemn as he takes in the tears I'm just now realizing are streaking down my cheeks. I expect him to get awkward in the face of my uncharacteristic display, but he doesn't. In fact, he shifts closer to me, hands drifting up my throat to cup my jaw. He tilts my face up, and uneasiness crawls through me at being so exposed to him. More so than I've ever been when he had me stripped completely to the skin.

"It's okay to let it go. You've done what you set out to do. I want to make this home with you. For our future. I want to build a life with you, Catriona."

He lowers his head until his lips press to my skin, following the trail of tears. He erases each one until my hands are gripping his wrists to keep from trembling. When he's done, my breath shudders over his mouth as it lowers to mine. A needy sound escapes from my throat, and it's all the invitation he needs to press me against the wall of shelves behind me. If they bite into my back, I don't notice. God, I've missed him. I've *needed* this. So much.

My arms go around his waist, needing something to hold on to as I'm rocked off center. His tongue invades and conquers, and I relent, letting him plunder until I'm a needy mess under him.

When I try to press closer, drown out my thoughts in the taste and impossible hardness of him against me, he pulls away, and I find myself leaning toward him, hazy and confused.

"Is that what you want?" he asks.

It takes me a minute to remember what he asked. "Yes, yes, a thousand times yes." My words are watery. I push to my toes and sob against his mouth. "Yes."

He kisses me until I'm trembling, then pulls away. His silver eyes ignite, and his body shudders with the effort of his eagerness and restraint. "Take off your clothes," he says, releasing my hands. Taking two steps back so he can watch me, he rests a shoulder on the wall to my left, arms crossed over his chest, legs at the ankles.

I don't think about it as I draw the baby pink dress up my thighs to tease the sight of my panties. Thank God it's a rare warm day. The sun coming through the windows keeps the interior at the perfect temperature. I can practically feel Aiden begging me to go faster. Just for that, I change direction and undo the buttons at my chest, letting the dress gape away nearly to my navel to expose the pale blush lingerie I have on underneath.

Aiden straightens, pushing away from the wall, but doesn't come closer yet. His gaze is fixated to the sliver of skin exposed down my ribs.

Moving from the buttons to my hair, I unwind it from the claw clip at the top of my head and shake the length out over my shoulders. In the past year, I haven't had much time to focus on personal care, so it's grown out nearly down to my waist. His eyes caress my exposed skin, trailing from my face to my dress to where it splits over my breasts.

"The longer you make me wait, the longer I'm going to tease you," Aiden says in a low rumble.

Sending him a wicked grin, I say, "Maybe that's my plan."

"My wife's a masochist," he murmurs.

I pull the dress over my head and let it fall to the floor by my feet—not because he tells me to, but because I'm eager to see what he has planned for me. He contemplates my half-naked body like it's his new favorite meal.

"This new?" he asks with faux innocence.

"You know damn well it's new, Aiden O'Connor. You had a truck full of lingerie delivered to the house last week. Do you like it?"

"I love it, *bhean chéile*. Now take it off, or I'm going to rip it off, and I'd hate to do that because I know how much you hate it when I ruin them."

Because he's right, I unhook the shelf bra and let it fall on top of my dress. I shimmy out of my panties next and kick them toward him. He catches them and shoves them in his pocket before he prowls to me. Delicious, dark fear rolls through me, causing my heart to kick up and my breath to come faster.

He doesn't say a word as he studies me, his gaze hard and hot. Pinned in place, I can only submit to his observation, my nipples pinching under his perusal.

Does it make me a terrible person that I enjoy his attention after all that he's done? Probably.

Does it make me enjoy it any less? Absolutely the fuck not.

His lips draw into a smirk, and heat pools low and thick in my belly. He takes my wrists one at a time and presses them into the shelves behind me. "Hold on to these and don't let go. Can you do that?"

What I want to say is, *Please, go faster, you're killing me,* but what I force out of my mouth is, "Yes." There is a delicious ache in my shoulders, but no pain. I am blissfully at his mercy. Thoughts muddled. Worries eased. His touch is magic, and all my urgent concerns melt away. I whimper at the rush, already putty in his capable hands.

"Good. You'll tell me if it becomes so uncomfortable you stop enjoying it." It's not a question.

"I will. I promise."

At my words, Aiden inches closer. "Have I told you how beautiful you are, little wife?" One hand traces the curve of my body from my hip to my throat. How can one touch steal the very voice from my throat? "Hmm? Have I told you? Or are you not answering because you want my hands on you? Want me to make you feel good so you don't have to think about anything else?"

A desperate whimper is his answer, making him smile in understanding. "Poor, sweet baby. I'll take care of you. Don't worry." I expect him to use his hand, to get a weapon of some kind to abuse my body into submission. But what he does instead rocks me more than anything else ever could. He gets on his knees.

"Aiden, I—" He has to know how much this kills me. How heady it is to see him, a powerful, dangerous man, kneeling in front of me.

"I'm going to ask again. Have I told you how beautiful you are?"

"I don't... No, I don't think so."

He plants a kiss above my clit. A gentle, teasing thing. So opposite to everything I've ever been told about the ruthless man in front of me that it knocks away the first lines of my defense, and I begin to tremble in his arms.

Aiden grins up at me as though he can read the panic flaring in my mind, and, fuck him, he probably can.

"You're beautiful, Catriona. Every part of you. Want to know why I get on my knees for you the way I have no other person? Why you could run to the ends of the earth, and I'd follow you there?"

His arms wrap around my legs, and his tongue delves into the cleft between. The frustration at not being able to move, at only being able to accept what he gives me, has me throwing my head back and panting at the ceiling. I forget his question as he devours my pussy for several bone-melting minutes.

He stops to kiss my thigh. "Because I'm yours. I've been yours since the first moment I saw you. I've been chasing you since that morning when I woke up and found my bed empty of you. You're a beautiful, vicious thing, and as much as I've fought it, it turns out my wanting you is the one thing in this world I can't seem to kill. So I've given up."

"Aiden," I gasp on a ragged breath. I'm hot all over. The bundle of nerves between my legs is screaming for his attention, and my heart pounds in my chest like it wants to break out from the cage of my ribs. I swallow hard and try to marshal my thoughts back into order, but I can't help looking down at him, where he's still kneeling for me, eyes on my face.

"I'm yours, Catriona. On my knees for you. I'd do anything for you, love. You understand?"

"I understand," I breathe even though it's the only thing I've ever wanted to hear from anyone. Pressure builds in my chest, and I realize how terrible an idea it was to let a man like him inside my heart. Not because I think he might hurt me; he wouldn't need to overpower me to do that.

No, because he sees me in a way no one else ever has, and now there's no more running from him. No more hiding.

His hands cup my ass cheeks and lift me to his mouth, where he licks at me like I'm the best thing he's ever tasted. The groan rumbling from him is buried in my pussy, against my sensitive clit, and I squeal at the rush of sensation. He's mumbling against me, one word, over and over, but I can barely hear him over the thundering in my ears and my own bellowing lungs. It feels like I've run a mile, but I've barely moved a muscle.

The word he's chanting finally registers. Yours.

Yours.

Yours.

Yours.

"Aiden," I protest, but that's all that comes out. I want to reach down to grip ahold of his hair, tell him it's too much, but I promised. And I'm not sure I want him to stop anyway.

Everything about him wrecks me. I expected him to fuck me, dominate me, show me how much I belong to him. To have him on his knees at my feet, feeding me pleasure with his mouth... it cuts me up inside until I'm a quivering, bleeding mess for him.

What man has ever, ever prostrated himself like this? What man has ever worshipped *me?*

The answer is simple.

None.

I force my eyes to open, needing to see him kneeling for me. To bear witness to this and sear it into my brain. It reorganizes something inside me down at a cellular level, and my brows furrow, trying to sort it out, but my neurons are too fried by his wicked tongue to piece it together.

"That's right," Aiden says, his chin glistening. "Do you get it yet, little wife?" At my shaking head, he smiles. "No? Well, we've got all the time in the world for me to convince you. And I promise... I can be very convincing."

I open my mouth to protest, but his tongue spears inside me at the same time as his fingers scissor over my clit, and all those protests wither, forgotten in the back of my throat, as a hoarse moan spills out instead.

He pinches the sensitive flesh until it throbs, then lets go, blood immediately rushing back to the space. He does this over and over as he fucks me with his tongue, and when I come, almost delirious, he drinks it down, a rumble of approval vibrating through his chest.

When I'm nothing but a quivering mess, covered in sweat and hanging limply, Aiden rises to his feet, hands at my waist to steady me. He makes soothing noises in the back of his throat, scattering kisses over my available skin. His praise filters through the white noise in my head: *You're so good. Such a sweet girl. Take it so well for me. You can take a little more. I've got you, love. That's it. Let me help you.*

When I can see through the haze of tears—I hadn't even realized I was fucking crying again—I see he's got me cradled in his arms. He spins my limp body around until I'm facing one of the windows between the shelves. My fingers grasp at the frame, arms stinging with renewed blood flow, but it's luscious, almost too much sensation.

I think he's going to fill me up and fuck me until I

scream, but no, he has more devastating plans for me than that. It would be too easy, and Aiden's never been easy.

There's the sound of rustling fabric, and I nearly sob again at the thought of him giving me skin. I've given up the thought of speech; I'm simply incapable. He presses his body against my back, and that's enough. I take long, deep breaths until I get myself under control, but of course, that's not what he wants.

"You can take more, can't you, baby?"

I nod, and I hate myself for it. But I'll take whatever he has to give.

"I'm yours, Catriona. On my knees for you. I'd do anything for you, love. You understand?"

For a man who could say those words to me?

I'd do anything for him.

Anything.

Take his punishments.

His pain.

Lie.

Kill.

There isn't anything I *wouldn't* do for him.

As though he knows it, his hand comes around to tease and tempt. Starting with my sensitive, neglected nipples. His mouth at my throat, he uses his fingers to pluck the tips into defiant peaks and nips at my ears until I can't tell which is riling me up more. I grind my ass into his crotch and he's so hard, I *ache* for him.

"Aiden, please," I beg.

"Please, what?"

"I want you inside me."

"Oh, I don't think so. Not yet. I want you crazy for me.

Want you to know what a day in my life is like since you stormed your way into it." His teeth ravage my neck, and he licks away my tears. His fingers are the devil's work, kneading and pinching my breasts and nipples until I think I could come only from his hands on them. My hips flex against him, pressing back into his heat, but he's an impenetrable wall, seemingly unaffected by my slow unraveling.

"Feel how desperate you are? How much you crave me? That's how I've felt every *fucking* minute since I met you. My thoughts have been of nothing but you for months. My dreams. My nightmares. I haven't been able to focus on anything but having you. Then you showed up at that fucking dinner, and I realized I couldn't have you. Not if I wanted to keep you safe. Don't you understand?"

He moves closer, shifting one hand until he can fit two thick fingers inside me. I whimper, sob, probably scream, and I hope to God no one can hear me. It's not like this place is soundproof, considering the open walls. People flit down the sidewalks outside the window. Cars rush by. And I'm falling to pieces above them. The thought that they could look up and see me fills me with lightning. Sparks travel from his fingertips to my skin. We're electric.

"I'm not going to stop. Not until you give me everything that you are. It may not be tonight. Or this year. Or five years from now, but I'm going to claim every piece of you, Catriona O'Connor. Because I'm yours, and you're fucking mine."

Fingers piston inside me, harder than I thought possible. Usually, I need a little working up to get there like this, but the orgasm bowls me over like a landslide.

I stiffen against him, a scream tearing from my throat.

My legs collapse like a house of cards, simply folding underneath me. I give half a thought to possibly slamming into the floor, but Aiden catches me against the safety of his body. Lips to my ear, he croons those words of praise again: *You're so good. Such a sweet girl. Take it so well for me. You can take a little more. I've got you, love. That's it. Let me help you.*

Carefully, Aiden unlatches me from the hook, then unwinds the restraints around my hands, which have turned a light shade of purple due to the slight restriction. My legs go around his hips as he cradles my palms in his, massaging to soothe and tease. Head resting against his chest, I finally become cognizant enough to hear the wild thunder of his heartbeat.

Without thought, my lips find his, tipping up and searching until our mouths fit together. With a sound of animal need, his tongue thrusts inside, filling my mouth with the heady taste of him. I drink from him, nipping at his lips, and conclude I'd never need to eat or drink or breathe again if only he'd spend the rest of my life kissing me. I could survive simply by stealing the very air from his lungs.

Slowly, almost delicately, the want for him ignites again, filling my belly with a slow burn that has me whimpering against his mouth, almost panicking, unsure if I can handle the intensity again.

"Yes, you can," he says. Jesus, is he reading my mind now? "You can be so sweet for me, *bhean chéile*. Won't you? Take every inch of my cock and scream my name like I know you want to. Because you know you belong to me. Don't you?"

"Please, Aiden," I whimper.

He only gives me dark laughter, unoffended, or perhaps more accurately, he's very aware I'm only holding on by a thread. I bite my lip to keep from saying something that'll make him stop. Or from saying exactly what I know he wants to hear. But it doesn't matter. His silver eyes gleam in triumph from whatever he can read on my traitorous face.

"Don't worry, love. It's all right. I'll take care of you." He takes my hands and cuffs them behind my back in one of his. His hold is loose—I could free myself at any time, but I don't dare when I see that he's unbuckling his belt and unzipping his slacks. His cock springs free when he shoves down his briefs. He's hard and leaking at the tip. My mouth waters at the sight of it, and I almost ask him to let me drop to my knees so I can worship him in return.

But then he's spreading my legs, hitching me up on the windowsill so I'm at the right angle. He smears the head of his cock through my arousal and allows the slightest inch to tip inside me. A ragged sound comes from his throat, and he throws his head back, gritting his teeth to maintain the tenuous grasp on his control. I twine my legs around his hips and pull him to me, catching him off guard, and with the loss of balance, he drives deep inside me.

My vision goes almost totally white as I take him in that one brutal thrust. I'm swollen, sensitive, and so close to the edge, a stiff breeze could shove me over. When he doesn't move, I blink around the room to get it to focus. His expression is part thunderous, part awestruck.

His free hand comes to my throat, where he presses until I feel my heartbeat thudding against his palm. "You'd deserve it if I made you soak my cock for the next hour. I could stand here all night, princess, and not move an inch. As soon as you got close to coming all over me, I'd leave you empty and clenching on nothing."

"Aiden, please, don't. I can't—"

His hand tightens on my throat. "What did I say about what you can take?"

He pulls out, and I thrash against him, afraid he'll make good on his threats. "No, don't. I promise I'll do what you want. Whatever you want."

"Whatever I want?" he asks as he thrusts back in. My eyes roll into the back of my head, and if I had my hands free, I'd cling to him for support. Instead, I slump against the window, arching my back to bring my hips closer to meet him. "That's a dangerous thing to promise me. I could ask for anything."

"A-anything you-you want," I babble.

"What if I said I wanted you to tattoo my name on your skin?" he muses, keeping his hips to mine and tilting, until the tip of his cock drags against a spot inside me that has me seeing stars. "It would only be fair because yours is on mine."

I give it half a thought. I don't have any tattoos, had never considered them because Father would have beat me senseless if I had, but I say, "I would. Wherever you want." I become obsessed with the thought of him on me permanently, where no one can take him from me.

This pleases him because he drops a thumb to my clit, coating it in my cum and teasing me with gentle strokes. "You would, hmm?"

I nod vehemently, testing his shackle around my hands, but now his grip may as well be iron.

"What if I wanted to tie you to my desk, spread over its surface, and leave you there while I work?"

Shivering, I don't hesitate. "Yes, Aiden, oh God. Please. Whatever you want. Tell me what you want, and I'll give it to you."

Aiden releases his grip on my wrists and I sob in relief, because now I can wrap my arms around his shoulders, pull him closer. I'd climb inside his skin if I could. His hips pin me against the wall as he drives into me with reckless abandon.

"I want you to say that you're mine. Tell me you're mine. That you won't leave. That you're going to keep me. Tell me. Tell me, Catriona, and I'll let you come all over my cock. Say it, pretty wife. You're mine."

"I'm yours, Aiden. I'm yours. I promise. I only want you. I'm all yours." The words are so similar to the night we met, it feels like I'm suspended in two moments of time.

"Now tell me you love me."

"I—oh my God, please."

"Tell me."

"I love you, Aiden, fuck."

He chuckles. "The mouth on you. You're stuck with me, *bhean chéile*, because I've loved you since the day we met, and I've loved you more every day since."

His admission breaks open a dam inside me. We collide. My arms go tight as a bowstring around him, giving him little room to maneuver, but it wouldn't matter, anyway. My pussy clamps down on him so hard it causes a breath to hiss out of him. He tries to move, but he comes instead. He shouts, but I don't know what he says because I'm screaming his name.

Just like he said.

"I love you," he breathes into my skin, stitches into my soul.

"I love you," I chant against his mouth.

Until death do us part.

EPILOGUE

AIDEN

A body lands at my feet as Catriona strides into my office, Eamon following her like the loyal little lapdog he is. I'd feel threatened if my wife didn't immediately come to my desk and sit her perfect ass on my lap. Eamon watches, rife with jealousy, like a cat staring after its favorite toy. I lift my brow at him, and he smiles, unrepentant. The slut.

"What's this?" I ask Catriona, nuzzling her throat and inhaling her scent. She must have just finished a lavender and honey latte, because I can almost taste it on her skin. I'd only left her a couple of hours ago, but I already want to take her back home and press her into our mattress.

Eamon sighs heavily, and we both ignore him.

The body on the floor jerks as they try to roll to their feet. I watch, amused, as my wife studies the bloodied form in front of us with an intense expression of satisfaction. My hold tightens on her thigh and hip. Maybe I should take her on a second honeymoon—somewhere with sun so she can wear as few clothes as possible. I make a mental note to ask Mara for recommendations. Before her commitment to Niall, Mara spent a good deal of time traveling... among her other pursuits.

"This is the first time I've brought a body to your feet," Catriona says, and I hide my smile at the pout in her voice. "I feel like it should get *some* praise."

I lean closer and press my lips to her ear. "The praise I'd like to give you shouldn't be shared in public."

She huffs out a breath and gestures to Eamon, who is only too happy to manhandle the person to their feet and toss them into the chair across from me. A few seconds later, having secured their arms and legs to the wood, Eamon accepts Catriona's approving smile like a cat with a treat. "It took King long enough to track him down. I thought you said he was the best," he says.

"We *are* the best," comes a voice I don't recognize from the doorway.

Eamon makes a sound of disagreement, but he's too busy helping himself to my whiskey to contradict the statement.

I'm too relaxed with Catriona in my arms to question the response. But when I look up, recognition dawns on me, and I realize the reason I didn't recognize the woman's voice.

"Took a while to track this one down. He's slippery," Gracin Kingsley says, with a nod at Senator Rory Gallagher, who is shouting behind a gag. "Found him trying to cross the border into Mexico."

"Which reminds me, we should take Owen to Mexico. He'd love to take a trip out to swim with the sea lions." Tessa

Kingsley, *née* Emerson, Gracin's wife, stands in front of him with a satisfied smile.

We've never met, and King says little about his wife and son, preferring to keep to business when we speak, but there's no denying the way he wraps a possessive arm around her waist. I knew enough of their story from my background research when I first started working with Gracin to piece it together.

"Whatever you want, little mouse."

Before, when I'd worked with King on other projects, I couldn't stomach the thought of attaching myself to a woman, living the kind of lives we do. I'd thought him even more reckless for having a child, who would constantly be in danger. But now, with Catriona safe on my lap, I think I understand the inevitability of this kind of obsession.

I see the mirror of my own in his eyes as he studies his wife like she's the only person in the room. Because it's the same way I feel about mine. Is that the way of it for men like us? The kind of men who have dealt with blood and death. When we find a woman worth having, they become our entire world.

A grunt draws my attention back to the restrained body and the conversation I'd tuned out.

"Why don't you come with us to the warehouse, and we can truly make this a party?" Eamon suggests after he's drained his drink and carved lines into Rory's skin with the edge of his knife. Not hard enough to draw blood, but enough to leave irritating, reddened marks in their wake.

"I do love parties," Gracin says, watching the glint of the knife.

Tessa snorts and presses her shoulder into his chest. "And I like to watch."

"Excellent," Eamon says with a loose grin.

"I hope you don't mind if we crash," Tessa says to my wife.

"Of course not. The more the merrier. Besides, we could use Gracin's help with some of the technological aspects, if you have the time. I'm happy to pay for—"

"Let Tessa help when you deal with this one," Gracin answers with a nod at Rory, "and we'll consider it even."

Eamon looks like he's won the lottery. After all, he usually works solo. It's rare that other people like to participate.

I should have never introduced them I say to myself as we transport Rory to the back of a van parked outside the casino. The warehouse is located by the river in a dead part of town. But it doesn't matter. Catriona recently bought the entire block, reasoning that the space could be put to better use.

Gracin pulls Tessa closer to his side as we enter the warehouse, but she merely smiles sunnily back up at him and tightens her arm around his waist. I don't ask, because it's not my business. Besides, if I showed any amount of concern for his wife, I have a distinct feeling it would earn me a knife in the ribs. I value my health at this point, especially when there may be a promise of a second honeymoon in my future.

While Tessa, Eamon, and I ready Rory on another chair, once again restrained, Gracin and Catriona huddle together, talking logistics in low voices.

"You know, I'm getting sick and tired of you always

invading my space. You said I could use this location whenever I wanted."

I glance over my shoulder at Mara's voice and raise a brow at the body she's dragging by the foot. Craning my neck, I try to get a glimpse of the man she's towing, but a mask obscures his face. I really need to reevaluate my taste in friends.

"Niall?" I ask nonchalantly, wiping the sweat from my forehead.

She snorts. "We're not that lucky." Nodding toward Rory, she says, "Do you need some help with that?"

Eamon is sulking a little as Tessa teases Rory with a pair of pliers. You'd think he'd be overjoyed to share his toys, but in this case, I think he wants to impress the couple with his prowess like some twisted form of a dick-measuring contest, but with instruments of torture. Or maybe how loud they can get Rory to scream.

"I think we've got it covered. What about you? Do you need any help?" I'm not the type to meddle in my friends' affairs, but I'm also not the type to stand idly by if they're struggling. And Mara has been struggling increasingly more since we solidified the arrangement with Niall Cleary. Probably even longer than that, considering how well she's always managed to lock down her emotions. After things settled when we returned from Ireland, I offered to deal with the situation for her, but she wouldn't hear of it.

"Do I ever?" she says with a toss of her short inky hair.

I know better than to push too much. Besides, if she needed help, she would've told me when I asked.

Because of this, I force her to meet my gaze. "I mean it. If you ever need anything, you reach out to us, yeah? Catriona would have me by the balls if something happened to you. And I swear sometimes you're the only thing keeping Eamon from coming completely unglued."

A small smile pulls at her lips. "Aw, I love you, too, Aiden." She pushes up on her toes to press a kiss to my cheek. "I promise I'm fine, but I think I'm going to take this to your other location so I don't disturb you. It seems like you have your hands full."

"Dinner on Sunday at our new house. You'll be there, right?" I holler as she reverses direction.

"Wouldn't miss it," she chirps back, heeled boots clacking against the concrete. "Even if it's still only half-finished."

Shaking my head, I turn back to Catriona, who is studying the computer screen with a delighted smile on her face. Her plotting and scheming turns me on like nothing else. It's a madness I could study for a lifetime and never seem to fully understand.

Maybe it's simply that the monster in me matches the monster in her. A balance we keep fed just enough so we don't unleash on the public.

Just on pieces of shit like her father.

Speaking of Rory, his eyes damn near roll in the back of his head, and Tessa cackles, slapping his cheeks with her empty hand until he jerks awake. Sweat coats his body like a slippery second skin. Tessa had ripped open his shirt to display his paunchy belly. Once upon a time, it must have been muscle, but glutton that he is, it has turned to fat, softened him like a pig for slaughter.

He meets my eyes, and his nostrils flare with fear.

Satisfied with whatever they've discussed, Catriona pats

Gracin's arm and nods with finality. "As long as you can make it look like an accident, it works for me."

"You're certain?"

Catriona eyes her father with determination. "Absolutely."

"How much do you want me to make it hurt?" Eamon asks, that manic gleam bright in his eyes. Like Mara, I can only hope his demons don't destroy what is left of him.

"Do whatever you like, but don't disfigure him too much. He was just so heartbroken over losing his wife and then his daughter nearly a year later, he couldn't take it anymore. Started drinking too much and drove drunk. The news will eat it up."

Rory shouts behind his gag, his eyes pleading with Catriona, but she only stares at him with the satisfaction of a job well done.

Now that we've crossed him off our to-do list, no ties are keeping us moored in the past. She can move on from his abuse, neglect, and control, and I no longer have Cian present to tighten the noose around my neck.

We are free.

The Kingsleys leave soon after, apologizing that they can't stay longer. Understandably, they don't want to leave their ten-year-old son alone for extended periods of time. I shake Gracin's hand and give Tessa a nod of thanks with a promise that I'll be in touch if we need their help again. Catriona guarantees the same if they ever have need of our now vast resources.

"Are you sure you don't want us to stay?" Catriona asks Eamon, as he settles in for a long night of what he does best.

"Course not, love. Get going. I'll take care of all this."

Catriona pauses for a second before she loops an arm around Eamon's shoulders. He has to dip down a little, even though Catriona is tall. His eyes close and he nods at whatever she whispers to him, then gives her a little shove. "I promise you have my permission. Now get out of here."

Catriona comes to my side, and I press a kiss into her lavender-honey hair. "What do you need his permission for?"

"Actually, why don't I show you?"

I lift a brow at the devilish gleam in her eye. No amount of convincing breaks her silence, and I spend the entire ride trying to distract her as she drives, so she'll let it slip, but she never does.

"Standard release. We make everyone who chooses to get someone else's name tattooed on them sign one. You wouldn't believe the number of idiots who get drunk and come in here trying to get the name of their one-night stand on their tits. It also has those amendments we talked about, since your additional payment already cleared."

Catriona flicks a mischievous look at me over her shoulder, her long blond hair swishing and begging that I wrap a fist in it. "No problem," she says to the woman. I didn't even catch her name because I'd been in a state of shock when we stopped at a tattoo parlor a few streets over from Bourbon Street. She'd managed to park the car and tug me out of it with very little resistance.

I've found there aren't many places I *wouldn't* follow her.

She fills out the paperwork, and the tattoo artist leads us back to a private room, closing the door to block the voices and pulsing rock music. Eamon has always done most of my ink, so this will be a first for me. Curious about what she has planned, I take a seat next to a reclining chair as she chats with the artist about the stencil and placement. Adrenaline still pumps through my system, so I'm enjoying the thought of watching her take ink a lot more than I should.

"You still sure about this?" the woman, Kaye according to her chirped introduction, asks.

"A thousand percent."

"It's your body," Kaye says with a shrug, and begins to pull supplies out of metal drawers. The gun, needles, ink, and antiseptic. A stencil lies on a moving tray, but I can't see what it is other than vague purple ink for the outline.

Catriona moves to me, dress swishing enticingly around her legs. She steps between my knees and rests her hands on my shoulders. "Any guesses?"

"I've given up trying to predict what you'll do, darlin'. I'm just happy to be along for the ride."

She smiles and dips down to stamp a kiss on my lips.

A few moments later, Kaye clears her throat. "Well, let me walk you through how to do this." She shifts toward me. "Let's go, big boy. You look like you know your way around a tattoo gun. Shouldn't be too hard to get the hang of."

My eyes collide with Catriona's. "I'm sorry, what do you mean?"

"You'll be giving her the tattoo. It's in a delicate location, and I've been informed you'd likely maim anyone who attempted it. Luckily, I'm the owner, and your wife here has paid generously for the privilege. It's a small tattoo, relatively simple, so you shouldn't have an issue with it. As long as you two don't run your mouths, it's her body to do with as she pleases."

A million thoughts blaze through my mind. Where is this tattoo going? What is it? Does she really fucking think I should be the one to do it?

Then I imagine all the places it can go, and how it'll look when it's all healed up. How it'll feel knowing I've marked her. Permanently.

Pushing to my feet, I move to Kaye's side as she explains the basics. I have to hope my brain has absorbed most of it, because the majority of my animal instincts are screaming at me to put needle to skin. She probably shouldn't have waved this in front of me. I'm no artist, but the dual notion of having her underneath any implement of pain and knowing she'll wear the tattoo forever is too enticing to comprehend.

"You think you got it?" Kaye asks after a moment of silence.

"I think I can manage," I reply, throat bone-dry.

Kaye hums in the back of her throat, her pierced eyebrow twitching with humor as she puts everything I'll need on the moving tray, along with a couple of bottles of water on the table next to Catriona. "I'm just gonna apply the stencil and then I'll scram. You can holler at me if you have any trouble."

I give her a jerky nod and freeze as Catriona climbs onto the reclining chair. Kaye adjusts it until she's flat, then positions the lights so Catriona's waist is fully illuminated. If I had any saliva left, I'd lick my lips in heady anticipation.

Kaye nods at Catriona, and she flips up her skirt to bare a simple pale pink thong. My hands tighten into fists. Thank fucking God we're in a private room. Thank fucking God she didn't ask Eamon to do this. I never would have heard the end of it. No wonder she checked with him before we left. She wanted his okay. The conniving little thing.

It takes me a few seconds to focus on what Kaye's doing, and longer to realize she's laying the stencil at the junction of Catriona's thigh and hip. She's had to yank the strap of her thong way up on the curve of her ass so it stays out of the way.

Then I finally comprehend what the stencil says.

Aiden. Fucking Christ.

It says *Aiden.*

She's tattooing my name on her.

I'm tattooing my name on her.

Like a fucking brand.

Like her name on my knuckles.

Indelible.

Undeniable.

Mine.

I chug down one of the bottles of water to soothe my dry throat and then snap on gloves. A few beats later, Kaye is gone and we're alone. I pull up the rolling chair to her side, tattoo gun in hand. Then I finally meet Catriona's eyes again, hoping she can't see the flare of nervous anticipation in mine.

"I'm not going to ask if you're certain. If you change your mind, I'll tie you down and make you take it anyway, no matter how much you struggle or how horrible it looks."

Her sunny smile disarms me, and I curse underneath my breath. "I'm not changing my mind. I want it. You're okay with this?"

"I've never been more okay with anything in my fucking life, darlin'."

"Good."

"Don't tease me. I don't want to fuck it up," I say before I click on the gun like Kaye showed me and concentrate on the stencil. "Don't move."

To her credit, she stays perfectly still. Which is better than I'm able. It's not an overly large tattoo, maybe two inches across and an inch high at the very most, in a simple but legible script. I'm sure it's not perfect, but by the time I wipe it clean for her inspection, it's the single most important achievement of my fucking life.

I lift a mirror so she can check it from all angles. When she tips her face up to mine, cheeks deliciously, perfectly pink, I place the tattoo gun and all the supplies on the tray and shove it away.

"Do you like it?" I ask.

"Do *you* like it?" She studies my expression, a furrow appearing between her brows. "I can't tell if you're into it or if you think it's a bad idea."

In answer, I take her by the thighs and yank her to the edge of the chair, ignoring her choked squeal of surprise. The movement causes the skirt of her dress to bunch at her waist and her already displaced panties to stretch even more. I take it one step further and twist the material until it snaps clean off.

Her hips are already lifting to meet me by the time I lower my mouth to her eager cunt. Groaning into her flesh, I lick her slit from top to bottom, relishing as her flavor soaks my tongue. One thumb hooks into her as I lift my head to say, "You're so wet, darlin'. Is this all for me? Do you like having my name on your skin?"

Hips bucking, she fists her hands in my hair and tries to

tug me back down. When I don't comply, she growls, and I smile against her inner thigh.

"If you don't put your mouth to good use, I'm going to take care of things myself. I've been daydreaming about this for ages. Now show me what a good husband you are for me and make me come."

I'd argue, but I want to taste her more, and we both know I like when she uses me to make herself come. This is no different.

Pulling my hair again, she grinds her pussy against my tongue, and I follow her like I'm a starving man and she's a feast. The wet sounds of her pleasure fill my ears, and I'm thankful for the distant beat of music. As much as I love others hearing how much she enjoys me, I prefer keeping her to myself. When she gets close, I cup her ass with my palms, pulling her up to my mouth so she's unable to wiggle away when she grows too sensitive.

"Fuck...fuck, Aiden, I can't. It's too much. Please, I—"

Oh, sweet wife. Begging is music to my ears. Careful to keep away from her fresh tattoo, I grip her to me and fuck her with my tongue until she lets out a soundless scream and feeds me her pleasure like the sweetest dessert.

"I'll take...that to mean...you do like it," she pants, when I've licked her clean.

Senator Rory Gallagher's tragic car accident is still all over the news two weeks later, but Catriona and I are thirty thousand feet in the air on our way to the Maldives. I'd wanted to go immediately, but she convinced me to wait until she had everything in place. Eamon was only too glad to manage operations in our stead. As much as I tried to impress upon him the need for discretion, Catriona gave him permission to bludgeon as many idiots as he liked.

Fuck my life.

"You've got to stop doing this," she says, climbing into my lap as soon as we're allowed to take off our seat belts. Bren and Tadhg are up front with the flight attendants and pilots. Unfortunately for Catriona, given all her earlier escapades, they've made it their life's mission to never let her out of their sight again. It's hell for her but gives me an unending peace of mind. Despite the Clans' agreement of peace, I know it's only a matter of time before someone tries to usurp my position.

"Doing what?" I say against her throat. A pink diamond glitters against her cleavage, and I dip my head to kiss it, reveling in her hitched breath as my tongue flicks out to taste her skin.

"Whisking me away whenever you feel like it. I do have a job, you know."

"That wasn't in the contract, darlin', so I'll whisk you away whenever I like."

She wiggles in my lap, and I clamp my hands down on her thighs to keep her still. "Don't you think it's time for renegotiations? After all, so much has changed."

"I'm always open to renegotiations," I say into the skin of her throat. "What do you want to start with?"

Chuckling, she lets me lick up to her mouth. When I break away, she's heaving for breath in order to speak. "Once I finish my clerkship, I think it's important I get my certifications in Ireland as well. I know you'll want to go back there at some point. Niall doesn't deserve to lead the families, and you know that. You'll need a good lawyer when you do. What do you think?"

It sounds like a good idea to me, so I click a button to lock the guest cabin doors, letting the flight attendant know not to disturb us. Catriona's wearing a pretty little sundress again—*fuck, I love her sundresses*—so all it takes is a little repositioning until she's straddling my lap and a swipe of my fingers and she's bare for me. Another few quick movements to unbutton and unzip my pants, and then I'm inside her.

Heaven.

"I take it..." she pants, "you like the idea."

"Move on me, darlin'." She doesn't hesitate, and I throw my head back against the seat. "You're going to terrorize every fuckin' one of them, aren't you? Whip them all into shape. My vicious little queen."

There will be some who will hate that I put her in a position of power, but that will only make it easier to get rid of them.

Catriona giggles, but her pussy tightens around me, and I know she enjoys the thought, too. Of being in control after a lifetime of suffering at her father's whims. A person like Cian could never grasp the idea of giving up any kind of control, but I've learned it's the most powerful thing a man can do. But a good leader knows when to protect his queen... and when to let her attack.

As she loses herself to the rhythm, I whisper in her ear about how much I want to come inside her, how good she feels, how much I'm never, ever going to let her go. How she's all mine and how I'm going to fuck her every day in our villa with the sun on her bare skin.

At first, I'm thrusting up into her, driving deep and hard using the leverage of my legs and my death grip on her hips, but it's not long until she presses me back into the seat and takes over once again.

And this is it.

This is why it'll only ever be her. Because she's the only person I'll ever be able to cede control to. She's the only one I'd ever let put a hand to my throat. She's seen the monster in me, the darkest, most evil, unforgivable parts, and curled up next to them like they were nothing. Conquered them. Accepted them. Loved me in spite of them.

She's ruined me.

"Aw, did that do it for you already?" she teases into my ear, when I can no longer watch as she takes me.

"You're gonna fuckin' kill me before we even get there."

Her dark chuckle fills my ears, making me shudder against her. I grab handfuls of her ass to try to control the heady motion of her hips, but she's relentless. Before I can ask her—beg her, really—to give me a second before I embarrass myself, she throws her head back, her nails driving into my shoulders as she loses it.

"Oh fuck, baby. Already?" I tease.

When she makes an absolute mess of my cock, dripping her sweetness all over me, I regret my words. I promised myself I'd get her off at least twice every time to remind her for the rest of her life she needs no one but me. But her soft whimpers and how soaked she is destroy that promise in seconds.

Soon, her mouth finds mine, and it doesn't take me long to convince her to move to the bed so we can do it again. The ten years—or less if she lets me renegotiate again—I promised to wait to fill her with a baby is a blink of time, and I'll need all the practice I can get until then.

Hours later, we tumble out of the jet and into a car half asleep. Catriona tucks into my side in the back seat and immediately falls back into a deep, restful sleep. Between traveling back and forth to Ireland to smooth over all the wrinkles of managing an organization as vast as ours, passing the bar, and preparing to start her clerkship with Judge Landry, she's needed this vacation much more than she's let on. It's not my fault if I have to sneak her onto planes to get her to take a break. Maybe in the future she'll listen to me when I tell her she's got too much on her plate.

I catch myself before I snort. *Not a fuckin' chance.*

Bren and Tadhg have a villa nearby, but not so close that we won't have our privacy. They follow in a car behind us, keeping watch. Catriona has her rings, but I feel better knowing we have backup here we can trust.

It's a short but jaw-droppingly beautiful drive from the airstrip to the secluded villa where we'll spend the next two weeks. Catriona is going to be disappointed when she wakes up and realizes she's missed it, but letting her rest will be worth it. Contentment steals over me as the sun begins to set over the vast blue ocean.

A few months ago, I never thought I'd be here.

Never thought I had anything to live for other than the next gruesome order from Cian. The next heartache I'd have to watch my mother endure. She may not be with me anymore, but at least she's at peace now. If there is a God or an afterlife, maybe she'll be there with my father. I've never been religious despite my Catholic upbringing, but I hope that's where she is.

The car comes to a stop at the lone villa on a curve of one of the islands. It's secluded from the rest of the resort, and that alone was worth the price of the booking. A long dock extends out into the turquoise expanse of the ocean, and the echoes of the waves can be heard from every room inside the villa.

Catriona stirs as I cross the threshold into the bedroom. I nuzzle her close to me as I collapse on top of the bed, not bothering with the sheets in the mild, sea-scented air. All I need is her next to me.

That's the last thought as I let exhaustion overtake me.

That I could die right here and be happy, because all I need is here in my arms.

Continue reading Mara's story in Kiss of Death now!

ACKNOWLEDGMENTS

When I started writing this book at the end of 2023, I did it by hand in my bathtub, scribbling in a notebook. The first scene I wrote is, surprisingly, still Chapter 1, where Aiden / Eamon confront Rory. It feels like forever ago and that scene wouldn't be the book it is today without some incredible people.

First and foremost, my husband Charlie, who does not understand my romance obsession, but supports it, and me, wholeheartedly. Thank you for your listening ear, even if you have no idea what I'm talking about.

To my daughters, Afton and Charlotte, who are the best kids in the whole world. If you're reading this, close the book and step away.

To my editors Amy Parsons, Kelli Collins, & Jenny Sims. I nearly walked away from this book so many times, but your insightful comments and, honestly willingness to put up with me, helped me keep going.

Alicia Winings. There aren't words for how grateful I am that you messaged me that day. I'm sure I test your sanity, but I'd lose mine if you weren't there with your level head and ability to keep me on task. Thank you.

To Justine Bergman from JAB Design who worked her ass off to create this cover. I appreciate the hell out of you for treating my last minute cover change with kindness and understanding. You are incredibly talented and I am so fucking lucky to have the chance to work with you. You are a literal badass.

As always, my eternal love goes out to my Book Junkies and Street Team for being along for the ride!

Thank you all!

ABOUT THE AUTHOR

 **Nicole Blanchard** is the New York Times and USA Today bestselling author of the TikTok-viral dark romance Toxic, a wildly addictive best-seller that has sold over 100,000 copies worldwide. Known for her morally gray antiheroes, off-the-charts heat, and jaw-dropping twists, Nicole's stories drag readers deep into love's darkest corners—where no one escapes unscarred.

When she's not crafting twisted love stories that break your heart and then heal it, you can find her soaking up beach sun with a glass of sweet tea, getting inked, or running a farm full of lovable misfit animals.

Visit her website www.authornicoleblanchard.com for more information or to subscribe to her newsletter for updates on sales and new releases.

facebook.com/authornicoleblanchard

instagram.com/authornicoleblanchard

amazon.com/Nicole-Blanchard

bookbub.com/authors/nicole-blanchard

goodreads.com/nicole_blanchard

pinterest.com/blanchardbooks

tiktok.com/@authornicoleblanchard

threads.com/@authornicoleblanchard

patreon.com/NicoleBlanchard

ALSO BY NICOLE BLANCHARD

DARK ROMANCE

Queenmakers Series

Little Death

Until Death

Kiss of Death

Standalones

Toxic

CONTEMPORARY ROMANCE SERIES

First to Fight Series

Battleboro Fire & Rescue Series

Friend Zone Series